Hous

Apart from occ
cooking in a girls
a secretary for a b   ...... and for a parlia-
mentary lawyer, Barbara Rowan has had a
lifetime's career in journalism. She took a
first degree as a mature student with the
Open University while in full-time work,
and after her husband died studied for her
Ph.D. at University College, Swansea.

She travelled widely in Europe with her
husband, particularly in Italy and Spain,
and lived for six years on the Channel
Islands. She now lives in Swansea.

Barbara Rowan

House of Sand

FONTANA/Collins

First published in Great Britain by
Victor Gollancz Ltd, 1986

First issued in Fontana Paperbacks 1987

'Our island is a "rock", but our house has become a house of sand.'

> *- Maurice Edmond de Courvel,*
> *hereditary Steward of the*
> *island of La Roque*

ONE

It was the beginning of the autumn of 1959. I had just returned to London after a six-weeks' assignment in Italy and the first news to reach me was of the death of my old friend, Maurice de Courvel.

I say 'old friend' but, twenty years ago, he had been more like a father to me than just a friend. And although I had only seen him twice since then, I had always been proud of the link that existed between myself and this kindly and distinguished old man.

I could not believe that he had committed suicide. Yet that had been the verdict of the inquest, a report of which I was shown in a coffee-bar on my way back to the office that yellow October day. I was feeling particularly unenthusiastic about going back that morning. I hadn't had a holiday for eighteen months and nine days. I felt stale – mentally, physically and spiritually – from the roots of my hair to my toenails. Furthermore, I had just had six sweating weeks under the still hot Italian sun, trailing round after a fat, greasy ball of brain, brawn and energy that added up to the great Italian film director, Nicolo Grandi, the purpose of the operation being to provide the magazine I worked for with one of those exclusive features on famous people at work that readers are supposed to revel in. As such assignments go, it had not been by any means the toughest, despite the sun and the inevitable exhaustion. Grandi, shorn of his protective layers of publicity personnel, had proved to be quite a fellow, and there was nothing phony about his genius. I am not a film man: the printed word is my business, but I have learned to recognize the true artist in any medium when I see him – or her; and Grandi was certainly that. I could almost have enjoyed the chore, except for the lack of holiday.

Which was why, the day after my return to London, instead of taking a taxi straight to the office, I took time out to wander down Piccadilly on foot and stop for a coffee en route. I drifted into one of those plush bars much frequented by pressed-suit executives and their secretaries and had barely sat down with my first cup and my morning paper when I heard a voice I knew.

It was a chap called Bill Adamson, chief pundit of a steel industry journal, whose offices were above a beauty parlour just round the corner. He made the usual jocular remarks aimed by those jealous members of the fraternity whose boundaries of research are in the main confined to the suburbs of Sheffield and Doncaster; then he slapped his morning paper down on the table beside me and said:

'You knew this chap, didn't you?'

I looked vaguely over the front page and he jabbed a finger at a point down towards the bottom of the second column. It took me a full minute to assimilate the dry heading:

Maurice de Courvel
Suicide Verdict

and I had to use a considerable effort of will to clear my brain sufficiently to read through the brief report that followed. When I had finished, I read it through a second time, slowly:

At the inquest on M. Maurice Edmond de Courvel, the distinguished French historian, held at Porte Hilaire on the island of La Roque yesterday, the jury returned a verdict of suicide while the balance of the mind was disturbed. Seventy-one-year-old M. de Courvel, Steward of La Roque, was found dead with gunshot wounds at his island home, St Michel, a week ago. An old-fashioned revolver, with his initials carved on the ivory handle, was found beside him. On a desk nearby was a letter addressed to his son and daughter.

M. de Courvel was said to have been 'extremely depressed' since his wife's death, after a long illness, two years previously. His son, M. Alain de Courvel, told the court that his father had shut up the family home shortly afterwards and had not, to his knowledge, entered it again until the day of the tragedy. He agreed that his father had suffered acute depression for a considerable time, and stated that neither he nor his sister, Mme Simone Corlander, had any doubt that the letter found on their father's desk after his death had been a 'suicide note'.

When the court closed, M. Guy Le Marnet, President of the Island Assembly (the La Roque Parliament), paid tribute to the late M. de Courvel's services to the island and spoke of the 'lasting pleasure and illumination' he had given to students of history.

At the foot of the column an Editor's Note read:

An appreciation of the work of Maurice de Courvel by his fellow historian, John Cumminge, appears on page 8.

I was hardly aware that Bill Adamson had sat down opposite me. It was as though a door had opened and I was looking through it down a long tunnel into my own remote boyhood. I could see the garden at St Michel and the plantations stretching away beyond on all sides, and the giant catalpa tree on the broad lawn in front of the house; in my ears was the sound of the sea, mingling with the hum of insects. The feeling of those far-off days was strong within me: the feeling of security in a tight, closed world in which time was in abeyance, the true and rightful feeling of childhood. I was torn from it by a reality that jarred.

'Did you know about it?'

With an effort I shifted my gaze to Adamson's face.

'No,' I said. 'No, I hadn't heard. I've been away.'

'I know. That's why I – '

He didn't finish. He looked uncomfortable for a second and then took a packet of cigarettes from his pocket, handed me one and said: 'If this is the first time you've heard about it, you won't want to discuss it now. I can get lost if you like; or else we can talk shop. Quite a lot's been happening since you went away.'

I nodded, grateful to him, and he plunged into a long narrative of recent events in our respective spheres.

After I'd left Adamson, I took a taxi the rest of the way to the office, and on the way tried to get my thoughts in order. In front of Adamson, I'd felt both guilty and foolish. It wasn't just that news was my business and I hadn't heard that one of the scholars of his day had committed suicide. It was something much more personal. I felt that, somehow, I had failed Maurice de Courvel. At the same time, I resented being told of his death by a more or less casual acquaintance. Unreasonable, since I'd lost touch with almost everyone on the island in the last ten years, and since I'd only just flown in to town. But then there was rage: bitter, seething rage – with Corby, my Editor! Damn him to hell! Why hadn't he told me yesterday when I'd phoned him? Why? Simple. Because Corby was a good editor, and yesterday I was due to wind up operations by attending as Grandi's guest at one of those lavish parties film people like to hold when they finally get a big film into the can. I had been expected to get some nice last-minute angles at that party – and Corby had meant to have them. And while I had sat, tied up in paper streamers, watching a real, live Spanish matador execute the *coup de grâce* on a boar's head on top of a table strewn with dirty plates and half-empty glasses, Maurice de Courvel had lain under a sheet in a mortuary, with a bullet wound in him that they said he'd put there himself. To hell with Corby! It was immaterial that there was nothing I could have done. He could have told me just the same. To hell with him!

Adamson had insisted on my keeping the paper and now I remembered the appreciation by Cumminge and turned to it. It was the usual thing: efficient, well-written and scholarly; cool without being indifferent. But it conveyed nothing of the real Maurice; for the reason, no doubt, that Cumminge had never known the real Maurice.

When I left the taxi, I went through the foyer of our office building like one of Sitting Bull's arrows. I wanted to get to Corby's inner sanctum before general office *bonhomie* had softened my mood.

In the event, I said very little. Corby took the wind out of my sails by being unusually remorseful and apologetic. I knew this only meant that he wanted something, but as I wanted more or less the same thing I decided it wasn't the moment to stand on principles. What Corby wanted was for me to go to the island, get the facts on Maurice and do him something rather special by way of an obituary. He knew my connections with the island and sensed a good story, with strong elements of mystery and lots of drama about what he called 'feudal lords: the last of their breed, governing from privileged positions, with arbitrary powers'.

'They governed well,' I pointed out.

'No doubt. But today that in itself constitutes a rarity. And besides, Angus, where else in the civilized world would you find another island paradise entirely ruled by one family?'

'Three,' I corrected.

'Yes, well, that's what it would be interesting to find out. Who *did* hold the balance of power? And why did this nice old man throw in the towel?'

He was right, of course. There *was* a mystery on La Roque. And I was the only one, with my special roots there and my links with the families, who would have the slightest hope of getting at the answers. There's a story told on the island that they used to meet strangers on the beach with bill-hooks and choppers. It may be apocryphal, but it's still a fact that the average Roquennais trusts no one from further than the next parish. Today, though, they know that the right word in the right place is sharper than the knife.

They can cut you down before your plane's landed, and you never feel a thing. All you know is that, after you've been a month in the place, you've had a wonderful time, been everywhere, met everyone – and learned that half-closing's on a Wednesday.

So it was finally agreed that I should leave for La Roque next morning, and five minutes after I'd left Corby all the available cuttings on Maurice de Courvel were on my desk. I gathered them up, left instructions about incoming mail and departed.

I studied the cuttings over lunch in the West End, reading the longest of them twice over:

Maurice de Courvel Dead
Found in Derelict House

Seventy-one-year-old Maurice Edmond de Courvel, the historian, and Steward* of the forty-eight-square-mile, privately owned island of La Roque, was found dead last night in the study of his home, St Michel, on the island's north coast.

Although the house and lands of St Michel had been in the de Courvel family for over three centuries, neither Maurice de Courvel nor any of his family had lived there for some years. The room in which the body was found was littered with furniture and books, covered with dust, and an old-fashioned revolver, with the initials, 'M.E.D.C.', inlaid in the ivory handle, lay on the floor beside the chair in which the dead man was found. It is believed that M. de Courvel, who had been living with his daughter, had gone to the house alone some time during the evening. Foul play is not suspected.

At the foot of the column, an explanation was given of the asterisked word 'Steward'. It read:

12

The Stewards, or Sénéchaux, of La Roque still rule the island under a feudal form of government that has barely changed since the island was bought by a de Courvel from Spanish traders some four centuries ago. Since then, the three island families of de Courvel, Le Marnet and Cartier have shared the ownership – and a considerable part of the government – of the island between them. Traditionally, the office of Sénéchal is filled by the retiring President of the island's Assembly. M. de Courvel, who retired from the Assembly in the middle of his second term five years ago, was succeeded as President by the island's Chief Justice, M. Guy Le Marnet. It is understood that M. Le Marnet will now become Sénéchal.

Over coffee, I lit a cigarette and sat back to think the thing out. For the life of me, I couldn't accept the picture of Maurice de Courvel, suicide, on the basis of what I so far knew. But then, neither could I see St Michel as a derelict shell. Obviously, I'd missed some large chunks of the de Courvel family story in the twenty years since I'd lived in their home. Again, I felt the nagging sense of guilt. Apart from the usual Christmas cards, with their conscience-assuaging messages scrawled hurriedly after the signature, there had been very little correspondence between myself and the family over the last five years or so. There was no significant reason for this. Lack of time was my own excuse – possibly theirs, too – added to the fact, in my case, that when you earn your living with the pen, figuratively speaking, you tend to develop a certain compensating reluctance to write anything more demanding in your spare time than the odd paying-in slip.

My last *real* visit to the island had been ten years ago, for the wedding of Imogen Le Marnet to Max Cartier. Everything had seemed perfectly normal. Yet – and for the first time an odd note sounded at the back of my brain – three months later there had been another wedding: that of Simone – Maurice's own daughter – to a chap called

13

Corlander, a wealthy hotelier. I'd found an invitation awaiting me on my return from an assignment and had spent a fortune telephoning to apologize. But it hadn't occurred to me then – as it did now – to wonder how it was that nobody had mentioned Simone and this Corlander character before. Whirlwind courtships were not exactly a tradition with old Roquennais families. The opposite, in fact. But what the hell – perhaps I was seeing bogies where none existed!

I said my last *real* visit was ten years ago. That's because the very last time I'd seen Maurice and Justine de Courvel had been for two hours only, five years ago, when I'd broken my journey back to London in January, 1954, after ten days down in Sierra Leone. I hadn't even gone up to St Michel on that occasion. Maurice had been in Porte Hilaire, attending the Assembly, so Justine had rung him after getting my telephone call and arranged for the three of us to meet for lunch at the Yacht Club. Beyond being reprimanded by both of them for cutting my visit so short, I'd had no intimation of anything amiss – or was it that I had been so busy with my own affairs that I had failed to see what signs there were? Justine may already have been ill – but she'd said nothing, and my undiscerning eye had perceived nothing out of the ordinary. When she died, three years later, the message reached me too late for me to attend the funeral. As for Maurice, in that winter of '54 he'd said nothing to me of his impending retirement.

Maurice's retirement: the more I pondered, the more I felt that this was the hinge upon which everything turned. All the mysteries and contradictions surrounding his death had their source, I was convinced, in whatever had led him to retire from the office of President of the island Assembly in mid-term. His lonely death in an empty room of that abandoned house was surely but the final phase in a drama that had had its beginnings many years before. The explicitness of this feeling brought me back to reality with a jolt. I saw that my bill had been placed on the table, and, picking it up, I stubbed out my cigarette, dropped some loose silver on the table and moved towards the cash desk, where I handed over the exact money and walked out into the cool autumn afternoon. A teasing wind had come up, the kind that often precedes rain. After Italy, I would have welcomed rain. Instead, in no time at all I'd be back under a blinding sun. God, how tired I was of the sun!

TWO

In the event, we landed on La Roque in a blinding storm, and, as we rolled on up towards the terminal building, I felt a distinct sense of relief at being safely down. At the best of times, La Roque seems a very small chunk of earth to be floating around on its own in such a large expanse of water. From the air, it's as if some optimist has produced a pocket handkerchief in which to catch an albatross. Nor, I've found, does it help much to know that the airport boasts an accident-free history; ten short years (before which time everyone arrived by boat) hardly establishes a firm sense of precedent.

As usual, the sheer boisterousness of the rainfall seemed to touch off in the locals a sort of fizzing effervescence that some of my fellow passengers, I noticed, found somewhat less than reassuring. Already confused by being met with the Deluge in Paradise, several of them blanched visibly as the inevitable welcoming party of officials, carrying huge, gaily striped umbrellas, descended upon us in a crescendo of volubility and hilarity.

There are no Customs to speak of on La Roque, the island's government remaining accommodatingly incurious as to what its visitors bring in besides their money. I was therefore in and out of the airport whilst most of my fellow passengers were still greeting their friends and relations, and the first taxi in the queue at the front of the building was all mine.

The fellow who jumped out from the driving seat to take my bags was familiar though now the black moustache and mop of wiry black hair was faintly grizzled with grey. The official-looking cap was strange on him, but if he had been dressed as Little Bo-Peep I should still have recognized him.

'Paulo, you old so-and-so! What's happened to the liquor business, then?'

'Señor?' He halted in surprise, a bag in each hand. Then, as

16

he stood there, a quizzical look on his face, recognition slowly broke through.

'Señor Angus! Mother of God!' He dropped my luggage with rather more abandon than I cared for, grabbed my hand and pumped it wildly. I could almost have believed the old devil was actually pleased to see me.

The last time I had seen Paulo Garcia he had been head barman at the Yacht Club in Porte Hilaire, a position he had held for as many years as I cared to remember. He had won for himself a special place in my father's heart by being, in his spare time, an enthusiastic and almost fantastically successful fisherman. It was strange to see him, as it were, out of water.

'They kicked you out in the end, then?'

He flashed a white-toothed grin that seemed to stretch from one ear-lobe to the other and pulled the cab door open with a flourish.

'Señor, I retire!'

I acknowledged the royal air with a slight bow, deriving both amusement and comfort from this evidence that at least *one* person on La Roque hadn't changed one whit.

As we drove off, he explained that during his last years of office his feet had played him up and he had decided to hand over to his son, Luis.

'You remember 'im, Señor? 'E was my assistant. 'E played a guitar very good.'

I said I did and he looked pleased. He went on to explain, at length and with considerable histrionic emphasis, that to drive a cab had always been his retirement ambition and now that he had achieved it he intended to carry on until – ' 'Ow you say, Señor?' – I suggested 'die in harness' a trifle unhappily and he seized on the phrase with delighted gusto.

Like most of the island's manual workers, Paulo Garcia was part, if not wholly, Spanish: in other words, a blood member of the island's founder race. His people it had been, who, more than four hundred years ago, had discovered the island, called it *Terra Verde* and had started the

17

first community of fruit-trading settlers – some thiry years before the wealthy merchant-captain, Raoul de Courvel, had arrived on the scene and, with a varying number of pieces of gold – according to which history in the Porte Hilaire library you prefer – bought the island for himself and his heirs. Since that day, the French way of life and its language have predominated – though, as to the latter, only just. There are, in fact, four languages spoken on La Roque: French by the controlling class and its aspiring sat-ellite factions; Spanish by the peasant farmers; English by a growing number of increasingly influential 'tax refugees'; and an orally-evolved and virtually unteachable explosion of sound known as 'Roquennais-French', which, merci-fully, is confined for the most part to those conversations of the plantation workers not meant for the outside ear. Those acquainted with the British skill for avoiding the tedium of learning other people's languages will not be surprised to learn that for quite some time now English has been the one language on La Roque that almost everybody speaks.

Paulo's own skill in that direction may have left some-thing to be desired, but he drove a cab, I discovered, with the same nice combination of dash and accuracy with which he had dispensed drinks.

'You come for 'oliday, Señor?' he enquired, turning in his seat to look at me, while negotiating a narrow hairpin bend and narrowly missing the airport bus trundling up from town.

'You could say that.'

'You find things different, I think. You know, Señor, about – ' He paused and half-turned again to look at me, concern written large on his expressive countenance.

'Monsieur de Courvel. Yes.' I stopped; then, on an impulse: 'Do you know why he died, Paulo?'

I'd expected *some* reaction, but what I got startled me.

A sound like the hissing of a trapped alley-cat came from his lips. He shook his head violently from side to side and then brought his huge hand down on the horn with such force that for a second we sounded like the Queen Mary

18

entering New York harbour in heavy fog. Finally, he spoke, nodding his head up and down as thought it were on elastic.

'There are *some*, Señor, who do! Sí! Sí! Sí! – ' an emphatic nod with each affirmative – 'but they won't tell you! Oh, no!' – now a shake – 'You know why, Señor?'

I said I didn't and he gave vent to a further explosive snarl. 'Because they are the sons of the Devil! That is why.' A few more nods and then a deep sigh.

To say the least, I was taken aback. 'But I understand', I said, 'that his family – '

I was not allowed to finish. ' 'Is *family*! Bah!'

The ferocity of this dismissal of Alain and Simone de Courvel, the close friends of my boyhood, startled and dismayed me. I suddenly felt a curious disinclination to pursue the matter further. But let loose a tiger and you have no choice but to run. My tiger had caught the smell of the chase and was in it for blood.

'When,' he demanded, 'is a family a family. Eh? When it desert you, eh? When it no longer care about you, eh? When it leave you die, an old man in an empty 'ouse? *That* is a family – eh?'

His face registered a deep, personal anguish and he took both hands off the wheel and gestured towards heaven. He brought them back again just in time to prevent us from plunging through a low brick wall and several hundreds of feet down into the sea and began to shake his head slowly from side to side in an expression, apparently, of an uncontrollable inner suffering.

'But – '

'No, Señor!' – I doubt if, in fact, he remembered I was there – 'A family it look after you! It care! It comfort you in trouble. When you are old, when you are no more strong, then a family fight for you. It keep you *up*!' – both hands in the air – 'not *down*, not leave you go away alone – Mother of Heaven! – like an animal, Señor, like an old dog, to die! No, no! Oh, no, no, Señor!'

I felt a sickness rising inside me. 'There must have been reasons,' I murmured.

'Certainly, Señor! There were reasons! Plenty reasons! For some, plenty *good* reasons! But for Señor de Courvel' – and here he directed over his shoulder a look of such balefulness that I could only hope it was by intent aimed at the 'some' to whom he had referred – 'all bad ones, Señor! All bad ones!'

I was silent. My mind was baulking at the implications. Allowing for the Spanish temperament, plus the possibility of more than a grain of some personal prejudice against the ruling class – which nevertheless did not seem to extend to Maurice de Courvel himself – there were sinister notes in Paulo's outburst that I could not explain. Grief I understood, knowing the immense respect and affection which all Roquennais had felt for the old man: shock, too, by reason of the way in which he had died; but this violent undercurrent of hatred of his family was something else, something inexplicable, and profoundly disturbing.

I began to wonder to what extent it would be prudent to continue discussing the subject with Paulo. If there had been such changes in the de Courvel family as his remarks hinted, better, perhaps, to seek some explanation of them from a less prejudiced source.

About half a mile out of town, Paulo's attention was diverted by one of those roadside 'incidents' so common on La Roque: in this case a confrontation between a tourist-driven hired car (identifiable by the customary large yellow L above the front number-plate) and an elderly Roquennais leading two mules and a cartload of compost. Paulo swerved violently on the wet road as he endeavoured to catch the drift of the altercation in passing and, before it was too late, to make some suitable contribution of his own. After that, the impositions of tourists in general and particular occupied him fully until he pulled us up on our noses outside the Hotel Place Royale. At that moment the rain stopped.

I had never before had occasion to stay at any of the hotels on the island, and was confident of not being known to any of the management or staff at the Royale. This was how I wanted it, and I hoped I would be able to avoid running into anyone I knew, or who knew me, until after I had been able to go up to St Michel and take a look at the place on my own. It was unlikely that I would be able to get inside the house, but I had a trained nose, better than any bloodhound's, for what in my trade as a journalist we are supposed to call 'atmosphere', and I was anxious to discover what, if any, of this ephemeral substance I would pick up at the place of my old friend's death.

I had a large whisky sent up to my room, drank it while I unpacked, had a quick shower, changed my shirt, and then went out in search of transport.

The Royale had its own car-hire facilities and I settled for a nicely inconspicuous cream-coloured Citroën and within ten minutes had signed all the necessary forms and a cheque and was on my way.

I found there had been some changes in the traffic routing in the town since my last visit and twice managed to go down one-way streets the wrong way before I finally got clear. Once out on the northern coast-road, nothing had changed. It was the same neat, clean countryside, steaming slightly from the recent rain and becoming more familiar with every mile. At Porte du Spain, about four miles out of town, I left the coast and began the climb into the lovely Arle Valley. Here, under the shelter of Mont Colombe, were the big banana plantations owned by families I knew, many of them with sons or daughters who had been among my personal friends.

The road took me along the shores of the only natural lake on the island, the water shimmering under a moist haze. The lake was a reservoir and a bird sanctuary, a beautiful place even at the height of the tourist season. As I drove along its banks, a sudden fierce nostalgia swept over me for those long-gone days of my boyhood in this place: the days when we had picnicked – I and the de Courvel twins, Alain and Jean, and their sister, Simone, and Imogen and Nicholas Le Marnet and the two Cartiers – here and on the banks of the Arle River where it ran down to the sea.

For a while, the reasons for my return to the island seemed totally unbelievable, as sights and sounds of the past floated back. I had been thirteen the year my father came to La Roque to write his last book. He had come alone, as my mother had died when I was seven and there was no other family besides myself, struggling my way through public school. In the long summer holiday he had sent for me and I had arrived, perspiring and puffing in my thick English flannels and school blazer. My father was staying at a small pension on the waterfront in Porte Hilaire, where he had made friends with all the fishermen, and the first night there I sat up in bed reading *Twenty Thousand Leagues Under the Sea* by the light of a lamp that flickered on and off every time I moved. That was the first and last book I opened that holiday. For a writer, my father was a very physical man, and he had planned for me a programme of fishing, swimming, walking and riding that in two days had me reeling into bed at night like a drug-addict. Moreover, he had some friends, he said, whom he wanted me to meet. He would have taken me to see them sooner, had not my pale English face made him ashamed of me. At all events, on the third day he took me up to St Michel and I met the de Courvel family for the first time. Maurice was one of my father's oldest friends, dating back to a chance meeting in Paris in their student days.

For me, the de Courvels and their world were earth-shattering. Not even the endless variations and uncertainties of life with my father had prepared me for the pattern of existence at St Michel. Life was lived in just two elements – air and water. Within a week I was at home in both, and my pale skin was so burnt by sun and salt that only my blue eyes and red hair distinguished me from the hordes of part-Spanish, part-French boys on the waterfronts.

I discovered that the de Courvels were not just a family, they were a dynasty: tightly interwoven with the two other island families of prominence, the Le Marnets and the Cartiers. These *were* La Roque: they always had been and it seemed then that they always would be.

I spent three more summers with my father on La Roque.

Towards the end of the third, he was drowned on a fishing expedition leaving me at sixteen completely alone in the world. With nowhere to go, it had seemed natural at the time to become absorbed into the de Courvel family; it was only much later that I had realized how much I owed to Maurice and Justine. The next three years were among the happiest of my life. The memory of them sustained me throughout the war in Europe and when my wife, Maggie, was killed in a London air-raid just one year and six days after we were married.

Now, as I drove in the yellow sun through the Arle Valley, an uncomfortable thought took hold of me. Over the years the whole de Courvel family had become illumined in my mind by the after-glow of happy memory. Occupationally conditioned as I was to facing realities, it was unnerving to think that I could have been guilty all those years of the blind idealism of youth. Yet the possibility was there.

Now the first plantations of the St Michel estate came into sight, flanking the road on both sides. And here was another surprise. They were as green, as flourishing and as full of activity as they had ever been. There was not a sign of the neglect and decay I had been given to expect. Baffled, I turned the car up the narrow lane that led to the gates of the house, and about twenty yards short of them, I stopped, turned off the engine and lit a cigarette. For some reason, I wanted to slow down my approach to the house, to come upon it gradually, on foot, with time to absorb whatever I would see.

I found the gates open, as they had always been, and I stood for a moment, looking up the broad, tree-lined drive. I could see the house itself standing sideways to the lane, the drive broadening out in front of it and bordered by a wide lawn which directly faced the front porch.

As I approached, I saw that it was here, round the house itself, that the changes I had anticipated were to be found. The garden had been long abandoned. The lawn was overgrown and one of the lower branches of the huge catalpa tree that stood in its centre had been blown down and was

23

hanging, gaunt and mutilated, in the long, straggling grass. I remembered how Nicholas Le Marnet and I had played chess under that very branch in the long summer evenings, how, above us, Jean de Courvel would sprawl in the fork of the trunk, reading, and how tea with strawberries and cream would be served to as many as a dozen people in the tree's shade on any day of the week as a matter of course.

I dropped my cigarette into one of the weed-choked beds, hoeing it in with the toe of my shoe. Then, I walked on up the drive past the two coach-houses, where a small van was parked, its back doors open revealing ladders and miscellaneous builder's materials. Near it, propped in some bushes, was a man's bicycle.

As I came level with the van, I noticed that further down the drive, just beyond the door of the house, a small blue car was parked and crouching just in front of it, almost hidden by the bonnet, was a little fair-haired girl, playing with something on the ground. Before I could decide what to do the child straightened up and came darting round the car towards me. She stopped in her tracks when she saw me, staring at me with wide-eyed apprehension and hugging to her chest a small frightened ginger kitten. Before I could draw breath to make some sort of reassuring noise, she darted back towards the house and disappeared inside.

This was it, then. In no time at all the alarm would be given and a reception committee would be gathering on the doorstep. It was annoying, but there was damn all I could do about it, so I confined myself to hoping that, with luck, the child simply belonged to one of the workmen. The odds that any of them would know me, even if I recognized any of them, were remote.

As I drew level with the house, I saw with a further shock just what those two years of abandonment had done to it. The Palladian-style portico was now a mess of unswept rubble, the creeper that had grown so elegantly round the pillars that supported the roof along the front of the house was tangled and trailing, and there was a large crack in one of the ground-floor windows.

The front door was open, but even without the presence of the workmen this would not have surprised me, as I had never known it to be otherwise except in the middle of the night. Inside the sight was even more depressing. The hall, once a lovely place of cool quiet, with shining, polished-wood furniture and Maurice's splendid old grandfather clock noting the seconds with sonorous dignity at the foot of the stairs, now looked like a builder's yard. Ladders, half-used tins of paint, lengths of timber and festering pieces of rag and old newspaper littered the floor. Everything looked dark and dingy, and there was an unpleasant smell of decay. The only cheering aspect was the fair-haired child, who was now standing at the far end of the hall, talking to the ginger cat, perched on some steps. She had forgotten all about me. The cat, however, took one baleful glance in my direction, leapt off the steps and darted up the passage leading to the kitchens. The child followed.

I could hear hammering now, and the sound of voices, but it seemed that the front of the house was deserted. On my left was the door of the study. This was the old man's room, the room in which he had lived out so much of his life and in which he had died. The door was shut and I stood for several seconds, staring at it. I felt exactly as I had as a boy when I had watched them bringing in the boat from which my father had been washed overboard. It was like standing on the brink of something so intimate to another's experience that a feeling almost of guilt took hold of one. Death was the ultimate individual knowledge. It could not be shared, any more than a key that is made to fit a certain lock can be used to open another.

Nevertheless, I was determined to enter that room. Only when I walked up to the door and turned the handle, did it occur to me that the door might be locked. But it wasn't. I pushed it open and stood with my hand still on the knob and looked into the room.

I could hardly believe what I saw: it could have been an auctioneer's storage room. The room was furnished exactly as it had always been, but a mass of furniture had been piled in from other parts of the house. All of it thrown together anyhow, one article on top of or alongside another in no sense of order that I could see. Directly opposite the door three bedsteads were propped in layers against what I recognized as the dresser that used to stand in the kitchen. Tables were piled on each other like trays, the tops resting on the feet of the one below, and the wells in between were crowded with bric-à-brac of every description, from paper fans to marble busts. Pictures were stacked three and four deep against anything that would support them, and the floor was covered – literally – with rolled carpets and with books. There were books everywhere: in piles, in rows, alone, open, and, over by the fireplace, a three-tier dinner wagon was loaded with them. And all this was in addition to Maurice's own huge glass-fronted bookcases which lined the walls of the room and which, I knew, included the books of French history he had written himself.

Almost at my feet lay a huge tome bound in black leather and with brass fastenings. I recognized it immediately and felt a dragging sense of depression at its present condition. This was one of the de Courvel treasures, the ancient family Bible, over two hundred years old, in which it had of more recent years become traditional for each eldest son of the family and his bride to sign their names upon marriage. I recalled being shown the signatures of Maurice and Justine de Courvel and thinking that one day Alain's name would appear there, alongside that of some girl as yet unknown to us. But Alain had never married, so Maurice's and Justine's names would still be the last to appear. I took a step forward, knelt and opened the book. The yellowed pages now had a grey film of dust, which I tried to blow away as I opened the massive covers. On the fly-leaf I found the familiar list of names, some of them thin, spidery and fading, others bold and black and seemingly indestructible, all speaking for the hand that had penned them so long ago. As I stared at them, a heavy sadness descended on me and I looked again round the room. Was this, then, what the de Courvel family had come to? Chaos, abandonment, an empty silence?

Then, as I still knelt, I heard a movement behind me. My skin pricked like a dog's and I raised myself upright and turned towards the door. A woman was standing there. At first, the spectacles and the strained lines between the eyes deceived me. Then recognition came, slowly, like a familiar place emerging out of a mist. I was face to face, after ten long years, with Simone de Courvel.

THREE

It was several seconds before either of us spoke. I was shocked at the change in Simone's appearance. Ten years was a long time between visits, but it wasn't exactly the gulf between youth and old age: yet, looking at Simone now, I was almost tempted to believe so. She had never been a conventional beauty; her mouth was too wide, but with her upturned nose and great grey-green eyes there had been a gamin, elfin quality about her that had always been appealing. Now, the fair, wind-blown hair seemed to have flattened into an untidy yellow, the eyes were lost behind thick-rimmed glasses and the once glowing skin had become pinched and strained-looking.

For courtesy's sake, I struggled for recovery. It was clear she was as stunned as I by the unexpected meeting. Her colour came and went and her eyes looked almost frightened. At length I managed a weak grin.

'Hello, Simone.'

It sounded flat even to me, and I took a step forward and drew both her hands in mine. Immediately, I sensed I had made a mistake. Her face went very white, and her hands, as cold as ice, shrank away from mine. I let go of her and the set lines round her mouth relaxed; she tried to smile.

'Angus – ' She stopped: then tried again. 'It can't be true! I – I don't believe it!' She drew a deep breath and shook her head.

At that moment, the little fair-haired girl came running up and stood behind Simone, staring at me. I saw the likeness between them and remembered: of course, there had been children – a boy who had died and then a girl. What was her name? It bothered me that for the life of me I couldn't remember. But something else bothered me, too. There was an odd look about the child. To me, it seemed something more than the wondering withdrawnness that is natural to some children. To have described it as a 'vacant' look would have been to overstate, yet there was something strangely and disturbingly lacking in the expression on the small, pale face.

Simone didn't appear to notice the child's arrival. She had made a big effort towards composure, but her face now was flushed and she began to talk with such nervous speed that, good though my French is, I had difficulty in keeping up with her.

'Why didn't you let us know?. . . It's so incredible!. . . I – we – someone would have met you. But it's so *long*! (a reproachful look, then contrition). Of course, we're as much to blame, but time goes so quickly . . . there's never a moment to write.' There was a pause for breath, and a long look, then she began again, this time rather more slowly. 'But how are you, Angus? You know – about – ' She became flustered once more and her glance darted across towards the fireplace where the old man's chair still stood.

'Yes,' I said. 'I'm sorry, Simone.'

As quickly as the excitement had risen in her, it drained away again; her voice, when she next spoke, was almost mechanical.

'Yes, you must have heard.'

'I didn't until yesterday,' I said. 'I'd been in Europe. When I got back, I saw the papers.'

'Ah, yes,' she said. 'The papers.' There was another pause. 'We were going to get in touch with you – but – ' Her voice trailed off.

'Of course,' I said.

Her eyes, apologetic, met mine; she was making a visible effort to pull herself together. 'We really ought to go somewhere where we can talk,' she said. 'I'd ask you to come home with us, but – ' She stopped abruptly and I sensed some acute discomfort in her.

'It's all right, Simone.'

'Oh, but no!' she cried, 'it's not! The only thing – ' Again she stopped, and now her face looked agonized. It

29

was then that the truth hit me with all the directness of a well-aimed poleaxe. She didn't *want* to take me home with her. She didn't want to prolong this reunion one second longer than was absolutely necessary. In a nutshell, she wanted me the hell out of here.

I fought off another numbing attack of shock and hastened to her aid.

'Actually,' I said, 'I'm afraid I've got to go straight back. I'm expecting a call from the office.'

'Oh,' she said. 'Really?'

If it hadn't been so tragic I could have laughed out loud at the thinly disguised relief in her face. Simone had never been our best actress.

'Well,' I said, 'you know how it is. I left a few loose ends.'

'You have to return soon, then?' She made a token grimace of regret, but the eagerness in her voice was palpable. I felt almost guilty at having to spoil it for her.

'Well, not immediately,' I said. 'I'm due a break, so I may stay on a few days.'

The split second of shock and dismay no longer surprised me, but neither did the obligatory smile that followed give me any comfort. What had happened to the warm, generous and uncomplicated friendliness that had always been inherently part of the Simone I had known? Where was the rapport I had once come to feel existed between us?

Well, now was no time for analysis. I owed her an explanation for my unheralded presence here, and it had better be a good one.

'I'm afraid I hadn't really taken it in, about the house being empty,' I said. 'I thought it was just press exaggeration. I know how they do things.'

'Oh, I see,' she said, 'you thought – '

'Yes,' I said quickly. 'I thought I should find someone here.' I smiled. 'As it happens, I did.'

She forced a smile in return, but underneath it her face was still bleak, as she stood twisting the strap of her handbag. The impression of some inward struggle was stronger than ever. Simone was being consumed by something much more than simple grief. But what? As I looked into her tired green eyes, I tried to recapture a picture of the girl I had known, but it was no use. She was gone for ever, and all that was left was this pale, anxiety-ridden woman who, at – what was it, thirty-four . . . thirty-five . . . already looked aged by some prolonged inner suffering. Suddenly, I realized that she had spoken.

'Sorry,' I said.

She gave a quick, surface smile. 'I only wondered,' she said, 'if you'd like to come out and have lunch with us tomorrow. Would that be possible? I'm sorry about this evening, but – '

'Tomorrow would be fine.' I wondered what it had cost her to suggest it. Probably she'd decided she couldn't put it off indefinitely, so, after playing for time, she'd get it over with. 'If you want to change your mind for any reason,' I said, 'give me a ring. I'm at the Royale. They'll take a message if I'm not there. If I don't hear, I'll take it it's O.K. You'd better tell me, though, how I find you.'

'Oh yes! Of course!' She started rummaging in her bag and I handed her the pen and small note pad I always carry around with me.

She propped the pad against the wall beside her, scribbled on it and then handed it back to me. 'It's easy to find,' she said. 'You turn left at the St George's Mission and then left again. Here – ' She took the pad off me again, scribbled some more and then handed it back, turning so swiftly that she collided with the child, who had come forward to try and see what was being written.

'I'll find you all right,' I said, and I wondered what on earth Simone de Courvel, wife of the wealthy Raymond Corlander, could possibly be doing anywhere near the St George's district of Porte Hilaire, which, if not actually a slum, was as near to it as made no matter.

'We must go now,' said Simone, and once again she cannoned into the little girl, who had now begun to look apprehensive. Simone seemed to remember her daughter for the first time, for she stopped, took the child by the shoulders and pushed her towards me. 'This is Hélène,' she said. 'I don't think you've seen her before.'

'No.' I bent and looked into the child's grave eyes. 'Hello, Hélène,' I said. 'How are you?' It sounded far more formal than I had intended, but somehow the child's stiff manner inhibited me. She didn't answer, but simply stared at me with those great grey-green eyes and with that curious empty expression. I was saved from any further attempts at communication by Simone, who turned the little girl briskly round and propelled her towards the door. To me, over her shoulder, she said: 'We only meant to come for an hour, but you know how it is.'

That was just it: I didn't. As I followed them out, I closed the door of Maurice's room behind us, wondering what, if anything, that room could have told me had I been able to linger there alone a little longer. Perhaps nothing. Perhaps there was nothing more to tell. Depression and suicide . . . somehow it seemed less unlikely now than it had before. But the basic questions remained.

Outside, Hélène broke away from us and ran ahead to the small blue car, where she began wrestling with the handle of the door. She stood back as I walked up and bent to open it for her. When she was comfortably installed, I went round to the other side, where Simone was already at the wheel.

'We'll see you tomorrow then, Angus.' She spoke lightly, but the anxiety was still in her eyes.

I nodded. 'Take care, Simone,' I said.

To my surprise, her head jerked up and for a moment she looked as though she were going to burst into tears. Possibly my alarm showed, for instead she smiled. But it was the uncertain smile of an injured child and in place of relief I experienced a violent sense of dismay. Something was wrong. Terribly wrong. But I had no idea what it was, nor what had caused it. And I had not the faintest clue how or where to look for the answers.

* * *

Before I returned to town, there was one more thing I had to do.

The village of St Michel stands another hundred feet or so above the Manoir, at the top of a long, winding hill that climbs up from the plantations to the headland called Point St Michel above the bay. I drove through the village to the far end, where the road begins to give way to the springy turf of the cliff. For it is here, alone and facing the sea, that the parish church of St Michel was built in the fifteenth century, its graveyard a part of the cliff itself, marked out only by a low stone wall and a few cypress trees.

I knew exactly where to find the de Courvel family grave, but, even if I had not, the great mass of fresh wreaths and flowers would have drawn me to it. I stood for a while, reading the newly-carved lettering on the stone:

> *Maurice Edmond de Courvel,*
> *Seigneur du Fief de St Michel,*
> *Sénéchal d'Isle de La Roque, 1954–1959,*
> *Président de l'Assemblée, 1949–1954,*
> *Mari de Justine de Courvel, née du Bois.*
> *Mort Septembre 28 1959*

And below this, in smaller lettering, under the de Courvel crest – an opened book borne between two soaring wings – the family motto:

> *'Mon Dieu et mon Espoir Voici'*

I had brought no wreath. it was not time for that. Perhaps, when I had discovered why he lay here, it would be time. But until then, flowers were not what I had come to offer Maurice de Courvel, and a wreath was not what his spirit asked of me.

Back in town, I garaged the car, showered and went in to dinner. I lingered over the meal and afterwards carried my drink into the lounge, where I pretended to read the local evening paper but in fact thought over my meeting with Simone and considered my next move. It was nine-thirty; for the majority of Roquennais, the night was still young. What I had decided to do now was tricky. It involved bringing together certain people and checking for reactions. Nothing more. But long experience of interviewing people had taught me that much could be learned from reactions. Especially those produced by the unexpected. And especially when certain of the people involved weren't exactly buddies. As, for example, Max Cartier and Alain de Courvel . . . As I remembered it, they'd never enjoyed an empathetic relationship. What had they now? I wondered.

I left the lounge and went into the telephone booth in the lobby. I looked up the number I wanted and picked up the receiver. I spoke in French and a courteous Spanish operator answered me in the same language and put me through. A man's voice answered my query in cool, impersonal French.

'I'm sorry, Monsieur, but Monsieur Cartier is not at home.'

'Do you know where I can find him?'

'Monsieur and Madame are at the Yacht Club, Monsieur.'

'Thank you.' I rang off, checked again in the directory and asked for another number. This time, I recognized the voice at the other end immediately.

'Hello, Alain. It's Angus. How are you?'

'Who?'

But *was* it surprise, I wondered? Or had Simone flashed him the signal? Before I could repeat myself, he came back to me.

'Angus! Good God!' It sounded genuine enough, but, if so, what was wrong with Simone's reflexes? She had had well over an hour.

'I'm at the Yacht Club,' I lied. 'I wondered if you'd care to join me.' I had to risk his refusing and asking me to go to him instead, in which case so be it. There was silence at the other end of the line and I could almost hear him thinking. He isn't coming, I decided. He considers the rendezvous

34

inappropriate in the circumstances and me tactless for suggesting it. Then I heard him draw breath.

'You know about Father, Angus?'

'Yes.' I had the grace to feel ashamed at what I was trying to do to him. 'It was in the papers. I'm sorry, Alain.' I was right. He wasn't coming. 'If you'd rather not – ' I began.

'It's all right.' To my surprise, he came back quickly, like a man who knows something is inevitable and wants to get it over with. 'I'll be with you in about fifteen minutes.'

I heard the line go dead, and felt myself in a curious way dismissed. It occurred to me that there was something odd in his *not* having asked me to go to his place. I'd never seen where he'd chosen to live since he'd left St Michel, though I knew he had a flat or house somewhere in the centre of town. It would surely have been more natural for him to have suggested we meet there? But the invitation hadn't come. Well, that suited me – but it was odd all the same.

The lounge bar of the Yacht Club was so full that for a second I had to stand in the doorway to get my bearings. It amused me to think that if someone from outer space arrived and demanded, 'Take me to your leader,' this is probably where they'd end up. It was the place where, on almost any evening of the week, and especially at weekends, almost all the really important representatives of island power, bar the very old, ill or tired, would be gathered. As now. The room hummed like a dynamo and glowed under the discreet lights as the talk rose from the groups round the tables and the colours of the women's dresses mingled with the occasional flash of jewellery.

Behind the bar, young Luis Garcia, in black bow-tie and trousers, white frilled shirt and a maroon jacket, was learning his father's trade the hard way, but he seemed well compensated by the raven-haired, bosomy barmaid down the other end of the counter. I ordered a Scotch from her and sat down on one of the stools to take stock.

Almost immediately, I spotted the tall figure of Max Cartier down at the far end of the room. He was standing beside a table, at which I could see Imogen in brilliant green, and a couple unknown to me.

I picked up my drink and began to make my way towards them. As I approached, Max took a vacant chair from the next table and sat down beside Imogen: whereupon all four of them began to laugh uproariously at something the other fellow had said. It was Imogen who saw me first. She stopped laughing, clapped a hand to her chest and sat for a moment looking at me, her mouth open. Then, as the others looked at her, she found her voice. 'Angus!' she cried.

For a moment, it seemed as if the whole room stopped whatever it was doing to look at me. But in the second it took me to get over my embarrassment everything went back to normal. Except, that is, for the four at the table in front of me. Her shock over, Imogen's delight was rapturous. Max, whose handsome face had first sagged with surprise – he'd put on flesh, I noticed – rallied with the charm and bonhomie one could always count on from him. I remembered how I'd always admired him for the things I lacked: good looks, wit and that supreme kind of self-assurance that could turn almost any situation that arose to its own advantage. Nevertheless, there had always been a bantering cynicism in him that at times could irritate, and even now, his surprise over, his face began to assume that lazy, half-mocking expression I'd once known so well.

After the greetings and introductions were over, I called a waiter and ordered drinks all round. Max pulled a chair up for me between him and the Englishman they'd called Tony Fellowes – a vacuous type if ever there was one, I decided – and I was put through a third degree as to my activities since we'd last all met.

Characteristically, it was Imogen who first grasped the nettle: 'You've heard about Maurice, Angus?' I said I had and we all agreed how sad it was. There was some augmentation of the theme, and while it continued I studied them both. Neither seemed to me to have changed much, except that Max now sported a military-style moustache, and *was* distinctly over-weight. Imogen, on the other hand, was as

36

beautiful as ever. The years had been as good to her as they had been cruel to Simone. It was easy to see her still as she had been as a girl: her long, almost black hair tied back with a wide, brilliantly-coloured ribbon. What a creature she'd been even then, her will and her personality dominating us all! Looking back, I realized that a large proportion of the response she had evoked in each one of us had been pure and simple fear. With Imogen, we had never known at any given moment where we stood, what might be expected of us, what humiliations awaited us if we failed to measure up to her ruthless spirit of adventure. At times, her utter disregard of danger had seemed to reach beyond the boundaries of mere courage into something mercilessly, almost sadistically, forgetful of either self or others. Hers, for instance, had been the dare that had sent Jean de Courvel striding into the sea at Mt Michel's bay on the night of his eighteenth birthday in an attempt to swim the four miles round the coast to Ste Marie Pier. We'd been discussing the fact that someone or other (damn him) had once done it, and Jean, who had been a good swimmer, proclaimed that it was nothing to write home about. Imogen had laughed derisively, whereupon Jean had simply got to his feet and walked towards the water. Despite our half-disbelieving cries to him to return, he had dived into a wave, emerging the other side to begin, slowly but inexorably, to swim out to sea. After a while, we'd packed up our picnic equipment, piled it and ourselves into a couple of cars and roared off up the coast road in pursuit. We'd crawled after him almost into Porte Hilaire, but there we had had to turn inland, and when we came back to the coast road again at Les Pyramides, the other side of town, there had been no sign of him. We had waited there so long that finally we'd decided he'd duped us and slipped aboard a boat at Porte Hilaire. Heaping abuse on him, we had then torn on round to Ste Marie, ready to denounce him loudly in the Dolphin bar. I don't think it had seriously occurred to any of us that he wouldn't be there. It had been Nicholas who had finally phoned the coastguards. They told him that Jean had been picked up in the Roads just off Porte Hilaire in a distressed condition. He had died before a doctor could be got out to him. Well, it wasn't Imogen's fault, I suppose, that Jean had had a weak heart. Who *could* have known it if he, himself, and none of his family had? For all that, I'd always had the uneasy feeling that Maurice had never really forgiven her. Certainly Alain hadn't, and I can't say I blamed him.

'You're thinner, Augus,' she was saying. 'You need feeding up. You must come and stay with *us*.' She gave her brilliant smile, but as I looked at her I realized suddenly that for the first time Imogen's magic had failed for me. Why, I didn't know. Passage of time? Perhaps. But I sensed it was something more: something to do with Simone, with the change I had found in her and the difference between what Simone was now and what Imogen was, and always had been: a survivor.

I realized Max was speaking and looked at him enquiringly.

'Where are you booked in?' he demanded.

'The Royale, but – '

'We'll pick up your things when we leave,' said Imogen. 'It will be all right, chéri, we know Corlander.'

Corlander? Of course, Simone's father-in-law owned the damn place. One more thing I'd forgotten.

'It's very nice of you,' I said, 'but I think I'd better stay put. I've got some unfinished work,' I lied. 'I promised I'd complete it over here.'

'No problem,' said Max. 'You can have my study. There's a typewriter in there, and I can get you a girl to work the thing if you like.'

'There!' said Imogen with malicious sweetness, 'one of Max's little girls. What more can a man give?'

Max frowned. He looked incredibly pompous and I had trouble keeping a grin off my face.

'What my wife means,' he said, 'is that I can detail someone to come to the house every day. No trouble.' He drained his glass with dignified detachment.

'Thanks again,' I said. 'But I really would rather not, if you don't mind.' *And* if you *do*, I thought.

Max shrugged. For him, the discussion was already forgotten. Imogen, however, had the look I knew well. She would try again later.

Fellowes raised his glass at someone over my shoulder and Max's eyes followed the other man's glance. He nodded, looking pleased at the diversion.

'Hello, Ray,' he said. 'Come and join us.'

A tall, thick-set man of about my own age, with a pink, rather fleshy face, moved up beside Imogen and bent and kissed the side of her neck.

'Greetings,' he said, raising his glass first to her and then to us all.

Imogen's smile was coquettish, but I had the feeling that she hadn't enjoyed the intimacy overmuch. 'You two don't know each other, do you?' she asked, waving a hand in my direction.

'This is Angus Logan, Ray. He used to live with the de Courvels before the war. Angus, this is Ray Corlander.'

I rose and took the hand he offered. It was wet where he'd slopped his drink over it. 'Oh, yes,' I said. 'I met your wife this afternoon. I expect she told you.'

There was a curious stillness. Corlander's face sagged into an expression of bewilderment. 'I met her at St Michel,' I offered. 'She had your little girl with her.'

Now, I sensed, rather than saw, glances being exchanged. But there was no mistaking the amused grin that spread across Corlander's face. He glanced towards Imogen. 'Before the war, you said?' Then he looked back at me. 'Time marches on, old boy. The lady you saw was undoubtedly my ex. The present lady's name is Phyllis and offspring we have none.'

I needed time to assimilate this, but I was not given it.

'You went to the house, Angus?' Imogen queried.

I nodded.

'That was a shock, too, I should think,' said Corlander. He laughed noisily, and I could have kicked his nice white teeth in. I found I disliked him intensely, and, recalling Simone's face, it occurred to me that it would be a pity if she was grieving at all for the loss of this particular piece of real estate. Perhaps he sensed my reaction: at all events, he made to turn away.

'We're at the Casino if you'd all like to drop in later,' he said. 'I must get back now.' He gave a comprehensive nod and wave, slopping more drink on to the table. 'See you.'

He hadn't gone more than a step, however, before he turned back, looking directly at me. 'Give my love to Simone when you see her again,' he said. There was a distinctly bantering look in his eyes now, and I must have looked what I was feeling because he broke into a self-conscious laugh before making off through the crowd towards the door.

There followed a second's rather special silence, broken by Imogen, who had apparently decided that the only way to deal with a potentially dangerous animal was to confront it head-on. 'You hadn't heard, then, Angus?' she said.

'No.' I hoped she wouldn't pursue the subject. For one thing, I didn't want to discuss Simone in front of the Fellowes; for another, I still wasn't sure I could respond sufficiently dispassionately. At the same time, I blamed myself for much of what had happened. If I'd kept in touch with the family, I'd have known the score, saving myself and everyone else a lot of embarrassment. As it was, all that could be said for the present situation was that at least it had given me an insight into what in all probability had contributed towards Simone's present condition. The thought of her married to Ray Corlander was both sickening and incredible.

'It never stood a chance, of course,' Imogen said.

I looked at her without speaking, and a faint, patronizing smile touched her lips. 'Well – I don't mean to sound unkind, Angus, but you know Simone. She's a sweet girl, always has been, but hardly a ball of fire, would you say?'

When I still didn't answer her, she began to look uncomfortable and went on the defensive. 'What I mean is, Ray's got a lot on his hands now. He and his father between them more or less run the entire tourist business on the island. It's a situation that needs a rather special kind of partnership.'

'You mean like a three-ring circus.'

Imogen's face froze and Fellowes' tiny wife gave a nervous whinny.

Alain de Courvel could not have timed his arrival more felicitously. Seeing his tall, thin figure in the doorway, I murmured an apology and got up and began to thread my way towards him.

He was lighting a cigarette when I reached him and glanced up at me over the top of his lighter. He seemed not to have changed at all, although the wariness that had always been a part of his dark good looks now seemed accentuated by a tension in him that I suppose was natural in the circumstances.

He returned my greeting with a nod and I led him over to the bar and ordered a Pernod for him and a lager for myself. I told him how shocked I'd been at the news of his father and he nodded again.

'I went up to the house this afternoon,' I said. 'I saw Simone.'

He extended an inviting hand towards one of the stools that had become vacant at the bar and when I shook my head sat down himself.

'Yes,' he said. 'I know.'

So either she *had* rung him or he had rung her, and he had decided to be frank. That was one obstacle out of the way at least.

'Why did he do it, Alain?'

He shrugged, raising his eyebrows as he did so, but without looking at me.

'I mean to find out,' I said.

His head jerked round at this and I think he would have said something, but at that moment Luis Garcia gave us our drinks and greeted us with much smiling enthusiasm. When he'd moved away again, Alain took his Pernod and began to sip it, and his face, I saw, now had a closed look.

41

'I'm over there,' I said. 'Shall we go over?'

He looked surprised, but obediently took up his glass and began to follow me across the room.

When we approached the Cartiers, however, I felt him stiffen and almost stop. Pretending not to notice, I pushed on, halting a few inches from Tony Fellowes' shoulder.

'Look who's here,' I said.

They all looked. Imogen smiled, but without warmth, inclining her head to Alain in a royal gesture of distant courtesy. Max rose, his face creasing into a faint, laconic smile.

'Well, well,' he said. 'Welcome, my friend.'

I glanced back towards Alain, and for the first time I felt a twinge of alarm. His face, as he looked at Max, had the hard look of granite. But that was not all. In his eyes, I saw the warning signals of imminent disaster. Whatever I had expected to discover in this meeting between these two, one thing was clear without the faintest shadow of a doubt.

In Alain de Courvel, a vague dislike, rooted in mere temperamental incompatibility, had turned to a reasoning, virulent hatred.

FOUR

Simone rang just after breakfast the following morning. She told me she had invited Alain to lunch, too, as she thought it would be a chance for us to meet.

Did that mean she hadn't heard of the previous night's fiasco? I was relieved, anyway, that Alain had accepted the invitation. It had crossed my mind that there was every possibility that I shouldn't see him again if he could avoid it, as, indeed, was no more than I deserved. Still, I could hardly have been expected to know that he and Max were not on speaking terms so any inadvertent meetings between them were not guaranteed to conform to the accepted standards of social etiquette. But I had deliberately engineered last night's meeting, knowing that Alain never *had* had much use for Max Cartier, that he hated Imogen for what had happened to Jean and that I just wanted to see what kind of chemistry the three of them put together would produce. Well, now I knew, and in the event it had proved embarrassing. Alain had left the scene immediately post-confrontation, and without the time-wasting preliminary of an excuse, leaving me to pick up the pieces as best I could, while Max, apparently overcome by some humour in the situation that had escaped the rest of us, gave vent to uninhibited mirth. Sick, and more than a little ashamed, I had left shortly afterwards.

I set out for Simone's just after midday. The St George's Mission is about half a mile from the centre of Porte Hilaire, and when I arrived there I began following Simone's directions and found that they led to a terrace of large, ugly and decaying houses in an untidy cul-de-sac. I wasn't surprised. This was one of the old, predominantly Spanish, quarters of the town, but the original Spanish

43

buildings had been pulled down at the end of the nineteenth century by a wealthy French eccentric and Anglophile named Pierre Boules. It had been the intention of this worthy, the head of a flourishing business empire in France, to endow the citizens of the district with a gracious community centred round the old Mission of San Antonio (re-dedicated at the old man's instigation, to St George), which in turn received a welcome injection of financial support from the Boules industries. The old boy had apparently been potty about 'La Vie Anglaise', including its current architecture, and the result was that, except for the heat and the brilliant sunshine, the present scene could have been any one of those seedy areas of lapsed Victoriana all too familiar in our cities back home.

Each house was fronted by a narrow rectangle of neglected garden, which, in most cases, appeared to be valued more as a convenient dump for discarded household paraphernalia. I was appalled at the thought of Simone living in one of these houses after the grace and elegance of St Michel. Someone, and I couldn't help feeling it should have been Alain, should have taken Corlander apart before allowing it to happen. I wondered who had handled the divorce. Considering that almost every male friend of the family was a practising advocate at the island Bar, her present situation suggested a degree of impartiality that would have been an example to Abraham on Mount Moriah.

Half-way down the street, I saw one of the dingy front doors open ahead of me, and a now familiar figure appeared at the top of the steps leading down into the garden. It waved and I waved back, just holding my own against a sudden almost overwhelming urge to go into reverse. Instead, I stopped the car, got out and began to walk towards the gate that led into the dreary little garden. A couple of Siamese cats had shown up alongside Simone in the doorway and now they stalked pompously down the path to meet me. I paused, ostensibly to acknowledge their characteristically noisy greetings, but, in fact, to compose myself sufficiently to greet Simone with the grace she deserved, and was certainly in need of. Once I came up to her, however, I realized that she had obviously made an effort to prepare herself for this second encounter. She had on a pale green dress, which gave her a rested look, and a pair of straw-coloured shoes, which I thought looked rather fetching beside the Siamese twins, who were now circling her legs. If it had not been for the residual strain in those grey-green eyes, Simone would have been almost pretty again. As it was, I could still feel a sort of wary anxiety in her as I approached.

'I'm not late, am I?'

She shook her head, smiling. 'Alain's not here yet.'

As she led the way into the house, I could see that she wasn't in the least embarrassed by her surroundings. For all that, I couldn't believe that she could actually have *chosen* them. How the hell, then, had she got here? I decided to take the bull by the horns.

'I met your ex-husband last night, Simone. I'm afraid I hadn't realized, and I'm sorry.'

She turned in the middle of the hall, and now there was a look of genuine amusement on her face.

'Oh, poor Angus! We really *have* been out of touch, haven't we? That's why I asked you to come here. Things are very different over here now.'

'I'd noticed.'

She gave a small laugh, but I sensed a touch of play-acting again now that we were getting back to fundamentals.

As I followed her across the hall, I suddenly became uncomfortably aware of a powerful and familiar odour. Cats. Simone didn't appear to notice it, and again I marvelled. She moved towards a staircase ahead of us, nodding as she did so in the direction of a closed door on our left.

'Lodgers,' she said. On the small landing half-way up the stairs, she paused. 'He's an artist. They have terrible rows.'

'They?'

'He and Rose. They're terribly in love, but every so often he gets these black depressions and they fight. She's been in hospital twice.'

It got better and better, I thought.

45

At the top of the stairs, she led the way into a room on the right which appeared to be her dining-room since there was a table in the centre obviously laid for a meal. As, however, there was also a piano, a settee and a large armchair in the room, it was difficult to determine what its precise designation, if any, might be.

Almost as if she guessed my thoughts, she said: 'This is where we eat.' Then, with a wry smile that contained the first hint of awkwardness, 'You must excuse the muddle. I wanted to keep as much as I could of the furniture from St Michel, but there just isn't room, and we simply can't afford storage.'

It was an understatement of classic simplicity. The room was dead square, with a window in the centre of one wall and the door at right angles to it, and there was barely room between the chairs round the table and the surrounding furniture to accommodate a pencil. It was probably the most uninteresting room I'd ever seen, its only fascination being that it belonged to Simone de Courvel, who had lived all the years I had known her in surroundings of the utmost beauty and charm.

The window was open at top and bottom, but even so it was oppressively hot. Below, I could see a narrow stretch of garden, and, beyond, the blue of the bay where it curved in towards the harbour at Porte Hilaire. A tanker was crossing at the moment, its progress so unnoticeable on the dead calm water that it looked almost like a toy.

'What would you like to drink?' Simone asked. 'Scotch? Wine? I *may* have some gin, if you'd rather.'

I said I would have wine and her face puckered anxiously.

'You're sure?'

'Absolutely.'

She smiled, giving me once again a fleeting vision of the old Simone. Then she went off along the landing out of sight, leaving me to contemplate my surroundings at leisure. Since there wasn't much to contemplate, I drifted out after her. I could hear her talking to someone and the sound of glasses being assembled on a tray, and I found her in what was obviously now her kitchen-cum-larder, a small room which I imagine would once have been a dressing-room, with a window that overlooked the street. Now, this room contained a sink and gas stove, plus the usual shelves and cupboards. Everything in the room that had a flat top was littered with plates and dishes containing odd items of food.

Simone was pulling bottles out from the bottom of one of these cupboards and talking at the same time to Hélène, who was sitting on a stool just inside the door, nursing yet another cat, this time a black-and-white with the look of a seasoned bruiser. At first sight of me, the animal leapt out of Hélène's arms and dashed out through the door and down the stairs, the child pausing only long enough to flash a reproachful look in my direction before taking off in pursuit.

Still kneeling, Simone turned to see what was happening.

'Oh,' she said, 'it's you.'

I nodded. 'Children and animals find me irresistible.'

She straightened up, holding the bottles up to the light to check how much was in them before putting them on the tray with the glasses.

'He doesn't like men,' she said. 'Well, he hardly ever sees any. Only Julian downstairs, and he's not exactly reassuring at times.'

'No.'

I took the tray off her as she was about to lift it and, to my surprise, she gave a flustered little laugh, like a schoolgirl receiving her first attention.

'Where?' I asked, holding up the tray.

'Oh.' She pulled herself together and, smiling again, moved past me to the door. 'We'll have it in the lounge,' she said.

I followed her into a room on the left of the kitchen and she took the tray from me and put it on a sideboard just inside the door.

This was a more cheerful room, with bright cretonne covers on the chairs, and the furniture, in general,

47

covers on the chairs, and the furniture, in general, consistent with the function of the room.

I wandered over to the open window and looked down on to the street, just in time to see Alain getting out of his car behind mine at the gate. As he came up the path, he looked up and nodded and I raised my hand to him.

'Good,' said Simone. 'I thought he might be late. He's not the best of time-keepers.'

He never was, I recalled.

We heard the front door slam, and Alain's voice as he came up the stairs, and then saw him stride past the open door of the lounge, carrying a large paper bag, which he apparently deposited in the kitchen. Contributions to the meal, perhaps?

When he appeared in the doorway, he looked first at Simone and then at me, but it was impossible to tell from his expression whether he felt any resentment towards me, or simply nothing at all.

Simone indicated the drinks and he poured himself a neat whisky. Glass in hand, he turned and looked straight at me, a slight, rather malicious smile on his thin, dark face.

'Don't misunderstand me,' he said, 'but wouldn't you, perhaps, have been better advised to have spent your little holiday in the Balearics, or Trinidad, or whatever?'

'Don't be silly,' said Simone. She smiled a trifle over-resolutely and I raised my glass to her.

'I've never been more serious in my life,' said Alain. 'Even Angus, blinded as he is by that English upper-class loyalty of his, must have observed a certain disarray in our affairs. Not to mention the sour smell of decay and corruption.'

'Since you mention it,' I said.

'There! What did I say? There's an honest man for you.'

'Also a very curious one.'

'My dear fellow, what do you want to know? Why I spat in Cartier's eye last night – metaphorically speaking, unfortunately – ? Oh, yes – ' as Simone looked at him, startled – 'the worst happened . . . our paths crossed.' To

48

me again, 'What else? Why Simone lives in this hovel – '

'It *isn't* a hovel! I like it here.'

Alain gave a short, rasping laugh, and I looked at her, unable to keep the incredulity out of my face.

A slight flush appeared on her cheeks, but she continued to protest. 'I mean it,' she said. 'I know what you're thinking – ' (Impossible!) 'but it's much nicer than you think. The people are *real*. They're warm. Most of them are very kind. They may knock the place up a bit from time to time – '

'And each other,' I murmured. 'Like your Mr and Mrs downstairs.'

'Oh, Rose and Julian aren't married!'

'Oh.'

'As I said, they're artists. Well, *he* is. Nearly all the folk here are. Or writers. That's something else that's changed since you were here.'

'Yes,' said Alain. 'The St George's district is now the Chelsea of La Roque, dear boy. Hardly any poor Spanish any more. Nearly all English throw-outs.'

I took the last sentence as it was intended, between the eyes, and felt both stung and puzzled. Simone reached out and pressed my hand, but I didn't look at her. I was looking at Alain. His face wore the cynical, sneering expression that matched his words, but underneath there was a hard, taut bitterness. I could both see it and feel it, and, even allowing for his natural inclination towards sarcasm as a form of humour, it alarmed me.

'At the moment,' I said, 'I'm only interested in finding out one thing.'

'Why Father committed suicide.'

'*Did* he? I mean, are you absolutely sure?'

'My God, yes! What did you think? That he'd been murdered?'

'It *could* have been an accident.'

'Not possibly. There was a note – I thought you'd read all about it in the papers.'

'I did. I just couldn't believe them.'

'You saw St Michel.'

49

'Yes. And I don't understand that, either. Your father – it wasn't like him. Whatever happened – money, whatever – he wasn't the type that runs out.'

'Well, he did. And I don't blame him.'

'Oh, for God's sake!' I was exasperated by the aura of fatalism they both exuded. I felt the pressure of Simone's hand in mine again, but when I looked down at her, she withdrew her hand and averted her face from both of us.

'Accept it, Angus,' she said.

'Why?' I demanded. 'Because *you* all have?'

'Because it's the way it was. Things were just too much for him. Mother's death, my mess of a marriage – which he never *had* approved of – '

'But which you *had* to go through with, of course,' interrupted Alain savagely.

'Yes. Which I had to go through with.'

'And – ?' I asked, still looking down at her.

'It was all too much. He became depressed. He began to lose his grip on things: the plantations first of all, then other things. We lost money, then began to get into debt. Father had never had a debt in his life. He couldn't accept what was happening to him. He couldn't face it.'

Alain gave a snort of derision. 'How *do* you face a boot in the back?'

I looked at him. 'Suppose you fill in the gaps,' I invited.

'Gaps.' He laughed sardonically. 'Very apt. Oh, yes, the *bon mot par excellence!* But one gap will do – it did for Father all right – one bloody big gap, created by certain shifts of position of our so-called bloody friends!'

'That isn't true, Alain.'

'Of course it's true! Damn it, Simone! Why won't you face facts?' His face was dark with anger, and he glared at her almost as if he could have struck her.

I remembered the words of Paulo Garcia: 'His family! Bah!' Now, here was Alain saying, in effect, 'His friends! Bah!' Which was right? Or, were both wrong? I could see that Simone was distressed, so decided to take a different tack.

'You said there'd been trouble with the plantations. I thought they looked fine when I was up there.'

'They don't belong to us any more. The house and the land round it are all that's left, and that only because we can't find a buyer – or, at least – ' She stopped, her discomfort obvious, and Alain gave vent to another short, bitter laugh.

'What she means is we could sell it tomorrow, only I've told her I'll kill her with my bare hands if she takes dirty money.'

'Meaning?'

'Meaning her ex. He and his unspeakable father would buy the place without a second thought if they got the chance. They already own the plantations. Oh, yes – ' as my mouth fell open – 'that surprises you, doesn't it? Yes, well, it's only a matter of time. We shall have to give in in the end, if only for Hélène's sake, but at least we can make them sweat for it.'

'But couldn't you find some other buyer? I noticed you're having the place decorated.'

'Oh, yes, well, Simone thinks if we tart the place up some English tax-dodger will snap it up, thus restoring family pride.'

Again the barbed thrust. Was it *me* he was out to get, or the whole Anglo-Saxon race? And, in either case, why? Or was it just an overspill of frustrated hatred?

'Well,' I said, 'isn't that possible?'

'With Corlander on the Housing Committee? Don't be funny.'

'You mean they'd block it? *Could* they? – God, there *have* been some changes!' Neither of them answered and there was a short silence, during which I vaguely thought I heard the sound of the piano in the other room. 'What do they want the place for?' I asked at last.

'Oh, they'd pull it down,' said Alain. 'Their latest idea, I believe, is a sort of holiday camp for the upper classes. Luxury chalets. Private railway down to St Michel Bay . . . all that sort of thing.'

'God Almighty!'

'Progress, my friend. Corlander Père has his own company in London now for handling it. If he gets the airport extensions through the Assembly, as looks likely, he'll probably open offices in Madrid and Lisbon, possibly even New York.'

'He'll *ruin* the place! The whole island, I mean.'

'*Will?*'

'Surely they're not letting him get away with it?'

Alain smiled: a patient, weary smile. 'What the hell do you imagine we've been talking about, Angus? You asked why Father died. He died in war.'

I looked at him. My brain still wasn't working any too clearly, but at last I felt I was beginning to see daylight.

'So it's *Corlander*,' I said.

'*It?*'

'Well,' I said, 'presumably Corlander and his son – ' I paused, glancing apologetically at Simone, but she was looking into her glass and appeared hardly to have heard – 'I mean,' I continued rather more warily, 'obviously they're the new order. Your father and all he stood for was the old. I can see how they'd crucify him.' I stopped. Suddenly I was no longer certain what I was trying to say. Something was wrong. Maurice de Courvel and suicide were as irreconcilable as ever.

Alain's smile now was broader, and he was shaking his head as though incredulous. 'My dear good friend – and for the moment I take it you *are* that – ' I didn't answer, but felt the irritation in me rising to a dangerous level – 'All right,' he said, 'don't get touchy, dear fellow. We'll take your sentiments for granted. But you really can't be as naive as you seem. You can't really believe it's as simple as that.'

'As what?'

He shrugged, spreading out his hands. 'Black and white. One God, one Devil. When has it ever been like that? Except, of course, when we were children.'

I stared at him. He was right. But what was worse was that, already, my half-formed but cosy little theories were beginning to crumble, and I was back where I'd started from – which was nowhere.

'You don't really imagine,' Alain was saying, 'that a man like Corlander, despite all his resources, as you put it, could have brought Father to his knees, alone?'

No. That was it. That was just what I *couldn't* imagine.

'So what, then?'

'So he had help, of course. The kind of help that's much more effective than all the open manifestations of wickedness put together: the kind that eats into your guts.'

'In other words?'

'In other words, the Brutus touch, my friend, the Brutus touch.'

I waited. But not for long. He took a swig of his whisky, and then it came: 'Cartier!' He almost spat the name.

I shook my head, bewildered. 'I don't get it. You said your Father sold to Corlander.'

He gave a mirthless laugh. 'Can you imagine it? He sold to Edith Cartier. She offered to take over the plantations to help Father pay his debts. It was the last decent thing the Cartiers ever did. Unfortunately, she died without taking the precaution of seeing that her charming son didn't get his hands on them. When he did, he sold to Corlander.'

I was stunned, and while I stood there, looking from one to the other of them, trying to grasp the implications, Alain helped himself to another whisky. When he turned back, the sneering look was on his face again.

'The poor boy had a few money troubles of his own. Strictly relative, of course, but they rather cramped his style. And if there's one thing Cartier's always worked hard at, it's acquiring style.'

I walked towards the window and stood there for a moment with my back to both of them, looking down into the street. I'd been more right than I'd known in insisting that I came to the island myself: for if there was one thing that was becoming patently clear, it was that the kind of trouble I'd walked into was not only very dirty but also very private.

'In your vast experience, my friend,' said Alain, 'this can't be the first time you've run across a little matter of strategic disinheritance.'

I didn't answer. I was thinking again of the look on Paulo Garcia's face when he had said: 'His family! Bah!' This was Maurice's son, his only surviving son. His pride? Or his disappointment? Had these hands, too, held a knife?

In the silence that ensued I once more became aware of the sound of the piano in the next room. Someone was strumming on it. It was a haphazard, fingering sound, with no definable tune, yet something about it held my attention. Despite its formlessness, there was a certain fluency, a certain order about it, and a curious kind of control. I turned round, looking enquiringly at Simone. She gave me a faint, uncertain smile. 'Hélène,' she said.

'Hélène?'

'She loves that piano. I tried to sell it last year, but she cried so I had to explain to the people that I'd changed my mind. Fortunately, they had children of their own, so they understood.'

'Which made it an expensive toy for a seven-year-old,' said Alain.

'Shouldn't she have lessons?' I suggested.

'Yes,' said Simone. 'I'm hoping to arrange something for her, but – well, these things take time.'

What she meant, I guessed, was that they take money.

Alain asked her when lunch would be ready, and she got up then and went out to the kitchen, telling us that she would call us when she wanted us.

I was glad of the break. I wanted time to assimilate what I'd so far learned, and from Alain's attitude I judged that he, too, was disinclined to go further into family troubles. For all that, there was still much that I was curious about: why, for instance, over the past ten years he had detached himself from his family, the running of the plantations, everything connected with St Michel. It had long been obvious that he didn't share his father's feeling for the traditions of the place, and that he'd never make much of an estate manager on his own. But with a good foreman like old Pedro Calvaro, who had served the de Courvel family for over fifty years – what had happened to Pedro? I wondered. Alain had always rather fancied himself as a writer, so it hadn't been altogether surprising to hear that he'd taken a job on the local paper. Nevertheless, when I asked him about it now, the tone of his reply was discouraging. It appeared that he considered his job a demeaning necessity, and that he had little but contempt for a community whose idea of an adequate news service was a weekly paper of the quality of that produced in some of our remote English country towns. As to the latter, I was professionally inclined to agree with him, but whereas I have always had the profoundest respect for the individuals who work on small-town newspapers, he, apparently, had none. It was all of a piece with the bitterness, amounting to malice, that seemed to form the major part of his general attitude to life these days, and I found it disquieting.

Lunch proved to be a disorganized affair. Simone kept jumping up and down for forgotten items of food or equipment, all the time apologizing in that schoolgirl way in which she had accepted my services as a wine waiter. Conversation was therefore desultory and on general lines. I learned that Max Cartier was hoping to follow his father on to the Assembly, and that Nicholas Le Marnet, who had married Max's sister, Stéphanie, was now senior partner in the family law firm and considered to be one of the most able advocates at the island Bar.

'He's unique,' said Alain. 'He's honest, more or less.'

It was the first charitable remark he'd made, all the more surprising since I gathered that it was Nicholas who had handled Simone's divorce, and that he and his father before him had been Maurice's legal advisers. I made a mental note to see Nicholas as soon as possible.

I also gleaned that the Corlanders, *père et fils*, were not only the biggest hoteliers on the island but also sat on most of the committees of the Assembly between them, which, of course, gave them a near monopoly of power; furthermore, that they and the Cartiers were close friends.

As I ate, and listened, I watched Hélène. I still felt that the child was strange, but I had begun to reassess the quality of that strangeness. The excessive 'withdrawnness' that had at first seemed almost sub-normal now seemed to me to arise out of something quite different: something which, in someone more mature in years, I would have described as total self-containment. But how could this be in a child so young? Hélène, it seemed to me, lived in a world that was not ours: yet it was a real, logical, thinking world; for some reason, she preferred to keep it locked away inside her. Out of harm's reach? Was that it? But if so, why? The thought worried me almost as much as if she had been simply retarded. I don't know an awful lot about children, but all the psychologists seem to parrot on in unison these days about early impressions and the effects on personality. What impressions had Hélène drawn from life around her that had led her to retreat into a bastion of self-sufficiency and to lock and bolt the door behind her? When – if – she emerged into our inadequate world again, what kind of person would she be? After lunch, I remembered the piano and asked her to play for us. The complete lack of diffidence with which she complied was astonishing. All she could manage was the same, haphazard strumming, but again I was conscious of that curious quality of order and control, and the absence of any sign of hesitation or uncertainty. On her face, I saw what I had expected: that a mask had dropped away, revealing the life stirring and feeling within. In its way, it was exciting: like watching an act of creation, or revelation, a unique and privileged experience. I didn't have long to think about it, for, as suddenly and decisively as she had begun, she stopped playing, her face closed into its normal expression of disinterest and, before I could say anything, she got up from the stool and ran out of the room.

Simone gave a self-conscious, apologetic little laugh, but Alain, I noticed, had turned to a copy of his own newspaper and I doubted if he had even been aware of the interlude.

He appeared, in fact, to have lost interest in all of us. I decided it was time I left, and after we'd drunk some coffee and I'd helped Simone with the washing-up I said so. She made a few polite demurs, which convinced me that she, too, thought the same. We were back, I decided, to square one.

As I went down the slightly odorous staircase, my eye caught sight of a small figure looking down through the banisters of the landing above.

'Goodbye, Hélène,' I said. 'Be a good girl.'

Her large green eyes never wavered from mine, but she made no reply; no smile came and she didn't attempt to come any further down. I was surprised she had even conceded this much, and so, apparently, was Simone.

'You're honoured,' she said as we went on down. 'She doesn't usually trouble to see guests off the premises.'

'Perhaps she feels I'm not really a guest,' I said.

We had reached the front door and Simone looked at me with something of the same expression I had seen at St Michel, followed by the same uncertain smile.

'Yes,' she said. 'You're quite right, Angus. You must come again – soon.'

Why, then, did I have the feeling, as strong as a mule's hind leg, that she hoped I wouldn't?

FIVE

Back in Porte Hilaire, I stopped the car under the walls of the old town church of Santa Maria de los Angeles and walked back through the narrow Rue Colombe into the Place de Justice. Here, alongside the parliament building and the chambers of the courts of justice, was another handsome white-fronted building, whose two massive wooden doors were open from nine in the morning until seven at night: the La Roque Central Library.

As I crossed the square towards it, I was aware of the scene around me with a feeling of pleasant nostalgia. My father had loved this place and had often sat here in the evenings at one of the tables under the oleander trees, sharing a bottle of wine with the local fishermen and farmers. Like so many of the small squares of rural France or Spain, it was a meeting place for people coming into town from miles around. Even at midday and early afternoon, as now, the centre of the square would be shaded by the trees, although all around it the white-walled buildings flung back the heat and light of the sun with an almost savage intensity.

I glanced up at the high dome of the parliament building, where the island's flag hung limply in the still air. La Roque had chosen for its heraldic emblem a device that always seemed to me to have been pinched from the Zodiac sign of The Fishes: a pair of cavorting dolphins, in white on a blue ground. The only difference I could see was that in this case each animal wore a crown and carried a large key in its mouth, symbolizing, I'd always supposed, the sovereignty of La Roque among islands and its possession of the wherewithal to unlock the doors of prosperity. The former hypothesis still seemed OK to me: the latter, I suppose, depended on your definition of prosperity. Once a fair, virtuous and modest motherland to some 60,000 souls, La

Roque now seemed hell bent on turning into a bit of a painted lady if all I'd so far heard was true. Mammon, it could be said, was in the process of dealing the dolphins a few well-aimed fourpenny ones. But there were signs that certain people cared: on my way out to St George's, I'd seen a couple of chalked wall slogans that had surprised me. One had said, 'End closed committees'; the other, more hackneyed but certainly more specific: 'Government by the people'. Who was behind these stirrings of radicalism, I wondered? How significant a force was it? Up until now, politics hadn't figured much on La Roque. Seigneurial rule had been just and economically viable, and most people seemed happy to leave things undisturbed. Not any longer, obviously.

On the steps of the Library I paused once more, glancing across to the opposite side of the square. There, almost in line with where I stood, were the windows of the firm of Le Marnet, Avocats et Avoués. I imagined Nicholas sitting there now behind the Venetian blinds: Nicholas, the honest law man. I toyed with the idea of going across to see him, but decided against it. A busy office, surrounded by clerks and secretaries, was not the place for the kind of discussion I wanted with Nicholas, and it was hardly fair, either to him or to his clients, to expect him to walk out on the rest of the day's scheduled work. Time, anyway, was not important now.

I explained to the Librarian, who didn't know me, that I had been acquainted in the past with Monsieur Maurice de Courvel, but that I didn't wish to worry the family at this sad time and should be grateful if he could let me see some copies of the local newspaper reports on Maurice's death.

I spent the next half-hour studying them. Except that they were fuller and more subjective than the ones I had seen in the London papers, I found them hardly more revealing. There was, however, one item in the account of the inquest that caught my eye. It appeared that an ex-worker on the St Michel estate, a man called René Le Duc, whose cottage was about two hundred yards up the lane from the Manoir, had heard a shot at about five minutes past eight on the night before Maurice's body was found. He had been certain of the time because he and his wife always had a final glass of wine at eight o'clock, and he had just looked at the clock and got up to go and fetch the bottle when they had heard the sound. Asked if he had taken any steps to investigate, he said that he had not because he had assumed that someone was shooting in the woods above the plantations. Local farmers often did; there was no law against it. As no one had admitted to being in the woods that night, it had been assumed that the shot Le Duc had heard was that fired by Maurice in taking his own life.

There was reference to the fact that Maurice had lived with Simone at St George's for the past two years, and some evidence from her as to his health, which she had described as very low. As might be expected, there were manifold tributes to Maurice's contributions to the island and to scholarship, but the only mention of his early retirement from the Presidency of the Assembly was a bald statement of face that told me nothing at all. I decided to follow this up elsewhere, and left the Library just as the clock in the tower of Santa Maria struck four.

When I checked in for my key at the Royale, the desk clerk came over all apologetic and told me that Madame Cartier had called to see me and on being told I was out had insisted on being given my key and going up to my room to wait for me. For his sake, I disguised my annoyance as well as I could. I knew just how imperious Imogen could be, and the fact that she and Max were close friends of the Corlanders would be one that the hotel staff could hardly be expected to overlook for the sake of some academic principle about a guest's right to privacy.

Nevertheless, as I went up in the lift, I felt my anger rising, and having to knock on my own door did nothing to assuage it. Curse the woman! She could at least have lifted the lock! But this would not have suited Imogen's theatrical temperament at all. Opening the door to me at last, she stood there, elegant in dark green velvet pants and a green

60

chiffon blouse, one hand against the lintel, the other spread wide, thus effectively barring my passage while, as she saw it, the full impact of the moment was absorbed.

'Angus, *chéri*!'

'Hello, Imogen.'

She took my arm. 'I want to talk to you, darling. You didn't mind my coming up, did you? I hate sitting in public places alone. I felt sure you wouldn't be long, not with all that work you have to do.' (I'd asked for that, I suppose.) 'I had some tea brought up. Will you have a cup? It's not too terrible.'

I shook my head. 'As a matter of fact, you could have had quite a long wait. I've been working in the library.'

She opened her eyes wide: the very picture of tolerant understanding. 'No *matter*, my sweet! I've quite enjoyed myself. I started to read one of your books. This one.' She picked up a paperback thriller from the settee. 'You don't mind, do you, darling?'

I opened my mouth to mutter some discourtesy about it being all the same if I *did* mind, but she wasn't listening. She chattered on inconsequentially for several minutes longer, hovering about the room as she did so like a bird after worms, while I wondered what, in addition to the therapeutic qualities of a quiet sit-down in someone else's bedroom, had brought her here. Eventually, she perched herself on the arm of the settee, accepted a cigarette and informed me through a haze of smoke that she had orders to see that I went out to St Cloud to have dinner with her and Max that evening.

'Orders?' I smiled. The idea of orders and Imogen in harness was ludicrous.

'But yes!' Her brown eyes under their green shadow opened wide again and she shook her sleek, dark head chidingly. 'It's very wicked of you, Angus, to hide yourself away like this. Nicholas and Stéphanie are coming. They're *enraged* you haven't seen them yet.'

This time, my amusement was audible. Nothing less like Stéphanie's quiet, matter-of-fact temperament could have been envisaged.

'It's rude to laugh at people,' she said. 'But no matter. I'll forgive you. So long as you don't let me down. There'll be one or two other people, too,' she added, flicking ash in the general direction of the ashtray I had placed on the table in front of her.

I glanced enquiringly at her at this, but either she felt the individuals to whom she had referred were not worthy of enumeration, or that to keep their identity up her sleeve was for some reason more propitious.

'Well – ' I hesitated, and she stepped in neatly to clinch the deal.

'Come as soon as you're ready, darling. Why not now? I've got my car outside.'

'I've some things to do. Anyway, I'll need my own car to come back in.'

'Oh, but you'll stay the night, of course!'

Her tenacity really was amazing. There was nothing for it but good old honest-to-God brutality. 'No of course about it, I'm afraid. I told you – here I am and here I stay.'

Two small lines of vexation appeared between the perfectly groomed eyebrows. 'Oh, really, Angus. This *is* absurd.'

'I do agree.'

She rose abruptly and I had the satisfaction of seeing that she was genuinely put out.

'Very well. Max will be furious, of course.'

Max, as she very well knew, wouldn't give a damn.

As suddenly as it had appeared, the chagrin was gone, replaced by a brilliant smile.

'We'll see you about seven, then. Don't be late, *chéri*. And – ' she touched my cheek with a cool fingertip – 'don't overwork. It won't get you anything in the end except night starvation.'

After she'd gone, I spent a few minutes cursing myself for letting her manoeuvre me, then resigned myself to the inevitable. After all, I'd *wanted* to see both her and Max on their own ground at St Cloud; I'd *wanted* to see who their friends were, and I'd certainly wanted to meet Nicholas and

Stéphanie again. It was simply that I *hadn't* wanted to do it all in one fell swoop, and under pressure. Nor so damn publicly.

I was late getting to St Cloud. After Imogen had departed, I yielded to an impulse to drive around town to take a closer look at some of the tourist developments that had sprung up since my last visit. Most of them were on the long curve of bay called the West Front that stretched from the harbour out towards the Bai des Palmes.

In the old days, the West Front had been a fairly exclusive residential area of large, handsome, white-walled houses set in big gardens full of green lawns, lemon trees and hibiscus. Now, most of these houses seemed to have been turned into hotels and chalets, and the rest pulled down and replaced by jerry-built structures housing night-clubs and bars. Dominating everything was the new Casino. Sitting circular and glittering white at the top of a wide flight of steps, and surrounded by phony columns and pillars, it looked for all the world like a giant wedding-cake, icing and all. It was encircled by an Italian garden of cypresses and vine-clad pergolas, and half-way up the steps there was a large fountain with terra-cotta naked ladies prancing around on horses in the middle of it.

Maybe it was the horses that did it, but suddenly I remembered that I'd parked my car in a restricted area. I wasted no time getting back to it, but at ten yards could see the small yellow slip tucked under my windscreen-wiper.

On La Roque, parking fines can be settled on the spot, or on the same day at the nearest police station, and all is forgiven. Failure to do either, however, renders a court appearance obligatory, in default of which the original fine is quadrupled, and a second offence can – and often does – result in the suspension of the right to drive on the island for an indefinite period. I therefore spent another half hour or so finding my way through the new traffic-routing maze to the building occupied by the Porte Hilaire Police Centrale, and another twenty minutes waiting while a noticeably under-occupied desk sergeant got round to dealing with my case. It was seven-fifteen when I finally made it back to the Royale and I still had to shower and change and drive the twelve miles or so out to St Cloud. I rang Imogen to explain, hoping it would annoy her, but she was unperturbed.

'It doesn't matter, my sweet. Dinner won't be before eight-thirty anyway.' You couldn't win with Imogen.

Forty minutes later I turned the car off the coast road above the Bai des Palmes and up the lane across the headland to St Cloud. The lovely old house looked exactly as it always had in Edouard and Edith Cartier's time. Standing alone, high over the bay, its main windows all facing the sea, it was simple, almost austere, in its beauty. It had suited Edith well: Edouard, too, despite the fact that because of the strong winds up here the family's plantations were a good two miles further down the coast road, where there was more shelter for the young plants. I was a little surprised that it apparently still suited Max and Imogen. I could only assume that the dignity and status that went with St Cloud compensated them for the sacrifice of more contemporary standards of comfort.

Certainly no one could accuse Imogen of being an unworthy châtelaine of this fine old house. The regal air always had come as naturally to her as fleas to a dog's coat and she'd added to this a dress-sense that was arresting to a point just sufficiently short of vulgar. Tonight, for instance, a focus of light in gold *lamé*, she'd turned every other woman in the room into a Little Dorrit.

As soon as she saw me, she left the group she was with and greeted me rapturously, stuck a drink in my hand and then proceeded to haul me round from one bunch of people to the next, introducing me to those I didn't know (whose name was legion) as the de Courvel's 'foster son'. Just as I'd begun to find this so powerfully irritating that some utterly unforgivable riposte started to tremble on my lips, she made off to greet someone else, leaving me, after a decent interval, to seek refuge out on the terrace.

It was there I found them: Nicholas and Stéphanie, who,

64

as soon as they saw me, detached themselves from the group they were with and came quickly over to meet me. The pleasure was mutual, and we laughed a lot as people do when their emotions embarrass them.

'We hoped you'd turn up,' said Nicholas. 'We'd have rung you at the hotel, but Imogen said you were playing hard to get and Stéph said this probably meant you wanted a little time to yourself for a day or two.'

I smiled at her. As kindly and understanding as ever. She hadn't changed much to look at either; a little plumper, perhaps, but still remarkably young-looking for a mother of four and still exuding that reassuring aura of quiet practicality and humour. It was hard to believe that she and Max were brother and sister. It wasn't simply that she was as fair and even-tempered as he was dark and mercurial; there was something fundamentally different in their whole attitude to life. Whereas Max's approach would always be oblique and tinged with the sardonic, Stéphanie met everything and everyone eyes front, and with a generosity and tolerance that had their roots in sound common-sense.

Nicholas had put on weight, too, and the look of mild harassment that had so often clouded his round, good-natured face now appeared to have settled in there permanently. With the steel-rimmed spectacles he wore, he looked, I thought, a little like a crew-cut Franz Schubert.

'I'd have been here for the funeral if I'd known in time,' I told them, and explained about my recent assignment.

'It must have been a shock to you,' said Stéphanie. 'You were so close.'

I sighed. 'Not so close as I should have been. Not by a long chalk.'

'*C'est la vie,*' murmured Nicholas, the harassed look deepening.

I looked at him; another odd brother-sister dichotomy here. Who'd have thought he and Imogen were from the same litter?

'I'd like to go up and see your father,' I told him. 'Do you think tomorrow would be all right?'

'Yes. He's already rung and told me to ask you.'

The good old grape-vine; it was as I'd thought: another thing that hadn't changed.

'Fine. I'll run out in the morning.'

Just then, Imogen appeared, towing behind her the unfortunate girl I was to take in to dinner. This turned out to be a petite Parisienne, tourist category, named Marie du Pré. She was, I guessed (rightly as it happened), a student, and, if you discounted a certain un-Gallic naïveté, as typical a representative of her kind as you can get. She had a bubbly sense of humour, and we got off to a good start when I tripped on the bottom step going in from the terrace and burnt myself with my own cigarette. This was probably the moment when she put me down as the archetypal ancient roué about whom she would endlessly amuse her friends at the Sorbonne.

It irked me that the arrival of the Corlanders, Ray and his wife, Phyllis, appeared to accord us the required sanction for entry into the dining-room, and I was therefore anything but enchanted when I found him facing me across the table, and the lady herself on my left. It seemed we were to be spared the paternal Bernard, who, I was told, had an important meeting to attend. Well, *someone* had to make decisions about naked ladies on prancing horses. Or the other way round.

Meanwhile, Phyllis wasted no time in getting down to the nitty-gritty.

'Ray tells me you lived at St Michel before the war,' she said over the prawn cocktail.

I gave her what I hoped was an expression of tolerably good humour and told her that Ray was correct.

'You know us all better than we know ourselves, then,' she said archly.

You can bet on it, I thought. I said: 'Well, I'm afraid I lost touch over the last eight or ten years. But Maurice was a very old friend of my father's, and he and Justine more or less brought me up after my father died.'

I felt the sympathy in the smile she gave me was genuine

enough. At heart, Phyllis Corlander probably wasn't a bad sort, but in her blonde ultra-sophistication I saw what Imogen's oblique reference had suggested: a self-assurance that was basically calculating – and hard. I sensed a nature that could turn to coarseness under the stress of extreme emotion. Phyllis Corlander would be generous when things went well, but I had the feeling I'd just hate to be around when something didn't. A smart cookie; Ray Corlander being what he was, Simone hadn't stood an earthly.

'You must have noticed a lot of changes on the island since then,' she commented.

'One or two.' If she was aware of the irony in my voice, she gave no sign, but I glanced up to see Corlander grinning across the table at me.

'Staying long?' he queried. His English was totally unaccented. It was impossible to tell either from his looks or his voice where he came from; all one could feel reasonably certain of was that his allegiances would be strictly saleable.

There was something slightly over-casual about his question and I took care to match it with my reply.

'No idea, really. Depends on how the mood takes me, you might say.'

Imogen's laugh rang out from the other end of the table, from where it was clear she'd been keeping tabs on us.

'Angus loves to play the dark horse, don't you, darling? I think he's here for *copy*,' she added, giving the word a melodramatic emphasis and raising her beautiful eyebrows in mock concern.

Everybody smiled dutifully, except my sturdy little Marie, who looked genuinely baffled.

'Copy?' she queried, looking into my face.

'I told you, *chérie*,' Imogen said, 'he writes. He's looking for something horrible to send back to his editor and he'll get paid fabulous sums of money for ruining all our reputations.'

'Delicious,' murmured Phyllis. She patted my arm lightly with her well-manicured fingers. 'Me first, darling.'

67

Her husband gave a snort of derision. 'You flatter yourself,' he said unpleasantly and then guffawed at the arch look of reproof she gave him. The artificial silliness of it all made me feel sick and I wished with all my heart that I was down the other end of the table, where Nicholas and Stéphanie appeared to be having a fairly rational conversation with the others. I decided that the best defence of my reason was frontal attack. I looked Corlander firmly in the eye.

'I understand *you're* running the St Michel plantations now.'

He was taken aback, but quickly reassumed the casual air. 'That's right. What's left of them.'

'They looked all right to me.'

'Oh, yes, of course, you've been up there. Well, we've got things more or less organized now, but it's been bloody hard going, I can tell you. Poor old de Courvel had let things go to hell up there. Long-standing orders cancelled. No plants coming on. Discipline gone to pot. It was a shambles.'

'What happened to Calvaro?'

He looked puzzled.

'Pedro Calvaro,' I said. 'He was Maurice's manager. Been with him since when.'

'Oh, the old boy with the moustaches. Oh, yes – well, all I can say is that he may have been a boy wonder in his time, but he was nothing but a thundering old fool as far as I'm concerned. No sense of the dynamics of change whatsoever. There's a helluva lot more these days than just knowing one end of a bloody banana from the other, you know. Times change, my friend. Times change.'

'So what happened to him?'

'Eh?' The pink, fleshy face showed bewilderment at my persistence in a subject that, to him, was clearly of total unimportance. He gave a short, embarrassed laugh.

'I haven't the least idea. I suppose he just – well – ' (he shrugged and grimaced) 'retired'.

'On pension.'

He didn't answer, but his face, I noticed, had gone a little dark.

'I'm asking,' I said, 'if he retired on pension.'

He looked me directly in the eyes now and his own were hard. 'Was he "entitled" to?' he countered.

'It depends what you mean by 'entitled'. He'd worked for the de Courvel family in one way or another since he was little more than a child. Maurice – and I know this for a fact – always intended him to have a pension. Plus a generous gratuity when the time came.'

He raised his eyebrows and a faint sardonic grin curled the corners of his mouth. 'Was it in writing?'

'I doubt it very much. There was no need. It was always understood. By everybody.'

'Well, by "everybody" I take it you mean the de Courvel family. But the de Courvel family don't own the St Michel plantations any more.'

'That's why I'm asking what happened to Calvaro.'

'Good God, man!' He was openly annoyed now. 'How the hell should *I* know? I don't do the office work. You'd have to ask Townsend.'

'Townsend?'

'My manager.'

'I'll ask old Pedro,' I said.

I knew then what the Buddha had meant by 'the roaring silence'. The quiet that engulfed the whole table fairly sizzled with significance. Imogen, the perfect hostess, finally broke the tension by turning upon Phyllis with a flood of small talk, and the rest of the meal passed uneventfully. My show of arms, however, had done the trick. Both the Corlanders were unduly subdued from then on, throwing each other watchful little glances from time to time, and leaving me strictly alone.

Back in the drawing-room over coffee, I steered Marie over towards Stéphanie, who introduced us to her companions, an airline pilot named Bob Dart and his girl-friend, Laura something-or-other, a Spanish lady of quite arresting beauty.

69

Dart raised his cup to me. 'After what you've just done, I shouldn't wonder if this stuff's poisoned,' he said.

We were joined by Nicholas, who touched my arm and edged me a little way from the group. He spoke quietly. 'Don't worry about old Pedro. He's all right.'

'He *got* his pension?'

'In a way. Yes.'

'I see. No thanks to Corlander.'

He patted my arm, smiling gently, his plump, dark face looking more like Schubert's than ever. 'Don't waste your time, Angus. Some things are best ignored.'

I looked him squarely in the face. 'Until it's too late to do anything about them?'

His good humour collapsed like a pricked balloon and I was instantly sorry. I'd no need to take it out on Nicholas. He was all right. He'd always been all right. He didn't deserve the kick in the backside I'd just given him. It was my turn for some arm patting. 'Forget it, old son. You know me. No damn sense of proportion.'

To my relief, he grinned again, and we turned back to the group. Stéphanie's gaze met mine. 'Angus, do come out on Sunday. The children want to see you again, and we'd all love it.'

'So would I.' It was the truth. I could think of nothing more appealing than a nice relaxing day with the Le Marnet family out at Bai St Michel. Maybe, too, I would get some entirely different slants on the situation from the man who had been the de Courvels' legal adviser and had handled Simone's divorce.

Towards the end of the evening I particularly noted one piece of conversation between Corlander and Bob Dart, with Max Cartier as a silent (and somewhat uneasy, I thought) onlooker. Dart had detached himself from the group I was with and gone over, rather deliberately, to where Corlander was standing in a party which included Max and the Fellowes. I heard him say: 'Hear you've missed the boat on that . . . deal.' I couldn't catch the word he used to describe the 'deal', but it sounded like a Spanish name, possibly the name of a company or an individual.

Corlander, who was standing picking the gold seal off a pocket-sized cigar, turned, saw who it was and grunted. 'That's what *you* think.'

'Well, they turned it down, didn't they?'

I couldn't make up my mind whether Dart's expression was truly one of malicious pleasure or whether the interpretation was wishful on my part, but if it had been any deal of mine they'd been talking about I would certainly have taken exception to the kind of smile he had on his face at that moment. Corlander didn't look too pleased, himself.

'If they know what's good for them, they'll think again.'

Words of wisdom, or a threat? And who were *They*?

Dart's smile became a grin. 'Always thought you had the committees in your pocket, old boy. Spot of rebellion flaring up?'

'You know damn well what the island laws are. It's simply a matter of convincing certain people that changes are necessary every hundred years or so (he was big on change). They're still living in the past. It takes time, but it has to be done by someone.'

'And you're the one, old boy, you're the one.'

'I intend to be,' said Corlander.

Dart raised his glass in mock homage. 'And a plague to all your enemies, *mon prince*. And God bless all who serve under you.' He drifted back in our direction and I carefully averted my gaze back to where Marie du Pré was explaining to the Spanish girl some of the intricacies of French fashion.

In retrospect, this little exchange seemed somehow important. Rightly or wrongly, I found myself linking the look on Dart's face and the obvious taunt behind his words with the chalked signs on the walls of Port Hilaire. There were at least some still left on La Roque who were not paying court to Mammon.

SIX

My visit next day to Guy Le Marnet at Mont Vert was an experience as traumatic as the return to St Michel had been. Short of seeing Maurice himself, no other human being could have recalled my boyhood to me more poignantly than this old man.

When I entered the room where he sat waiting for me I had to make a conscious effort to free myself from the old familiar feeling that, somehow or other, my sins had found me out. But, when he got up from his big leather chair near the window to greet me, the illusion was destroyed. He seemed to have shrunk in stature and he moved with obvious difficulty. Guy Le Marnet was frail as well as old, his face lined and thin, and the bones showing white under the skin of his hands and wrists; but his manner was as dignified as ever and his welcome as warm. He grasped my hand strongly in his own while he looked into my face. His brown eyes, I saw, were very much alive. He spoke firmly, in faultless, almost accent-free English.

'Angus, my boy! I am so glad to see you! So very, very glad! Sit down, dear boy, sit down. They're bringing in some coffee in a moment. Unless, of course, you'd prefer – No? I've said we're not to be disturbed on any account. Sit down, my boy. It takes me a little time these days . . .' He lowered himself with difficulty into his chair again and, when he was down, heaved a deep sigh. 'Old age, my son. Put it off as long as you can. Spoils everything.' He sighed again. Then, suddenly, he jerked up his head and his chin jutted defiantly. 'But never mind all that! Tell me how *how* are. Successful, I know. Oh, yes, I've read your work. You've done well, my boy. Maurice always said you would, you know. He kept telling us so, and he was right.' He paused. He put his elbows on the arms of the chair and

72

pressed the tips of his fingers together, looking at them as he did so. 'I miss him, Angus,' he said.

We neither of us spoke for a moment, then I leaned forward in my chair towards him. 'Would you tell me about it, sir?'

The sharp brown eyes met mine. 'That's what you've come for, isn't it? I mean to the island. I'm so glad. I prayed you would. Things are very bad here, Angus. Nothing is as it was. Nothing. Things are changing all the time, but not for good. They say it's progress, but they're lying.'

'They?'

'There are people here now who have made a lot of money out of the island. Still are. They've done it the easy way, by taking short cuts, by exploitation of the worst possible kind. They're not interested in the island as we were. It's not their home, their blood. All they care about is profit. They are *buying us up*, Angus. Literally. Root by root, field by field. And it's a one-way transaction. Hardly any Roquennais family can afford to buy, or even rent, land or property for themselves any more. Prices have been driven up to such an extent that the only people who can afford them are the rich *immigrés,* or those who are calling the tune.'

'If it'll make it any easier for you, sir, I'd mention that I've met Corlander *fils*. The paternal relative is no doubt a larger and even noisier edition.'

'And a richer one.'

'No doubt. Where do they come from?'

'Who knows? Originally, I think, from somewhere in the Low Countries, but they seem to have lived everywhere. They belong to the world. They are symbolic, you might say. The parents, I believe, suffered in Germany during the war. Very badly, one suspects. Unfortunately, they're making up for it at our expense! You'd never met them before?'

'No. Heard of them, of course. In Maurice's letters, he'd mention from time to time things like the new casino, for instance, but I simply didn't take in any of the implications.'

'No. Why should you?'

'Who else is in on the Big Take?'

'It's hard to say, my boy. But it isn't merely *things* they're buying; it's people. They're buying people.'

'And those that can't be bought?'

'Are very few. Resistance can carry a high price. As Maurice found.'

I looked at him speculatively for a moment. 'You agree it *was* suicide, sir?'

He drew another deep sigh and his face sagged. 'Unfortunately, it was never open to doubt. Absolutely none whatever.' He glanced up at me. 'There was a note, you know.'

I nodded. 'Yes, I read the report in the English newspapers.'

'They said what was in it, the note?'

'No.'

'It was addressed to Alain and intended for him and Simone jointly. As his executors, we were given a copy of it. Nicholas has it in the office, but I made a personal copy of my own, which I have here. I'm sure neither Alain nor Simone would mind your seeing it.'

He levered himself up and went across to his bureau. He opened the desk lid and then, taking a key from his waistcoat pocket, pulled out one of the small drawers inside. From here he took a small folded piece of paper and brought it over to me. Here, in Guy's thin, spidery handwriting, was Maurice's last token of intent to his family. It was brief and its intimation seemed all too clear:

By the time you get this it will be too late for you, or anyone, to undo what has to be. I can only hope that in time you will both come to understand and forgive me. Had there been any other course, I would have taken it, but for those of us whose ways are the old ways events have moved too fast and too inconsiderately. I no longer see any hope of saving anything of the life we once knew, and it therefore seems pointless to continue fighting. Our island is a 'rock', but our house has become a house of sand.

I am sorry. You must make whatever you can of what is left.

Your Father

I read it through several times in silence and then handed it back to Guy, who took it without a word and returned it to its drawer. Not until he had lowered himself into his chair again did he speak.

'They say he couldn't have suffered physically, Angus.'

I said nothing and another silence fell between us. What Guy Le Marnet's thoughts were, I couldn't know, but, for myself, I felt a chill inside me.

There was a knock on the door and Guy's man, Pierre, entered, carrying a tray. He placed it on a small table and carried both together over to the side of Guy's chair and proceeded to pour out two cups of coffee.

'Thank you, Pierre,' said Guy, making a visible effort to pull himself together. He raised his hand in the old servant's direction. 'You see, Angus,' he said to me. 'He still looks after me: he and Berthe, and she still cooks like an angel. Where I'd be without them, I just don't know.'

I glanced up at Pierre, who was smiling indulgently as he manipulated the cups. It occurred to me that he must be nearly as old as Guy, and possibly as frail, if the truth were told, but clearly in his own eyes he saw himself as the stronger of the two, the protector, the one to be reckoned with if need should arise. I had already seen this in action. When he had opened the door to me on my arrival, it had been several slightly uncomfortable seconds before suspicious wariness had given way to a reserved welcome, and this despite the fact that he must have been expecting me. Pierre was a man for whom no amount of personal recommendation would mean a thing until he had satisfied himself, by some internal mechanism known only to himself, that a person or a situation was admissible. Watching him, I pondered for a moment on the changing fashions in human values. In Britain, the cult of so-called 'social equality' was bringing nothing but hostility between 'boss' and 'worker'. Here, in this still feudal society, men like Pierre, Pedro Calvaro, Paulo Garcia, fulfilled their functions not only without complaint but with something near to love. In theory, it was all wrong. In practice, here, theory seemed to lose its validity.

After he had seen us comfortably settled with our coffee, Pierre departed. Guy picked up his cup and saucer and settled back in his chair, stirring thoughtfully.

'Maurice made a new Will just over a year ago,' he said. 'With so little of his estate left, the old Will had become worthless. Also, he was concerned about Simone and the child. In his new Will, he left what was still intact – virtually only the house and gardens – to her, with the proviso that, should she sell, the proceeds should go to her own immediate needs and those of the child, the residue to be added to the trust he had formed for Hélène shortly after her birth.'

'And Alain?'

'Alain was not mentioned in the second Will. I think he had understood that for some time.'

Had he? I wondered. How far had Alain and his father drifted apart? How much mutual understanding *had* there been left at the end?

'Had you ever suspected that he might take his life?'

'Never! Not that! We knew how things had been going with him, of course. Nicholas was still acting for him, but it was extremely difficult because Maurice would not talk of his problems and therefore put himself beyond any advice that might have been given, for what little it would have been worth. We were continually having to negotiate sales of land for him: at first, small plots here and there, then more. Finally, the plantations. I don't know whether you knew this, Angus, but Edith Cartier bought them. In the condition they were in, it was a most generous act of

76

friendship on her part. But by then, of course, it was too late to do anything with the money except pay off debts.'

God, if only I'd known!

'And the other plots? Who bought *them*?'

'Oh, various farmers. Mostly, they were a way of paying off bills in kind. If it could only have stopped there. When the plantations finally went to Corlander – ' He sighed. 'And I'm afraid it's only the beginning. They want the house, too, and the land immediately round it, so that they can turn the whole estate into some kind of spectacular tourist venture. One rumour has it that it could be another casino – you've seen the one in town, I expect. Others say he plans to build luxury chalets right down to the beach, with shops and bars, etc. – a kind of holiday village – like he's done down on West Front: "Coney Island", Nicholas calls it – '

'Not even as innocent, I'm afraid. More Las Vegas out of Blackpool.'

Guy nodded. 'And then there's the social damage. The plantations don't mean a thing to them, but they're obliged by our laws to continue working them as agricultural land for three years from the date of purchase – that gives them just under a year to go. After that, apart from anything else, all those poor devils up there will be out of work.'

'Couldn't Maurice have protected the position – so far as the house is concerned, anyway – with a provision restricting its use?'

'As a private residence, you mean? He could have, but there are always ways of getting round such things. In any case, I think he gave a great deal of thought to the various alternatives that faced Simone on his death. You realize, Angus, that, apart from a very little capital left in the bank, one or two land rents still left her on the estate and the little she gets from Corlander – '

'*Little!*'

'Yes, I know.' He hesitated, looking at me. 'You'll think it strange, I know, Angus, but we couldn't persuade

Simone to press her case at all. Despite his open infidelities, we had the utmost difficulty to get her even to agree to the minimum settlement the court could allow.'

It was worse, far worse, than I'd imagined. Unbelievable, in fact. Pride, I supposed. I said it aloud, but Guy shook his head.

'No.' He hesitated again. 'No, it wasn't that. Simone blamed *herself*, you see – ' He raised his hand as my head jerked up. 'I know – we all felt the same. It was shameful, pathetic. But when she married this man, she was infatuated with him. She wouldn't listen to a word against him. Even when they separated, it was the same. She felt she had failed and had only herself to blame for what had happened.'

I stared at him, speechless. My feelings were dangerously near the surface, and Guy sensed it, waiting and saying nothing. Eventually, I said: 'You can't surely mean that the bastard put in a defence?'

'He claimed extenuating circumstances. He said Simone had neglected her responsibilities and failed to make a proper home.'

'God's teeth!'

'And Nicholas had the greatest difficulty in stopping Simone from agreeing with him, publicly. You see, Angus – ' he looked at me with something like a plea in his eyes ' – the sheltered life she'd led, plus a perhaps unusually shy nature, had made her almost abnormally diffident. It is probably true that, by *his* standards, she didn't measure up to all the social requirements of this marriage – '

'Great God in heaven! I don't believe it!'

'No. Well, Ray Corlander lives the kind of life you read about in books. He's a highly self-dramatized individual – '

'He's a bastard.'

He gave an ironic smile. 'Well, certainly his Napoleonic image of himself requires a background in which our gentle Simone never had the smallest hope of surviving.'

'Then why the hell – all right, she was infatuated with

him – but as gallantry is clearly not one of the attainments he'd lose much sleep over, why did *he* marry *her*?'

'Oh, undoubtedly he saw the marriage as a short cut to his plans, and Simone as a prestigious acquisition. In a way, I was surprised he gave her grounds for divorce. I think, in the end, he'd just got so bored he couldn't stand it.'

'From what you've said, I'm surprised she agreed to divorce *him*.'

'She didn't want to. But she had no choice, really. He was so open in his disloyalty to her. Even more to the point, though, she felt, I think, that she was holding him back. I've often wondered – though I doubt if it would have made any difference – but there was a son, you know, Angus. Before Hélène. He died soon after birth. He would have been about ten now.'

'Yes, I heard.'

'So you can understand how concerned Maurice would be that what was left of St Michel should go to Simone. You may wonder why he didn't just sell – to an outsider, I mean – and put the proceeds in trust for her. I wondered that myself. I can only think he may have hoped for some miracle – even perhaps a fresh marriage. I don't know. It's one of the mysteries his death leaves us with. But to give up a home your family have had for hundreds of years – '

'He must have realized that she'd *have* to sell in the end.' I paused, thinking. 'I don't know, it just doesn't gell somehow.'

He shook his head. 'The only interpretation I can put on it – and I've thought about it endlessly – is that he felt that where there was life – for her – there was hope. Desperation works on an instinctive level; we can't always give it a rational formula.'

We were both silent for a while. I was still thinking, trying to make some sort of sense of everything I'd heard. Eventually I told him about my visit to St Michel and my meeting with both Simone and Alain (though *not* of my subsequent ambush of the pair of them).

'They seem resigned to selling,' I said. 'But of course it's going to take a bit of doing to find an outsider mug enough to buy a house surrounded by land right up to the front door, so to speak, that's down for development by somebody else.'

'Precisely.'

'So Corlander's offer's the only one she's likely to get. And he knows it.'

'Yes.' His face was heavy and we both fell quiet again.

Eventually, Guy stirred, and I thought I detected a new sharpness in his face.

'There's still one thing that stands in his way,' he said.

'Yes?'

'It isn't *much* of a hope, I'm afraid, but it's something – the Land Purchases Committee.'

I recalled Dart's words to Ray Corlander. 'I think I've heard of it. What does it do exactly?'

'The LPP was set up by young Cartier's grandfather when he was President, to stop just what these people are trying to do today, buy up traditionally agricultural land for non-productive or personal profit-making purposes. The way it works is quite simple. All purchases are examined by the Committee and have to have their permit; if plantations or farmland of any kind are included, the purchaser has to undertake to continue to work them as such for a clear three years. It isn't perfect, but it gives a breathing space, and it does prevent exploitation from being easy. Up till now it's worked fairly well.'

'And now?'

He sighed. 'Lately, the Committee itself seems to have lost its teeth – or acquired a few false ones.'

'Infiltration from interested parties.'

He nodded. 'Mind, there are still a few good men trying to hold the structure together, but it isn't easy. When loopholes occur, it takes time to legislate against them. Time we can't afford.'

'Technically speaking, can the Committee veto a sale altogether?'

'Technically yes. So far, it's never had to, but there's a test case pending right now.'

'I think I've heard of that, too.'

'A family called Iturbi have some land out at Point Rouge. Bernard Corlander bought some of it about two years ago. So far, he hasn't developed it, although the plot he acquired wasn't restricted, so he could have if he'd wanted to. But now we've discovered why. He wants the rest of the land, and the house itself, for a hotel and night-club and he's offered the Iturbis a lot of money.'

'So they want to sell, and the Committee have turned him down.'

'Twice. He's got one more chance, and from what I've heard he's been doing some powerful lobbying – of one sort or another. He's arguing on a technicality – that the sale of the rest of the property should come under the permit he's already gained on the previous purchase. If he brings it off, it will give him a springbroad for all subsequent negotiations he sees fit to enter into.'

'Including St Michel – if he can bring Simone to heel.'

'Exactly. This Iturbi business is crucial for us. Even if Corlander's application fails the third time, he can still take it to the Grand Council for a decision. In the old days, their rulings were sound and reliable. Nowadays, who knows.'

'These Iturbis . . . they make a living from the land they still own?'

'In a small way, yes. But, as I've said, Corlander has offered them an inflated price. I rather suspect, too – though I've no proof of this – that he's managed to get some other hold over them. His methods are believed to be quite unscrupulous when circumstances dictate, but so far it's been impossible to catch him out.'

'When the balloon goes up, he's not there.'

'Precisely.'

'I take it the Grand Council is some sort of court of appeal?'

'You might call it that. It's a select committee composed

81

of senators, elected by vote of the Assembly and headed by the President. In cases of impasse, or contention, it can be appealed to for a judgement, which is tacitly accepted as final. You see, Angus – ' he smiled wryly – ' I know it's been said – I've seen it in some of the foreign newspapers – that we're a feudal society, and I suppose inasmuch as we're probably the only completely privately owned territory of comparable size still in existence in the world, the definition is inevitable. But there are other forms of feudalism on this earth today far worse than any practised here. Since you were last with us, we've built many more schools, a splendid new hospital just outside Porte Hilaire – you must go and see it – clinics in the country areas, mobile libraries: and we had plans for much more. I say "we", but you understand I mean the Assembly. Always, we've worked within the structure of our laws, and they've stood the test of time. The people have been content up to now.'

'And now?'

'Now they're being seduced with promises of quick riches: lured into selling their land, turning their backs on the old traditions. But only a few will profit. The rest will find they have been disinherited – by their own greed. They'll find tourism cannot give them *all* jobs, and when they look round again, for their land and their homes, they'll find everything's gone into immigrant property deals in which they've had no part whatsoever. This is the new feudalism of today. Men like Corlander give nothing in return for what they extract, only a complete and irrevocable enslavement. And now, with Maurice gone, and Edith Cartier, who is to hold them. I?' He gave a bitter little laugh. 'They have me precisely where they want me.'

'How's that?'

'Well, you see, according to our constitution, when the Sénéchal dies, or retires, the next to succeed him is the President of the Assembly. In this case, myself. It has always been a workable way of ensuring succession

throughout the Assembly and of bestowing the final acco-
lade, as it were, upon a man who has given the best part of
his adult life to the island's service. Unfortunately, that is
about *all* the Stewardship is.'

'You mean it carries no powers?'

'None whatever. In a way, I suppose you could say the
Stewardship is what you call a "rubber stamp" job, but
we look upon it as an honour, too.'

'The ermine instead of the axe. We have it as well.'

He smiled. 'Yes. Politics has become very subtle these
days.'

'This was Maurice's *second* term as Steward, wasn't it?'

'Yes, and had he lived, and had it been constitutionally
possible, they would have voted him in again. I've absolutely no doubt about that. He was President for five
years, you know. He asked to be relieved before his final
term was up.'

'I know. I've been thinking about that. *Why* did he,
sir?'

Guy shook his head. 'We never really knew. Officially,
he gave health reasons. But he was as fit as any of us.
Personally, I believe it was a kind of despair. He'd begun
to see how things were going, both in his private life and
on the island itself, and felt he could no longer carry on.
Or rather, perhaps, that others – and in this, of course, he
was desperately mistaken – were better equipped to deal
with the responsibilities of the office. The President, you
see, as head of the legislative and the Council, *does* have
certain powers – limited, but mostly effective. That's
what I meant when I said they had me where they wanted
me.'

'Yes, I see that. But where St Michel is concerned, it's
bad luck on Simone *either* way, isn't it? I mean, is there
any point in stopping Corlander buying, if she can't sell
anywhere else?'

'Only that it's unlikely that Corlander will want to continue to run the plantations indefinitely. If he doesn't get
hold of the house within a reasonable period of time, he

may throw up the idea and agree to sell the plantations to someone who was prepared to buy the house and land together as a going concern.'

I nodded. 'On the other hand, if he hangs on, and Simone gives way in the end, he could always argue, I suppose – like this Iturbi business – that an offer for the house should come under the same consent which covered the purchase of the plantations. Yes?'

'Yes.' He smiled wryly. 'You've grasped the subtleties very well. Now you see why this Iturbi case is so vital. Somehow, we just have to stop him here, but *how* . . .' He shook his head and relapsed into silence.

Neither of us spoke for a while. For my part, I was busy trying to absorb the gist of what he'd been saying. The important point, I realized, was that, as from now, his presidency was ended. Therefore his powers. He would be succeeded – by whom? I asked him.

'The present Chef de Justice, next in line, is Stéphan Cartier. Max's uncle. You remember him, perhaps?'

'Vaguely.' I recalled a hawkish-looking man, with the dark, thin features of the male Cartiers, but with a predatory quality lacking in Max's basically lazy personality.

'Stéphan is an unknown quantity,' said Guy. 'If I were to be completely uncharitable – '

'I wish you would, sir, it saves time in the end.'

He smiled. 'Yes, well, with Stéphan Cartier one can only guess which side of an issue he will take when it becomes clear which side is winning. It is then reasonably safe to lay a small wager.'

'And right now you'd chance a dirty great big one that he'll swing over to Corlander once he's in the saddle.'

'It's very possible, I'm afraid. Yes, very, very possible.'

We were silent again for several minutes, during which the only sounds in the room were the firm but gentle ticking of the fine old ormolu clock on the mantelpiece and the clink of Guy's spoon in his saucer. I wondered why I had not come to see him first. I realized it was because I had been so keen to see St Michel, and, arising out of that visit, Alain and Simone and the Cartiers; but only now, in the presence of this old man, Maurice's oldest living friend, was the picture beginning at last to slide into focus. Guy Le Marnet was too civilized to say that he hated the Corlanders as individuals, but it was clear that he loathed and detested everything they stood for. This would have been Maurice's feeling, too: added to which would have been the intense personal involvement resulting from Simone's unhappiness. Just *how* bitter had his antipathy been? Enough for a fight, certainly. But then, why had he given up while things still remained to be done? Why suicide? Somehow, it was still as unanswerable as ever.

I looked at Guy, who was gazing out of the window, presumably lost in his own thoughts of the past.

'How did Maurice's troubles actually *start*, sir? His financial troubles, I mean. It – the whole idea – seems so unlike him.'

Guy sighed. He rubbed his forehead again, slowly, from side to side, with the middle finger of his right hand, still gazing in front of him out over the gardens. 'It *was* unlike him. Completely. I suppose – ' he sighed again, leaning forward on his elbows and staring, now, at his feet stretched out in front of him, 'it was a bit of this, a bit of that. First, there was Jean. I know it's a long time ago, but for him it never really healed. He'd had great hopes of Jean – of both the boys – but Jean – ' He paused again and I wondered if he was trying to avoid suggesting that, somehow, Alain had been a disappointment to his father. Presently, he continued. 'You see, I know it's archaic in the world you come from, my boy, but here, for us, for our three families, in particular, a son has a special significance. Maurice seemed fortunate indeed; he had two. The inheritance was secure. Then one dies. So, eventually, he begins to pin his hopes and plans on the other. But gradually he realizes that no common ground exists. Alain has always been his own man. As he grew older, it became more and more apparent that he had different interests. He took this job on the *News* and we began to wonder if

85

he was going to become interested in politics, in administration. But lately—' He broke off and I waited. 'Well, lately,' he continued, 'he seems to have withdrawn into himself, become bitter, unapproachable.'

I nodded.

'If you've seen him, you'll have noticed. I've wondered sometimes if he has some serious worry of his own. There's a woman, you know. They've lived together for some years, but her husband won't give her a divorce. Whether that has something to do with it – but I'm digressing. The point is, Maurice had to face this – this second death, you might call it, the collapse of all he'd hoped for.'

'But surely, so long as the plantations remained in the family, it didn't really matter. They could always be run by a manager. Old Pedro knew the business inside out. I don't imagine Corlander is involving himself very personally in them, but he appears to be making them pay.'

Guy's look was reproachful. 'You know better than that, Angus. To Corlander, St Michel is just what you've said, a business. To Maurice, it was his life, his family's heritage. If you haven't understood that, then we've been wasting our time.'

'Yes, I do know, sir. I'm sorry. It's just that every time I think about this whole damn business – '

'Yes. But consider, Angus. I've told you how he felt about Jean, about Alain. Now, on top of this, Simone takes up with Ray Corlander.'

'God, yes! I'll never understand *that!*'

'Nor did Maurice, nor any of us. But there was no reasoning with her. The marriage nearly broke Justine's heart. She became ill shortly after – ' (My heart fell. As long ago as that!) – 'We only realized at the end what she'd been through, what they'd both been through. It's my belief that Maurice always felt that the worry of Simone's marriage was the cause of Justine's death. He watched her struggle and finally fail, and all the time this marriage followed exactly the same pattern. Simone was

86

humiliated by this man, Angus. Openly. It was agonizing for us all. For Maurice – well, I leave you to imagine. For a while, he retreated into his books. He lost all interest in practical affairs. I think the knowledge that he was in debt came to him as a surprise. The selling off of land, all the rest, followed. In the end, there was a sort of inevitability about it all.'

I felt cold again. And sick. And frustrated. I wanted to break a window or step on somebody's hands. Instead, I sat with the sour taste of anger in my mouth, seeking still for an enlightenment that would not come.

'Why in heaven's name,' I demanded, 'didn't Simone stay at St Michel after the divorce?'

He grimaced. 'Pride, I suppose, my boy. It *is* understandable.'

'Hell, yes, but – well, frankly, sir, that place she's got in town – God, how Maurice must have loathed it! I can't help wondering if maybe he would have survived if only they'd stayed on at St Michel together.'

'Who knows. But suffering makes people do strange things. Like an animal in pain that goes and hides away in some dark place where you can't reach it. I suppose it's an instinct as old as life itself. And as unreasoning.'

'Maybe you're right.' I thought again. 'About Hélène – '

'Ah, you've noticed Hélène.'

'Yes. What's wrong? Has anything been done about it?'

'Well, she's been seen by doctors. They say there's nothing wrong with her.'

'She's not retarded?'

'Not in the strictly clinical meaning of the term. Withdrawn, but not retarded. On the contrary, they all agree that there is considerable intelligence there. She's like a lamp with the switch turned off. The light is there, but something has turned it off. They hope it's only temporary.'

'In the meantime, though, isn't she losing a lot of very formative time?'

'They say not. They say she's storing her experiences:

87

that nothing is really being lost, and that there's every hope that in the right circumstances she will rediscover the need and the will to communicate. At the moment, that is what is lacking: not the ability to do so, but the desire.'

'Yes. Yes, that does pretty well describe it.' But what, I wondered, would be the 'right circumstances'? I was about to say something about what I'd seen at St George's, but Guy suddenly leaned forward in his chair and the expression on his face stopped me.

'Angus,' he said, 'I want you to find out why Maurice died.'

I stared at him, my mouth sagging foolishly. 'But – I'm sorry, sir, but I thought this was what you'd been trying to tell *me*!'

'And it satisfies you?'

'Well – ' I broke off, shrugging helplessly. 'Well, no, I suppose it doesn't. But I'd thought – '

'You thought it did me.'

'To be honest, yes.'

He grimaced. 'I've tried to accept it. Heaven knows I have, but – well, the truth is, Angus, I've told you *what* happened, and how it happened, and the generally accepted reasons why it happened, and it would all be explicable and understandable enough if it had been almost anyone but Maurice de Courvel. But in the last few years, Angus, he and I came very close. We were the last of our time, if you know what I mean. He was a much cleverer, wiser man than I, but we shared a great deal; so much so that when there was something we *didn't* share, I was aware of it. You understand me?'

I nodded. 'And there *was* something?'

'Over the last year, yes. Something was worrying him – no, that isn't the right word – *eating into him*, something that was different from all the things I knew about. I was so certain of this that once or twice I tried to draw him out, but each time I sensed such an anguish and conflict within him that I couldn't bear it. In the end, I decided he would either speak to me of his own accord, or

88

whatever it was would remain his secret to the grave. And that, of course, was what happened.'

'But if *you* couldn't find out what it was, sir, what hope have I?'

'I don't know. But you might. You're the only one, I feel, who could. Nicholas, Alain, I – we're all too close. But you, Angus, with your training, your knowledge of people – above all, your disinterest – '

'Hardly that, sir.'

'Oh, I don't mean in that sense. I know your regard for Maurice; it's because of that I'm asking you. But you, my boy, come here "clean", if you know what I mean, free of involvement. If anyone can discover what it was that Maurice feared, I believe you can.'

'Before you said "worried": now, you say "feared". Which was it, sir?'

He hesitated. 'A little of both, I think. But it is strange you should ask that. I don't think I recognized until now – at least, not consciously – that there *was* fear. Now, I feel sure there was. Yes, Maurice was afraid of something.'

When I took my leave of Guy he insisted on accompanying me round the corner of the house to the drive. Pierre hovered watchfully in the background, and when I got into the car and Guy began to walk back towards the terrace, I spotted Pierre hurrying towards the car. As I started the engine, he broke into an awkward little trot and I put my head out of the window, waiting for him. He came up, breathing heavily and red in the face.

'Take it easy, Pierre.'

'Pardon, Monsieur.' He smiled apologetically. 'I am not so young now.'

'Just as well to remember it.'

'Monsieur Angus, I am so glad you have come. Madame and I are very worried.'

'You, too, Pierre?'

'Monsieur, it is for Monsieur Le Marnet. We believe he could be – ' he hesitated, looking uncomfortable.

'Yes?'

'Well, forgive me, Monsieur, but we believe he could be in danger.'

I looked at him quizzically, but there was no mistaking the genuine concern on his pink, perspiring face.

'They wish to harm him, Monsieur. We are sure of it. Forgive me, but we are sure.'

'What's happened, Pierre?'

'Two things, Monsieur. Accidents, Monsieur Le Marnet thinks, but we do not. We are afraid – ' He stopped, looking back towards the house, his face agitated and fearful.

'Of what?' I demanded.

He hesitated again. His initial impulse to confide in me seemed, now, to be in conflict with an instinct to hold his tongue. I waited, and presently he arrived at a resolution.

'We are afraid, Monsieur – for his life.'

SEVEN

I woke to the sound of bells. I'd forgotten how many churches there were in Porte Hilaire and how exuberantly they greeted the Sabbath. I got up, put on my dressing gown and threw open the balcony windows.

Below, the harbour square lay deserted in the yellow morning sun. New order or no new order, it looked as if the average Roquennais still believed that God had made the world in six days and rested on the seventh.

There were no lorries and no people; the weighbridges stood empty and silent, their glass-fronted office doors locked and shuttered. You could almost believe that the whole world had stopped in its tracks to listen to the only sound that remained, the wild, ancient voices of the bells.

Nor was their message ignored. Even as I stood there, a 'church bus' came trundling in and deposited its load in the centre of the square. On Sundays, the only buses running on La Roque were the church buses. Unlike the 'cinema buses', which every night took circuitous routes through the lanes taking people home from the last performances, the church buses only ran to and from the outskirts of Porte Hilaire itself. But they were always full, as this one was now. All the men were formally dressed in their best dark suits, redolent no doubt of moth-balls, and the traditional beret, the sombreness relieved only by an occasional buttonhole. Their womenfolk, an arresting contrast, wore their brightest cotton dresses and most brilliant headscarves, and many of them carried bunches of freshly picked flowers. As for the children, they were a mobile aviary of colour and chattering sound as they moved across the square: little girls in white with coloured sashes, and carrying more flowers, little boys strutting like young magpies in solemn black and white, enlivened by bright red, green or blue ties.

How long would it last, I wondered, this simple acceptance of old values and even older traditions? How many
'church buses' were there still to run on La Roque? How
much unquestioning faith, religious and social, remained? I
watched until the last splash of colour, the last straight,
dark back, had moved round the corner of the railings of
the Town Church. Then I turned back into the room,
noticing for the first time how dark it was.

During breakfast, I was called to the telephone. It was
Stéphanie to say that the children wanted to know whether
they should wait for me before going down to swim.

'Certainly not. I'm too old to bathe on a full stomach.'

'But it's half-past nine!'

'So? The day's in its infancy. Only *I'm* not. If your brood
think I'm arriving in a loin-cloth and swinging on branches,
you'd better disillusion them – fast. Even Johnny Weiss-
muller probably wears contact lenses and a top denture
these days.'

She rang off, laughing, and I returned to my meal.

Over my final cup of tea I thought about what Pierre had
tried to tell me. I didn't feel inclined to take the old man too
seriously. I hadn't managed to get much out of him in
support of his dire prophecy, except that on one occasion
Guy had fallen from his library steps, which had subsequently been found to be mysteriously broken, and on
another that he had given himself a shock with his electric
razor, discovered later to have a frayed connection. Neither
incident seemed particularly bizarre in its context, given the
average age of the three present occupants of Mont Vert.
Nevertheless, I decided that a careful word with Nicholas
on the subject wouldn't go amiss.

Before I felt the hotel, I bought two dozen yellow roses
for Stéphanie, some cigars for Nicholas and the largest box
of chocolates I could find for the children. I wondered why
the assistant gave me a curious look until I remembered that
it was the second time in three days that I'd bought yellow
roses (a safe colour, I always think) and chocolates to go
with them.

On an impulse, and because it was partly on my way, I decided not to go direct to Cap St Michel but to take a quick look at the Iturbi farm at Point Rouge. Accordingly, I drove out to the Point and after making some enquiries of a group of children playing on the roadside, found the farm at the top of the hill overlooking the bay. As soon as I saw it, I realized its attraction from Corlander's point of view. It stood on high ground, looking down over the sweep of its own fields straight across one of the most famed panoramas on the island. As its name implies, Point Rouge is celebrated for its sunsets. Most evenings, the whole expanse of the bay turns to molten fire, and every window along the shore becomes a glittering prism. Tourists go gaga about it, and even islanders of a romantic nature tend to make their way down to the Point on leisured evenings to sit on the turf of the headland just above the lighthouse and watch the sun's slow burial below the darkening horizon. It was inevitable that sooner or later someone would come along and exploit these natural pyrotechnics. So far, the only hotel on the shore below Point Rouge was too low, geographically speaking, to afford the best views. Higher up, most of the land was agricultural. If Corlander succeeded in his application, he would have added a gold mine to his empire.

The Iturbi farmhouse, built of the natural pink stone of the island, was long and narrow and low-roofed, and it had a bit of garden in front of it facing the sea. I drove on past the gate that lay open to the yard and then stopped the car and began to stroll slowly back. I had some vague idea of turning in at the gate and, if accosted, saying I had lost my way, but as I drew near to the farmyard I saw two figures walking across it towards the lane where I was. Retreat was out of the question, so I continued to approach, trying to look as much like a tourist as possible. We all drew level at the gate together and I looked up casually, trying to take in as much as I could of the situation without attracting attention. One of the men, a tall, gaunt-faced, bad-tempered-looking fellow, with the dark skin and hair of the Roquennais, I took to be Iturbi himself, or one of his family. His companion, who appeared to be doing all the talking, was, by contrast, short, squat and paunchy, and wore thick-lensed glasses.

Iturbi seemed barely to notice me, but as I sauntered on I noticed that the other man's head turned in my direction. Although I couldn't be sure, because of the thickness of his glasses, I fancied he was giving me a more than cursory once-over, and for some indefinable reason I felt a spasm of disquiet. He was talking in Spanish with an accent I took to be French. A French farmer? Interested in buying some stock? Only a handful of the farmers on the island were French, but they were the ones with the money. Or maybe it was the local vet. Or the bloke about the hole in the barn roof. Or come to swap an old sow for half a dozen hens.

I walked on down the lane, forcing myself to move slowly and casually, and continued on down the hill almost until I reached the main road running round the bay. There, to put a fine aesthetic touch to the exercise, I made a play of looking around the terrain before turning and beginning to climb back up the way I had come. I had barely gone a yard when I saw a dark blue Renault coming down the hill towards me, and as I flattened myself against the bank for it to pass I was aware of a pair of thick, pebble glasses turned in my direction. Conscious that I had made somewhat of a thundering mess of the whole operation, I plodded on back to where I'd parked the car and set course for St Michel.

On the way, I had to pass the lane that leads to the airport and there I made another rapid decision. As it was Sunday, there was no guarantee that the man I wanted to see would be around, but when the terminal building came in sight I saw the car I wanted parked at the end of the cab rank. I drew up nearby, got out and strolled over to the driver's open window.

'Hello, Paulo.'

Señor!' He cast aside the paper he was reading and made to get out.

'It's all right. I don't want to go anywhere. Just the pleasure of your company for a few minutes, that's all.'

'But of course, Señor!'

He looked at me quizzically. 'You enjoy your 'oliday, Señor Logan, yes?'

'No.'

'Oh.' He had expected a routine run and was disconcerted.

'I don't like changes, Paulo. They confuse me. This island now – everything has changed.'

'Ah, sí.' He nodded ponderously. 'Sí.'

'So many new faces, new names. Difficult to keep track.'

He nodded again, sagely, waiting now, I sensed, for whatever was coming.

'You might be able to put me right on a few points.'

He spread his hands wide, bland innocence settling on him like the dew. 'A pleasure, Señor.'

'Good. Let's start with the Iturbis.'

It was as if I'd tampered with the primeval dawn. Sweetness and joy died a sudden death and the darkness of Satan showed on his face. 'Iturbis? You say Iturbis, Señor?'

'I do.'

'You want to know about Iturbis?'

'Confound it, Paulo, that's what I said.'

He looked at me for a full minute without replying and his eyes were like two hard, black buttons in his dark, corrugated face. Then, suddenly, his lips curled into a snarl and he spat, clearing me and the car with consummate skill.

'Iturbi! Whole family bad!'

'Is that just your opinion, or is it a consensus?'

'Señor?'

'What's wrong with them?'

'Señor – ' He looked round him uneasily and I realized I was asking rather a lot of him in the circumstances. He nodded to me to come closer to the window, while he himself drew further back into the car. 'Why you want to know about Iturbi?' he asked.

'They're selling their farm, I believe.'

He stared at me for a moment and I could have sworn that I saw relief come into his face. 'Sí.' he said. 'Sí. They sell their farm, to Señor Corlander.'

'Who's having to fight the Assembly to get it. Do you think he *will* get it?'

He shrugged. I had not been mistaken; he was very much more relaxed now.

'Certainly, Señor. He will get the farm.'

'In spite of the Assembly?'

He shrugged again.

'Why?'

His button eyes regarded me shrewdly for a moment and he pursed his lips.

'You said there had been changes, Señor. It is true. The Assembly, it is like a dog that is old – it growl, but there are no teeth.'

'Old? Or sick?'

He glanced at me for a second, then looked fixedly ahead of him. 'Perhaps so, Señor.'

'There's no perhaps about it, is there? Look, Paulo, I haven't time to shadow-box with you. I'm putting my cards on the table. I'm here to find out why Monsieur de Courvel took his own life and I'm going to do just that, so anyone who doesn't like it can take fair warning. But I need help. I need people I can trust. Now, you knew my father. He thought of you as a friend. He trusted you and you trusted him. Now *I'm* trusting you, whether you like it or not. Do you understand me?'

A range of expressions, from shock through deep concern to a kind of despair had passed over his countenance during this speech and now, slowly, he began to shake his head solemnly from side to side, while his eyes avoided mine.

'You won't help me?'

'No, no, it is not that, Señor!' He faced me squarely now and his face was anguished. 'Why you ask about Iturbi?' he asked.

'Simply because they happen to be the only handle I've got so far to loosen out a few facts about the people who're running this island now. There's something going on there, isn't there? Iturbi's willing to sell his birthright, and it's

96

more than just a question of being offered a good price, isn't it? I can smell it from here.'

He hesitated. I felt he was on the brink of a decision. Finally, he temporized. 'It could be, Señor. Sí, it could be.'

'All right. Have it your own way. If there *is* something else – just *if* – what would it be likely to be?'

He made a show of thinking about it, eyebrows raised, his hands stretched out on the steering-wheel, his eyes averted again. 'Much smuggling on the island,' he said. His voice was so low I wasn't sure for a moment that I'd heard aright.

'Smuggling?' I stared at him. 'You mean the Iturbis?' Light began to dawn.

He shrugged, still looking ahead of him. 'Some say,' he said.

'I see.' I began to think aloud. 'If Corlander knew about that – could prove it – but in that case why should he bother to offer them a decent price? Unless, of course, he didn't want folk wondering how he'd managed to get something for nothing.' I was silent for a moment. 'So that's it,' I said.

Paulo threw me a deprecating look. '*Could* be,' he said.

'Could be, nothing, you old devil! You know damn well it is. Now, how would Corlander find out, I wonder?'

'Señor Corlander know everything.' He looked at me sideways. 'He more than *know*,' he added darkly.

'*Does* he then!' I looked at him for a moment. 'What you're suggesting you couldn't prove, of course. You're wise to be careful. But don't worry. As far as I'm concerned, Corlander can be Captain Morgan and Old Nick rolled into one just so long as it's got nothing to do with why Monsieur de Courvel died. On the other hand, if it *has* – '

His head jerked round and alarm showed in his face now. 'No, Señor! It is not so!'

'You're very sure.'

'Sí!' Immediately he regretted the emphasis and tried to back-pedal. 'I do not know why Señor de Courvel killed himself, Señor Angus, but I know it is not that.'

'You know *something*, though, don't you?'

I regarded him in silence for a moment. His face had sagged and his whole appearance had taken on a kind of hangdog misery. But he didn't answer me and eventually I straightened up. 'O.K.,' I said. 'We'll leave it at that for now.' I moved away from the window.

'Señor!'

I stopped and looked back at him. He was leaning out of the window and his eyes were imploring. He was clearly having trouble with his conscience, but I wasn't prepared to make things easy for him.

'Señor, be careful.'

'Why, Paulo?'

'Señor. Do not trust anyone. Not *anyone*. You understand?'

'No. Should I?'

His misery now was deperate, but the struggle within him was clearly not going to be resolved by any further discussion, so I gave him a brief nod and turned away.

As I drove out from the car-park, I glanced back through my mirror. For a moment he was directly in my line of vision and I saw that he was still sitting there, gazing after me. I could no longer see the expression on his face, but the intensity of his emotions seemed to pour out from him like air from a burst balloon. Paulo Garcia knew a great deal. But he wasn't telling – yet.

It was several hours later, while I was sitting on the terrace in the garden of the Villa Valeuse resting after my swim with the Le Marnet children, that I remembered the look of relief on Paulo's face. I glanced at Nicholas, sprawled out in a canvas chair nearby.

'Is there much smuggling on the island?' I asked him.

He looked surprised, then he grinned. 'Somebody been offering you a nice little bit of silver?'

'Not yet. But somebody looked a bit worried when they thought I knew something I didn't. I came to the conclusion that smuggling was what it was all about.'

He smiled again and gave a wry shake of the head. 'Could well be. It's what the sociologists call endemic.'

'A problem, then.'

'Well – ' he pursed his lips in a speculative fashion. The typical lawyer, I thought, slightly amused. 'It depends,' he said, 'on what you call a problem.'

Stéphanie appeared, carrying a tray, with nine-year-old Marguerite a few paces behind and bearing a large jug of something or other with infinite care. We both jumped to our feet to assist in laying out plates and various items of food on a couple of patio tables, and Stéphanie moved back towards the house.

'Put the lemonade over there,' she directed Marguerite with a wave, 'and go and call the boys.'

It had been like this ever since I'd arrived. People whose friends have large families, or whose own quivers are full, will know the feeling. Coherent discussion of any kind is out of the question. A sentence of six words is a sustained one. Anything longer will be lucky to get beyond the first comma. What conversation there is has a staccato quality, like gunfire punctuated by shellbursts, the latter consisting of sudden frantic commands, such as, 'Put that down!' or 'Don't touch that!' or – quite simply – *'Drop it, I tell you!'*

On the whole, Nicholas and I had been well blessed. We'd managed something like fifteen consecutive minutes of uninterrupted discussion, during which Marguerite had gone to help her mother in the kitchen and the boys had returned to the beach to whet their appetites further for a picnic lunch. We'd dealt with the little matter of Pierre, which Nicholas was no more disposed than I to take too seriously, and we'd discussed his father's health, which we agreed needed watching. Nicholas said that he or Stéphanie, often both of them *and* the children were frequent visitors to Mont Vert, and I was faintly surprised that Pierre, who had done a four-minute mile to reach me in the drive there, had apparently made no effort to confide in Guy's own son. Why not? Didn't want to worry him? It was possible. Or supposing . . . Which brought me back to Paulo and the Iturbis.

I decided to settle back and enjoy myself. The Villa Valeuse is designed for such a reaction and it would have been excessively churlish to deny it its due. From this flag-stoned terrace, alight with roses and backed by the wistaria-clad walls of the beautiful long, low-roofed house, you could see clean over the bay to Cap St Michel at its other end. This was the loveliest bay on the island: a shining mile-and-a-half curve of sand, surf and palm trees, sitting in the green lap of Mont Colombe and sheltered to the south, east and west by the mountain's sun-baked slopes. Where the beach bordered the promenade wall, the sand was soft and white like flour, but further out towards the sea it became a smooth, hard carpet of honey-gold. The narrow, palm-lined promenade ran the entire width of the bay, from the luxurious two-hundred-room Hotel Rivage d'Or on the Cap to the slightly smaller but even more exclu-sive Hotel de Bai just below us to the left. In between, behind tall white walls, inlet with little wrought-iron gates, were the gardens of the beach-side villas, separated here and there by the open terraces of cafés and bars, their coloured umbrellas shining in the brilliant sun. As always, a life-saving breeze from the northern sea took the edge off a temperature that would otherwise have been strictly for the lizards.

Abruptly, these sensual delights were shattered by remembrance of Simone. Irrationally, I almost for a second begrudged Nicholas and Stéphanie their happiness. But only for a second. If life had added little to my knowledge over the years, it had at least relieved me of a few illusions, one of the most primitive and strangely enduring being that by robbing Peter we can pay Paul. I now knew that if human beings shared anything in this world, it was, para-doxically, the common condition of essential separateness. I had learned to live with the prickling panic that the aware-ness of this fact always aroused in me, but how to nullify the panic – that was another bag of tricks altogether.

'About Hélène,' I said. I should have known better, of course, but Marguerite still hadn't returned with the boys, and Stéphanie had joined us now and was sitting beside me, her short fair hair rising and falling in the breeze and her kindly face smiling its sweet, serene smile. Nicholas looked blank at my question, but in her intuitive way Stéphanie had followed me unerringly. 'Yes,' she said. 'There *is* a problem.'

'Any theories?' I asked. 'Apart from the obvious, of course.'

'The marriage, you mean?' She drew a deep breath. 'Well, inevitably it's the one most favoured officially. And really, it's difficult to know what else *could* have caused it.'

'How did she get on with her father?'

'I don't think he really registered, if you know what I mean. You know what realists children are. Artificial situations – and people – even in fiction, unless they're *meant* to be artificial, bore them. They turn aside, which can be worse, I think, sometimes than explicit rejection.'

'Yes. Guy said almost exactly the same thing. He said she'd "withdrawn".'

She nodded.

'What about Corlander's attitude to *her*?'

She shrugged. 'I think he could take her or leave her.'

'So he left her. And now they share a mutual indifference.'

'Yes. Except that indifference in children is more dangerous – it can be such a mask for other things.'

I looked at her thoughtfully, conscious that Nicholas was now giving me another of his guarded 'lawyer looks'.

'Did you ever hear her play the piano, Stéph?'

She smiled. 'Well, I know what you mean, of course. She certainly loves that old horror of theirs.'

'I wondered about getting her some lessons.'

For a moment, she was taken aback. Then, the expression on her face changed from surprise to delight. 'Angus! How clever of you! Do you know, I believe you may be right! It just simply never occurred to me! But you may just be right!' She looked across at Nicholas, shaking her head. 'We should have thought of that, Nicko; we really should, you know. I tell you what,' she said, turning back to me, 'I know someone who might be able to help. I did think at one time of sending Marguerite to her, but frankly that child is hopeless. But Hélène – shall I ring this girl? Her name's Louise Rochas. I could make an appointment for you to see her.'

'Well – ' I hesitated, wondering suddenly where I was going. Then, hell, why not! It couldn't do any harm, surely. I nodded. 'I don't see why not,' I said. 'Mind, she may not want to take it on when she realizes the problems.'

'Oh, she will, I'm sure. She's very good with children, and they like her. I'll give you her number before you leave.'

I nodded again. There it was then. Whatever I'd come to the island for, it certainly wasn't to get piano lessons for little girls, but life was like that. Plain bloody ludicrous.

After lunch, Nicholas suggested a walk along the cliff road, and the entire Le Marnet family rose as one to join us. All, that is, except Stéphanie, who asked to be excused in the interests of domestic efficiency.

So off we went: Nicholas and I, accompanied by fifteen-year-old Guy, a tall, slender boy with a lean, tanned face and Nicholas's dark eyes; and ahead of us, diving this way and that like wasps after jam, the other three, their voices shrill and clear above the variety of sounds rising from the beach below. I noticed a battle for dominance between Marguerite, exuberant and extrovert, her fair hair flying, and Edouard, at thirteen, a younger edition of his father – short, sturdy, round-faced and solemn. Against his almost ponderous self-assurance, the restless energy of the little girl took on an aggressive fire. A contrast with all of them was the youngest member of the family, twelve-year-old Simon. Stéphanie's contribution, this, all right: the same light hair, clear, direct gaze and friendly good humour. There was a maturity here beyond his years, but at the same time an adventurousness that reminded me uneasily of the young Imogen. In the water, Simon had been a formidable combination of crab and torpedo; on land, he was goatlike, leaping from one craggy shelf to another on the cliffside, totally, it seemed, without fear. Neither did Nicholas seem to fear *for* him – or else he was resigned.

Ten years ago, this narrow road leading from the Villa Valeuse out along the eastern arm of the cliff to the convent of St Damien had been no more than a sandy track. Now the surface had been made up, and several new villas had been built on the ascending slopes opposite the cliff. From one of these, as we strolled along, the biggest St Bernard dog I'd ever seen came heaving his several tiers of flesh at an incredibly jaunty pace. From the children's reception of him, I deduced he was an intimate of some standing.

About ten yards from the convent gates, Nicholas paused opposite a very large villa still in process of construction. It stood on a shelf of land surrounded by palms and conifers, its huge, empty windows gazing out across the expanse of the bay. I sensed some restraint in Nicholas's manner as he stood looking at it, almost, I could have sworn, a hint of distaste. When he caught my eye, however, he merely smiled. 'This is the newest,' he said.

'Very nice. Who does it belong to?' But I'd guessed even before he spoke.

'Corlander.'

'Which one?'

'Ray.' He paused. He appeared to be wrestling with something inside him, and then to come to terms with it. When he spoke again, his voice sounded more relaxed. 'As you probably know, he and Phyllis live at the Rivage d'Or. Bernard owns it now – and the Bai.'

It was my opportunity and I took it. 'Is there anything – or any*one* – they don't own? Your father gave me the impression he didn't think so.'

His natural worried look deepened. 'Yes, I know.' He hesitated again and I waited. 'Well, frankly, Angus, I dislike the Corlanders as much as he does, but – well, perhaps not so unequivocally as he.'

'You mean you think what they're doing is justified. Is that it?'

He grimaced and ran a hand through his frustrated crop of crew-cut hair. 'Not altogether. I think Ray's every kind of a swine and therefore needs handling with a very long stick. But it's Bernard that's Mr Big. He's repulsive, too, but that doesn't necessarily make him Public Enemy No 1. He doesn't give a fig for our traditions, it's true, and he's no altruist, but neither were the old sea-dogs who founded this island in the first place. In the final analysis, it's what the people *want* that will count.'

'And you think they want a change?'

'I don't know. I simply don't know, Angus. All I'm saying is that the right of a society to experiment, to change, has to be accepted realistically.'

We walked on to where the road ended at the gates of the convent and I sat down on a ledge of rock and lit a cigarette. I offered one to Nicholas, but he shook his head.

'You called Bernard Mr Big,' I said. 'Did you mean politically?'

He gave another of his grimaces. 'Well – I suppose – yes, he's got a certain following. Mostly among the traders and bankers, and, of course, the tourist industry, which is more or less his creation, anyway. There's something that calls itself the "People's Party". It's not directly Corlander-led, but everyone knows he's behind it. It's clever, really. The "People's Party" sounds a popular movement, doesn't it? But in fact, it attracts people like Max Cartier. It's big business, and it's elitist. But that's not the face they show the world.'

'No. What they show the world are chalked signs saying "Government by the People".'

He nodded. 'Not *all* those signs are theirs, though. There's another movement getting under way. I don't know much about it, because at the moment it still seems to be a bit subterranean, but it seems to be a mix-up of intellectuals and working-class Spanish – '

'Whose slogan is "End closed committees".'

He smiled. 'That's about it. But what else it is I don't know.'

'Probably they don't either – yet. But it might be interesting to see if they find out. And that'll depend on the kind of leadership they've got. How involved was Maurice in all these shenanigans?'

'*Maurice?*'

'Well, I take it he probably shared your father's views about the Corlanders and what they represent.'

'Oh, undoubtedly, but – well, all this is still very new – the political infighting, I mean – Maurice retired from public office years ago.'

'So you don't think his death was in any way connected?'

'Oh, good God, no! I think it was purely personal. I don't think Maurice was ever a political man in that sense of the word. I think, like Father, he took seigneurial rule for granted: the divine right of kings, and all that.'

I didn't answer him, and we strolled back up the lane the way we had come. As we neared the Villa Valeuse, Nicholas suggested that instead of turning straight in we make a round tour by going on down to the church and back along the beach to the steps leading up to the garden. Neither Nicholas nor Guy, I noticed, seemed the slightest bit concerned that we had now lost the other three, last seen careering down one of the rocky tracks to the beach, followed by their hefty friend in a cloud of dust.

We stopped between the bushes of red and white camellias along the sea wall in the graveyard and gazed over the beach below. A favourite tourist pastime, this: as, indeed, the little Church of the Fishermen here at St Michel was categorized as a 'must' in every island brochure; not only because it was very old and very beautiful, with its traditional lych-gate and lovely mellow stone, nor even because of its specific dedication to the island's fishermen, but because of its setting. The view from between those camellias really does have to be seen to be believed. It was the same view that I'd enjoyed from the terrace of the Villa Valeuse, and I enjoyed it again with the same intensity, not unmixed with some deep and rather sad nostalgia.

Eventually we wandered on, leaving the graveyard under

the stone arch that led on to the slipway to the beach. Opposite the arch, on the other side of the slipway, there was a high brick wall surrounding a large house, barely visible over the top. This was the original convent of St Damien, two hundred years old, but long deserted by its holy inmates, who had preferred their present, more secluded, quarters. The house had had a number of owners since. In my youth, it had been occupied by a family called Cotarde, a retired Parisien banker and his family. Their sons, Raoul and Charles had been among our beach-party friends. As we picked our way down the slipway, I was about to ask Nicholas what had become of the Cotardes when a voice behind us addressed him in somewhat guttural French.

'Bonjour, Monsieur Le Marnet.'

We halted and turned. A short, burly man was standing at the small wooden door let into the wall of the old convent, obviously about to go in. He had spoken to Nicholas, but I saw that it was at me he was looking, and a curious tingling ran along my nerves as I gazed back for the second time that day into those thick pebble glasses.

Nicholas bowed: a stiff bow, and his face looked suddenly cold.

'Monsieur Corlander,' he said.

EIGHT

It would be difficult to say which of us was the most surprised. Corlander's expression was enigmatic, but, looking at him, I concluded it always would be, no matter what the situation. He had the kind of flat, heavy face that put you in mind of two-day-old custard. Eventually, as he made no move to retire through the gate, Nicholas was compelled to introduce us.

Corlander acknowledged the courtesy with a curling up of his thick, rubbery lips that I took to be a smile. 'Monsieur Logan and I have already met,' he said in English, with an accent that was thickly overlaid with Germanic overtones.

Nicholas turned a faintly interrogative glance in my direction and I nodded. 'Our paths crossed, you might say.'

'Yes. Very aptly put.' Corlander's grin broadened, exposing the disagreeable sight of a row of large, uneven yellow teeth, with two flashes of gold, one on either side. The bloke really hadn't much going for him. The Villain of the Piece personified, you could almost say.

'That lane is so narrow, Monsieur Logan,' he was saying. 'I was afraid of running you down. You liked Point Rouge?'

'Very much.'

I was irrationally irritated by the 'Monsieur'. Corlander wasn't French, whatever else he was, and since he'd chosen to speak to me in my own language, the French title seemed an affectation.

'I have always thought,' he said, 'that anyone spending a holiday on the island would consider it a highly desirable place to stay. You agree?'

'Well, you can't eat a view, of course.'

'Ah.' His eyes widened appreciatively at this apparent

empathy between us. 'My own feelings entirely! I see you are a realist, Monsieur Logan.'

'I try to be.' And you're bloody pedantic – and patronizing into the bargain.

'I take it, then, you would agree that it is a pity to waste such a beautiful spot?'

'I hadn't exactly thought of it as wasted.'

'Ah, but it is. Many holidaymakers, Monsieur Logan, would like to stay in Point Rouge, but at present they can only go and come away again. Oh, a few stay down on the coast road there (he dismissed Point Rouge's sole hotel with a contemptuous shrug), but what is there for them to do? Point Rouge, Monsieur Logan, is a typical example, one of so many, of how the island wastes its opportunities.'

'Like South Wales before they discovered coal.'

He smiled. 'Oh, we have *much* better plans for Point Rouge, Monsieur Logan. I would like to tell you about them one day – but now, if you have time, I would very much like you to come in and meet my wife.'

I was startled. For a moment, I thought of declining with as much grace as I could muster. But curiosity won.

'I should be delighted,' I said.

I felt, rather than saw, Nicholas's round, good-natured face, which had worn its habitual expression of slightly worried concern during this exchange, jerk towards me in surprise. Corlander noticed it, too.

'You were not in a hurry, I hope, Monsieur Le Marnet?'

The answer to this was so patently obvious that Nicholas could only murmur a polite disclaimer.

'Good,' said Corlander. He pushed open the wooden door in the wall. 'Follow me, if you please.'

On the threshold, Guy hung back, uncertain as to his inclusion in these adult courtesies, but Corlander gave the boy his rubbery smile and piloted him inside.

Here was the Cotardes' garden much as I remembered it, except that down below the lawn directly opposite the house, at the point where the garden came to an abrupt end some forty feet above the beach, there was now a paved terrace, with tables and chairs set out under red and black umbrellas.

Two sets of French windows opened on to the path bordering the lawn, and Corlander led the way to the first of these and turned in. After the bright sun outside, the room within seemed unusually dark and I was temporarily blinded. I could see only the back of Corlander's grey linen jacket ahead of me, and, not realizing that he had stopped almost immediately upon entering the room, I cannoned into him and was compelled to apologize. I then realized that the reason for our abrupt halt was that just a few feet from the open windows was an armchair, and seated in it an elderly woman.

'You have visitors, Dorothea,' he announced. He pronounced it 'Doro-taya'.

The woman in the chair sat with a book resting in her lap, and, as my eyes became accustomed to the contrasting shade, I saw that I was being studied by a pair of the most piercing dark eyes I had ever seen. In a face that was dead white and hawk-like, the effect was chilling. If myopia was Corlander *père*'s cross in life, Nature had certainly compensated him in his choice of mate. Madame, I felt, would see all. And then some.

I murmured a polite greeting and took the hand she extended – albeit without enthusiasm, I felt – towards me. It lay damp and cold in mine, and I was as glad to get this part of the formalities over as she obviously was.

'Monsieur Logan used to live with the de Courvel family,' Corlander explained to his wife. 'You remember Simone speaking of him, Doro?' He turned to me. 'We didn't come to the island until after the end of the war, Monsieur Logan, so we didn't have the pleasure of meeting you. Simone, however, often spoke of you.' To his wife again he said: 'You remember now, huh?'

If she had heard him, she gave no sign. Her eyes still studied my face, but at no time during the introductions, or since, had her own moved a muscle. Obviously, Madame Corlander believed even less than her husband in the conventional social gestures.

No one asked us to sit down, so I gathered, with intense gratitude, that we weren't expected to linger, and began to edge back as imperceptibly as possible towards the window. The heavily furnished room, Madame's cold, formidable stare, the sight of her white, bony hands, covered with rings, gripping her book, and Corlander's oppressively benevolent presence looming over us, all combined to create an atmosphere of inhibiting tension. I felt as though we had stepped into a world in which the bay outside, and all its bright sunshine and movement, had no part. Moreover, under those glittering eyes I began to feel more and more the kind of personal discomfort that a toad must feel in the long seconds before a snake moves to devour it. God knows what inanity I might have been compelled to utter for my own relief had it not been for Guy. Having managed to get no further into the room behind his father than the step of the window, he suddenly lost his balance on this and clattered forward, pushing Nicholas into the back of a chair.

'Pardon, Madame! Pardon!'

The boy's flushed, apologetic face sought hers and, to my profound gratitude – unmixed, I'm sorry to say, with any compassion for Guy – I saw her eyes move from me to him. Surely now, I thought, she would utter – it would not have surprised me to hear some ancient Flemish curse descend upon the hapless infant – but still nothing came and poor Guy blushed into an intimidating silence.

After a few seconds, however, Corlander spoke as if nothing had happened. 'Monsieur Logan is staying at the Royale,' he said, and in some curious way it occurred to me that he was impressing upon his wife a certain significance relating to this interview that was entirely lost on the rest of us. 'You are comfortable there, I hope?' he enquired, turning towards me.

'Perfectly, thank you.' I took another very small step back towards the window.

'You are staying long?'

I jumped. The question had come in a harsh, heavily-accented female voice, scarcely above a whisper. I turned to the woman in the chair. 'Nothing would give me greater pleasure,' I said. 'But I doubt it very much.'

'That, as you say, would depend, yes?' Corlander's voice seemed to have dropped a tone.

I smiled. He had the same talent for provoking me as his son: yet the two, I now realized, were utterly different. Ray Corlander could sit up nights inflating his ego with helium, but at year's end all he'd be would be a small man out of breath. His father was a different proposition altogether. Behind the half-blind eyes, the soft voice, the unemotional manner, there lurked all the hidden dangers of a minefield. This was the type of man who, having no need of self-reassurance, would contrive to let his enemies' own weaknesses effect their destruction. As he moved among the ramifications of his world, like a spider garnering flies, speed and silence would be his way, and, at the end of it, there would be no sign of his hand. To such a man, another's suicide might well seem a happy fortuity.

'You will find many changes on the island,' he said, still in the same soft voice.

'So everyone keeps telling me. I won't pretend I hadn't noticed.'

'It would be interesting to know how they strike you, Monsieur Logan. So many people resent, and resist, change, wouldn't you agree? But life *is* change. In general, this is the sign of a healthy society, is it not?'

'Some people might feel it depends upon the change.'

'Yes. There, you know, Monsieur Logan, I have always felt that your Jeremy Bentham was right: "the greatest good for the greatest number".'

'And the Jesuits? The end justifies the means?'

He smiled, bending towards his wife, but still looking at me in an arch fashion that I found extremely irritating. 'You hear that, Doro? Monsieur Logan is a philosopher.'

For a moment, I struggled with an almost overwhelming desire to boot him up his grey linen backside. Perhaps he picked up the vibrations. At all events, he straightened and his face became serious again. 'We will leave her now,' he

111

said. To his wife: 'We are going now, Doro. Do not read too long. It is bad for your eyes.'

He shepherded us towards the French window, standing back himself to watch us through. 'Your family keep well, I trust, Monsieur Le Marnet?' he enquired.

Nicholas, in process of following Guy out over the threshold, was taken by surprise. He half-turned, gave another of his courteous little bows and then, turning back again, tripped over the step. I felt my friends were not exactly adding lustre to the occasion.

Outside, after we had moved out of earshot of the woman in the room, Corlander paused.

'You will forgive such a brief meeting, I hope, Monsieur Logan. My wife tires easily. As you see, she is confined to her chair, and in such circumstances life can pall. Nevertheless, she appreciates it greatly when people take the trouble to call on her occasionally.'

I was surprised, and suddenly discomfited. That Madame Corlander was an invalid and that her husband was capable of sounding like a normal caring human being were both facts that had till then escaped me. Was it conceivably possible that I had misjudged him?

At the gate, he stood back while we filed through on to the slipway.

'I hope we shall meet again soon, Monsieur Logan. Meanwhile, I wish you a pleasant stay on the island.'

'Thank you.' I could think of nothing else appropriate to say, so I imitated one of Nicholas's correct head-bobs and followed the others out.

We heard the heavy wooden door close behind us as we went on down towards the beach, but none of us felt inclined to speak until we had progressed along the sands well past the Corlanders' garden wall.

'And what', I asked then, 'was that all about?'

They both grinned, and Nicholas shrugged. 'You might call it a reconnaisance, I suppose. I was surprised you accepted the invitation.'

'I was curious. I still am. What the hell was his game? It

wasn't just so Madame should experience a new lease of life, which would understandably result from a meeting with Angus Logan. (I was gratified that Guy, at least, found this funny.) So what?'

Nicholas gave another shrug.

'And what did he mean about her and the chair business? Is she disabled?'

'She's an invalid. He was just assuming you knew. They always play it like that. I don't know what's wrong with her. They don't talk about it, but rumour has it they were both in concentration camps in Germany during the war and that's when it happened, whatever it was. He's nearly blind in one eye, too. We've always assumed it stems from the same source. They tell you nothing. The only thing you can be quite certain of is that if you get in their way, you're dead. Figuratively speaking, of course.'

'Of course?'

He met my glance with an amused smile. 'Unless I'm mistaken, a moment ago you were asking yourself whether you hadn't perhaps heinously misjudged him. No?'

I looked at him for a moment and then grinned. 'All right. I admit the man baffles me. Part of me says he's a bastard, another part – Drat it! With his beastly son I knew where I was!'

They both laughed, but as we went on across the beach I had the feeling that whatever it was that had been going on back there in that shadowed room in the old convent of St Damien, it wasn't funny.

I left the Villa at about nine o'clock, after a family supper served in a delightful room with pale green walls and light woodwork, and wide French windows that opened out on to the terrace where we'd sat earlier. 'You must all come and spend an evening with me in town,' I told them when they saw me off, and they said they would, and the children ran alongside the car until I turned off at the end of the lane past the church.

This time, instead of going up 'La Verderie', the steep,

tree-shaded lane to the left of the church which I'd come down that morning, I took the road through the bay and the wider, more gradual ascent of 'La Pompe d'Haute' at its western end. At the top, instead of turning right, back to town, I went straight across the main road and into the first of the tortuous maze of lanes that I knew, if I remembered them correctly, would take me up to the Manoir itself. Sunday, I felt, was a good day to visit St Michel. There would be no workmen there and I had no scruples about taking advantage of a broken window catch, or any other unconventional means of access that might present itself. It was a beautiful evening, with at least an hour and a half of light left in the sky.

When I reached the house, however, I began to think that my journey was wasted. The downstairs windows at the front were all shuttered, and for the first time in my experience the door was locked and bolted against me. The next two windows round the side of the house were equally impregnable, and at the back the garden was so overgrown and littered with builders' rubble that I could barely find a way through to the only windows that remained, the two opening on to the kitchen. Even before I reached them, I could see the shutters across them, but as I wrestled to disengage myself from the straggling limbs of a neglected lilac tree, I caught sight of another window, hardly wide enough to be called such. This not only had no shutters but, as I discovered when I finally lurched out from the hostile undergrowth, had a broken catch and was held fast by nothing more than a piece of stick sloped against the frame on the inside.

Some judicious work with a penknife, followed by a good hard shake or two, delivered the *coup de grâce* and the window fell open. Getting myself through it was another matter, and there was a point, halfway, when I had time to speculate on how I would explain my elevated and spread-eagled presence to a builders' foreman in the morning. I finally solved the problem and descended into the little butler's pantry with such speed that I pitched right across it and hit my head on the partly open door. I remained sitting on the floor, leaning against one of the lower shelves, while I got my breath back and gingerly felt my head. It felt sticky and my fingers came away smeared with blood. Marvellous! Now I'd have to explain to everybody how I'd come to get a hole in the head that showed.

When I had recovered and the bleeding appeared to have stopped, I emerged into the littered passageway outside and stood for a few seconds, listening. My entrance had been about as stealthy as a cavalry charge, but there was no sign of movement anywhere, and eventually I went on up the passage and into the hall where I paused again and considered. Should I go straight to Maurice's study and complete the snoop which Simone had so unexpectedly interrupted? Or should I first quickly reconnoitre the house? I finally decided on the latter. I'd no idea what, if anything, I was seeking, beyond perhaps the intangible substance of inspiration, and in an empty house there was likely to be precious little of that around.

In the event, I was startled to find some of Maurice's clothes still hanging in a wardrobe in an otherwise empty bedroom – dismal evidence of Simone's irresolution. Most of the rooms were bare of all but the odd chair or cupboard, as I'd expected. But at the very top of the house I found a box-room loaded to the door with bric-à-brac and ancient personal junk; there were long-forgotten snapshot albums, riding gear, all musty and tarnished, tennis racquets with broken strings, chipped ornaments, hat-boxes, still inhabited – floppy old panamas, dented and soiled, ladies' straws with half a garden round them, even a top hat, collapsible by design and still in tolerably good condition – and endless items of presumably worthless jewellery. In another small room next to it there were even more incredible things: trunks crammed with perfectly good household linen, some of it embroidered with the family initials, and tea-chests, with nothing more than a sheet of old newspaper on top, stacked with enough superb china and porcelain – Sèvres, Dresden, Meissen, Royal Worcester,

Derby – to give several poor Roquennais families a handsome new start in life. I came away dismayed, and curiously ashamed, though whether of myself or the apparent careless profligacy of the de Courvel family I couldn't possibly have defined.

It was as I emerged again on to the top landing that I fancied I heard something. I stopped and listened, but there was nothing but the sound of my own breathing. I went down into one of the lower bedrooms and looked out across the front of the house, but in the shambles of garden round the trailing limbs of the catalpa tree I could see nothing untoward. I turned back into the room, and then I heard it again. It was like a door being shut, but muffled, as though somewhere away from the house. But St Michel had no near neighbours.

Down in the hall, I stopped once again to listen. I wondered if it could have been a car door. The thought of being caught a second time snooping where I didn't belong spurred me to make short work of the butler's pantry window, and egress, I discovered, on to the soft ground outside, was a good deal easier than entry had been. I pulled the window to after me, hoping it would be decided that the stick had slipped by accident, and moved cautiously away round the side of the house towards the front drive. Once there, I felt better. There was nothing particularly sinister about taking a stroll through an empty garden for oldtime's sake. In any case, now that I was outside the house, the idea that the sound had been that of a car door being shut struck me as the most plausible explanation, and the car could well have been way down the lane somewhere. I cursed myself for being panicked out of a chance to revisit Maurice's study, but decided it couldn't be helped; I didn't fancy a second encounter with the butler's pantry, and in any case I now realized that my head was aching abominably.

I stepped off the grass on to the drive and walked boldly past the front of the house towards the lane. I was nearly there when I heard the sound again – loud and unmistakable this time. I stopped and turned. I had just passed the stone archway that led to the two coach-houses and, as I looked back, I saw a figure standing on the step of the furthest one, a hand still resting on the handle of the door which had just been pulled shut. I walked slowly back, and still the figure remained there, silent and motionless.

'I'm sorry if I startled you,' I said.

But it was not shock nor bewilderment that showed in the face that looked back at me. To my surprise, the expression uppermost on Simone de Courvel's face as she stood on her own property, confronting me, the trespasser, was guilt.

NINE

'Could I speak to Señorita Rochas, please,' I asked.

'Por favor, un momento.'

I waited. Down the phone I could hear sounds of brisk activity: doors opening and shutting, men's voices giving instructions to one another in Spanish. A busy household, obviously. Presently, the background sounds were cut off and a woman's voice spoke in my ear. *'Sí?'*

I answered in French and was relieved to find that Señorita Rochas spoke it fluently. I told her, briefly, who I was and what I wanted, and she said ah, yes, Madame Le Marnet had already telephoned her about it. Would it be convenient if I called to see her at about ten o'clock, she asked. I said it would and put the phone down again, wondering vaguely whether I ought to approach Simone first or afterwards. I finally decided to leave it until I'd heard what Señorita Rochas had to say.

I couldn't stop thinking about the look I'd seen on Simone's face the previous night. She had accepted my explanations and rambling references to 'Memory Lane' so mechanically that I'd been certain she hadn't really been listening. Her chief concern involved herself in some inexplicable way, and her insistence on explaining her own rightful presence there merely added to the sense I had of having stumbled on something distinctly odd. She had been painting some furniture, she said, in one of the flats above the coach-house, in the event, I gathered, of it ever being let, and had come to close the windows she had previously left open. She'd come up in a friend's car, she said, and had planned to catch the last bus back from the top of the lane. She had accepted my offer of a lift, but all the relaxation that had been established between us during my visit to St George's had gone again. Perhaps it had just been the result of an heroic effort of will; anyway, we were clearly back to square one.

We hadn't talked much on the way back to town. I'd told her of my visit to the Villa Valeuse, and from then on we'd confined ourselves to trivia. Dropping her at St George's, I'd asked her on an impulse to join me for lunch next day at the Royale. 'Bring Hélène, of course,' I'd said, remembering in time that she would have to.

'She has lunch at school,' she said.

'Oh – well – I'll pick you up at quarter to twelve. Time for a drink first.'

'Oh, I don't think – I'm sorry, Angus, I – perhaps another time, if you don't mind.'

'Of course.'

She'd given her tremulous smile by way of answer and we'd parted. But I'd lain awake most of the night, wondering about her. Bitterness I could have understood: even a certain vicious will to be revenged on life. But this petrifying resignation, heavy with self-criticism, was something else again. Guy had been right. She was blaming herself for everything. Worse – she was ashamed of herself: of her surroundings, her handling of her affairs: even, deep down inside her, of her daughter. Yes – I felt it with a growing horrible certainty – she was ashamed of Hélène. And probably hating herself all the more because of it.

I found the Rochas house halfway up the Arle Valley: a pleasant, renovated farmhouse in the middle of field upon field of flowers. Market gardeners, Stéphanie had said. And in a fairly big way, it seemed. For miles around the house, there was a blaze of living colour, and further on down the sandy drive I could see several sheds, packing sheds – by the sound of women's voices. Opposite the house, a man was slowly moving down a field bright with carnations, while a very small boy and a black and white puppy romped on the grass verge nearby.

When the door opened, I got a surprise. Instead of seeing someone whose appearance accorded with this earthy, workaday setting, I found myself looking at a young woman, possibly in the early thirties, whose looks, poise and grooming would have delighted all the fashion editors I knew. I was further surprised when she spoke to me in fluent English, with only the slightest hint of accent.

'Mr Logan? How do you do? Louise Rochas. Please come in.'

I followed her into a cool, tiled hall and across it into a small sitting-room overlooking the back of the house. Here again, it was cool, the windows already shaded by Venetian blinds. There were books on shelves round the walls, and a baby grand piano and music stand over near the window.

We sat down opposite each other in comfortable black leather armchairs and I told her about Hélène. She smiled when I described the strumming, and there was a kindness in her eyes that told me a lot about her. They were warm brown eyes, in a face that showed delicacy, intelligence and wit. I liked, too, the way her dark hair framed her features in a soft, natural way, and the stillness in her, unusual in her race.

'So you'd like her to have a few lessons,' she said when I'd finished.

'Well, I thought it might help. Even if it doesn't, it'll be something she'll enjoy doing. She does seem to have this thing about music.'

She nodded.

'You see,' I continued, 'I more or less grew up with her family long before she was born. I feel – well – a sort of avuncular responsibility if you follow me.'

'Yes,' she said. 'I can understand that. Madame Le Marnet mentioned the connection. And one of my brothers remembers your father.'

'Oh, really?' That was interesting. I suddenly realized that my father might have had certain insights into the de Courvel tragedy which I lacked and I wished he was around to give me the benefit of them.

'I expect, then,' I said, 'that you know as much about Hélène and her family background as I do.'

'Not really. Though, of course – ' she smiled again – 'in an island the size of this, people often know each other better than they sometimes give each other credit for.'

It was a shrewd remark and I wondered how much it was meant to convey.

'Señorita, if you know Hélène de Courvel at all – ' I stopped, embarrassed at my clumsiness – 'I'm sorry, I mean Hélène *Corlander*, of course – if you know her at all, you'll know she won't be an easy pupil. It's only fair you should understand that. Nevertheless, she's got what seems to me – and I'm not a musician, I'm afraid – some kind of a natural aptitude. What other kids see in dolls and teddy-bears, she apparently sees in her mother's old piano. Of course, you'll be used to parents proclaiming their children's talents, but in this case there *is* a difference; I don't know how to explain it, but I can feel it. Maybe it's got no permanent value, but I think she should be given the chance to put it to the test.'

'So do I, though whether I'm the person to help her do it – '

'I'm sure you are. The problem, I'm convinced, is psychological, not intellectual. I don't think you'll find her unteachable.'

'Very few people are. And nothing breaks through barriers like music: I suppose because its sources are possibly so very ancient and elemental. Indeed, they seem to transcend time altogether. Technique, too, in some strange way.'

She spoke lightly, and smiled as if her own thoughts amused her.

'I think you're right,' I said. And then, because I didn't want to risk boring her by outstaying my welcome, got to my feet. 'I should mention that I've still got to talk this over with Madame Corlander, but I can't see any reason why she should object. May I ring you?'

'Please.' She had got up, too, and we moved together towards the door. On the way, I noticed a guitar resting in one of the chairs. 'You play?' I asked, nodding towards it.

She smiled. 'For pleasure only. Most of us do. For the French here – and the English, of course – it's not really considered a classical instrument.'

'Barbarians, the lot of us.'

Her smile broadened. 'Oh, I wouldn't say that, Mr Logan.'

I grinned, holding the door for her as she led the way out into the hall again. Then, as I followed her, a door opposite us opened and a young man emerged. When he saw me, he stopped, apparently surprised, and inclined his head. '*Por favor, Señor*,' he said, and was about to retreat until Louise Rochas put out a restraining hand. She turned towards me.

'This is my brother, Felipe, Mr Logan.' She spoke to him in French. 'Monsieur Logan used to live with the de Courvel family when we were children. You've heard Enrique speak of his father.'

'Ah!' A brilliant smile broke across the young man's face and he stretched out a hand to me. '*Enchanté*, Monsieur! We had heard you were on the island.'

'*Really?*'

Louise laughed. 'As I said, Mr Logan, a small island.'

'You're not kidding.'

Rochas gave a sage shake of the head. 'You underrate yourself, Monsieur Logan. Ever since Monsieur de Courvel died, there has been much speculation as to whether you would come.'

I must have looked as disbelieving as I felt, for he went on protesting with increasing intensity. And suddenly I began to suspect that his appearance in the hall at that precise moment had not been as accidental as it had seemed. For a second I was annoyed. Why were these people manipulating me? First Corlander, now young Rochas, dangling me on their respective pieces of string, waiting to see which way I would jump.

Then, as I looked at Rochas, and from him to his sister, I knew I was wrong to connect them even remotely with the motivations of the Corlanders. Felipe's next words confirmed this – and, at the same time, startled me because they were almost the identical words used by Guy le Marnet at Mont Vert.

'We hoped very much you *would* come, Monsieur.'

'Why?'

'Because, Monsieur, everyone knows you were a son to Monsieur de Courvel – ' I winced. Fine son! – 'And Monsieur de Courvel's ghost needs a son.'

It was a calculated insult to Alain, but young Rochas' dark eyes never wavered from mine and his expression remained politely grave. I looked at him with interest, standing there poised like an athlete. I couldn't help feeling that the island needed men like this: men who would meet challenge with something more than mere emotion, men prepared to fight, but in whom aggression would always be tempered with intellect and sensitivity. In a vague way, his appearance reminded me of someone, but at the moment I couldn't think who. In the eyes, the high forehead, the light ivory-coloured skin, and in his basic gentleness of manner, Felipe resembled his sister, but there was also a tigerish quality that kept me slightly wary: and, despite my instinctive trust in him, faintly hostile, provoked, no doubt, by the implicit criticism – conveyed in his words and manner – of people who had once been close to me. I didn't mean it to, but the hostility sounded in my voice when I spoke.

'Everyone on this island talks in riddles. If you've got something you want to say to me, Señor Rochas, I'd take it as a personal favour if you'd make it quite clear.'

For a second, Louise looked distressed. She glanced quickly from one to the other of us and made a deprecating gesture with her hand. 'Mr Logan, please forgive us. Felipe, you have no right – '

'No, wait.' I held up my own hand. 'Your brother does have a right, Señorita. I think Monsieur de Courvel would interpret it as the right of a friend.' I turned towards him. 'Well, Señor?'

'Monsieur de Courvel was murdered, Monsieur.'

I literally *heard* his sister holding her breath. My eyes never left his.

123

'Impossible.'

'No, Monsieur. Not in the way I mean. There are more ways than one to kill someone.'

I should have felt relieved, but I didn't. 'If you're saying he was persecuted, hounded, literally *worried* to death, O.K., I might agree you could be right. But there's not a damn thing you, or I, or anyone else can do about it now.'

'I think so, Monsieur.'

'Look,' I said, 'if this is vendetta talk, I'm not interested. I'll admit, since you obviously care, that I *did* come here to try and find out why Monsieur de Courvel took his own life. I'll admit I'm beginning to think he *was* hounded, and I'll agree that that can be a form of murder, taken far enough – and provided it's deliberate – '

'You doubt that, Monsieur?'

'I doubt everything, Señor Rochas. Everything – and *everybody*.'

A faint smile flickered across his face. 'I respect you, Monsieur.'

'But let's be clear about one thing,' I continued. 'I'm not the classic figure of the avenging son, or any of that sort of thing. I'm not going round this island screaming for blood, no matter who might want me to. And I'd further advise anyone whose fancy lies that way to re-examine his motives. If there's one thing less calculated to serve that decent, honourable old man than a blood hunt in his name, I don't know what it is.'

'You misunderstand me, Monsieur.'

'I'm glad to hear it.'

'You are right in saying I care,' Rochas went on. 'But it is not only for Monsieur de Courvel. What I, and many others, also care about – as Monsieur de Courvel himself did – is what is happening now on this island, what is to come now that he and his kind have gone. Have you looked around you, Monsieur? Have you seen what is already happening? Good land changing hands like – what do you say – hot potatoes. Whole plantations slowly disappearing, here a bit, there a bit, and in their place hotels, bars, nightclubs. Soon, the whole island will be a fairground, and we – ' jabbing his chest with a forefinger – 'we who were born here, we shall be turning the handles while others empty the tills!' His face shone with the intensity of his feeling and his eyes were hard. Suddenly, I felt myself wishing there were a hundred of him. It was Guy all over again – but a young, vigorous, down-to-earth, hard-hitting Guy, with time and muscle on his side. It wouldn't bring Maurice back, but it was the nearest thing to an effective threat to his enemies – if they really did exist – that I'd heard since arriving on the island. For that reason, if for no other, I was prepared to listen to him, though Rochas now hardly seemed to care whether I did or not.

'They tell us, "Look what we are doing for you". "Look how much money we are spending." But what do we see? Better houses? Better jobs? More schools? Hospitals? Opportunities for a fuller life, more security? Of course not, Monsieur! These we were beginning to get when the Seigneurs governed. Now – ' he gave a contemptuous jerk of the head – 'Look around you, Monsieur Logan.'

'You said you and "many others" cared. How many others?'

'I speak for all true Roquennais, Monsieur.'

I smiled. 'There's many a politician that's said that: some that have even believed it – until they lost their deposit.'

'I'm not a politician, Monsieur. I'm telling you what I know the ordinary, working people on this island feel. People like myself, my family, and our friends. They are all of them sick to the heart.'

'Then why don't they do something about it?'

'Things are never as simple as that, Monsieur.'

'O.K. But how hard are they trying? I'm not calling you a liar, Señor Rochas. I'm convinced you believe every word you say. But human nature's funny. There's no time a man shouts loudest about evil and wickedness than when he's got his own hand in the till.'

The colour flared into his face and I grimaced an apology. 'All right, don't get me wrong – all I'm asking is, if you're right about the people wanting something better, how is it they're not out in the streets with banners?'

'Monsieur Logan, let me prove this to you. Come and meet some of our friends. I think they would convince you that what I've just told you is true.'

'You don't have to bother about proving anything to *me*.'

'True. But if I did, perhaps you would agree to help us.'

'I? How?' This was not what I meant. What I meant was *Why*? But I shrank from both the brutality of the question and the possible answer.

Rochas hesitated. There was a hint of desperation in his face now. 'You are a writer, Monsieur. You have travelled a great deal. Also, you know this island. You could – you could advise us.' I knew this was not what *he* meant either, but he was playing the same game: holding his fire and waiting to see what my response would be.

'When do your friends come out to play?'

The brilliant smile returned to his face.

'This evening, Monsieur. If you will come here, say, at about eight o'clock, I will introduce you to one or two people who would be happy to meet you. You will find it interesting, I'm sure.'

'There's just one thing – ' I said.

He looked at me enquiringly.

'I'm an outsider here. And that's the way I intend to stay. Just so long as your friends understand.'

He gave a little gesture that might have meant anything. 'Until tonight, then,' he said, smiled at us both and turned and strode briskly back into the room from which he'd come.

Louise looked at me ruefully. 'I don't know what you must think of us,' she said.

I grinned. 'I'm told – and I believe it – that you are a good music teacher, Señorita Rochas.'

She laughed.

'As to your brother, he may not know it but he's a good politician. Incidentally, what else does he do? Somehow, I don't take him for a gardener.'

126

'He is a law clerk: with Cartier et Fils.'

'*Is he indeed!*'

'He's been with them since he left school. Felipe was the clever one. Both he and Enrique, my elder brother, went to the Town School, but Enrique came back to the farm, with Carlos, my other brother. Felipe was more ambitious. To be fair to him, he has done well. He is honest, Mr Logan, and he has gained some influence among the Spanish landworkers, and even one or two people in Porte Hilaire.'

'And you? Has he convinced you?'

She smiled. 'He is my brother. But, yes – I think much of what he says is true.'

'Such as?'

'Felipe is trying to get the ordinary working people on the island to see that they've got to do things for themselves. He feels there should be more Spanish representation in our government, both local and central – not for nationalistic reasons, but because so many of these people *are* Spanish and no one speaks for them.'

'Is *he* prepared to?'

'I don't know. I mean, I don't know how far he's prepared to go. He was speaking the truth when he said he wasn't a politician. He's been asked if he will stand as a Député for this Parish. The elections are next month, so he will have to make a decision soon.' She sighed. 'In a way, I hope he won't.' Her face had gone a little bleak and I felt for her.

'I know,' I said. 'But some people haven't any talent for side-stepping. If I read your brother aright, he won't be walking away from any fights. I think you'd best just check up on the sal volatile.'

Her smile returned and she held out her hand to me. 'You've been very generous, Mr Logan. I hope you won't regret it.'

I took her hand and grinned back at her. 'I hope so, too. I'll let you know about Hélène. This evening possibly.'

It sounded nice, that. All of a sudden I realized why I'd let Felipe persuade me to return and meet his friends.

TEN

Under normal circumstances, I shouldn't have telephoned Simone at all. I should simply have got into the car and gone round to see her. But nothing about Simone seemed normal these days, and after the previous evening's incident I was uneasy. If I went to see her, what kind of reception would I get? No two occasions seemed to find her the same. The girl with whom I had once felt so close, who had always held a special place in my growing world, was now a woman I couldn't seem to reach on any but the most superficial level: a woman who seemed determined to be more untouchable than a nun, more negative than a closed grave.

So what? Why should I care? The hell of it was, though, that I did!

'So you see,' I said, 'I thought it would be like eight birthday presents rolled into one. Make up for past lapses, if you know what I mean.'

'Well, it's terribly kind of you, Angus.'

'Not really. Low cunning, I'm afraid. You see, when she's a beautiful young matron, with grown-up children of her own, her dear old Uncle Angus will always know where he can move in his coat-hangers for the odd week or two.'

From her laugh, I sensed she had relaxed again.

'Tell you what,' I said, 'why don't I pick her up from school for you and tell her myself.'

'Oh, I – I think perhaps not, Angus. She has this arrangement with the school bus, you see. She might get confused if I rang and tried to alter it at short notice.'

'Of course. Stupid of me. Never mind. Another time.'

'But – Angus – '

'Yes?' I'd been about to ring off, but I stopped.

There was a pause. Then – 'Come and see us again,' she said.

Well, well! *Plus ça change, plus c'est la même chose?*

My return to the Rochas farm had a feeling of inevitability about it. I tried to analyse it, but couldn't. All I knew as I drove up the sandy drive again towards the house was that I was there in response to some irresistible compulsion.

I wondered that there weren't any other cars in the drive, but when Felipe opened the door to me he told me that his friends would be along later. He'd told me eight o'clock, he said, so that I could meet people individually, as they arrived, rather than in a group. It intrigued me that he should take such care over the encounter.

As he led the way across the hall, I could hear from behind the closed door of the music room the sound of some unfortunate scales being inhumanely executed and, during a merciful pause, Louise Rochas' voice gently but firmly admonishing.

Rochas opened the door of a room on the other side of the hall and we entered what I took to be the family dining-room, since there was a long, highly polished table running down the centre of it, with several straight-backed, leather-seated chairs drawn up around it. He pulled out one of these, indicated to me to sit down, and went over to a sideboard opposite, where he mixed some drinks and handed me one. It was Scotch, with the merest dash of water, and I wondered, since he hadn't asked me my preference, how the hell he'd known that this was it. For some reason, tiny, totally irrelevant details like this always bother me and I was still fidgeting over it when he came and sat down at the table.

He glanced around him and then spread out his hands in an apologetic sort of way. 'I'm sorry, Monsieur, if all this looks a little to you like a committee meeting. It's simply that this is the only room – except the music room – that's big enough to accommodate us all. Not,' he added hastily, 'that this little party represents our full strength. All you'll be meeting here tonight are just a few of our closest neighbours and friends. There are others, more influential than these, but, as I said, this is just a gathering of friends.'

'That being so, could we drop the "Monsieur"?' I asked.

He smiled and raised his glass to me, and we both drank.

At that moment, the door opened and a tall man entered the room, looking around him with a diffident smile. I took him to be in his early forties, though with these lean types you can never tell. His face was so thin as to be almost emaciated, his cheekbones two sharp ridges from the ears down.

Felipe introduced us. 'This is my brother, Enrique,' he said.

For a moment, all I could do was stare. In my job you get used to life's incongruities, but this was ridiculous. After one brother who looked like a bantam-weight and was a clerk, here was another who was a horticulturist and looked like something between an elf and a mediaeval saint, sandals and all.

But when I gave him my hand, I was forced to an instant and painful reappraisal. His grip was like a steel trap.

'Señor Logan,' he said, and then followed up with a little speech in Spanish, of which very little except the fact that his voice was as firm as his hand registered with me. I must have looked as blank as I felt because Felipe gave his brother an exasperated look and said something which caused Enrique to spread out his hands to me and launch into a long and effusive apology in French.

I gave him my best Gallic shrug. 'Think nothing of it,' I said. 'By the way – '

He had begun to move away, smiling, but now he paused, looking at me enquiringly.

'I understand you knew my father.'

'Ah, yes!' He nodded warmly. 'Twice – ' he raised two fingers – 'twice we went fishing. With Paulo Garcia, barman at the Yacht Club. You know? Yes? Ah, yes.' He sighed, appearing for the moment to be lost in private reminiscence. 'Twice,' he repeated, and with another smile wandered off towards the window, where he stood awhile, hands in pockets, before beginning to circle the room in a

vague sort of way. I began to entertain the wildest specula-
tions as to the nature and appearance of brother Carlos. No
one had mentioned a father: nor a mother, for that matter.
Were they dead? I wondered.

I glanced across the table at Felipe. 'I'm told you've been
asked to put up for the next Parish elections.'

He drew on his cigarette and blew the smoke up into the
air between us. It was impossible to tell from his face
whether the prospect pleased or displeased him. Eventually, he sat back in his chair, grimacing slightly. 'You
have a phrase, I think – about stretching out the neck.'

'That's right. As phrases go, one of our more relevant
imports.'

'In this case, certain people want the neck to be mine.'

'And you? What do you want?'

Enrique stopped walking up and down and regarded his
brother with a quizzical smile. He appeared to be as interested in the answer as I was.

Felipe shrugged. 'I don't know,' he said.

Enrique resumed his walking, and out in the hall a bell
rang. Felipe excused himself, not without some relief, I felt,
and went out. He reappeared a few seconds later with two
men, the elder of whom I recognized immediately.

I got up and held out my hand. 'Pedro! Pedro Calvaro!
How *are* you, my friend!'

To my embarrassment, the old man's eyes filled with
tears. 'Señor,' he said, and for a moment could get no
further, though his leathery old face was a veritable jig-saw
of a smile. I took his arm and propelled him towards the
chair beside mine, then realized that Felipe was waiting to
introduce me to his other guest, a dark, burly, middle-aged
chap, whose Sunday suit wouldn't have fooled a short-
sighted cow at ten yards; this was a farmer without a
shadow of a doubt. There was no smile on his swarthy face,
but a shrewd, appraising look, intended, clearly, to winkle
out all faults and weaknesses in whatever – or whoever –
happened to be its object.

'This is our next-door-neighbour,' said Felipe. 'Señor

José Orthoz. You passed his farm as you turned down from the main road.'

'Senor Orthoz.'

'Monsieur.'

Mercifully, it looked as if everybody had been primed before-hand to address me in French – a fact which was going to save us all a lot of heartache.

I wanted to have a few words with old Pedro, but not wishing to give offence to the farmer I offered him a chair, and was relieved when he indicated his intention of going round the other side of the table. Calvaro now was wreathed in a blanket of pipe smoke, his eyes half-closed as he peered up at me. I sat down and raised my glass to him.

'A votre santé, mon ami. Ça va?'

The nut-brown face creased again with pleasure so that the skin seemed to run up in rivulets into the grizzled white hair above the ears. His whole head was white now, and, bent over his pipe, he seemed a very old man, a disquieting reminder of just how long it had been since I had spent any time on the island.

Unfortunately, conversation between us was not very rewarding. Pedro seemed to have lost most of his English and his French wasn't a lot better. I learned that he'd lost his wife a couple of years ago and was now living with his married daughter. I gathered his involvement with the Rochas family went back to a long friendship with their father, who had been killed in a road accident several years ago. The Rochas' mother, I learned, had died in the same accident.

'All is not well here now, eh?' I asked him slowly and carefully.

He shook his old head sadly, removed the pipe from his mouth and sighed.

'Is that how Monsieur Maurice felt, too?'

For a second, his shrewd black eyes held mine, then he put the pipe back in his mouth, drew on it for a minute or two and, almost imperceptibly, nodded.

I was trying to think how best to proceed when we were

132

interrupted by two more arrivals: a middle-aged man, tall and spare, with the sharp, dark looks of the Roquennais-Spanish, and a lad about twenty, of the same height, build and looks in a suit that had possibly fitted him a couple of years ago.

'This is José's brother, Juan,' said Felipe, 'and his son, Ramon.'

'You're late,' José called out accusingly, but Juan merely raised an eyebrow and, after a word with Calvaro and me, lowered his tall frame into a chair, leaving his son to collect their drinks.

'There's only Rodriguez and Castro to come,' Felipe told the others, 'and as they may be a little late we may as well get on. They have to come from town,' he added for my benefit.

So what about *Carlos* Rochas? I wondered. Wasn't he a member of the party? If not, why not?

Felipe kicked off by reminding everyone that I was visiting the island as a courtesy to the de Courvel family, and continued: 'I invited him to come here tonight because I felt his concern over the death of Señor Maurice gave us all – he and us – some common interest. He's asked me to make clear that he has no wish to become involved in our island politics, but I don't think he will mind my saying that I nevertheless feel very strongly that he would agree with us that what happened to Señor de Courvel cannot be altogether separated from what has been happening to the island as a whole over the past ten years or so. Our problem now is to identify the dangers that still exist, and that we feel are increasing every day, to others.'

There was a general grunt of agreement, but José Orthoz made a snorting sound and stabbed the air with his pipe.

'Why don't you speak clear, heh? Why don't you say what we all know – that it killed him, heh? And it will kill us all, one way or another, if we sit on our backsides and let it!' He glared inimically from one to the other of us and there was a moment's uncomfortable silence, in which I felt a treacherous sense of the comic lurch dangerously near to the surface. Fortunately Orthoz didn't seem the telepathic type.

'So?' he demanded. 'What is wrong with that, heh?'

'Nothing,' said Felipe. 'Except that it doesn't explain anything.'

'*Explain!* Bah! Who wants explanations! Anyone can *see*.'

'Not really,' I said. 'Forgive me, Señor Orthoz, I understand only too well what you feel, but at a first glance the situation here is *not* clearly as you portray it. In fact, a visitor to this island at present could be forgiven for taking away an impression of great and growing prosperity. You have more and better hotels, entertainment, commercial activity. The tourist and consumer industries, I would say, are booming. You say your problem is to identify the dangers to the rest of the folk here. I'd say that could be truer than you think. In fact, I'd go so far as to say that you've first got to be sure that the majority of people would agree with you that the things you're on about *are* dangers.'

'*Exactement*,' said a soft voice, and Enrique got up from the table and began pacing up and down again.

Meanwhile, the entire Orthoz family looked to be on the point of explosion. With commendable speed and adroitness, Felipe headed them off.

'It's a fair point,' he said. 'The reason Corlander's been so successful so far is that he's been able to persuade a few people that what's good for him is good for them. And in the short term it *is*. But only for a time, and only for a few, and we shan't know how high the price has been until the island we've known all our lives has gone for ever. *That's* what we've got to get across. But it's not going to be done simply by ranting about the present situation, or continually harking back to the past.' He paused, but no one spoke. José sat with his head bent on his chest, wrestling, no doubt, with subterranean rumblings, while his brother examined the surface of the table with unblinking attention. Only Pedro behind his pipe and Enrique, now lost in contemplation of the scene beyond the window, seemed totally at ease.

134

'You see,' Felipe continued, ' – the Seigneurs knew this – if you want something to prosper, then *all* must profit, or, ultimately, none can. I don't mean, of course, that everyone's got to profit to the same extent and in the same way. A man with one field will be rich with two: with three, he'll feel a tycoon – but give him six and it's likely he'll be bankrupt in a week.'

'Yes,' I said, 'I remember Maurice saying something like that once. He said – if I've got it right – something about excess being an imbalance. I remember it reminded me of Aristotle.'

Felipe smiled, but José gave me a look of such baleful incomprehension that I felt obliged to throw a life-line to my image before it was lost without trace.

'What I'm trying to say,' I went on, 'is that, since you're not going to be able to put the clock back, you've got to decide whether a pinch of compromise wouldn't be worth a ton of conflict – because, make no mistake about it, that's what it would be – a whole heap of trouble; these people you're up against are powerful *hombres*, and they aren't going to step down for you, not this week nor next.'

'So!' snarled José, 'we're not going to step down for *them*! Not this week, nor next!' And he nodded his head at me with supreme satisfaction at his own verbal adroitness.

Felipe, I decided, was going to have his work cut out here. And I wasn't helping much. I should never have come. Dammit, I wasn't on the island to play politics! I was here to find out why Maurice had killed himself, and a fat lot I should achieve if I went round antagonizing the local populace.

'No,' said Felipe quietly. 'We shan't step down: not while some of our oldest friends are being seduced. And those that can't be seduced are destroyed.'

I looked at him, and suddenly I felt a creeping weariness invade my body. These people were all so certain – as was Guy, as was Alain, as was Paulo Garcia – that Maurice had died by treachery. I realized now that secretly I had clung to the hope that I would be able to disprove it – or, at least, to

135

rationalize it to proportions that could somehow be accepted. And I could then go home more or less content in the knowledge that all that had happened here was that a sad old man had killed himself for no more sinister reason than that he was sad. But it wouldn't wash. In my gut I knew it, and I felt sick.

'Destroyed,' I said, 'is a strong word.'

'As I said, Angus, there are more ways than one – '

'Yes, yes, I know.' I felt a rising impatience. I didn't want any more philosophy. 'All right,' I said, 'accepting that your theories of corruption, and all the rest of it, are correct, accepting all that, where does it get us? Which one of you can produce a shred of evidence? Particularly of the fact that it had the slightest connection with Monsieur de Courvel's death? Well?' I looked round the table. '*Can* you?'

'Uh?' José Orthoz looked bemused and I doubted if he had followed half of what had been said.

'No,' said Felipe, 'we can't give you proof. We can only show you people who have bled a little. People like old Pedro here: turned out after a lifetime of service without so much as a *sou* for his old age except what charity could offer him. Do you think that was what Monsieur de Courvel intended?'

'I know damn well he didn't, but I'm surprised all the same that there was nothing in writing.'

'Some things do not need writing. And those are the things that can get conveniently forgotten after a man has made a hasty decision to die. Oh, we could tell you many other things – of people who were under some kind of pressure one minute and the next were in trouble with the police. And of others who *should* have been in gaol, but for whom miracles worked. You'd be surprised, my friend! Believe me!'

I took out a cigarette and lit it, looking at him through the smoke that drifted between us. 'Well,' I said, 'what do you want me to do? Even supposing I can do *anything*.'

He leaned forwards across the table towards me, and I

136

sensed that everyone in the room was watching him.

'Two things, Angus. One – ' He pointed an index finger towards me – 'get us Alain de Courvel – '

'Eh?'

'Get us Alain de Courvel. Two – ' Another finger shot out – 'persuade Monsieur Le Marnet to decline the Stewardship – at least for another year – to stay on as President just that bit longer.'

'But surely that's not possible. I mean, constitutionally.'

'There's nothing against it. Absolutely nothing. I have checked the legal position as far back as our written records go. There is nothing to say that a President whose term is not completed cannot, if he wishes, choose to remain on in office for his full time. There is nothing to say that the Stewardship, which is purely a figurehead appointment, anyway, cannot remain temporarily vacant – or even, if it were wished, that someone else, other than the incumbent President, should take it. All these procedures have been traditional. Nobody has ever sought to vary them because up until now there has never been any need.'

'But he's an old man! This is a war you're fighting.'

'All we ask, Angus, is a little more time. With Monsieur Le Marnet holding the power of veto in the Assembly, we would have that time. We *must* have it if there is to be any hope of stopping these people. Will you do it?'

'Hell, Felipe, I don't know!' I was worried. It was one thing to offer my own support, but to have any hand in pushing an old man nearly eighty in front of a juggernaut was quite another. For the first time I realized just how far Felipe and his supporters were prepared to go.

'I don't think I can help you,' I said at last.

'Angus, *think*.'

'No, *you* think, blast you! I came over here because one man killed himself. I'm not staying to hand out the knives for another – and then perhaps another – to go the same way. How many martyrs do you want? No, *you* think, and then tell me what you take me for.'

'We need Monsieur Le Marnet,' growled José Orthoz.

'Then you ask him, my friend.' I looked round on them all. 'Why haven't you, anyway, if you're so sure you're right?'

'If we have to, we shall,' said Felipe. 'But we may not be able to convince him. You could.'

'And Alain?'

'Alain de Courvel and his newspaper could be worth an army of men to us.'

'So why isn't he?'

Enrique gave an explosive sound. I suspected strongly that it was derisory.

'Because,' said Felipe, 'he sits, as you say, on the gate.'

'Fence.'

'Pardon? Oh, yes – very well. He sits on the fence and he does nothing. It is not right for a son.'

'I'm not here to teach Alain de Courvel his filial responsibilities. Where he sits and how he sits are his business.'

'No, it is *our* business: the island's business. He cannot escape the fact that he is a de Courvel. He was born to certain rights and privileges. In return, there are duties.'

'I understand that for years now he's shown a certain disregard for those facts.'

'Yes. He wants to be like other men: to earn his living and at the end of the day call his soul his own. Very reasonable – if he were not Alain de Courvel.'

'Oh, but surely, in these days – '

'These days have nothing to do with it! This is not your outside world, Angus. This is La Roque. This is our way of life and these are our traditions.'

'Well, all right – but what about approaching de Courvel yourselves?'

'We have. Many times.'

'And?'

'He won't listen. He thinks we are troublemakers.'

I grinned. I believed him!

'And what makes you think he'll change his mind for me?'

'He must at least listen to you. You are, after all, practically brothers.'

138

I laughed out loud, and to my surprise I noticed that Enrique also found this funny. Felipe, however, remained grave, and the Orthoz family appeared unmoved either one way or the other.

'Sorry,' I said, 'but I really do doubt, you know, if Alain sees it that way. However – ' I leaned forward, resting my arms on the table and stared for a second into the polished wood. Something told me I was on the brink of letting myself in for one hell of a lot of trouble. I sighed. 'Well,' I said, 'so far as Alain's concerned I'll have a word. Just so long as you realize that the end-result is likely to be precisely as if I'd done nothing at all.'

Felipe's face cleared and that brilliant smile of his, with which he had first greeted me, reappeared.

'Thank you, Angus. That is all we ask.'

There was an impatient movement next to him and I saw that José Orthoz, clearly not a man for compromise, was glowering at me. 'We need Monsieur Le Marnet,' he growled.

'Sorry,' I said. 'I can't help you, and what's more – '

Before I could finish, the doorbell rang again, and this time Enrique, who was still standing, placed a restraining hand on his brother's shoulder and went out.

He came back almost immediately with two young men, one tall and very thin, with a trim black moustache: the other a thick-set individual, with black, oily hair brushed straight back until it shone, and with a slight scar over one eyebrow. All three looked agitated. Enrique wasted no time on introductions, but turned straight towards his brother and said something to him in Spanish.

Felipe rose, glass in hand, looking at him, and I felt tension run round the table like an electric charge. Then the young man with the moustache began to speak in rapid Spanish, and immediately there were exclamations from all round. On José's face I saw a look of livid rage. Only Felipe remained still, but his olive skin seemed to have gone white and his dark eyes shone like hard metal.

'What's wrong?' I asked.

He didn't answer immediately, and I thought he wasn't going to. But then his voice came, quiet and completely controlled.

'The Committee has been sitting. They have agreed the Point Rouge sale.'

I stared at him. There seemed to be no answer that I, a stranger, could make.

'It was not due to be heard for another week, at least. Somehow – no one asks for explanations any more – they have managed to get it brought forward. The Committee's decision comes before the Assembly for ratification in two weeks' time. Unless a miracle occurs, it will, of course, succeed – and that, my friend, will be that – one more victory for Monsieur Corlander: one more battle lost.'

He turned again to the young man with the moustache and spoke to him, presumably for my benefit, in French.

'Monsieur Le Marnet's acceptance – it has been received?'

The young man shook his head.

'No?' Felipe looked surprised.

'Not, anyway, before we left. Perhaps now, who knows? It was expected today, but – ' He shrugged – 'today, tomorrow. What does it matter?'

There was silence for a while, then Felipe lifted his glass and drained the contents. 'To Monsieur Le Marnet,' he said. 'If he accepts the Stewardship, we may as well give up, I think. If not – ' He looked at me and smiled. 'How *are* you on miracles, my friend?'

I didn't know the answer to Felipe's final question, but I decided to put it to the test forthwith. It was time, anyway, that I took a look at Alain de Courvel's present life-style. But, first, there was something else.

As the meeting broke up, I cut my responses to the two late arrivals – introduced as Antonio Rodriguez, a school-teacher from Porte Hilaire, and Jaime Castro, a clerk like Felipe in one of the town's law offices – and touched old Pedro's arm as he moved towards the door.

'I'll take you home,' I said.

He smiled, but paused uncertainly, glancing towards Juan Orthoz and Ramon.

'It's all right,' I said. 'I'll explain to them.'

I lingered as I did so, hoping, as we passed through the hall, that the door to the music room would open. It didn't, and we left to an extravagant misinterpretation of the waltz theme from *The King and I*.

Once we were out in the quiet lanes leading to Calvaro's daughter's cottage near the de Courvel plantations, I took the issue squarely on, speaking slowly in correct French so that he could follow me.

'Pedro, you knew Monsieur de Courvel and my father were very close friends.'

'*Sí, sí*,' he said warmly, nodding his head in approbation.

'And you know how Monsieur and Madame de Courvel cared for me after my father died. I owe them a great deal.'

I glanced at him and our eyes met. His were wary. 'Sí,' he said.

'I owe them enough,' I said, 'to try to find out why Monsieur Maurice died in the way he did. I have asked many people this question, but nobody seems to know the answer: people who had known him all their lives, who were close to him; they just don't seem to know the answer. I find this very strange.'

I paused, glancing at him again, but now I could see only the side of his brown, sun-beaten face as he stared in front of him through the windscreen.

'You were with him for fifty years, Pedro. You knew him better, probably, than anyone else. Can *you* tell me why he took his own life? Was it what they say – his debts, Madame's death, Madame Simone's marriage? – Or was there something else?'

It was such a long time before he answered that I began to wonder if, in fact, he was deaf and hadn't heard a word I'd said. Then I heard him draw in his breath in a long sighing sound, almost as though until that moment he had been holding it. I could still see only the side of his face, but now

141

his head dropped a little and his gaze was no longer in front of him, but downwards on to his own knees. From the hidden, deep-lidded eyes I gained an impression of ineffable sadness. At last he spoke: 'I can tell you nothing, Señor Angus.'

I stopped the car at the edge of the grass verge, turned off the engine and faced him.

'Pedro, I have to know. You must see that.'

Still, he didn't look at me. 'There is nothing to know, Señor.'

'That isn't what you meant, is it? There *is* something, but you won't – or can't – tell me. That's it, isn't it?'

He half-turned towards me, tried to smile, but, seeing the look on my face, failed. We sat in silence for about half a minute, and all the time I stared at him fixedly, willing him to speak: but he had turned his head away again and remained mute and unhappy, looking down. At length, I put my hand out to the ignition and turned it on. 'Very well,' I said, 'you win, old friend. But in case you should change your mind, you know where I am.' I looked at him again. 'You see, Pedro, I intend to know whatever there is to know about this business. And I *shall* know – eventually.'

I jerked at the starter, but the engine stalled and in the pause before I tried again I heard his voice. I stopped with my hand still on the knob. 'What did you say?'

'Nothing, Señor. Only that it is a pity.'

'You're damned right it's a pity! Do you know, Pedro, I used to think this island was heaven on earth, and everyone on it just one halo removed from an archangel. Well – for the record – I've changed my mind. I was very, very wrong. You're all on your knees, all right, but to a man who knows nothing about you and cares less. God Almighty, if *this* is what Maurice de Courvel knew, no wonder he took the quick way out!'

I pulled savagely at the starter again and the engine roared into life. But I let in the clutch so fiercely that it stalled again and we jerked to a stop.

I paused, both hands spread on the wheel in front of me.

'Forgive me, old friend.'

Immediately, he turned towards me, his face an agonized mixture of reassurance and remorse.

'No, no, Señor! It is true! All you say is true!'

I shook my head. 'No, Pedro. A little, perhaps, but not all. And I've no damn right, anyway, to criticize you, or anyone else. For God's sake, where was *I* these last ten years!'

I started the engine again, and this time we moved off in an orderly manner. In the five minutes it took to reach his cottage neither of us spoke. But before I could get out, he stopped me.

'Señor Angus!'

I looked at him questioningly. His black eyes glistened with an emotion that seemed to electrify him. But for the gnarled, trembling hands and the silvery stubble that lined his jaw and chin, I could have taken him at that moment for a much younger man.

'Señor Angus! For Señor Maurice's sake, do not go further!'

I stared at him.

'I beg you, Señor! For the love of Our Lady, let it – let *him* – lie in peace!'

'What *is* it, Pedro? Tell me.'

For a moment he seemed to struggle with himself, and I became a little alarmed. He was an old man and I had put him into hell. But then I remembered another old man and another hell and my heart hardened.

'What is it, Pedro?'

But even as I spoke, I knew it was no use. The moment was already passing. The light died in his eyes as I watched and he seemed to shrink within himself.

'There is nothing you, or anyone, can do,' he muttered. 'Only harm.'

'Harm? No one with a clear conscience has that to fear from me.'

But he only shook his head, over and over again.

'Only harm,' he repeated. 'Only harm.'

143

ELEVEN

I didn't know the address of Alain's flat in Porte Hilaire, so I parked the car behind the Town Church and looked him up in the telephone directory in one of the kiosks along the wall there.

It turned out that he lived only a stone's throw from where I was standing: Rue Royale, No 302. This was the long, straight road that ran down behind the Palais de Justice into Harbour Square. Once, its handsome houses had been homes for the island's wealthiest families; now, most of those families had moved out of town and the beautiful old houses, with their polished wooden doors and shining brass, had been turned into law offices or mere *pieds à terre* for the town's more prominent business men. Did Alain de Courvel now see himself as one of these?

As I emerged from the road alongside the church, I found that No 302 was almost immediately opposite, and, crossing over, discovered Alain's name and apartment number amongst those on a small plate beside the door. I rang the bell, and, while I waited for someone to answer, turned to look across at the walls of the Palais, wondering idly as I did so whether Apartment number three afforded Alain a view of his father's old state chambers; and where, if anywhere, he garaged a car.

Somehow, I was surprised when the door was opened by a woman. Correction: by a woman who, if she was a professional housekeeper, I was Little Orphan Annie. Mid-thirtyish, maybe, with a striking, intellectual sort of face, relieved from severity by a humorous gleam in her light brown eyes and a quizzical half-smile in the corners of her mouth.

I must have *looked* taken aback, because the smile broadened.

'*Je peux vous aider, Monsieur?*'

'I beg your pardon. I – um – I may have pressed the wrong bell.'

Still on the wrong foot, I'd spoken in English, but before I could correct myself she replied in the same way with just a hint of accent.

'You wanted?'

'I was looking for Monsieur de Courvel. I *thought* I'd pressed number three, but – '

'You did. But I'm afraid he's out at the moment. Can I help at all? Or would you like to come in and wait? He shouldn't be long.'

She had stepped back as she spoke and was holding the door for me to follow. Belatedly, the facts of the situation had begun to filter through. This must be 'the woman' Guy had mentioned. I could see what Alain saw in her, but what did she see in *him*? I wondered. Perhaps I was about to find out.

'Well,' I said. 'If you're sure you don't mind.'

'Of course not, Monsieur Logan.'

So. There it was again. For somebody trying to be inconspicuous, I was about as underexposed as the Invisible Man trapped by a faulty zip.

Smiling weakly, I stepped past her into a small, rather dark hallway, taking up my position on the edge of an oblong Persian rug while she shut the front door. When she turned, there was an amused look on her face. 'Forgive me,' she said, 'I know you, but you don't know me. I'm Madeleine Le Brocq. As soon as you said you wanted Alain, I realized who you were. He mentioned you were here. Shall we go upstairs? I'll lead the way.'

She moved towards the staircase on the right of the hall and I followed her up to the first landing, where she beckoned me through some double doors. We were in a small parquet-floored hall, occupied chiefly by a long, polished wooden chest, on which stood a white telephone and a large vase of flowers. To left and right of the hall were more double doors, the right-hand pair standing partly open and leading, from what I could see, into a lounge. This was the room she led me into: a tastefully, but not extravagantly, furnished room, with French windows standing open on to a small balcony above the Rue Royale. Opposite, were the high walls of the Palais de Justice, with, to the right, the shuttered windows of the Steward's apartments. In this room, it would be hard for Alain de Courvel to forget his inheritance.

Madeleine Le Brocq gestured towards one of the leather armchairs near the window. 'Please,' she said. 'Can I give you a drink? Or would you rather have coffee? I've got some on as a matter of fact,' she said as I hesitated.

'Well, if you're going to have some yourself – '

'I am.'

'Then I'd be glad to join you. Thank you.'

She must have been telling the truth, because I barely had time to glance around the room before she was back again, setting the tray of coffee down on the table between us. While she poured it out I had an opportunity to study her. She wasn't what you'd call a pretty woman; her face was too long and sharp, her mouth too thin, but there was a magnetism about her that was powerfully effective. It was a magnetism part sensual, part cerebral. I'd caught a glimpse of Ayer's *Language, Truth and Logic* among the books on a shelf beside my chair; she probably knew the damn book by heart.

'You're a journalist, too, I understand,' she said as she handed me my coffee.

'Well, opinions differ. I agree with whichever's the nicest.'

When she really smiled, her face was transformed, and my respect for Alain went up several notches.

Sipping our coffee, we embarked on a comparison of past and present values, brought on by my remarking upon the many changes I'd seen on the island. Just as I was beginning to hope to pick up a few pointers to current de Courvel thinking, however, the telephone rang. She put her cup down and with a murmured apology got up and went out into the hall, leaving the door ajar. I could hear her speaking in rapid French as clearly as if she were still in the room. *'Mais, Chéri, où es tu? Tu fais quoi? Quel dommage! Combien de temps – ? Non. Ne te fâche pas! Mais, écoute – il y a quelqu'un ici qui te demande. Oui. Monsieur Logan. Oui. Très bien. Je vais l'indiquer. Oui. Je vais l'expliquer. Bien.'*

I heard her put the phone down and she came back into the room.

'It was Alain. It seems there has been one of those crises. You'll know all about that, I expect. He didn't say what it was, but they've been waiting for something or other.' She gave a puzzled frown. 'I wonder what.'

I had an idea I could have told her, but said nothing.

'Well,' she said, her face clearing, 'he's on his way now. He *was* going on somewhere else – that's why he phoned – but when I told him you were here he said he'd send someone else. He should only be about five minutes.'

I was a little surprised. Consideration for *my* convenience – or anyone else's for that matter – hadn't struck me as particularly noticeable in Alain before. Why now?

None the less, he was true to his word: within ten minutes we heard his key in the door.

As he entered the room, a look passed between him and Madeleine that I recognized; it was strictly 'Thee and Me' stuff: all superfluities instantly disposed of and complete understanding established in a second. Even amongst husbands and wives, it was a look by no means frequently seen. It told me plenty about this particular relationship. By contrast, the glance he gave me was full of questioning.

'You've heard, then? Did *he* tell you?'

He misinterpreted my stare of incomprehension and became impatient. 'For God's sake, Angus! I must know what he thinks he's doing!' He glared at me as though he felt that whatever was bothering him was all my fault.

'By "he", I take it you mean Guy Le Marnet. And I'm only guessing, but I imagine that what's put the cat among the pigeons is that he's decided not to stand down. Is that it?'

147

It was his turn to look blank. 'You mean you didn't know? You haven't seen him?'

'*Should* I have? Today, I mean. When I saw him a couple of days ago, the subject didn't arise.'

'Oh. Oh, I see.' He turned abruptly and went and mixed himself a drink from the sideboard. When he looked round again, his expression was deflated. 'I'm sorry, I took it for granted that that's what you were here about. But – ' and now he looked suspicious again – 'how could you have guessed if you didn't know anything about it?'

'I didn't say I didn't know *anything* about it. As a matter of fact, I did, and that *is* why I'm here.'

His face went dark again with sudden irritation. 'Look, what the hell – '

'Hold on, for God's sake, I'm trying to tell you.' I paused, casting an apologetic glance at Madeleine, who was looking from one to the other of us with a mixture of amusement and anxiety. 'The point is,' I said, 'I've been spending the evening with a chap called Rochas and one or two of his pals.'

'*Mon Dieu!*' He turned away in exasperation and walked over to the window.

'O.K.,' I said, 'you don't approve of them, but at least listen to why I came here because it's even more relevant than ever now.'

He gave a sardonic snort. 'I can imagine!'

'Alain. Please.' It was Madeleine. But he ignored her, turning back to face me with all the old spite on his face.

'I can imagine! All the things they consider *I* ought to be doing, and Guy Le Marnet ought to be doing: everyone, in fact, who stands to lose the most. Oh, yes, I can imagine!' A sudden thought struck him. 'If they've got anything to do with this – '

'They haven't.'

'How do you know?'

'I know.'

'They're mad, those people. They think you can run an island on Boy Scout principles. They think you can fight vested interest with idealism. They're pathetic, I tell you.'

'Well – you could be right. The point is, Guy appears to agree with them. So what are you going to do about it?'

He looked at me almost, I felt, with hatred.

'Do you realize what you're saying? Do you realize what that foolish old man is doing? Have you the slightest conception of what any of this means? What life is really like here now?'

'I'm learning every minute. Though I'm not quite sure what. Where do *you* stand? Right, left, or on the fence?'

I hadn't meant to be quite so insulting, but he'd begun to irritate me.

I'd expected him to go into one of his hypercritical tirades; instead, he turned away towards the window again and stood there, silently fingering his glass. I'd half-begun to think he was going to ignore me completely and had made up my mind to abandon my project, make my excuses to Madeleine and leave. But then he shifted slightly and threw an oblique glance at me over his shoulder.

'You disappoint me, Angus.'

I didn't answer and after a moment he turned fully round and faced me and I saw that he had composed himself again into what I had now come to regard as his 'prevailing look', that of slightly contemptuous mockery.

'You talk,' he said, 'as if the little melodramas by which people seek to convince themselves they have free will in this world had any relevance here. It's doubtful if they ever have had *anywhere* – but *here* – ' he gave a sneering, pitying smile – 'on La Roque – believe me, my friend, when all your phony, half-baked reactionaries have done their puny, pathetic worst, we shall be as much closer to stopping the direction of things on this island as the Galilean Inquisition to making the sun go round the earth.'

'Now, that's an interesting analogy. I hadn't exactly seen Corlander *et al* as prophets of natural laws, nor radical dissenters in the role of reactionaries. Quite a turnabout. If I follow your logic correctly, everything that's now happening here is part of some predetermined evolution. Yes?'

'Why not? Feudalism died out three hundred years ago everywhere else. Isn't it time it did here?'

'Ah, yes, but that isn't the argument, is it? As I understand it, it's not the demise of feudalism that bothers some people here: it's the particular pattern that's taking its place.'

'So. Some people will like it; some people won't – and a lot of those will simply use it as an excuse for their own personal power game. They'll win a certain support, because some people love a part in a drama. But nothing significant will come of it. Nothing. If you want to spend your time over here making desperate and doomed sorties with the Rochas boys in the interests of some fictitious 'save the island' campaign, that's up to you. But leave me out of it. I see no virtue in wasted effort, and I abhor failure.' With that, he drained his glass and turned back towards the cabinet. Madeleine, I noticed, was watching him uneasily.

I was tempted, for her sake, to let him off the hook, but I couldn't.

'How the hell,' I asked, 'can you call a campaign "fictitious" if it's about people's lives? And how do you know effort's wasted until it's been spent? – And if you don't mind my asking [*and* if he did], since you hate failure so much, how come you're so keen on playing Humpty Dumpty?'

For a second, he seemed to freeze, except for a tiny involuntary spasm in the corner of his mouth. Then he drained his glass and turned and put it down beside the bottle on the cabinet. He still had his back to us when he spoke.

'I really don't think, Angus, that there is any point in our continuing to discuss this.'

It was a dismissal. I was supposed to kiss hands and leave. Nothing would have given me greater pleasure, but I had made a promise and I was now galled enough to want to keep it.

'I'm afraid you're right,' I said. 'Pity. Because I came here specifically to ask you something.' I paused, but he

150

still didn't move. 'About this young Rochas,' I said, 'contrary to the impressions you seem inclined to form, I met him purely by accident. He can hardly be blamed for imagining I might have some sympathy for his views about things here, and therefore I don't think his asking me to meet some of his pals can be seen as particularly untoward. I confess I wasn't all that keen – there's a lot to be said, I agree, for staying in out of the rain, especially when it doesn't seem to be *your* rain – but *having* met them, some of them, I can't simply dismiss them, as you apparently do, as being a bunch of futile idiots. Nor, on the other hand, did I find them particularly formidable. Reactionaries? Well, if you mean by that folk who are worried about their livelihood, their standards of living, the trend of things around them – well, yes, I suppose you could say that. But they struck me as being very ordinary sort of people. I almost felt afraid for them. Almost, but not quite. Because there *is* something pretty amazing about ordinary people in the end, isn't there? The trouble is they're like elephants, they don't know their strength – which is what gives all your tyrants and dictators, and all the pig's orphans of politicians their little run for their money. But in the end it's the ordinary people who count. If you consider it impious of them to expect your support, you must put it down to the well-known inability of such people to know where to draw the line.'

By the quick blink of his eyes and the way his nostrils moved I knew I had stung him, but apart from those small movements he remained still and unresponsive.

'Where I come in,' I continued, 'is that they hoped I would have some influence in persuading you and Guy to endorse their efforts to achieve some sort of representation in the Assembly. In Guy's case they clearly had no need to worry. In yours, I wonder they gave themselves the trouble. It's astonishing how deluded we allow ourselves to be about the things that mean a lot to us. These people, with their touching belief in the standards which your father and Guy, and those of your families before them tried to maintain, actually *trusted* you. Oh, they knew you didn't like them much, but they thought that when the chips were down blood would count. *Your* blood. Old-fashioned, I agree. And tiresome. But, as I said, they're very ordinary people.'

Sarcasm has never been my favourite form of attack, but it was either that or hitting him in the face, which, in present company, was no alternative at all.

'So,' I concluded, 'what am I to tell them?'

He didn't raise his eyes, nor move from where he stood, but I heard him draw a deep breath and slowly let it out again down his nose. His lips opened.

'To go to hell,' he said.

Madeleine bent suddenly as though she were in pain, and I don't know what I might have said or done if she had not been there. As it was, I stood and stared at him for several seconds and then made for the door. Neither of them came down to see me off.

TWELVE

'So you've heard,' Guy said. 'And you've come to tell me what you think of me.'

'Yes. Unless, of course, what I've heard is a complete misinterpretation of your actual intentions.'

'I hardly think so. The astonishing thing, Angus, is that no one has ever thought of it before. I suppose the need simply never arose. But it shows how blindly we follow precedent in this life. Nothing has ever been written down, you understand, yet every President has always unquestioningly followed established procedures. It was you who showed me the obvious alternative.'

'*I!*'

'Well, shall we say it was *through* you. It was going over it all with you, explaining our traditions and customs. Afterwards, I began to look at it all in a detached way, as a stranger would. And suddenly I saw the answer staring me in the face.'

'But don't you see, sir, if you stay on they'll crucify you.'

'They'll try, of course.' He shrugged.

'Try, *nothing*! You've said, yourself – '

'They are powerful, yes. But I have no alternative, Angus. Now I see there is a way, I have to take it.'

'No, you don't. You can follow procedure and use your influence behind the scenes.'

'Influence for influence, my boy, they can run rings round me. When greed or fear are aroused, something much more potent than persuasion is needed. I shall fight them with the law, Angus. If they defy that, at least the island will know the kind of choice it has to make.'

'Yes, but is it ready for that kind of choice? How do you know that your action won't be misunderstood and end in the very result you're trying to avoid – tipping the island into Corlander's lap? Nobody ever recognizes tyrants in the beginning. Napoleon, Hitler – history's full of the blighters who got away with it for a tediously long time simply because people couldn't see them properly in the glare of the spotlight.'

'All the more reason I must try. As for being misunderstood, well, it's a risk I must take. I can't let what happened to Maurice go unchallenged. I can't let it happen to others.'

'But that's exactly – ' I stopped, but he knew what I was going to say and smiled.

'I shan't end as he did. Don't worry. Not because I'm stronger, but because I've been more fortunate in other ways so far.'

'Maybe. But look, sir – how many people on this island even remotely connect Maurice's death with Corlander? Even if you stood in the middle of the Place de Justice and denounced him for the mercenary empire-builder he is, how many do you think would really believe you? You've said, yourself, the man never puts a foot wrong. He's never there when the gun goes off. So who's to believe his hand's on the trigger? One or two, yes. But *enough*? Enough even for a start? Incidentally, some of those who *would* believe it asked me to try and use my influence with you.'

'To what end?'

'To persuade you to do the very thing you're doing. They didn't contact you last night, I suppose?'

He shook his head. 'No. But there you are, Angus. Doesn't this prove that I'm right?'

'Not to me, it doesn't. Can't you see, sir – ' I felt a desperate need to head him off, but I also sensed the grim certainty of failure – 'if you can't nail the man for sure with *something*, there'll be no second chances; he'll have you – and the island – for breakfast. And what have you got right now? Well, ethics are great stuff, but you can't fight a tiger with a treatise. And beyond that, it's all a matter of interpretation, really, isn't it? I mean, one man's piracy is another man's good business. Cash in the bank, prosperity for the island, and all that. Can you honestly convict Corlander of a single illegal act and make it stick? If so, then fair enough, I take back everything I've said and I'm with you to the hilt.'

Guy looked at me for a long moment. He looked worn and tired and my heart went out to him.

'And if we can't?' he asked.

I took out some cigarettes and offered him one. To my surprise he took it, and I lit it for him and we looked at each other through the smoke. A bleak smile appeared on his face.

'It's no use, Angus. I've made up my mind.'

There was another brief silence, and then I stood up.

'Will you promise me just one thing, sir?'

He looked up at me questioningly.

'If anything should happen, anywhere around you, that strikes you as the least bit – shall we say, *unusual* – will you let me know immediately?'

This time, his smile was full and open. 'Unusual things are always happening to me, dear boy.'

'You know quite well what I mean, sir.'

'Yes, but you have no need to be concerned on that score. Of that I'm sure.'

'Nevertheless . . .'

'Very well. I promise.'

I had to be content with that. I let him ring for Pierre to show me out because I knew the old man would want to see me before I left. Sure enough, as soon as we were safely away from the breakfast room door, he stopped in his tracks and looked at me in concerned query.

'You'll have to watch him, Pierre.'

He didn't answer and I realized that this was an entirely unnecessary injunction.

'That's my telephone number,' I hastily scribbled it down, 'Call me *any* time – day or night – if you're worried about anything.'

'M'sieur.'

He put the number carefully away in an inside pocket.

As I went down the steps, a car swung on to the sweep of

asphalt in front of the house and I recognized Nicholas behind the wheel. He pulled up a few yards from where I had parked the Citroën and got out. I waited for him at the bottom of the steps and he looked up at me comprehendingly.

'I'm wasting my time, I suppose.'

'Unless you've brought a chloroform pad and a ball and chain, yes.'

He stood still, looking past me at the house, as though willing it to do something that neither of us could accomplish. His face was sallow with anxiety.

'Would it work, do you think, if I suggested he moved in with Stéph and me for a time?'

'Doubt it. You could always try insisting, of course, but even then I think he'd slip out of the bag somewhere.'

He began rubbing his forehead up and down with two fingers in a gesture that reminded me instantly of Guy, himself. Then he sighed.

'What *are* we to do, Angus?'

I was tempted to say 'start praying', but restrained myself.

'Immediately, nothing. There's nothing you *can* do. But in the long term, two things – simultaneously – watch out for him, and try to get *something* – any bloody thing – on Corlander that'll stick.'

He looked desperate. 'It's hopeless, Angus.'

'I know, I know. He's the Virgin Mary. But there *must* be a weak spot somewhere. Have you ever looked at the smuggling racket? Really closely, I mean?'

'Smuggling?' He looked blank.

'I've heard rumours.'

'Connecting Corlander?'

'Just rumours,' I said.

He thought for a moment. Then he shrugged.

'That's about all there would be to it, too, I think. In any case, smuggling on La Roque – well, it's like rain in England. It's been going on for so long, it's part of the balance of Nature, you might say. No one worries any more.'

156

'Unless they get wet.'

He looked at me, but said nothing.

'As I said, all I've got is rumour, but the way it comes across is that some people are being blackmailed on account of their involvement in smuggling – by the very people who are running the rackets.'

He looked startled, but still didn't speak.

'Neat, really. You tempt somebody into doing something illegal, and then you send in a different face who threatens to expose them unless. Not new, of course. But neat.'

'Good Lord, Angus, this is La Roque, not Sicily! Anyway, if it's *that* neat, what hope have we got of nailing anybody?'

'Well, hell, you could try! You know what the alternative is, don't you? Anyone who thinks this is a feudal island hasn't seen anything yet. Corlander's got the smell of the labour camps in his nostrils. Only it isn't he who's going to sweat this time. He's waited a few long years to reverse the tables, and now this is it.' I stopped, struck by the pattern of thought that had taken hold of me. Yes: perhaps I had come nearer to the truth than I had realized. 'It is a funny thing about suffering,' I said: 'This idea that it ennobles. In fact, it can be a kind of festering that goes on until it's destroyed everything, including itself. That can take an awful long time, Nick.'

He was still staring at me and I shrugged involuntarily, trying to shake off the sense of malice that had taken hold of me.

'Sorry,' I said. 'Whether the man's evil, or ill – or just plain greedy – I don't know. But as far as the island's concerned the result is going to be the same – and it won't be democracy.'

He came to then, pulling himself out of the mesmerism of all the new, unacceptable ideas I'd been planting in his mind.

'Well, O.K.,' he said, 'but it's Father I'm worried about at the moment.'

'So am I. But you can't separate him from the whole: not any more. He's stepped outside the family circle. Quite knowingly and deliberately. If you want to help him now, you'll have to join his army.'

Despite himself, a faint smile appeared at the corners of his mouth, and, seeing it, I felt irritated. Worried as he was, he still hadn't taken in the extent of the danger.

'I'm not joking,' I said. 'Whether you like it or not, your father's just made explicit something that's been with you for a long time. You're living in a divided island and heads are about to be counted on both sides.'

'You make it sound like civil war.' The smile still lingered, but now it was a trifle embarrassed. 'Somehow, I can't see people like old Pedro Calvaro wielding pitchforks in the Place de Justice.'

'I hope you're right. But just in case you're not, you'd better make up your mind where you're going to stand. You may not get time to check it with the book.'

Driving back to town, I felt sorry for Nicholas. I'd been less than friendly, but I was still irritated by his cautious lawman's refusal to face obvious inferences. Despite his regard for his father, he was still not prepared to take the issue beyond the narrow realm of the family. He was sitting on a barrel of dynamite, into which his father had just tossed a lighted match, and his chief concern appeared to be whether there was still honey for tea.

After I'd parked the car at the hotel, I went over to the Yacht Club bar for a drink. Young Luis Garcia greeted me with an enthusiasm reminiscent of his father, and then, without waiting for me to order, proceeded to pour me a large Scotch.

'Thanks, Luis. How's things?'

He grinned and shrugged, extending one hand palm upwards, making a little tilting movement with it from side to side.

'Like that, eh?'

'You found the meeting interesting, Señor?'

'Meeting?'

'Last night. At the Rochas farm. I was not able to come, but I hear, today, you are there.'

Which set me thinking: Felipe had been right; they still needed the combination of Le Marnet and de Courvel. Well, I'd failed with Alain: with Nicholas, too, as far as cold steel was concerned. So who was left? I weighed the question carefully in my mind, then, draining my glass, got up , nodding towards Luis, who was now down the other end of the counter.

'Fill her up again, Luis. Be back in a minute.'

I went out to the foyer, where, in a recess near the swing doors leading out into the square, there were a couple of telephone kiosks. The one I came to first was empty, but just as I put out my hand to open the door, a shadow loomed between me and the light coming in from outside. I glanced towards it and saw that the man coming in through the doors was Tony Fellowes. Behind him, another shadow bulked and before I could exchange greetings with Fellowes a familiar voice spoke my name.

I let the door of the kiosk fall to; no need, now, to ring. The man I'd been after stood there before me, his dark, handsome face alight with such geniality and good will that, had I not known him of old, I should have been flattered. As it was, I was content to be grateful for his fortuitous arrival.

'Hello, Max,' I said. 'What'll you have?'

'I was about to ring you,' I told him when we'd returned to the bar. 'I thought it was time we had a little talk.'

He looked surprised and suddenly wary. I ordered him a drink, grateful that Fellowes had tactfully discovered some friends of his on the other side of the room.

'You've heard, of course, what Guy Le Marnet is planning to do.'

He pursed his lips. 'I've heard a rumour, yes.'

'It's no rumour.'

He raised his eyebrows as acknowledgement, but said nothing.

'Whose side are you on, Max?'

'Side?' The old bantering smile returned. He took a swig from the glass which Luis had just placed in front of him. 'It's no affair of mine, old man.'

159

'I want to know,' I pressed, 'whether you're going to support him.'

'In what?' Irritation had provoked a response at last. 'I can't stop him going on in office, even if I wanted to, if that's what you mean.'

'You know damn well it isn't. He's going to collect a lot of flak. I want to know where you're going to be standing. You know why he's doing this.'

'That's where you're wrong, I don't. With all due respect, I think his brain's turned.'

I stared at him in silence and he began to bluster, but I wasn't listening. It was the reaction I had feared from him. The past flooded over me, momentarily paralysing all volition. We were boys again, he and I, and I was grappling with the dissatisfaction he had always aroused in me whenever a particular issue had to be faced. Everyone had an opinion about it, except Max; everyone was prepared to fight one way or the other, except Max; in short, everyone cared one way or the other, except Max. I had failed here, too. Max Cartier, like his Uncle Stéphan, would sit on the fence until he saw which way it was falling. Then, agile as a toad, he'd jump.

I felt him fidgeting beside me and pulled myself together. 'I'm sorry,' I said. 'I should have known better.'

Immediately he looked relieved. The smile returned. Complacency resettled itself on his features like a fly returning to a favourite piece of meat.

'Don't mention it, old boy. It's I who should be sorry.'

'Sure.'

But the irony was lost on him. He spread his hands in a gesture of mock appeal.

'I *mean* it! We're old friends, you and I. A lot of water, as you say. I'm sad you find me somehow lacking. Oh yes – ' he stressed as though I had contradicted him – 'you do. I can see it. The trouble is – don't mind my saying this – but you always did take things too much to heart. It was a bad thing about Maurice, but – believe me, he had no enemies but himself. He and Guy – ' he shrugged in weary resignation –

'It's no good, Angus. Change is inevitable. You know that. This island's moving out of the eighteenth century into the twentieth all at once. Such a big jump, it hurts. Bound to. But it's got to come. You of all people must see that. It just *has* to come. It will be to everyone's advantage in the end.'

It was the longest speech I could ever remember Max making. He was sweating a little, too. I stood up, draining my drink as I did so, and immediately he placed a restraining hand on my arm. 'Come and have some lunch with us,' he said.

It was ironic; I had been going to treat *him*.

'Er – no, thanks. I have to move on.'

'Then dinner this evening.' His face was alight now with an eagerness to make amends.

'I don't think so, thanks. I'll see you.'

'Of course.'

He turned away then, a hurt, rather puzzled look on his fleshy but still elegant face, and, as I left him there, staring at his glass, I knew that between Max and me a significant moment had come and gone; the links that had once held us, however loosely – the old sentimental links of our shared boyhood – were now finally broken.

There was a message for me at the hotel to ring Felipe at his office.

He answered the phone himself and told me he thought I might be interested to know that he had decided to stand for the St Michel Deputyship. There was to be a meeting in the village school that evening and he asked me if I would like to go. I said I would.

'You know, of course,' he said, 'about Monsieur Le Marnet.'

'Yes. I did my best to stop him, but he's on your side – theoretically, anyway.'

'He is a very brave man.'

'He's a fool. What's worse, he's a very old fool and therefore very vulnerable. I don't mind telling you, Felipe, I'm not a bit happy about him.'

161

'He will have every decent man at his side.'

'It's his back I'm worried about.'

'You needn't be. We shall watch out for him.'

'Frankly, I don't see how you can. But there it is, since I can't stop him, I suppose I'll just have to try and keep up with him. That's why I'll be at this meeting of yours. But look, Felipe – I've said this before and I'm saying it again – I'm not here to play politics. Don't bank on anything from me that doesn't connect directly in some way with my personal commitments. You follow?'

'I follow,' he said. But I knew he didn't.

It was nearly midday, but I felt a powerful disinclination to lunch at the hotel, so drove out to a secluded bay on the west coast of the island and parked in the shade of some palms on a stretch of sandy grass above the beach. After a while, I got out of the car and, turning my back on the sea, climbed up a rough track between olive groves until I found a shady place to sit. I had to think. Things were beginning to happen that I'd had no means of anticipating, and into which I was being drawn like it or not. Meanwhile, the problem that had brought me to the island remained unanswered. *Was* there any connection between Maurice's death and the upheavals threatening the island, as Guy and Felipe had suggested, or should I be looking for something else, something that Guy himself appeared to have sensed but which had eluded him? Something private and personal to Maurice and his family? How far was I justified in involving myself in island politics, however important to the people I was coming to have some concern for, if they brought me no nearer the truth about Maurice?

The trouble was that the more I thought about it the more confused I got. The whole thing seemed like a tight knot, to which no loose end was visible anywhere. Perhaps it was too soon. Perhaps the best thing was simply to play along, follow anything that presented itself and see where it led. Well, O.K., wasn't that exactly what I *had* been doing? And where was I? God knew. I didn't.

162

Except for one thing. An image – no more – but it kept returning persistently to my mind, blotting out rational thought: an image of St Michel, of the house as it was now, derelict and empty. *And Maurice's study*. The bare rooms upstairs: the clothes hanging in the cupboards. *And Maurice's study*. I knew I had to go back. It was absurd. There was nothing there but a deserted house, full of junk and memories. I had seen all that mattered on my first brief visit. My second – which I had made because of this same bedevilling urge – had only confirmed the fact. Why, then, this odd compulsion to go back yet again? Why the nagging feeling that here, and only here, the answers lay? Suddenly, and perversely, I was glad about Felipe's meeting. It meant there would be no time tonight. By tomorrow, who could say, something else might have cropped up.

A surge of hunger reminded me that round the next bend of the coast was Saracen's Point, and just up the hill from there was one of my father's old haunts, *La Bonne Fourchette*, where, at a table out on the patio above the bay, you could get one of the best meals on the island and excellent wine.

It was the best idea I'd had all morning. Long after I'd finished eating, I sat on, watching, between clusters of bougainvillaea, the energetic antics of post-prandial bathers on the beach below; gradually, all the tensions that had been devouring my nerves for days on their own account let up, and a pleasant sensation of well-being took their place.

When I got up, I realized that I had made a decision. Not a big one, it was true. But a decision.

THIRTEEN

Simone opened the door to me with what I was almost tempted to interpret as pleasure. It appeared to be endorsed, albeit cautiously, by one of the Siamese cats, who transferred himself from her ankles to mine, sniffing exploratively.

'If you were thinking of making a pot of tea,' I said.

She smiled. 'Without sugar. And just a dash of milk.'

I was surprised. It was an odd thing for her to have remembered.

'I'm sorry about the other night, Angus. You must have thought me unfriendly.'

I pretended I hadn't understood her. 'Um? I'm afraid I'm not with you.'

'On Sunday, I mean. Out at St Michel. I thought at first, you see, that you were one of the workmen, come back for some reason. I was worried in case something was wrong. Normally, I never see anyone there in the evenings. Not that I'm there very often (a touch of over-hastiness?), but I had this furniture to paint, you see. I think bathrooms and kitchens should be light, don't you agree? I mean, if we *should* decide to let it go.'

'Oh, yes, rather.' But I was intrigued. Why did this trivial incident bother her so? It required no explanation whatsoever, yet for some reason she was going out of her way to provide a quite elaborate excuse for herself. On an impulse, I put out a hand and touched hers. It was icy cold.

'You worry too much, Simone. Don't. Life's too short.'

Immediately, the colour rushed to her face and I felt her hand draw involuntarily away from mine. Nevertheless, there was a shine in the great grey-green eyes that knocked twenty years off her in a second. Looking at her, I wondered how I could possibly have missed the fact that, basically, she was still lovely in her own special, unconventional way.

When she returned with the tea, we sat opposite each other in the two big armchairs and chatted for a while about general things. I didn't mention the developments concerning Guy, nor my visit to Alain, and neither did she. I had decided not to drag her into any of these political problems from now on unless she herself seemed to want to talk about them. She'd got difficulties enough, I felt; her overriding need now was for security, not challenge. I wanted to protect her if I could. And this, I realized, was how I had always felt about Simone.

We were on our second cups before I decided to risk the question I wanted to ask. I put it circuitously.

'I was surprised your father moved out of the old house. Wouldn't it have been pleasanter for you both if *you'd* moved in there with him?'

Immediately, her expression froze and her gaze flickered away from mine. She passed her tongue across her lips before answering.

'We felt a smaller place would be more convenient. Also – Father knew I had made friends here. He didn't want to break that up.'

'The people downstairs, you mean.'

'Well – yes – and others, of course.'

There weren't any others. She knew it, and she knew I knew it.

'You came here straight after you and Cor – er, Ray – split up?'

'Yes. We'd had a suite at the Rivage d'Or. He and – and Phyllis – still have.'

I nodded.

'But why here?' I pressed. 'Wouldn't it have been better to have gone back *then*? To St Michel, I mean?'

'Oh, no.' But she said it too quickly. There was something here. I could feel it between us. But I also knew that I was torturing her. I couldn't go on. Abruptly, I changed the subject.

'Have you had a chance to speak to Louise Rochas yet? About Hélène?'

Her eyes came slowly back to mine and a faint smile touched her lips. Momentarily, she was safe again.

'Yes,' she said. 'She rang me. I said I would take Hélène up there tomorrow evening on the bus.'

'The bus?'

'I've had to take the car into the garage. There's something wrong with the ignition. Señorita Rochas said I could stay there while she talks to Hélène.'

'Well, we can do better than that. The Logan Elite Club Service is at your disposal. No gratuities to staff, please.'

'Oh, no, Angus! I can't ask you to do that.'

'You're not. Don't argue with the driver, please. It's bad for morale. What time?'

'We agreed six o'clock. Because that's the only convenient bus. But if you'd rather – '

'No. Six will be fine. I'll pick her up at ten to.'

I helped her wash up the tea things and then she insisted on taking me down to see what she called her 'garden', a singularly uninteresting stretch of sun-baked grass, bordered by two perfectly straight strips of soil in which a few flowers were making an heroic battle to survive. Here and there, I saw the neatly raked hollows of cat latrines, and on the edge of the 'lawn', contemplating the death struggles of what had once been a piece of rustic trellis-work, there squatted a hideous green plastic toad.

Simone gave a little giggle. 'Hélène's. She won him at a party. Isn't he awful? She calls him Mr Timms.'

'Hi, Mr Timms.'

She giggled again. 'Would you like to stay to supper?' she asked suddenly.

I smiled at her, touched somehow by the change of attitude.

'I would, awfully. But unfortunately I can't. I've promised to meet some people.' Oddly, I found myself reluctant to tell her that one of them was Louise Rochas's brother.

'Oh,' she said. 'Never mind.' But she had curled up

again, like a plant in a draught, and I cursed Felipe and his pals to hell.

'Look,' I said, 'can I come another night? I mean,' I pressed, 'would you like to suggest one?'

But it was no good. The moment had passed.

'I – er – I'll have to let you know,' she said.

She came out with me to the car, stopping at the gate to make a lot of fuss of the Siamese (whichever), who was giving a good imitation of a bassoon player while he washed his private parts.

I got into the car, conscious that everything had gone wrong. I'd intended to invite her to come and have dinner with me at the Royale one evening, but now I couldn't because it would look as if I were trying to make amends. God, how complicated we human beings had made communication between ourselves!

The little village school at St Michel was flaunting a large white banner on which, in bold, black-painted letters, was Felipe's name, followed by an appeal in Spanish for support for his nomination and an announcement of the evening's meeting. A line of cars stretched on both sides of the gates leading to the playground, and bicycles were propped against the walls; characteristically, none of them was padlocked.

I had to drive some way down the lane before I could find a space to park, and as I walked back towards the gates I saw a familiar tall figure walk his bike across the road and leave it leaning against several others. Like me, Enrique was cutting it a bit fine.

I caught him up at the gates and he gave me his gentle smile.

'Full house,' I commented.

He made a wry grimace. 'What is there to do on La Roque in the evenings?'

I grinned. He was probably right. Nevertheless, whatever their motives, the locals of St Michel had turned out in force. Inside, all the seats in the hall appeared to be

167

occupied and little groups of people were clustered along the back and part way down the sides. Enrique and I tucked into a space near the door and I glanced around. Felipe and a couple of men I didn't know were already sitting on the platform, and I could see the Orthoz family and old Pedro down in one of the front rows. There was no sign of Louise, but I'd hardly expected there would be. All told, there couldn't have been more than half a dozen females in sight, most of them tough, elderly peasant women, here, no doubt, as much from curiosity and a hope of a little harmless entertainment as anything else: which was probably true of most of the men, too.

I was probably the only person in the hall who was downright bored from start to finish, for two-thirds of the proceedings were conducted in Spanish. Although I usually find it more convenient not to admit it, I can, when the chips are down and providing there are no over-layers of dialect, make enough sense of the language to catch the general drift. Roquennais-French – worse, Roquennais-French-cum-Spanish – is another matter. And here, a large part of the dialogue, including almost all the questions from the floor, was rattled off in this bizarre fashion. The overall effect was rather like trying to follow a foreign film with no sub-titles, only to have it lurch into complete gibberish at all the most interesting points. Once or twice I caught an amused smile from Enrique, further provoked by the fact that on my other side an elderly farmer kept prodding me in the ribs with his elbow, inviting my support of his approval of something Felipe had said.

Given all these difficulties, I wasn't in much of a position to judge, at the end, how the meeting had gone, though the pervading climate seemed friendly, and Enrique looked quietly pleased. He led the way down the hall to where the others were, and I was introduced to Antonio Rodriguez and Jaime Castro, whose arrival at the farm the previous night had been somewhat lacking in the formalities.

Felipe and the two who had been on the platform with him were standing nearby, chatting to some of the audience.

Seeing me, Felipe brought the two men over and introduced us. André Laurent, shipper, Porte Hilaire: small, bald-headed and thin-faced, with a trim, dark moustache and keen eyes – the kind of face that gave nothing away, except perhaps the strong impression that there was, at least, something to be given. Marcel Despard, lawyer, in the office of the Advocate General: a bland, genial manner under a smooth crown of white hair. Reminded me of a bull-terrier of my acquaintance. Good-natured. Positively exuded friendliness. But nobody ever believed it: take him into any pub in town and he'd clear it in two seconds flat. Amusing. Despard gave me the same funny feeling.

'How did it go?' I asked Felipe.

He gave a wry smile. 'It's difficult to say at this stage. But I think we have a chance.'

Despard said we definitely did, but Laurent said nothing. He looked at me, I felt, as though he were trying to put a price on me.

'This parish carries *two* deputies, I understand,' I said. 'How's that likely to work out if you get in – helpful or otherwise?'

'Felix Charbonnier has criticized seigneurial rule for keeping us tied to the past, as he sees it. He's an uncertain quantity. But not a very strong one. I doubt if he'll give us much trouble.'

Laurent spoke for the first time. 'I don't think we should be complacent about Charbonnier. He can be manoeuvred.'

His voice was quiet, but there was something in it that ran along my nerves like ice-water. I looked at him thought-fully. This wasn't a man to waste his time with either irre-sponsible trouble-makers or foregone lost causes. If he felt that Felipe was worth backing, then it was odds on he was probably right. Despard, too. These men weren't fools. But neither were they necessarily whiter than white. They could be playing a little game of their own. I'd seen it too many times in too many parts of the world. You find a popular figure. Put him out front. Let him do all the work. And then, when the time's ripe, you clip him over the ear – or, better still, get somebody else to do it – and then step briskly in over his head.

I sighed. My trouble was, I'd lost all that nice, fresh innocent trust that makes the world go round. It was sad. But it was better than a kick in the teeth. *Someone* had to watch out for idealists: and Felipe – like Guy Le Marnet – was an idealist.

I'd intended waiting until I got Felipe alone before I told him of my visit to Alain, but José Orthoz barged in at that moment and asked me straight out if I'd done anything about it.

'Yes,' I said, 'but he won't play. I did warn you.'

Orthoz gave an angry snarl, but to my surprise turned on his heel without saying any more, presumably to go and take hell out of his brother. Felipe gave a resigned nod, but he looked less downcast than I'd feared, still upheld in all probability by the euphoria engendered by the meeting.

'We don't need him now,' said Laurent. 'Not now Le Marnet has made his move.'

Despard smiled as if he were humouring a child. 'Le Marnet is a very old man,' he said. 'One way or another, they will annihilate him.'

'My point precisely,' I said.

But Laurent remained unhumoured. 'I wouldn't be too sure of that,' he said.

And again there was something in his voice that made me look at him: something that made you feel that his opinion would not be too far from the truth.

Once or twice, I'd seen old Pedro looking at me, his weather-beaten face creasing into a gentle smile whenever I caught his eye. But when I finally looked round for him, hoping for a chat, I saw that he was moving away ahead of us with the Orthoz family, and some sixth sense told me that right now Pedro didn't want any more *tête-à-têtes*. It was surprising how many people gave me that feeling these days.

As we emerged into the open, Felipe turned to me, detaining me with a hand on my arm.

'You must come back and have supper with us. Louise insisted.'

Now he was *talking*! I tried, however, for courtesy's sake, to look hesitant. 'Well – '

'You must,' he insisted.

'Certainly,' said Enrique.

So I gave in. Gracefully. And before anyone could change his mind.

Louise, it seemed, *had* insisted. 'I told them,' she said, 'that if they came back without you, they would go hungry.'

'I assure you, no arm-twisting was required.'

'Good. It's the very least we can offer you by way of compensation.'

'Oh,' I said, dashed. 'I'd hoped you'd invited me for myself alone.'

She smiled. But she didn't rise to the bait.

Felipe led the way into a sitting-room with French windows opening out on to the front of the house, opposite the flower field in which I'd seen the man working while the little boy played nearby. Dusk, now, was giving way to night. Outside, it had still been possible to distinguish colours, deepened under the gathering shadows, but here in the lamplit room everything beyond the open windows was wrapped in dark, impenetrable blue. Out of this, as we sat, drinks in hand, a tall figure loomed. He wore faded blue linen trousers that looked as if they'd never seen an iron and a white cotton shirt, soil-stained, and open almost to the waist. Smells of earth and human effort were noticeable in almost equal proportions.

'Carlos!' protested Louise.

A self-deprecating smile came to the face of this giant of a man, and in response to Felipe's introductions he came over to me and gave me his hand.

'*Perdóneme, Señor.*'

I winced. His grip was precisely what I'd expected from someone with shoulders on him to fit a barn door.

'*No importa,*' I managed weakly.

171

'*Sírvase. Tengo mucho gusto de encontrarlo.*'

'*El gusto es mío.*'

'Well!' exclaimed Louise, laughing. 'You are a fraud, Angus! You *can* speak Spanish.' But she said it in English, into which, with relief, I followed her.

'The odd phrase only. And, believe me, it gets odder.'

'Please,' said the giant, abasing himself, 'I no know.'

He stood for a few more seconds, uncertain as a school-boy at a housemaster's tea-party, then bowed himself out of the room, still smiling repentantly in my direction.

'Well,' said Louise with a fond smile which I should dearly have loved to have thought was for me but which I knew was for her brother, 'that was Carlos. You must forgive him. He's a little shy. It's absurd at his age, but we shall never change him.'

'No,' I said, remembering the grip on my hand, 'I rather doubt if you will. Except,' I added, 'one day, something looking not much bigger or tougher than a feather duster will come along, and he'll be putty in her hands.'

This time, she smiled for *me*. 'I hope so,' she said.

FOURTEEN

That night I dreamed I was a boy again, back at St Michel, but there seemed to be something wrong with my eyesight, because I couldn't see anything clearly. I seemed to be straining to focus on things through some kind of film stretched across my eyes. Added to which there was a sense of some undefined horror lurking somewhere just out of sight. The feeling was instinctive, but the emotional reaction was palpable. Maurice was locked in his study, and though I knocked repeatedly there was no reply. Scared, I took the stairs two at a time up to the old 'Playroom', but Alain wouldn't put his book down, and Simone just sat nursing a great, blank-eyed doll and smiling. Eventually, the doll turned into a huge, obscenely grinning green plastic toad, but still she went on nursing it and smiling, and in the end it was the smiling that did for me. Feeling that all hell was behind me, I dashed out into the garden, calling out for Calvaro.

I woke wet through and with my head feeling as though it had been test-run to destruction. I threw the bedclothes back and gingerly heaved myself out on to the edge of the bed, where I sat waiting for my nerve endings to stop their May-Day semaphores and my heart and blood pressure to unlink themselves from the main arteries of the cosmos. All these effects were physiological, wholly disproportionate to the imagined events that had triggered them off, but a powerful argument still that Mind governs Body. Eventually, I put out a shaking hand to the bedside light, finding it only after I'd sent my travelling clock crashing to the floor. A splash in cold water seemed a good idea, and afterwards I sat down again on the edge of the bed and lit a cigarette.

I wondered about the dream, particularly as the preceding evening had been singularly pleasant. By the time I'd left the Rochas farm around midnight, I'd felt as if I'd known the family all my life, and was dangerously near to pledging them far more than mere token support in their fight against the new order. As it was, I'd agreed to turn up at a special protest meeting about Point Rouge in a couple of days' time. The meeting was planned to give explicit definition to Guy's stand on the Presidency and was therefore, I agreed, urgently necessary. It was also potentially very dangerous, as I'd tried to explain to Felipe.

'If you win the kind of approval you're looking for, you do know what it could mean, don't you? Not just for you, or even Guy – God help him – but for the island. There'd be no going back. Are you ready for this if it comes? Really ready, I mean. With time, effort, money – which means the right kind of *friends* as much as the right number of red corpuscles.'

He hadn't even blinked once. 'Yes,' he said. 'We're ready.'

Louise had come out with me to the car and we'd wandered down to the gate bordering the carnation field. In the cool night air, the scent was a clinging pall of sweetness. 'Don't worry too much about Monsieur Le Marnet,' she said. 'He has to do what he's doing. The island is his life. Whatever happens – and we can only pray it won't be bad – he would never know peace unless he knew he'd done everything in his power towards what he thought was best for the people here.'

I looked at her. In the moonlight, her dark hair and eyes shone as though lit from inside. It seemed suddenly absurd to be standing there talking politics. But with her brothers all lined up in a row behind us like full-backs on a football field I felt inhibited.

So be it. But there was something else too. I couldn't have defined it, but I'd found myself thinking of Simone.

As a result of my disturbed night, I overslept. Accordingly, I skipped breakfast and at ten o'clock, still feeling sluggish and disinclined to face the world, I rang down for coffee and brioches to be sent up to me. I was on my final cup when the telephone rang; it was almost eleven.

As soon as I heard the voice the other end, my stomach contracted.

'What is it, Pierre?'

'M'sieu, you told me to ring if – '

'Yes. What's happened? Is Monsieur – '

'He is all right, M'sieu, but something bad has happened on the plantation. A man has been stabbed.'

'Tell Monsieur le Marnet I'll be with him in ten minutes. And Pierre – '

'M'sieu?'

'Don't let him out of your sight.'

Pierre met me in the drive at Mont Vert; his face was whiter than ever and he was breathing fast. I looked at him, concerned; he was Guy's first line of defence: if anything happened to Pierre. . . .

There'd been trouble, he told me, between two of the plantation workers. One had accused the other of stealing some money. There had been a fight, in which several others had joined. Eventually, someone had pulled a knife and now one of them was in hospital.

'Is it serious?'

'We are not sure, Monsieur. The hospital says little. But Monsieur Le Marnet is very worried.'

He led the way to the drawing-room, where Guy was standing at the window, looking out into the garden. He must have seen us in the drive, for he lost no time in preamble. Turning, he said:

'You've heard?'

'Yes. What exactly happened?'

He shook his head, bewildered disbelief on his face. 'Something that has never happened before at Mont Vert in all my experience.'

'Yes?'

'Fighting. Serious fighting. A young fellow – Santana, Angelo Santana – was stabbed. They say he'll be all right, but you can't be sure, can you? And how could such a thing

175

have come about?' He looked at me, anguished, appealing for enlightenment, but I had none to offer. I asked Pierre to produce some brandy, and I made Guy sit down and pulled up a chair opposite him.

'These two men – Santana and – '

'Montez – Raymondo Montez.'

'What was the argument about?'

'Montez said Santana had stolen the lottery money – '

'Lottery money?'

'Yes, we have one every month now. The men save something from their pay packets and hand it over to Molina, the foreman. Once a month he puts it all into the lottery for them. It gives them more chances.'

'Yes, I see. And this Santana – was he *likely* to do such a thing?'

Guy shook his head again. 'If I'd had to pick out the *least* likely – apart from Molina himself – I'd probably have chosen young Angelo. He's hot-blooded – he might even have had the knife, as Montez swears he did – but stealing . . . no, I can't believe it.'

'So why did Montez think so? What's he like, this Montez?'

'Well, there's been a bit of feeling between them for some time. About a girl. She'd been going with young Angelo for quite a while. Then suddenly switched to Raymondo. You know how these things are. He's older than Angelo; knows how to make a girl feel important. She was flattered, I expect, because Montez, by all accounts had been playing the field a bit. Anyway, young Angelo didn't like it. There'd been a few arguments, but nobody had taken it seriously.' He grimaced. 'Until today.'

'And today Montez says Angelo pinched the kitty. Why?'

'Because it was found in Angelo's coat pocket in the Shack. Where they hang their clothes. All rolled up in an elastic band the way Molina keeps it.'

'All still intact?'

'Yes. Apparently, Molina keeps it at home until all the

176

money's in. Then he brings it in with him to work and rides into town in his lunch-hour and places it in the lottery.'

'Where does he keep it till then? While he's working.'

'In the Shack. In his coat pocket. Everybody's always known it. That's the point, you see. We've never had anything of this kind before. There's never been the slightest question of dishonesty. Nor fighting. Nothing serious, that is. Occasionally, you get a couple of youngsters losing their tempers, but nothing like this. Never. Never.' Again he shook his head, his face bemused and drawn. It was clear that this had upset him more than any of his political problems.

'I think I'd better go and see this young Santana. Is he allowed visitors?'

'Would you, Angus? I'd be so grateful – Yes, I believe they are letting his mother see him, anyway. Perhaps, if you said you had come on my behalf – '

I nodded. Pierre came in with the brandy then, but after he had given Guy a glass and had pulled a second towards him I stopped him.

'Not for me. I'm going now. But I'll be back.' I got up, turning towards Guy, who was sipping his brandy, lost in his worries.

'Have the police been brought into this?'

'I'm not sure. Montez was making threats. But Blanchard hasn't rung me yet. So perhaps they were just that – threats. I hope so for Angelo's sake.'

'I'll check back as soon as I can,' I said. 'Meanwhile, don't worry too much, sir.'

He did his best to smile, and I followed Pierre out into the hall. Before going out on to the steps, I stopped and looked at him.

'Well, Pierre, you know these people. What do *you* think?'

'Angelo Santana never took that money, Monsieur. Nobody would even have thought such a thing – before.'

'Before?'

He gave a bewildered grimace and shook his head.

'Not even Montez?'

177

'Eeh! – ' it was a disparaging sound – 'Montez is just a great – what do you say? – a great – ' He blew out his cheeks and hunched his shoulders, looking comical for a second.

'Ball of wind.'

'So! Montez is nothing. Nobody takes any notice of him.'

'Except the ladies, by all accounts.'

He grimaced. 'Ah, well . . . But *knives*. . . . ' More head-shaking. It was the best he and Guy together seemed able to offer. As elucidation, it wasn't much.

'Well, *somebody* pulled one. And Montez says it was Santana. So Montez is either mistaken, or lying, or – what?'

He didn't answer, and I left him there, standing looking after me as I went down to the car. By the time I'd started up, however, he had gone; I had no need to wonder where.

All the same, as I drove back to town I felt uneasy; two old men and an equally old woman made up a pretty vulnerable ménage in present circumstances. Perhaps it *would* be a good idea to try and persuade Guy to move into the Villa Valeuse for a while. Splendid. But academic. He'd never agree.

At the hospital, they told me that Santana's mother was with him, but I could join them for just five minutes. As soon as I saw him, I realized that Guy had been right. Angelo Santana had a swarthy, boyish face under a thick mass of untidy, black hair, and right now his eyes were huge with the shocked appeal of a hurt puppy's. As he lay sprawling under the white sheets, swathed in bandages, he looked about as capable of treachery as Billy Budd or the Queen of the Fairies. Immediately I had sat down in the chair which his mother pushed forward for me beside the bed and began to explain the reasons for my visit, a look of such anguish spread itself over his face that the emotional possibilities filled me with foreboding. My alarm increased when he began to vibrate the air between us with a torrent of excited Roquennais. Apart from the fact that I couldn't

178

understand a word, I was concerned about what all the explosions would do to his constitution. To my relief, his mother – a tiny, wiry soul with the face of a Spanish gypsy and, I deduced, the temper to match – turned on him with a stream of rebuke that stopped him in mid-sentence as effectively as if she had taken an axe to him. Most of it was in pure Spanish, but at the end, for my benefit, I suspected, she suddenly changed to French: *'Imbecile! Maladroit! Speak to Monsieur properly, or else keep your big mouth for snoring, like the pig he must think you are! Fee!'* At this final ejaculation she turned in my direction, her leathery brown hands spread out in a gesture of hopeless resignation, her black eyes fierce with apology. I tried to make some reassuring response, but before her quailing energy I felt almost as weak as her silly son, who now turned his dog-like eyes back to me and shrugged helplessly. Whereupon he winced with pain and then grinned in wry contrition.

'It hurts?' I asked.

He gave a self-deprecating grimace and spoke in halting French: 'A little. But it is nothing.'

'Montez says you pulled the knife first. Is that true?'

The anguish returned to his face. 'No! No, M'sieu! It is not true! I swear it! Someone took it.' He paused. 'They must have,' he added lamely.

'Montez? Did Montez take it from your belt during the fight? *Was* it your knife?'

He nodded. 'But I don't know whether it was Raymondo. There was much – many people were joining in. I couldn't tell, M'sieu.'

I was silent for a moment, looking at him. Call it instinct if you like, but I hadn't the slightest doubt that he was telling me the truth. There'd been a fight and someone had yanked the knife from his belt, but who?

'You and Montez were bad friends,' I said. *'Could* he have done it? Pulled a knife on you?'

He tried to shrug again, looking more unhappy than ever. 'I don't know, M'sieu.'

'Does he carry a knife himself?'

'Sí. We all – for cutting – ' He trailed off helplessly.

I got up, but before I turned to go I looked down at him. 'Did you take the money?' I asked.

For a moment, I thought he was going to try to leap out of bed. But pain overcame him and he sank back, shaking his head in rage and frustration. 'No,' he muttered. 'No. I swear it!'

In her chair, his little old mother was shaking her head, too, pride and resentment in her fierce gypsy eyes.

'O.K. O.K.' I said, 'that's what Monsieur Guy believes. But I had to ask.'

On the way out, I asked the sister-in-charge about Santana. He had lost a lot of blood, she told me, but he would be all right.

'No danger,' I said.

'No,' she said, an amused smile in her eyes. 'No danger.'

But there *was*. Only it wasn't the kind of danger we were talking about. Something much more subtle had been effected at Mont Vert. There had never been any intention to kill, or even gravely injure, Santana. The knife had been pulled on *Guy*. The memory of the look on his face: the worry, bewilderment, shocked disbelief, uncertainty, all confirmed it. He had never had anything like this before. Between the plantation workers at Mont Vert there had never been anything but friendliness, tolerance and goodwill. Now, suddenly, there was suspicion and distrust. Someone, somewhere, hadn't wasted any time. But it was only the beginning.

I was positive of it when I saw Montez. At my suggestion, Guy sent a message out to the man to come to the house. The formality of it was feudal and ponderous, but I felt it wouldn't do any harm to let Montez see that Guy Le Marnet, far from being an old man alone, was still a force to be reckoned with; moreover, he had a hired gun or two of his own.

I got the impression the point was taken, although Montez wasn't giving anything away. He ponced into the room with all the aggressive charm of a flamenco dancer,

180

and after flashing a wary glance in my direction pulled up in front of Guy with a slight bow and a brilliant smile. Considering he'd put the whole place in an uproar and one man in hospital, he certainly had style.

On the basis of the possibility that shock tactics might loosen Montez's tongue, I had asked Guy not to explain my presence. If the chap thought I was some kind of official investigator brought in by Guy, perhaps he'd scare and then make mistakes in an effort to cover his tracks.

Or perhaps he wouldn't. With eyebrows raised to about one sixteenth of an inch short of insolence he spun me a yarn about how he'd gone back to the Shack during the morning to answer a call of nature and seen Santana hanging around there alone, and how later, when Molina discovered his loss, he, Montez, saw Santana trying to slip out through the door, looking guilty.

'What do you call looking guilty?' I asked him in French.

'He kept looking back over his shoulder, Señor. He seemed – ' He shrugged, pulling the corners of his mouth down in what was apparently meant to be an imitation of a man shrinking in the face of imminent exposure.

'What did you do then?'

'I called him back.'

'Just *called*? Or did you put a hand on him . . . stop him by force?'

'Not at first. But he took no notice, so I just touched his arm, no more.'

'And accused him of having the money?'

'No. I asked him why he was in such a hurry to get away when the rest of us were worried about the money.'

'Was it then that you – and I understand it *was* you – suggested that everyone should empty their pockets?'

'Sí, Señor. It was the obvious thing to do.'

'Did Santana do it willingly?'

'Well, he – ' For the first time he looked uncertain.

'*Did* he? Or did you have to force him?'

'He grumbled . . . tried to make excuses . . . said he was in a hurry.'

181

'But he emptied his pockets just the same, yes? Of his own accord.'

More hesitation.

'I don't hear you, Montez. Are you saying yes or no?'

A scowl took over from the oily unctuousness, and he spoke a shade more loudly. 'He did, Señor. But there the money was! There it was all the time! He robbed us. His own workmates! He was a thief and a liar!'

'Which you proceeded to tell him.'

'Then he pulled his knife on me. I tried to get it from him and it dropped on the floor. Otherwise, Señor, I would have been dead by now!'

I let this piece of dramatic speculation pass.

'You said you'd found Santana alone in the Shack during the morning.'

'Sí.'

'And *you* were there to use the toilets.'

'Sí. They are at the back.'

'So what would be odd about Santana doing the same thing? Everybody who used the toilets would have the same opportunity to go to Molina's pocket. Yourself included.'

A haughty sneer replaced the remains of the scowl on his face. 'But the money was found in *Santana*'s pocket, Señor.'

'Yes. I've been thinking about that. Can you prove you didn't put it there? Was there anyone else in the Shack when the two of you met?'

His jaw shot out and his whole body seemed to vibrate with suppressed fury. I sensed Guy's dismay, but it was the only way I could make this man understand that I suspected him and that if anything else happened at Mont Vert I'd be looking in his direction.

'Look, Montez, I know what the score is between you two. I know about Santana's girl and the bad blood between you. You had as much reason to have it in for him as he for you.'

He made a muted sound of derision, looking at me obliquely down his long nose. 'Why should I care about

Santana? Anita prefers *me*. I think *nothing* about Santana! Pooh!' And he lifted his head and made a blowing noise.

There seemed no point in prolonging the interview. If there was any way of proving that Angelo had been framed, and that someone else had drawn the knife, I would have to look for it somewhere else: for what good it would do me, which, I suspected, knowing these people, wouldn't be much. For the moment, I could only hope that I'd made enough waves to warn off those whom I was certain were behind Montez's accusation against Santana and the subsequent fracas. The worry that still nagged me was as to how much this business would affect the old harmony at Mont Vert, and Guy himself to whom each worker was an individual whom he cared about and whose respect and loyalty he had taken for granted for as long as he could remember.

Before leaving, I made one more effort to try and persuade Guy to give up his plans to stay on in office. I might have saved myself the trouble.

'Oh, really, Angus!' He smiled now with chiding tolerance. 'I can't believe that all this is part of some sort of terrorist campaign. No. The suggestion is ludicrous.'

'You said yourself that strong-arm methods had been used against others.'

'Well, yes, but this is so – so *crude* – so fantastic.'

'Possibly. But the psychology behind it is far from crude. It's very clever indeed.'

He looked at me questioningly.

'Whoever planned this – oh, yes, I'm certain it *was* planned, sir – knows you well enough to realize that attacks on you personally would be as futile as they would be dangerous, to *him*. Your reaction to that kind of attack would be to soldier on, unless I'm very much mistaken, which, in time, would bring the whole island to your side to a man. *This* way – getting at you through the people who serve you – now, that's pretty subtle. Apart from the disruption it causes, everyone knows the concern you have for your people here. Oh yes, this is a subtle move all right.'

The doubt was still on his face, but he didn't answer, and I pressed the point home.

'You do realize, sir, don't you, that if I'm right – and I'd lay my life on it – there's going to be more, and other people as well as yourself are going to suffer.'

It was a long time before he spoke, but when he did all the incredulity and questioning had gone from his face; in their place was a mixture of sadness and weariness greater than any I had ever seen on any living human face before.

'If you *are* right, Angus – which is worse, to lose the battle or the war?'

I could have told him. But I didn't.

FIFTEEN

I spent the rest of the day trying to get a lead on what and who were behind the business at Mont Vert, but by the time I was due to go and collect Hélène I'd discovered just one thing: your average Roquennais was as clam-mouthed as he'd ever been. Not even appeals on behalf of Guy, revered by most of his workers and respected by all, got me anywhere, though I walked round the plantations all day, speaking to each man individually in the hope of establishing confidence. In the end, I collected as many versions of the affair as there were participants, roughly, the variations being dependent upon whose side the informant happened to be, or possibly upon his own complicity in the culmination.

Reacting simply to instinct – there being a singular absence of any basis for rational decision – I came away feeling even more convinced than ever that Santana was innocent of all but a few defensive haymakers, and that I'd been lied to more times in one afternoon than there are fleas on a hedgehog: furthermore, that at least some of the lies were on Santana's behalf. More than one man, for instance, swore blind that Angelo had never gone near the Shack all morning, though on being checked back upon later Angelo freely admitted to having visited the toilet and seeing Montez there. It was the same with the knife: against Angelo's own affirmation, several of his pals swore blind that he never carried a knife, had never possessed one and wouldn't dream of such a thing. Only a totally innocent man could have such crass friends, and, having them, would fail to plug the holes they left for him to fall through. For his part, Angelo seemed not only totally unaware of the implications but actually rather touched by his pals' combined show of loyalty.

'They are not telling you the truth, M'sieu,' he explained unnecessarily. 'But – ' with a smile of tolerant affection – 'they mean well.'

'The knife *was* yours?'

'Oh, *yes*, M'sieu! Certainly!' He said it as though any other answer would have been an indefensible slur upon his manhood. He looked weary, however, and I noticed that the nurses were watchful, so I left before anyone decided to throw me out.

When I arrived at St George's that evening, Hélène was waiting for me in the front garden. She had on a crisp blue and white cotton dress, which looked as if it might be her best. Beside her on the grass, where she was playing with one of the Heavenly Twins, was a leather music-case, one of those traditional affairs that fasten by slipping a metal bar over the handles. It looked very large and professional for a small girl who didn't play a note of music, and I wondered whether Simone had gone up to St Michel and unearthed it from somewhere specially for the occasion.

As I got out of the car, Simone herself came out on to the front doorstep. She gave a little wave and started to come down the path.

'We're ready.'

'So I see.' I grinned at Hélène, who promptly buried her head in the cat's neck.

Simone's smile was apologetic, but in the glance she threw towards Hélène I fancied I saw something else. It was gone before I could identify it, but for a mere flash of a second I felt I saw some sort of desperate harassment: or was it merely irritation? Whatever it was, there was no trace in her voice, when she spoke, of anything but motherly defensiveness.

'She's shy. She'll be all right in a moment.'

'I know. Me, too.'

The child looked at me then. A long look . . . appraising . . . checking to see whether I was making fun of her. Deciding – what? No smile, but – dared I hope? – a suggestion of empathy?

'Coming?' I asked.

She placed the cat gently down on the grass, and then picked up the case and came towards us, jumping the intervening strip of anaemic flower border like a young gazelle. As she landed, she looked at me again, but still didn't speak, and then moved away from us towards the car.

I watched her for a moment, then turned towards Simone.

'O.K.?'

She hesitated. 'Is it all right?' she asked. 'I mean, Señorita Rochas said I might come with her this first time, just to help her get settled. After that – '

'Well, of course,' I said. 'I'd taken it for granted.'

'Oh. Oh, well – thank you – we'd better go, then, hadn't we?'

'Yes.'

There wasn't much conversation on the short journey up to the farm. For my part, I was wondering what had gone to produce in Simone the mammoth, almost grotesque, inferiority complex which now seemed to be afflicting her personality like a disease. How much was due to her disastrous marriage? To the 'humiliation' Guy had mentioned, which she had suffered at Ray Corlander's hands. Simone had been a quiet, sweet, generous-natured girl . . . no extrovert, but with her own innate confidence and, at times, a bubbling sense of fun. Drawing her out had never been easy: she had always inhabited her own private world. But in the right circumstances she would flare suddenly with unexpected light and life.

There was a sleek white Mercedes in the Rochas drive when we arrived.

'Now, there's a car,' I murmured.

Simone didn't answer, which I attributed to typical female philistinism, but I noticed her glance at the car more than once as we waited for the door to be opened. When it did, it revealed both Felipe and Louise the other side, and, with them, someone who was apparently just

187

departing. My first reaction was that I'd seen the chap
before somewhere; my second, an awareness that Simone
was as filled with apprehension as she had been when
she'd first clapped eyes on *me* a week ago at St Michel.
Now what? I wondered.

The stranger seemed taken aback, too, but he recovered
quickly and a broad smile came to his face. It was then
that I remembered him. Charles Cotarde, brother of
Raoul, of St Damien. I don't think he'd noticed me,
though; he was too taken up with Simone.

'What a pleasant surprise!' he said. 'How *are* you,
Simone?'

She smiled back at him and murmured some reply, but
her unease was palpable. Whether knowingly or otherwise, it was Louise who came to the rescue.

'This really *is* a reunion!' she said. 'Let's go back in and
do it properly.' And she ushered us back through the
house and into the big room overlooking the flower fields.
By this time, Charles had remembered me and we were
both wrestling with the mental shock that the lag of time
always produces on these occasions.

Felipe managed to find a bottle of excellent Graves and
we got down to the serious business of reminiscence with
reinforced fervour. Charles, too, it seemed, had been
away from the island a lot since the war. He and Raoul
had gone to France soon after the outbreak and joined the
French Army. In '46, they had returned home, but Charles
couldn't settle and had returned to Europe, learned to fly
and taken a job with an airline, which, somewhat disillu-
sioned, he still held. His visits home were purely vaca-
tionary. And now – he shrugged – there didn't seem much
point.

'No one left.' I knew the feeling.

He nodded. 'When Raoul died, I sold the house. I think
it was probably a mistake, but at the time I just wanted to
make a fresh start.'

'Yes.' I understood that, too. 'When did Raoul die?' I
tried not to show it, but I was shocked. Both the brothers

had been about my own age. No time to go putting up the shutters.

' '49. He'd collected a few bad ones in the Ardennes. They invalided him home for a spell. He got back in time for the French withdrawal and was one of the lucky ones – like me – at Dunkirk. But it had done for him. Chasing Rommel in the desert didn't help either.' He stopped there and I didn't pursue the subject. It wasn't the time for old soldiers' tales.

He turned to Simone, his face alight with pleasure at seeing her again. 'Raoul often mentioned you in his let-ters. I even began to hope that you and he – ' he broke off with a wry grin. 'Ah, well – there we are, that's life, as they say.'

She nodded and then bent her head, making a motion as though to brush something off her skirt. But not before I had seen the glint of tears in her eyes. I was at first astonished and then dismayed. Possibly Louise had noticed, too, for she suddenly got up and said that women must work while men talked and if Madame Corlander would like to go with her they'd get started.

After they'd gone, I learned the reason for Charles's visit. From Bob Dart, a fellow-member of the local flying club, he had heard about the new political divisions on the island and had come to offer Felipe his support.

'Not that I can do a hell of a lot,' he said, 'but the changes on this island are all happening too damn fast and I'm not sure they're the right ones. Being away from the place so much, you notice it all the more.'

I nodded. I knew what he meant. But I didn't want to talk about politics then; I wanted to ask him what he'd meant about his brother and Simone. I wanted to know what had caused that sudden glint of tears. But now wasn't the time. Even if I could have headed Felipe off from the burning question of Guy and the Point Rouge issue, I could hardly discuss Simone's personal affairs in a threesome, and not only would Cotarde not have answered, he'd take damn good care to see me first in future. So I listened to Felipe's plans for the meeting next day in the Town Square and told them about the Mont Vert affair.

'You think it was a set-up?' queried Cotarde.

'Don't *you*? Over sixty years his memories go back of the running of that estate. Nothing like it ever happened before, either in his or his father's time. Now, suddenly. Just after he decides to do something that could block the Assembly on a vital issue. What do *you* think?'

Cotarde's expression was wry, but he still looked doubtful.

'Angus is right,' said Felipe. 'It's obvious. You'll never prove it, though,' he added, turning to me.

'I know. I'm just hoping that if I crash around enough, I'll destroy all the cover – for the next time.'

They both looked at me. But neither spoke. Then Cotarde said how sorry he'd been to hear about Maurice, and we skirted round that for a spell. This led, fairly naturally, to a steady flow of youthful memorabilia, and we were still at it when the women returned.

When the door opened, it was Hélène who came in first. Her face was slightly flushed and her eyes still held that curious gleam of vitality that I'd first seen at the old piano at St George's. Behind her, Simone looked like a child that's just seen Santa Claus. Quite suddenly, I felt an almost irresistible urge to grab her and hold her as tight as I could without actually breaking her into little pieces. It was a moment I was to remember for the rest of my life. Other things were to happen that were much, much more significant than this, things that would advance my knowledge of Simone Corlander far beyond this tremulous, piercing moment of insight. But it was then that I truly loved her – and at the same time knew that, by the world's poor definition, I would *never* love her. Moments like this come without warning, and they pass so quickly that, seconds later, it is as though they had never been. All the same, I felt oddly shattered as I turned to look at Louise.

'How did it go?'

'Oh, I think we're going to get along very nicely.' But it

was in the smile she gave me that I read her full, professional report. The interview had been a success. Hélène
had impressed her and I'd been right. The lessons were on.

I turned to Simone again. 'You're happy about it?'

'Oh, yes,' she said. 'Señorita Rochas actually got her to
play a *tune*! In *one* visit! I couldn't believe it.'

I could.

'It was only to let her see what could be done,' said
Louise. 'She won't be playing any more tunes for a while.
I've explained to her that first she's got to learn where all
the nuts and bolts fit in.'

'That's where *I* came unstuck at her age,' chuckled
Cotarde.

Me too. But then, I hadn't had Louise Rochas to teach
me.

On the way out, I made the casual suggestion to Cotarde
that if he hadn't anything better to do we might join up
later in town for a drink.

'Splendid,' he said. 'Why not come up to the Club? I
usually put up there nowadays. There's quite a decent bar.
Members only, of course, but guests allowed.'

I nodded. I knew the Flying Club bar: wooden chairs
with tattered old cushions in them round tile-topped
tables; the air thick with smoke and tall stories, including
some that would even shock a Merchant Navy stoker. In
the main, a masculine world, except for a few hardy wives
and resolute girl-friends. A world far from Corlander's
terra-cotta statues and the gold-lamé milieu of Imogen
Cartier: which was how I wanted it.

Back at St George's, Simone invited me in for some
coffee and I followed her up to her chaotic little mess-deck
of a kitchen and put out the cups and saucers while she
busied herself with the percolator. Almost immediately,
we heard the sound of the piano.

'That's a good sign, anyway,' I said.

Simone's smile was anxious. 'You won't be disappointed
in us if it doesn't last, will you?'

'The moment Louise Rochas reports that a mandatory

resentment towards scales has turned into something more fundamental, we call the whole thing off. Meanwhile, let's do what *she's* doing – play it by ear.'

In the old days, we would have groaned in unison at the pun, but Simone now seemed to dwell in a world in which all such mundane ineptitudes that we allow to pass as humour had no part. Like 'Alice', she had had to shrink so much to enter that world that there seemed to be almost nothing left of her. For the umpteenth time I wondered what had made her choose Corlander for a husband, what on earth she'd seen in him.

Almost as if she'd been following my train of thought, she said:

'How odd it is how people always expect logical conclusions.'

'Meaning?'

'Charles. Just because Raoul and I went out together a few times, he's got us in front of the altar. It could only happen on La Roque. It would seem ludicrous in *your* world.'

I forebore to tell her that, in my world, if a couple were seen more than once together, opinion on the whole would skip the altar in favour of a more comfortable place.

We carried our coffee into the sitting-room where, rather to my surprise, she pursued the subject of her own accord.

'Poor Raoul! He was in a terrible state when he came back. I felt so sorry for him.'

So that's what it had been. Pity. Well, it wasn't enough, true, for a lasting relationship – but it *did* explain the tears. All the same, I couldn't help feeling that Raoul, with all the unmentionable horrors of the walking wounded, plus the nightmares, would have been a far cosier stable companion than the nauseating Ray. Unfortunately, it could no longer be proved.

'Simone,' I said, 'I want to ask you a favour.' Here goes, I thought. This was going to be tricky.

She looked startled. 'But of course.'

'It's about St Michel. I'd like to go inside the house. Alone. For old time's sake. You understand? Would you let me borrow a key?' Hell, I couldn't keep *on* taking headers through pantry windows!

As I'd feared, she looked dismayed. And, I thought, a little fearful. But of what? The same thing that had caused her guilt-ridden anxiety on the coach-house steps? Whatever that was.

'Call it nostalgia,' I persisted. 'But I have this urge to see the old place again and to try to imagine it as it used to be. A sort of farewell odyssey, if you like.'

She was struggling with herself, I could see that. The colour had flared into her face when I had first put the question. Now, it had died away, but her eyes were still wide and full of a searching apprehension.

'Of course, if you'd rather not,' I said. If it had to be the pantry, so be it.

'Oh, no – ' She was pulling herself together as if her life depended on it. 'Of course you can have a key. I've got a spare upstairs. I'll get it.' She put her cup down on the small table between us, and before I could say another word got up and went out.

She seemed to be rather a long time away, so I took my coffee into the next room, where Hélène was still strumming on the piano. She paused only briefly as I entered, then went back to the attack. As usual, the sound was haphazard, formless, yet strangely assured and controlled.

I drew up a chair beside her. Then I began to tap out on the keys nearest to me the only primitive tune I could remember how to play: 'Yankee Doodle' – or thereabouts. She stopped playing and watched my fingers. Then, after about the fourth recital, she began to tap on the keys down her end. It wasn't perfect, but I helped her and we got it right. She stopped then, and looked into my face.

'You're going to have to work awfully hard,' I told her. 'Can you stick it out?'

She didn't speak, but after a moment, almost imperceptibly, she nodded. Twice.

'Good,' I said. 'Because I'm going to be rooting for you. All the way. O.K.?'

At that moment, Simone came in, holding a large key tied with a loop of string.

Hélène looked at her, and then back again at me.

'Are you going to marry my mother?' she asked.

SIXTEEN

It was one of those moments that sorts the men from the boys, and it left me paralytic in the nursery. I felt sorry for Simone, too. In the event, she coped remarkably well. After the initial moment of shock, during which her face went first white and then a lovely shade of rose, she merely bestowed on Hélène a small disparaging shake of the head, as though all the silly child had done was get the day of the week wrong, and on me a rueful smile. 'Poor Angus,' she said, 'you go to all this trouble and this is what you get!' And then she laughed. It was the first time I had heard her do so since I had arrived on the island. It was still not quite the old Simone but it was a start. Hélène considered her for a moment in grave silence; then, even more astonishingly, a smile came into her eyes and moved gradually down to the corners of her mouth. A moment later, a strange little sound, half gasp, half an impeded sigh, was heard. Hélène was laughing.

The only thing left to do seemed to be to join in.

To my intense relief, the Flying Club bar was almost deserted when I arrived there some twenty minutes later. Apart from the plump and elderly steward – in his shrunken striped pullover with an off-white shirt and no tie – there were only three people in the room: Cotarde, propping up the counter with a pint in front of him, and two chaps in earnest conversation at a table down the far end of the room. Every so often, the vibrations of a plane landing or taking off caused the little building to shake as if under subterranean attack. My instinctive reactions made Cotarde smile. 'Interested in going up?' he asked.

'No, thanks.' The firmness of my tone made him grin even more broadly and I grimaced shamefacedly. 'I know, I know. Scared as a flea on a vampire. But that's my nature, I'm afraid. Dedicated to deeds of derring-don't. No goose need fear what I might say to it.'

'Aren't you keeping rather odd company then?'

'Meaning?'

'Felipe Rochas. La Roque's first full-blooded revolutionary.'

'Funny you should say that. I'd be inclined to agree, but what he's being denounced for is being a *reactionary*. Holding up progress, and all that. I gather you don't accept the interpretation.'

'Well, it depends on what you call progress, doesn't it?'

'Ah, yes indeed.'

'Maybe when you're away a lot, like I am – you, too, for that matter – this business of change can be a shock. I don't own anything here any more. I have no particular interests, or people, for whom I feel responsible. Yet it bothers me. Perhaps our roots are stronger than we imagine, yes?'

I nodded.

'You come back, expecting to find at least a touch of *home* about the place you've grown up in, and instead it's like dropping down on another planet. Even that would be tolerable if the place were habitable, but – well, have you seen what they've done to the West Front?'

'Yes. But what really bothers me is what they're doing to *people*.'

He gave me a shrewd look. 'The de Courvels, you mean.'

'Well, obviously they concern me most, but I suspect there are many others. In fact, I more than suspect,' I added, thinking of Calvaro.

He took another quick look at me and I caught his eye. 'When did you last see Maurice de Courvel?' I asked.

He drew in his breath, thinking hard. 'Oh – must have been – two, perhaps three, years ago. If you mean did I see any significant changes there, though, the answer, I'm afraid, is no. But then I didn't see a lot of them by that time.'

'Simone? Did you notice anything there?'

He looked suddenly wary, and I decided it was time for candour.

'You talked about changes. Well, our little Simone, I think, has changed most of all.'

He nodded. 'Sadly, yes. But, again, if you were hoping I could provide any clues, I'm sorry. I just don't have any. Except, of course – ' He hesitated.

'Yes?'

'Well, I admit it shook me when I heard that she'd suddenly decided to marry Corlander.'

'Because you'd imagined that she and Raoul – ' I left the question in the air.

He sighed. 'I don't know, Angus. I really don't know. For a while there did seem to be something there. But I shouldn't have said what I did to Simone just now. I was a damn fool. I don't think there was really ever much hope.'

'Why not?'

He shook his head again. 'Poor old Raoul was a mess. Physically and to some extent mentally. And he knew it. I used to be afraid sometimes that he'd just bale out one day. I'm fairly certain it was Simone who kept him strapped in there, but he was worried about her. Felt he had nothing to offer a woman on a long-term basis. Yes, he was in a bad way.'

'Do you think she was upset, too?'

'God knows. After Raoul died – '

'*How* did he? I mean, was it sudden?'

'Yes. Chill. Pneumonia. His heart packed in.'

'And then? You were saying – '

'Yes, well then she married Corlander. It was the speed of it that got me. But I suppose he caught her in a weak moment and just moved in with the red roses.'

'Pity he didn't move *out* again a whole lot faster.'

He grimaced. 'I'll drink to *that*.' And he raised his glass and drained it accordingly.

After I'd replenished for both of us, I returned to the attack, trying to find out how he felt about Alain and what he knew about smuggling activities on the island. As I'd expected, he had nothing to offer about Alain since he hardly ever saw him, and his reaction to the second question was rather like Nicholas's had been. Smuggling went on, as it always had, but in the absence of any concrete evidence it was probably best forgotten.

'On the other hand,' I said, 'anyone with evidence could use it.'

He looked at me quizzically.

'You scratch *my* back and I won't put a knife in yours.'

'Ah – ' His face cleared. 'Blackmail, you mean.'

'Could work like magic if you wanted to buy someone out and they refused to sell.'

'You're surely not thinking of the *de Courvels*!'

'No. But I am thinking of its theoretic possibilities in a lot of other cases.'

'Better *keep* it that way. You'd never in a million years get it to stick. From what I've heard, it runs in families, and loyalties run deep. If you came within a square mile of a confrontation, the best you could hope for is that the rest of the tribe would close ranks with nothing more damaging to your carcase than a mass of false alibis. I wouldn't like to bank on it, though.'

'I think you're probably right. But I still think that somebody with a lot more to go on than I've got, and a lot more in the way of incentives, is finding this a pretty profitable way to operate.'

As more people began to drift in, the conversation became general. Meanwhile, a resolution began to form in my mind and around nine-thirty I stood up and made my farewells, promising to meet up with Cotarde again before his leave was up.

Outside, with the departure of the sun, the evening was fresh and clear. A good two hours remained before dark and the key to St Michel was heavy in my pocket.

This time, I left the car right outside the front door, and it occurred to me that the reason Simone hadn't spotted it when she had gone to the coach-house on Sunday was because on that occasion I'd driven on a few yards and

198

parked under some overhanging bushes. Now, my sense of legitimacy sustained me right up to the moment when I fitted the big mortice key into the lock and stepped through the open door into the littered hall. As I moved across to the study, however, a totally irrational feeling of guilt returned. This was Maurice's room, his private place. What the hell was I doing here? What did I expect to find that would justify such crass intrusion?

I needn't have worried. After I'd poked about fairly aimlessly, and with an increasing sense of futility, for about half an hour, the truth hit me. I was on the wrong track. The room was a paradox. Loaded with lumber, stacked wall-to-wall with memories, all it actually had in it was emptiness. There wasn't a sigh or a whisper left to tell me anything about the tragic event that had occurred here. I stood for a long minute in the open doorway, looking around me. Then I let myself out of St Michel and locked up behind me.

Outside, I lit a cigarette and wandered over to the edge of the overgrown lawn and stood staring at the trailing limb of the big catalpa tree. I was reluctant to leave. Realization had failed to come within a hundred light years of anticipation, and yet I still had this strange pricking of the thumbs; something still told me that if I was to make any kind of a breakthrough in this riddle, it was here and now. In my pocket I felt the key under my fingers. Should I go back in? Try again? – To hell with it! I dropped my cigarette on to the gravel, ground it under my toe and then picked up the stub and flung it into the bushes beyond the grass. With more resolution than I felt I walked back to the car, got in and started off again down the drive. As I drew level with the low wall in front of the two coach-houses, I slowed to a halt and sat staring at the freshly painted yellow door of the one to the right of the arch that led through to the stable-yard. This was the door at which I'd seen Simone on Sunday. She had been painting furniture, she said. Well, it was true that the outside of the place, too, had had recent attention. Like the door, the window-sills, both top and bottom, were newly painted. So why did I feel she had been making excuses, trying to put me off something?

I cut the engine and got out. It was obvious that the door would be locked, of course, so there wasn't much use in trying it. But I did and it was, and both downstairs windows were shuttered. I moved towards the archway, topped by its now defunct clock, noticing how the grass had grown between the cobbles under my feet. Looking through towards the small stable-yard beyond, an incident from the past flashed through my mind. The de Courvels had not been the kind of horsy folk found among their class back in England, but there *had* been a couple of rather over-fed ponies kept especially for the children, and I remembered the bigger one in particular, a black fellow named Robin, because he'd been startled by a gun one day when I was out on him and bolted. I had never jumped on a horse before, but that day I sailed over a stile and a small brook before my weight, hanging by this time under Robin's chin, finally brought the panicked creature to a halt. We had shared a moment of deep empathy, Robin and I. Four rolling white eyes had met and locked in those mad moments while I had hung under his neck. For old time's sake I could at least take another look at where the nice old soul had once eaten his oats.

There was a clammy feeling of decay under the arch, and, beyond, the stable-yard looked desolate. Stable doors were off their hinges, or left standing open, revealing dark and musty interiors littered with long-discarded junk. One contained a shabby old doll's perambulator lying on its side, one wheel broken, but still holding a grimy black plastic doll, naked except for a pair of faded blue satin drawers. In another, a rusty sewing-machine stood with its handle dangling from its side like a broken limb. Most ironic of all, framed in one doorway was a rocking horse. The top half-door above its head was closed, but the bottom stood open and the creature, either by accident or wry design, straddled the centre, its garish eyes staring boldly ahead as though challenging its fate. There was something almost frantic about those eyes, as though, trapped within this thing of wood and faded paint, there was a living, feeling creature panting to be free of the dead and dying rubble around it. I shuddered and turned back towards the archway. Not all the yellow paint in the world could revitalize this place for me. It was ghost-haunted by all the sorrows and regrets for a past that was gone for ever.

It was then that I noticed the downstairs window of the 'yellow' flat. It was clean and freshly painted like the one at the front. But there was a difference. It was open! A simple sash window, open a good foot at the top. I approached it with all the caution of an animal sniffing the lure, but neither sight nor hearing gave warning of any danger. I discovered that the bottom half of the window lifted easily and almost soundlessly, and I hesitated no longer than it took to say 'Act of God' before sliding in over the sill to negotiate a sink top littered with paint pots, jars containing brushes and a débris of stained rags and screwed-up newspaper. I was in a small kitchen and the reason for the open window was obvious. Simone had been telling the truth about the painting; the room had clearly been newly decorated, and standing on newspapers on top of the table in the centre were a small wooden stool and a cork-topped laundry box, both of which had been recently painted white. Despite the air coming into the room, the smell of paint and spirit was strong.

The kitchen door was open and I moved cautiously out into a narrow and rather dark hallway that led directly to the front door. On my right was a staircase, while on the left near the front door was a room that contained nothing but a pair of cretonne-covered armchairs and a matching settee forming a lonely trio in the middle of the uncarpeted floor. Despite the shadow cast by the closed blinds, I could see that here, too, the paint was fresh. Once, I remembered, this whole lower region had been a tack room. Now, it had been divided into two sections by the wall that separated this room from the hallway, and the civilized staircase replaced the rough flight of wooden steps that had led up out of the corner. I felt a tremendous admiration for

Simone as I looked around me. She was right. These coach-houses could be made into two quite pleasant homes.

It was as I moved towards the stairs that I began to feel guilty again. It was all very well to tell myself that the circumstances of Maurice's death justified all this poking about in other people's business, even criminally breaking into their property. Perhaps it did. The trouble was that there was no possible way I could be sure. Equally there was no way I could turn back. Meanwhile, here I was again, facing another of those compulsive moments of decision which seemed to have haunted me ever since I had arrived on the island. I was standing on the upstairs landing. I had passed a small bathroom and toilet, and next to them a bare room, presumably a spare bedroom, and now I faced a closed door. This would be the main bedroom, no doubt empty like the rest of the house. But I couldn't be sure. And the guilty feeling had now turned to an almost physical nausea. But everyone, they say, has his price, and some-where along the dark, mysterious line that stretched between Maurice and his inheritors I had reached mine. Once again, I was about to open a door on to a private world to which, by long neglect, I had forfeited the right to access.

Like the room below, this one was shuttered; but there the similarity ended. This was no half-finished room, reeking of paint and bare of furniture. There was a chintz-covered settee against the wall beside the door, two easy chairs each side of the window opposite, and between them, a small folded table with a healthy-looking plant in the centre of it. On the left, in a natural alcove, there was a divan bed, covered with a green-patterned linen counter-pane and topped by green and cream velvet cushions, while at the other end of the room a long glass-fronted bookcase-cum-bureau took up most of the wall. The room was car-peted wall-to-wall with a plain carpet of soft apple green. Near the bureau there was a cream-shaded standard lamp and beneath it a portable magazine rack was full. Clearly, this was a room that had been lived in, possibly for some

202

time. One reason for this, of course, could be that Simone intended it as a sort of show-piece for prospective buyers. Yet, as I stood there, looking about me, this idea faded before the growing conviction that here, in this room, I had somehow reached the end of the road. Whatever it was that St Michel had to tell me, it was here, awaiting recognition. It was a feeling that defied all reason, the undiluted stuff of basic animal awareness. But awareness of what?

I walked over to the bureau. It was locked, for which, perversely, I was relieved. On top of it, in the centre, there was a row of about a dozen books held between a couple of polished wooden stands. It was an odd collection, part French, part English. Proust's *A La Recherche du Temps Perdu* sat beside Baudelaire's *Les Fleurs du Mal*, Daudet's *Tartarin de Tarascon* next to Gautier's *Le Capitaine Fracasse*; then came four nineteenth-century English classics – the two elder Brontës in identical bindings, with George Eliot's *Adam Bede* and Thackeray's *Vanity Fair*. A slim edition of Michelangelo's *Sonnets* was flanked by Kafka's *Metamorphosis*, and finally, tatty and dog-eared, a French edition of the *Chanson de Roland*. They were all books I had seen in the main house years ago. Had they been specially chosen, I wondered. Or just scooped up in a moment of indecision? The Gautier, I knew, was a particular favourite of Simone's, or at least had been in the days when I had known her better, the days when she had been light of heart and there had been no constraint between us.

I wandered back towards the bed and turned back the cover. There was a blanket underneath and two pillows, but no sheets. I sat on the edge and gazed about me. The only other living thing in the room – the plant in its pot – looked back at me. It had delicate, silver-speckled leaves and the soil below was moist and dark, the whole thing bright with healthy living. It was this, plus the locked bureau and the books, that most convinced me that this was no mere showroom. Was it, perhaps, a sanctuary, a place of escape, a hidy-hole, such as we had had as children, no more and no less? The unmade bed suggested that it was not used overnight, and the lack of identifying detail of a personal kind indicated a possible desire for secrecy. It was an explanation that fitted Simone's strange attitude of guilt when I had caught her here. It was understandable that a grown woman, the mother of a young child, would feel embarrassed by the exposure of such an apparently juvenile lapse.

So why wasn't I satisfied? Why did I still feel that in some dread, mysterious way this room was somehow associated with Maurice's death? Something still rankled. Reason was satisfied; instinct was not.

As I sat there, my eyes turned once more to the bureau and suddenly memory flooded back. I had seen this piece of furniture before. I remembered wet days in the play-room at the top of the old house, where most of the furniture discarded from downstairs had usually found its way. This old bureau had stood over in the corner near the window, the keys in those days left in their locks. At some time in its long life the desk-lid had received a blow, causing a split in the wood, which I could see in the flap from where I sat. It had also had another injury, I recalled. Part of the wood along the bottom edge of the lid had broken away, leaving a small gap, unseen as long as the lid was closed. It had been Max who had discovered this. He had kept it a secret until the evening when the girls, trying to prevent us from seeing a certain cherished photograph, had rushed to the bureau as a last defence. Then, when they were seated on the floor triumphant, the key hidden somewhere about their persons, he had proceeded to demolish their illusions of security with a piece of bent wire.

I passed my fingers gently along beneath the lid. Sure enough, the gap was still there. What was more, as I bent to examine it, I noticed that a piece of paper was protruding very slightly through it. If ever there was a hostage to fortune, this was it! In my guilty haste, however, I was not as dextrous as Max had been and the paper caught and tore. Damn! I could only hope Simone would think she had done it herself. Straightening up, I saw with satisfaction that, in fact, only a portion at the top of the sheet had been lost; the rest was intact.

Just what I'd expected to find I'm not sure. I had lived long enough to know that secret places don't always reveal secrets. But this was the apotheosis of anti-climax. The paper was a receipt – the date of which I had left behind the flap, together with the name of the firm – for two cans of white paint, a couple of brushes and some turpentine. I swore. It was no more than I deserved, but I felt that the fates were against me, a sensation that was considerably reinforced by the length of time it took me to work the damned paper back where it belonged. Even with a piece of wire, my shattered morale could never have sustained another go at that thundering desk.

Depressed and dissatisfied, I glanced mechanically at the books again. *Did* they have any significance, or were they merely misplaced orphans from the collection in the main house? I pulled one out at random and it opened automatically. A slip of paper was caught in the centre-fold. On it, in pencil, was a date: '3rd May 1950'. I drew the slip out and turned it over, but the back was blank. Keeping my thumb in the marked page, I turned the book over in my hand and looked at the title on the front. It was George Eliot's *Adam Bede*, and when I looked back at the open page I recognized the description of little Hetty Sorrel's tragic quest for a pool in which to drown herself among the 'grassy fields' of Stratford-upon-Avon. Deluded little Hetty, burdened with her basket and her unborn child: Hetty, the uneducated country girl who ran away from her village after being seduced by the young squire, and who was later convicted of having killed her baby by abandonment. Suddenly I froze. Imaginative recollection reeled before the impact of shattering speculation. I placed the book back on the shelf and turned and walked towards the door. There, I stood for a moment, looking into the room.

It was impossible. I *knew* it was impossible. But there were two facts I had to know. And I had to know them before another twenty-four hours had passed.

SEVENTEEN

Stéphanie looked troubled when I faced her across the table in the pleasant green dining-room at the Villa Valeuse next morning. I'd phoned her from the hotel immediately after breakfast and asked if I could go out and talk to her and she had responded with her usual warmth. Her only concern was that Nicholas had already left for his office.

'You could catch him there if you need to,' she said, but I assured her that it was her I wanted to see, and she told me to come as soon as I liked.

'Something's happened,' she said as we sat down together.

I had intended merely to ask her two simple questions, not to regale her with the sordid details of my protracted perfidy at St Michel. But Stéphanie is a person who invites confidence and before I knew it I'd launched into the whole story, beginning with my first visit, when Simone had walked in on me in Maurice's study, continuing with my adventures with the butler's pantry and ending with last night's unpardonable prying in the coach-house flat. But when I came to the discovery of the slip of paper in *Adam Bede* I stopped. The thoughts it had brought to my mind were such that not even to Stéphanie could I put them into words. From the sudden intensity with which she looked at me I felt she sensed something, and to ease the tension I offered her a cigarette, lighting one for myself when she shook her head. Through the first spiral of smoke my eyes met hers.

'Stéph,' I said, 'when did Simone's little boy die? I mean *exactly* – the date. Do you know?'

For a moment she looked taken aback. What she'd expected I don't know, but it wasn't that.

'Well,' she said, and then stopped, frowning as she

consulted long-faded memories. 'He was born in the late spring. April, I think, or early May. And he only lived about a week or ten days.' She pushed her chair back and stood up. 'I'll get you some coffee,' she said. 'And while you're drinking it I'll look it up for you.'

'You've got a note of it somewhere?'

She smiled. 'I'm a diary-keeper,' she said. 'Not one of your great Victorian kind: just the usual day-to-day trivia – with, of course, the not-so trivial. But I've found it useful to keep back copies. I'll go and see what I've got.'

I thanked her, smiling, but while she was gone I felt a mixture of relief and foreboding. I hadn't wanted to worry Guy with my questions, and I'd had reservations of different kinds over everyone else. But for lots of reasons I now felt I'd made the right decision in coming to Stéphanie. All the same, I couldn't make up my mind about how much I should tell her. I trusted her implicitly, and reason told me that her counsel would be sensible and sound, but some ancient loyalty to Simone went deeper than reason.

I got up and, walking over to the window, stood there, looking out over the sunlit terrace and, beyond, to the deep blue of the bay. It wasn't yet ten o'clock, but already the sea was littered with bright blobs of colour as holiday-makers swam, paddled, canoed and sailed in the bright water.

I was still standing when Stéphanie returned, carrying a tray holding a jug of coffee, with cups and saucers and milk and sugar. There was also, on one corner of the tray, a small cream-leather book. She poured out one cup of coffee and slid it across the table. Then she picked up the little book and began turning the pages.

'Here you are,' she said eventually. '24th April. "Simone's baby born. Boy, Eleven a.m." '

'Where?'

'At home. St Michel. She and Ray were living there then.'

I walked back towards my seat. 'And it died?'

She turned the pages again and slid the opened book across the table towards me.

I sat down, staring at the diary as I did so. A heaviness was upon me. Stéphanie hadn't mentioned the date this time. But I knew it already. And I was right. When I finally grasped the little book and turned it over, I saw, above Stéphanie's small, firm handwriting, the unequivocal black figure '3', and, in the top-left corner of the page, the message, 'May 1950'. Besides the '3' Stéphanie had written, 'Simone's baby dies. St Michel. Pneumonia'.

I closed the book and pushed it back across the table.

'Thank you,' I said again.

Stéphanie was busy pouring herself some coffee and she didn't speak until she had finished. Then, drawing her cup towards her, she glanced over at me. 'Does it help?' she asked.

I nodded. 'In a way.' I paused, stubbing out my cigarette in the ashtray she had provided. *But what way, for God's sake?* I glanced towards the diary and then at her. 'Pneumonia,' I said. 'Was that the official diagnosis?'

'Well, yes, but I don't think they really knew *what* the cause was. Apparently, he'd been a bit feverish and snuffly for a few days, and then, well Simone found him dead in his pram. The poor girl! It was terrible for her. She seemed to lose her grip on things, kept wandering off for hours on end. No one knew where.'

I looked at her sharply. 'Wandering off?'

'Yes. She seemed confused. She couldn't seem to stay in the house. We went searching for her once or twice. Once we *did* find her. It was very worrying.'

'Where did you find her?'

I had already guessed.

'Down by the Arle.'

Yes. So that was how it had all begun – with the baby: all the strangeness, the tension, the anxiety – *and the guilt*?

'And the precious Ray? What was *his* contribution while all this was going on?'

'Well, he went through all the appropriate motions when the baby died, of course, but – '

'But not very convincingly.'

208

'Well – to be honest, Angus, there were times when I felt that Nicholas was more upset about that poor little child than he was.'

'Stéphanie – ' I hesitated on the brink, still desperately uncertain of myself. I looked at her and she waited, saying nothing.

'Look,' I said, 'I'm not quite sure about this, but I feel that that baby's death had something to do with why Maurice took his own life.'

The only indication of surprise in her was a faint flickering of her eyes; and still she remained silent.

'I can't explain this,' I said. 'I just feel it, and I also feel that Simone is in a lot of trouble still. To tell the truth, I'm bloody worried about her. This whole damn thing is all tied up on itself in such a way that I feel if I pull one loose end – always supposing I *see* one – God knows what will come down round our ears.'

We sat in silence for a while, then very quietly she said: 'In that case, do you think it would perhaps be best to leave things as they are?'

I sighed. 'You mean let the dead bury the dead.'

'For the sake of the living. Yes.'

'For the sake of the living.' I sighed again. 'I just wish to God it was that easy. The trouble is that one of the living doesn't see it that way. Guy Le Marnet is going through hell because he feels somehow he failed his old friend, who couldn't tell him at the end what had gone wrong. Now, Guy wants to *know* what was wrong, and, if possible, see it put right. Or, at least, see Maurice put right.'

She fell silent again, and I knew the time had come for question number two.

'I met Charles Cotarde yesterday,' I said.

'Ah, yes, we heard he was back.'

'He told me something rather interesting.'

Her eyebrows went up enquiringly. I decided to cut the corners.

'He told me he'd half-expected his brother, Raoul, to team up with Simone.'

She nodded. 'I think most of us did.'

So there *had* been something in it.

'They saw a lot of each other then?'

'For a time, yes. And then it seemed to stop, but – ' She paused.

'Yes?'

She smiled. 'Well, you know what small, closed-in communities are like. People started saying that they had a secret meeting place, but no one ever worked out where.'

Except me. *I'd* just worked out where. A cherished place, kept intact for almost twenty years.

'Why the secrecy, though?'

'Well, again it's only speculation, but it *could* have been because Raoul had decided that marriage was out of the qustion – he was a very sick man, as you probably know – and he didn't want to put her in a more difficult position than she already was.'

So much for wishful thinking.

'Did you get the impression that the affair was important to them both?'

'Well, I'm not sure it *was*, strictly speaking, an affair. Raoul was – ' she paused.

'OK. Relationship, then.'

'Yes. I think it was important. But then it all suddenly seemed to end.'

'How suddenly? When did Raoul first appear on the scene?'

'About a year after the end of the war – yes, 1946: in the summer.'

'And they began seeing each other more or less immediately?'

'Well – more or less. It's difficult to remember exactly. I know it went on for about two years, and then seemed to stop, and the next thing we knew she was marrying Ray Corlander.'

'So that would be in '48–'49?'

'1949. September. I remember because Max and Imogen were married in the spring.'

'And Simone's son was born in April, 1950.' I did some mental calculations. And then did them again. Stéphanie forestalled me.

'Yes. She hadn't been well and he was premature.'

'I see.'

I felt sure I did, too. If the putative Corlander first-born wasn't Raoul Cotarde's son, I'd take a running jump off the top of Mont Colombe. Had Stéphanie ever entertained a similar thought? Had *anyone*? Maurice, for example? Not that that alone would have accounted for what he did. Even the old feudal families of La Roque had moved a little further into the twentieth century than that. On the other hand, they wouldn't have treated it with equanimity either. Moral considerations aside, a bastard line on the female side probably made an awful mess of the ancient rules of primogeniture. Yes, it would have been awkward, but there had to be more to it than that.

'How did Simone seem to you afterwards?' I asked. 'I mean, after the baby was born?'

Stéphanie hesitated, clearly uncertain of her ground. When she spoke, it was haltingly. She was, I felt, trying desperately hard to marshal certain basic instincts into some kind of rational order.

'I don't think any of us quite knew where we were with Simone after she married Ray Corlander,' she said. 'She was – *distant* – yes, that's what it was. She seemed – well, as if she had – as if she were living in some other dimension. If you met her, sometimes she would speak, sometimes she wouldn't. It was as if she hadn't seen you, or was pretending not to. She was like a kind of puppet, not quite in control of her own life, if you know what I mean.'

'This was even *before* the baby was born.'

'Yes. Afterwards I only saw her once before it died. What I did notice, though – ' She paused again.

'Yes?'

'Well, she didn't *show* us the baby.'

'How do you mean?'

'Well, usually a mother gets a lot of pleasure out of

211

showing off a new baby, especially the first. But Simone didn't seem to care whether we saw it or not.'

'You *did* see it, though?'

'Once, yes. A dear little soul, but terribly tiny. I saw it in its pram under the big tree in the garden at St Michel, and I remembered thinking how sad it was for Maurice that unless a miracle happened this was all that would be left of the de Courvels, and even that wouldn't have his name.'

I nodded. 'But why a miracle? Simone and Ray could have had – *did* have – another child.'

'I know. I can only tell you that at the time I just didn't think they would. I never saw two people less ecstatic about each other. It was as if they'd made a pact more than a marriage.'

Something inside me jolted. *A pact*. Had Corlander somehow discovered that Simone was pregnant and blackmailed her into marriage for what he could get out of the family connection? Before I could think that out, something else came to me. I remembered Guy's words about Simone being besotted with Corlander. Now, here was Stéphanie suggesting almost the opposite. Which was right? Were either of them? I decided to put Guy's notion to the test.

'That's interesting,' I said. 'Nick's father seems to have formed a quite different impression.'

'Yes, I know. At the beginning, we all did. But after the baby was born. . . .'

'He also said she insisted on taking all the blame for the divorce.'

'Ye-es.' Stéphanie hesitated and looked troubled. 'That's true, I suppose, but. . . .' She stopped again, looking down at the table and frowning as she clearly tried to work out how to proceed. Obviously, something didn't quite gell.

For me, however, it was beginning to. If Corlander had blackmailed Simone into marrying him, it explained everything: the marriage itself, her oddness with Hélène, her retreat into herself, her fears and anxieties, and her massive sense of guilt. But there was still one thing, dammit, it *didn't* explain. I was thinking of what Stéphanie had said about the baby. Would a woman ever feel guilty or ashamed of the child of the man she loved? Were the sexual proprieties on La Roque still so archaic that a woman's natural feelings would be inhibited to the extent Stéphanie had indicated? Well, it was possible, I supposed. Given the extra ingredient of a subsequent forced marriage. It was at this point that I remembered. No, that was impossible. Maybe Simone had *felt* like poor Hetty did. Simone had not killed her own child. Of that I was as certain as I could be of anything in this whole bag of worms. Hang on, though: *did* Hetty Sorrel kill her baby, or was it only assumed that she had? Hell, it was years since I'd read George Eliot. Well, I wasn't going back into the coach-house to find out. I looked at Stéphanie, whose eyes, I saw, were now directed towards my face as she waited quietly for me to sort out my deliberations.

'I suppose,' I conjectured, 'you haven't got a copy of *Adam Bede*?'

If she thought I'd flipped, she didn't show it.

'We *may*. I'm not sure. I know we've got *The Mill on the Floss*. That won't do, I suppose? No. Well, I kept a lot of old books, hoping the children would come to them in time. Help yourself to some more coffee while I go and see.'

She was back more quickly this time, carrying an ancient-looking green-bound volume. 'There you are,' she said, sliding it across the table towards me.

'Brilliant,' I murmured. 'You're a treasure, Stéph.'

I opened the rather dog-eared book with its thick, rough-edged pages, searching, towards the end, for the bit I wanted. Meanwhile, Stéphanie watched me, showing none of the curiosity she must have been feeling.

It took me some little time, but at last I found the pages in which I'd found the slip of paper bearing the date of Simone's baby's death. I read cautiously, listening with an inner ear for the nuances which might have had a particular significance for Simone:

She chose to go to Stratford-on-Avon again . . . for she remembered some grassy fields . . . among which she thought she might find just the sort of pool she had in her mind . . . death seemed still a long way off, and life was so strong in her . . . at the very moment she was picturing to herself the bank from which she would leap towards death . . .

There followed the bit about how Hetty's face had changed, from one of the smiling happiness to one which was 'the sadder for its beauty . . . with the passionate, passionless lips'. Then:

At last she was among the fields she had been dreaming of . . . Hetty's heart gave a great beat as she thought there must be a pool there . . . She was frightened . . . at the long night before her. If she *could* but throw herself into the water!. . . The horror of this cold, and darkness, and solitude – out of all human reach – became greater every minute: it was almost as if she were dead already, and knew that she was dead. . . .

I turned more pages. The culmination, I recalled, came further on, with Hetty in prison for the murder of her child. I searched with a diligence I had not shown for a nineteenth-century novel since my student days. Here it was. In prison, Hetty tells the saintly Dinah Morris that she didn't mean to kill the child. She had listened all night to its crying after abandoning it in the fields and she had hoped someone might find it. Her account of her feelings struck me with particular force:

. . . 'I don't know how I felt about the baby. I seemed to hate it – it was like a heavy weight hanging round my neck; and yet its crying went through me, and I daredn't look at its little hands and face. But I went on to the wood, and I walked about, but there was no water'. . . .

I closed the book and sat for a moment, trying to throw off the oppressive sense of desolation which, for all its somewhat archaic melodrama, the little scene had produced in me.

I remembered Stéphanie then and wondered what I could say to her. I trusted her utterly, but some deep feeling for Simone held me silent. I still needed to know more.

I tapped the copy of *Adam Bede*. 'Can I keep this for a day or two?' I asked.

'Certainly.' Stéphanie's expression still gave nothing away of the grave doubts concerning my sanity which she must surely by now have been feeling. She smiled. 'I'm glad we still had it. So many of these old books seem to disappear as one gets older. If there's anything else . . .?' She left the question unfinished.

I shook my head. 'Not for the moment. But thanks, Stéph.' I got up. 'I owe all sorts of explanations, but at the moment. . . .'

'You owe us nothing,' she interrupted quietly. She walked with me towards the door, where she put a hand on my arm. 'We don't want explanations, Angus. Just tell us – any time – what we can do.'

I bent and kissed her lightly on the cheek. 'I promise,' I said. 'Meanwhile,' I added, 'your protegé has started music lessons. I'll keep you informed of progress.'

In the event, I took Stéphanie at her word, and, back in town, telephoned Nicholas and asked him if he could spare time to drive out to La Bonne Fourchette to have some lunch with me. I chose this particular rendezvous because I figured that almost anywhere in town would make us vulnerable to interruption from his scores of professional colleagues and acquaintances. He said he would meet me there at one-fifteen and I decided to spend the intervening time checking on the situation at Mont Vert. This turned out to be just as well because I there learned something that added considerable urgency to all the matters in hand: Guy had convened a special emergency meeting of the Grand Council to discuss the Point Rouge sale and it would be held in the following week.

'Couldn't it be sooner?' I asked him.

He shook his head. 'A number of people are out of the island.'

I felt a flicker of dismay. A lot could happen in a week.

'Will you do one thing, then, sir?'

He looked at me quizzically, eyebrows raised.

'Go and spend a few days with Nicholas and Stéphanie. No – ' as he gave a disparaging smile – 'I'm serious, sir. This is all being extremely tough on them. It would relieve their minds – mine too – to know you were somewhere safe, at least until this particular decision has been made.'

He hesitated, the wry smile still on his face, then he shrugged his surrender. 'Well, if you put it like that. . . .'

'I'll ask Pierre to pack a few things,' I offered, moving towards the door before he could change his mind. 'And I'll ring Stéphanie,' I added as I passed into the hall.

As I'd known she would be, Stéphanie was delighted with the manoeuvre, and Pierre almost broke into a gavotte as he moved towards the staircase.

'I'll be back this evening to run you down there, sir,' I told Guy when I returned to the study.

He nodded, the resigned smile reappearing on his face, but he was sitting now in his chair near the French windows and the sagging of his shoulders told me that his underlying mood was heavy. I promised myself there and then that if anyone put the boot in on Guy Le Marnet, I would personally alter their vital statistics irreparably.

There was no sign of Nicholas when I arrived at La Bonne Fourchette, so after reserving a table in a quiet corner of the terrace overlooking the beach, I went to the bar and ordered a Scotch. I was about to have it topped up when he arrived, looking even more flustered than ever. He'd been in court all the previous day, he told me, which had played hell with his normal routine. I told him apologies were unnecessary and ordered another whisky. He congratulated me on having persuaded his father to go to the Villa Valeuse until, as he put it, 'after that damn Council'. Stéphanie had rung and told him, he said, and they were both immensely relieved.

'Me, too,' I said. 'It was either that or me moving in on him, which, apart from the fact that I hadn't been invited, would have put an extra domestic burden on the Bouchiers.'

He nodded, took a sip of his drink, and then sighed. 'It's all one hell of a mess,' he said.

Comment seemed superfluous, so I suggested we took our drinks out on to the terrace. There, I came straight to the point.

'I want to talk about Simone,' I said. 'She bothers me, Nick. Every time I see her, I feel either she's stretched out on a bed of nails or else floating out to sea in a bucket. You handled the divorce, didn't you? Your father tells me she insisted on taking all the blame, wouldn't put up a fight; he felt she was under the carpet to the sod, infatuated from start to finish. Do you agree? I mean, how did *you* see it at the time? You must have had a fair amount of discussion with her and formed some idea of the state of her mind.'

His furrowed face took on the look of a newly-ploughed field as he wrestled with this unexpected avalanche of questions. He took a gulp of whisky and then gave a small grimace, composed in equal parts of wry amusement and self-deprecation.

'I'm not much good at this sort of thing,' he said. Professionally, I try not to think too much about what's going on in people's minds. I just answer questions and do what they tell me to do.'

'Oh, for God's sake, Nick! We're talking about a kid we grew up with! You must have had *some* idea whether she thought this cow-pat had roses in his navel.'

He grimaced again, took another swig of whisky and drew a deep breath as he considered.

'Well – Well, she certainly seemed keen to marry him, and she certainly refused to defend herself adequately in the divorce proceedings. All the indications were that she was – yes, that she *was* very taken with him.'

'But?'

He nodded. 'Yes, you're right. There *was* always a doubt in my mind, I admit. We'd all thought her inclinations lay elsewhere.'

'Raoul?'

''M. And it *did* seem a bit odd. But I suppose we all thought she had accepted the inevitable where poor old Raoul was concerned and that maybe Corlander caught her on the rebound and she was a bit captivated. The man does have a way with the ladies, you know. Oh, yes – ' as he saw the expression on my face – 'you may find that difficult to believe, but it's true, and Simone was always a little impressionable, as you'll remember.' He grinned. 'We always thought she fancied *you*, for instance.'

'Well, she doesn't now.'

'No, well. I doubt if she fancies anyone very much these days. But with Simone it never was easy to tell.'

I was silent for a while, thinking carefully about my next move. Then I decided to take the plunge.

'Nick, could there have been any *other* reason why she wouldn't fight Corlander? Why she *couldn't* show anything but loyalty and affection towards him? Could that have been so from the very beginning, from when she married him, I mean?'

Now, he looked plainly baffled, and I knew it was the point of no return.

'Could she have been under some pressure to comply? Some threat?'

He stared at me, his mouth hanging open, his dark eyes behind their glasses fixed on mine with a bemused expression.

'God dammit, Nick! *Think*! She'd been in love with Cotarde – you all thought that – suddenly she ups and marries King Rat in dancing shoes. Her first baby is two months premature. At the time of its birth she seemed unnaturally disinclined to take either it or her once so-desirable husband to her bosom – that's how Stéph saw it, anyway – and then, publicly, in the blaze of the divorce proceedings, she does a sudden quick change into the role of the loving, dutiful wife. What I'm asking you, Nick, is: *Was our little Simone blackmailed?* First, *into* marriage, and then out of it.'

Mystification gave way to incredulity. 'For what possible reason?'

'Because she was a de Courvel, dammit! And Corlander wants the de Courvel estates.'

He continued to stare at me for a full second, and then, as the shock hit him, he began shaking his head in disbelief. 'Surely not. Surely not,' he murmured.

I let it sink in. In any case, now I'd put it into words to someone else, the implications of it were having a curiously unnerving effect on me, too. If I was right about this, what had Simone had to do to ensure that her secret was kept safe? Had it been just a question of passing on snippets of information gained as a result of confidential discussions with her father, or had she had to try to influence him in some way? In what way? Had Maurice come to suspect it? To lose faith in her, as he had already lost faith in Alain? It would certainly explain the slow disintegration of spirit in him, which in turn would explain the neglect of vital interests and commitments. Would it also, though, explain suicide? I still couldn't see it. Unless – Supposing Corlander, finding Simone's efforts less than ideally effective, had added some pressure of his own, something to do with Simone. . . . I felt a quickening inside me. I remembered those games we'd played as children: 'You're cold – now you're getting warmer – now you're *really* warm – now you're *hot*!' I'd be damned if I wasn't at least getting warmer. I was suddenly aware that Nicholas had spoken.

'Sorry?'

His mouth twisted down with some inner distaste. 'I was thinking of the meetings we had before the divorce. I remember feeling this sense of urgency, the need to get it over with quickly. I felt if we didn't she would be ill. There was so much tension in her.'

'What kind of tension? She was miserable, you mean? Sad?'

He screwed up his face. 'It was more than that. In Maurice, too.'

'Maurice?' Again, the quickening.

'I went up to see her at St Michel one day. She'd gone back there with Hélène towards the end. Maurice waylaid me on the way out. He said – ' He stopped, closing one eye in the effort of recollection.

'Yes?'

'He said, if I remember the exact words – "Get her away from this man" – yes, that was it. "Get her away from this man. Never mind anything else, just get her away from him." At the time, it all seemed natural enough.'

'Now, you feel perhaps there was something more behind it?'

He shook his head again. 'Oh, I don't know, Angus. The trouble with all this business of reading people's minds is that so often it gets to be a case of reading something *into* them.'

'Yes, I know.'

'We have a preconceived idea of what someone's feeling – which is usually what we think *we'd* be feeling in similar circumstances – and, well – ' He shrugged. 'That's it.'

'Yes.'

I was content to let it rest there. He'd told me what I wanted to know: that even in Nicholas's careful lawyer's mind there was, once he thought about it, more than one possible explanation for Simone's attitude at the time of the divorce. It *could* have been unrequited love – or it could have been something very different.

I returned to Mont Vert in time to join Guy Le Marnet over a pot of tea. Then, after as much fuss from both the Bouchiers as if he'd been going to open up a new sub-continent, we set off for the Villa. There, he had a predictably warm welcome from Stéphanie and a rapturous one from his grandchildren, all of whom had gathered in

220

the hall for the occasion, and I eventually left feeling that at last I'd managed to do something right. I'd shut one stable door, at least, before the horse bolted.

Which just goes to show how wrong you can be.

EIGHTEEN

There was a telephone message for me back at the Royale to call Felipe, which I did with a mixture of relief and foreboding. I'd had enough drama for one day. All I wanted now was a quiet drink in the bar and an even quieter night's sleep. At the same time, I felt it was going to take more than that to enable me to work out my next move. Direct approach to Simone herself seemed out of the question. Yet what else remained?

Felipe's call gave me the excuse I needed to shelve the problem for the time being. It was to tell me that the meeting in the Town Square was fixed for the following evening at seven-thirty.

'Louise wondered if you'd like to come back for some supper with us afterwards,' he said.

My heart lurched pleasurably. 'I should indeed,' I said.

'Good. I'll tell her. If you've time, why not come up and have a drink with us beforehand? Say about six-thirty?'

Better and better. I told him he could count on it, and I went to bed, if not exactly more relaxed, at least with rather different feelings of anticipation.

I spent most of the next day like a tourist. I'd been nearly two weeks on the island and, except for the day with the Le Marnets at St Michel, I'd hardly set foot on a beach, let alone spent any time in the water. I chose a remote bay on the north coast of the island called Pointe Oseille, which, because of a tricky current, seldom attracted more than two or three swimmers, mostly Côte du Nord locals who for the most part only appeared in the evenings.

I think I was under the illusion that if I could distance myself from the problem that preoccupied me it would somehow slide into some sort of focus. In fact, all it did was slide out of sight altogether as sun and sea did their work. I'd bought some bread rolls and cheese en route, together with a couple of apples and a half-bottle of medium-dry Bordeaux, and around midday I collected these from the car and took them out to a shady spot on the rocks. I remembered the countless times I'd done just this with my father and then, later, with the de Courvels and the others. Suddenly, it all seemed a millennium away, but, oddly, at that moment I felt no emotion about it. Whether it was the effect of the wine, or the sun, or a combination of both, who knows, but the whole temporal and spatial dimension – and I with it – seemed curiously suspended and for the short time it lasted nothing appeared important.

After I'd finished the second of the apples, my swim-trunks were dry enough for me to pull my shorts on over them again, and I then decided to return to the car via a stiff climb up the rocks to the top of the headland and down again over the short, springy grass. By the time I slipped back into the driving seat of the Citroën, I was hot again and exhausted, but feeling better, mentally and spiritually, than I had in days.

Back at the hotel, I had a pot of tea sent up to my room while I showered and shaved and I drank it in my dressing-gown as I debated whether more roses or a box of chocolates would be the most appropriate offering on this occasion for my hostess. Bearing in mind the nature of the Rochas family business, I finally decided on the chocs and collected a discreet-looking box on my way out through the foyer at about five-thirty.

In my eagerness I was too early and stopped the car just before I got to the lane leading down to the farm and spent ten minutes in impatient meditation, hoping against hope that none of the family would find me there. I needn't have worried, for when I eventually drew up in front of the house the windows of the room overlooking the fields were open and I could see all three brothers gathered together there with glasses in their hands. At the sound of the car they turned and all three strolled out through the French windows to meet me. Clearly, someone had impressed on Carlos the importance of the occasion, for he had discarded his working clothes in favour of a tight-fitting black suit and white open-necked shirt, and his black hair was oiled back on his head so that it glowed. All the chap needed was a red cape and a rose in his teeth.

But it was Louise I'd come to see, and it was Louise who sent my nerve-ends spinning when she entered the room just as we trailed in through the window. She looked even more elegant than ever in a plain, sleeveless dress of some silken material the colour of dark coffee, her only jewellery a simple gilt brooch and matching ear-rings. Her hair shone as brilliantly as her brother's, but softly. I knew then that this was a woman who was going to play hell with the nice, uncomplicated, self-indulgent world I'd built up around myself since Maggie died. When I produced the chocolates the look she gave me confirmed it.

'Are you coming with us?' I asked her. I had no great hope of her reply, but was nevertheless disappointed when she shook her head. 'I have a lesson at seven-thirty,' she said.

Carlos nodded his head in emphatic approval. 'Politics are no good to man or animal,' he observed, 'but to *woman* – !' He made an expressive gesture with one hand and his face screwed itself up into a look of utter distaste.

Louise threw him an indulgent smile. 'Carlos thinks there's only one thing worse than a politician,' she said, 'and that's a woman politician.'

'He could have a point,' I murmured.

Beside me, Enrique laughed softly. '*All* politicians are a load of old women,' he said. I glanced at him, surprised. This was my own opinion, with certain embellishments, but I hadn't expected to hear it expressed in this house. Seeing my look, he grinned. 'If you're thinking of Felipe,' he said, 'people who give other people artificial respiration are not necessarily doctors.'

Just as we were preparing to leave, the telephone rang. Enrique went to answer it, and, when he returned, spoke to his sister in rapid Spanish. She nodded and then glanced at me, smiling. 'My infant is not coming,' she said. 'I may as well join you after all.'

'Good,' I said, trying for a casual air. 'I'll drive you, if I may.' But I knew, as I looked at her, that my face was giving me away, and I just didn't care.

The square was already beginning to fill up when we arrived. Someone had rigged up a small platform down at the end opposite the Town Church, and here we found a tight little group of Felipe's supporters, including Laurent and Despard and the Orthoz brothers. To my surprise, until I remembered the obvious reason, I spotted Alain de Courvel moving around among the crowd. He was eventually joined by a photographer, so the local press clearly meant to do justice to the occasion. Nevertheless, I was surprised that Alain should feel it of sufficient importance to warrant his own, rather than a junior's, presence. After a while, I murmured an excuse to Louise and strolled over to where Alain was standing, one hand in his pocket, the other holding a half-smoked cigarette, which he occasionally drew on as he looked around him with morose concentration. As I came into his line of vision, he looked at me without enthusiasm.

'An interesting thought has come to me,' I said. 'Do you think,' I went on, 'that your father could have been blackmailed?'

I hadn't had the smallest intention of asking him this. It just came out, as though in automatic response to some inner pre-programming. Alain's response was dramatic. His face darkened and when he spoke he stuttered in his effort to control his emotions.

'I've wa-warned you, Angus. I've had en-nough of this.'

'O.K.,' I said soothingly. 'O.K.'

'It is *not* O.K. You may have your reasons for – for all this, but it is clear to me that they have nothing whatever to do with paying your – your – respects to my father.'

'On the contrary, they have a *great deal* to do with it.'

'I am not interested!' His eyes, fixed on mine, glittered with an almost vicious rage. 'Will you understand that? I am not interested. I do not wish to talk about it. It is finished. Over. There is nothing we can do about it and I prefer that you do not insult our family with suggestions that there were things in our lives that were – were – ' he searched for the word he wanted, hunching his shoulders in frustration – 'open,' he finished, 'to such people as you imply.'

'Oh, for God's sake!'

'Yes. For God's sake. You will leave this matter, yes?'

It was not a question. It was a command, but he was being so melodramatic that I could barely resist a smile. Fortunately, at that moment we both became aware of the figure that had quietly approached and now stood between us. Which of us was the more surprised, I don't know, but pleasure, at least, was more manifest on my side than on his.

'*Now*, anyway, I'm glad I came,' I said.

Madeleine Le Brocq smiled, but then her expression became grave.

'We may all change our minds, I think,' she said. She nodded towards the back of the crowd. 'There are about half a dozen ugly-looking clowns down there that look to me as if they are out for trouble. Two of them are drunk already and I think they will need watching.'

Alain turned. 'Where?'

'Down at the back there. In two nasty little groups. Unfortunately, they are carrying banners in support of Señor Rochas, but I doubt if they are really friends of his.'

'I'll take a look,' I said.

'No!' Her hand came out and held my arm. 'Don't, Angus. I may be wrong, but in any case the police will take care of them if it is necessary. With these people, it is best not to interfere unless you know them.'

I hesitated, glancing at Alain. The last thing I wanted was to precipitate trouble.

'She's right,' he said. 'Leave it to the police.'

It occurred to me that I hadn't *seen* any police, but I

226

supposed they were bound to show up sooner or later and decided to follow advice.

Alain left us to join the photographer, who had gone over to the other side of the square, and I looked at Madeleine, liking what I saw. She was bareheaded, like Louise, and although there was a certain severity about the black dress she wore – despite its green silk scarf – that was entirely absent in Louise's gentler, more susceptible appearance, nevertheless the same kind of human warmth was here. It had emerged in the sudden, impulsive gesture of protection towards myself, and was indeed evident in the mere fact that she was here at all, and again I wondered at the relationship between her and Alain. In particular, it intrigued me that in his present embittered frame of mind he was able to hold such a relationship intact.

Realizing that my study of her might seem to her to have become a little intense, I grinned and nodded back towards the group I had left. 'Will you join us?' I asked her.

She shook her head, smiling. 'Thank you, but no. I shall not stay long. Crowds terrify me. It is foolish, I know, but there – ' she arched her fine, dark eyebrows and gave a Gallic shrug of self-deprecation.

'I don't blame you a bit,' I said.

'If it becomes unpleasant,' she added, 'bring Señorita Rochas over for a drink. I shall be happy to see you both.'

I stared at her, lost, for a moment, for an appropriate reply, and before I could think of one she had gone. Once again, that unerring Roquennais awareness had taken me by surprise. By some divination known only to herself, Madeleine had become acquainted with the fact not only that I knew Felipe Rochas' sister – a fairly obvious deduction for her to have arrived at – but that I knew her well enough for there to be some degree of social pair-bonding between us. I wondered if any Roquennais couple ever had to bother to put up the banns in church.

Louise, I saw, was deep in conversation with the group around her and I strolled over to join her.

'I've just had an offer of sustenance if things get rough

here,' I told her, drawing her away from the others.

She looked up at me, surprised, and I gave her the gist of Madeleine's message, playing down the bit about the bruisers in the crowd.

She laughed. 'Madeleine was always practical,' she said.

'You know her?'

'Oh, yes. We were at school together.'

'How long has she – ' I hesitated. 'I mean, she and de Courvel?'

'Oh, it must be almost ten years now.'

Ten years! I was amazed. I must have looked it, for she went on in a low voice, 'Madeleine had a bad time. Her husband – he owns a small vineyard on the south coast – won't give her a divorce, but he's no good. Our laws aren't very helpful towards women in such cases, but Nicholas Le Marnet managed to get a separation order.'

'How did she meet Alain?'

'Oh, I think that happened when Pedro – that's her husband – got into some particularly unpleasant trouble with one of his women workers that got reported in the paper.'

I was still thinking over this piece of information when I became aware that things were happening. Felipe had climbed up on to the platform and had begun to speak through a megaphone, to accompanying shouts of '*Olé!*' and '*Bravo!*' from the crowd. I was as usual left fairly stranded by the language problem, nor could I judge much how it was going by the response of the crowd, for all public speaking on La Roque is traditionally accorded a noisy display of emotion, be it approved or otherwise. However, the natives immediately around me seemed friendly enough, and Felipe, I thought, looked about as confident as anyone could reasonably be expected to be whilst trying to speak in a wind tunnel.

What subsequently happened, therefore, I was never quite sure. All I could recall afterwards was that one minute we were standing there, watching Felipe and listening to his voice and the surging, mainly sympathetic responses of the crowd, and the next that something that felt like a battering-ram seemed to come rearing from somewhere behind us, hurling us forward amidst a crescendo of nerve-racking sound.

By instinct, I grabbed Louise, pulling her forcibly up from her knees and towards me, and, as I did so, there was a sudden, terrible sound of shattering glass. I felt something hard and sharp on the side of my head and a warm wetness down my neck. I remembered dragging Louise frantically away from beneath the platform towards what I hoped was the relative safety of the alley-way beside the Palais de Justice, but before we got there I passed out.

When consciousness returned, I was swimming up from the bottom of the ocean. I felt exhausted and slightly sick when I eventually surfaced on the couch in Alain de Courvel's sitting room. Madeleine and Louise were there, though it took me a little time to distinguish them properly as both my eyes seemed intent on functioning independently of each other.

In between bouts of pain and swigs of something hot and very sweet which I was told was tea, I learnt what had happened. Apparently, some thug screaming support for Felipe had broken a bottle on the back of my head as fighting broke out all over the square. Louise and I had been rescued by Alain and his photographer, Michel Ormond, the latter having sustained a black eye in a fruitless defence of his camera which had been torn out of his hands and smashed to the ground. So far as was known, no one had been seriously hurt, but a lot of damage had been done and Felipe and some of his immediate followers had been arrested.

This was disturbing, but my immediate concern was for Louise. I asked her if she was all right in a voice that grated like that of somebody with a botched throat-cut. She said she was, but I was still anxious and tried to sit up, a manoeuvre I immediately regretted.

'You are not to move,' Madeleine said. 'Alain got a doctor to look at you before bringing you here. He said you would be dizzy for a while, but he was fairly sure there was no real danger. However, he said you were to remain absolutely still until he had been back to see you again. Ah,' she said as a bell rang out in the hallway, 'that will be him, I expect.'

It was. A tall, lean-faced young man with thinning hair, who looked at me with an amused expression. 'Back to the living,' he quipped cheerfully as he examined my eyes and then probed happily around at the back of my head and neck. In no time at all he straightened up and closed his bag with a decisive snap.

'You'll do,' he said, 'though I should take things very easy for a day or two. Just in case.'

Just in case of *what*, for God's sake!

After he had gone, I managed to get as far as the bathroom, where I changed into one of Alain's shirts, thoughtfully provided by Madeleine in replacement of my bloodied one. The sight of myself in the mirror was disconcerting. My face looked as if I'd stumbled inadvertently into a nest of incensed hedgehogs. It was covered in cuts of varying sizes, including one quite deep gash down the left side of the forehead that was still oozing slightly. To complete the picture, a sizeable bump had appeared just behind and above my left ear. I grimaced, and immediately all the gashes were maliciously mobilized. I remembered something else I'd said to Henry Corby about the natives of La Roque. I'd have at least one good scar to prove it.

Back in the sitting-room, a jug of coffee and a plate of sandwiches had appeared, and I was managing to do some justice to these when we heard the front door slam and the sound of feet on the stairs.

Alain's appearance, when he entered the room, was hardly more elegant than my own. He had what looked like the best part of a bag of flour over his back, and the rest of him was grubby and dishevelled. He cast an appraising eye in my direction and for a second I almost thought I detected an element of sympathy.

'Quite a picture,' he said.

'Thank you. I understand I owe it to you that it didn't get hung.'

A faint smile came to his lips and he and Madeleine exchanged glances in that special way I had noticed before.

I looked up at him carefully. 'Are *you* O.K.?' I asked.

He shrugged, looking down at his clothes. 'As you see. Nothing worse, I'm glad to say.' He glanced at me again and this time the smile could almost have passed for a grin. 'Your face really is charming,' he said.

'I know. I trust the gent who did it will be taking his breakfast off a tin plate in the morning.'

'Probably not. Your friends may be, though, unless they're extremely lucky.'

'But dammit, they were attacked! It was a deliberate, put-up job. You saw it yourself!'

'I know. And I've got most of their names – though unfortunately not their pictures. The trouble is they were masquerading as Rochas supporters, and they faded out like morning mist as soon as they'd done what they'd been paid to do.'

'You do agree, then, that that was what it was – a put-up job?'

'Oh, certainly. But in the absence of what Blanchard calls "concrete evidence" he's just holding those he sees as the ring-leaders – your brothers, I'm afraid, Señorita Rochas – and one or two others who were foolish enough to get drawn into the actual fighting. I've given him my version of what happened, and the names I took. He'll question them, of course, I've no doubt, and they, of course, will deny it, and since it's their word against mine and Ormond's they're pretty certain to get off with a caution.'

'And Felipe? You can't seriously imagine he'll be *charged*?'

He shrugged again. 'I don't know. If Blanchard considers he can work up a case – As he sees it, none of it would have happened if there had been no meeting. Therefore, he holds Felipe Rochas responsible.'

'So if a building falls on you, it's *your* fault for being underneath it!'

'Well, I suppose if you've put up the building yourself in the first place, it *could* be – but I'm not arguing the ethics of that.' He helped himself to a sandwich. 'I've spoken to Le Marnet. He saw some of it from his office windows. Not enough to be very helpful, unfortunately, but he says if your brothers *are* arrested, Señorita, he will act for them. Even if they're not – ' he pulled his mouth down – 'it can still be bad for them. Under our law they can be kept in custody up to six days pending the police investigation, which is not an amusing prospect.'

The sheer injustice of the situation was so blatant that for a moment all I could do was sit and stare at him in silence.

'The Orthoz have a farm to run,' murmured Louise worriedly, 'and Tonio Rodriguez teaches. It may get him into serious trouble. Jaime, also. He's an accounts clerk at Maillard's and they're very old-fashioned. All their staff have to have references as long as their arms.'

'Well, there's nothing quite so old-fashioned as a jail sentence,' said Alain with dark humour. 'But don't worry too much. If Jaime de Castro loses his job, I'll see he gets another. Unfortunately, I can't promise the same for all of them, but I'll do what I can.'

It was clear that something more had happened to Alain in the last few hours than collecting half a bag of flour and a smashed camera. I looked at him appreciatively and noted that Louise was doing the same.

'You'll print what *really* happened?' I asked.

'Yes. Rocard won't like it; staying clear of unpopular issues is his idea of objective journalism, but he's not getting away with it this time.'

I gathered he was talking about his editor. I had never worked out just how big Alain was on his paper, but clearly he was able to challenge the Chair with a certain amount of impunity.

'What effect is this likely to have on Felipe's chances for the St Michel deputyship?' I asked at length.

'You mean,' said Alain, 'how are we on martyrs?' He shrugged. 'Like most communities, we dote on them – especially the really dead ones. The living are not always so lucky. Much will depend on which way the wind is blowing when Corlander lights the wood under them. If it's in our faces and it smells bad, we *may* just let them burn.'

It was the first time any of us had mentioned the name we all felt to be behind what had happened; now Alain dropped it quite casually, as though its relevance was not in the slightest doubt. I studied his face closely and for the first time it seemed to me that there were signs there that the bitterness within was no longer merely a corrosive element, but was being channelled into some positive line of thought and action.

'We *are* right, I suppose,' I said, 'about who was behind this? I mean, it couldn't have been just what it looked like – a bunch of drunks out for an evening's entertainment.'

'Not these particular drunks,' he said. 'As I said, I know them. I know their connections. Three of them actually work for Corlander. All of them have what you might call a dubious history.'

'There wasn't a fellow called Montez among them, I suppose? Raymondo Montez?'

He glanced at me. 'As a matter of fact, there was.' He paused. 'It struck me as strange.'.

'Yes?' I was extremely interested now in what he would say.

'Montez works for Guy Le Marnet.' He stopped suddenly, and we both looked at each other. I nodded. For the first time, something had clicked between us. I was certain now that he was no longer fighting me. He probably still had reservations about some of my inferences, but this wasn't one of them. *Someone* – and I blessed him – had certainly punched one hell of a hole in Alain de Courvel's defences. Daylight, it seemed, was streaming in by the minute.

'What's his weakness?' I asked. 'Smuggling?'

'God knows. But if you're thinking of tackling him on that score, forget it. You'll need more than a confession

233

from a frightened man. And proof is not going to be quite so easy to arrange.'

'So everybody keeps telling me. But if I can persuade him that his future would be rosier on someone else's plantations – '

'And get yourself hauled in for threatening behaviour? Blanchard would throw the book at you, and they'd love that.'

He was right. A silence fell, broken eventually by Madeleine.

'Neither Bernard Corlander nor anyone else would have got anywhere on this island if people hadn't let him,' she said. She looked from one to the other of us and her voice, when she next spoke, had an uncomfortable edge to it. 'It's always the same, isn't it? Human nature. No objection to eating the meat so long as someone else butchers it.'

The brutal choice of metaphor was startling, coming from her. But then, how well did I really know her? For that matter, how well did I know anyone here? Even Louise. I looked at her, and what I saw in her face made me change my mind. It was not difficult to know Louise. Everything she felt – apprehension, anxiety, compassion, tenderness – yes, tenderness – was all there, burning in those dark, beautiful, intelligent eyes. I smiled at her and an answering tremor touched her lips. I trusted Louise. I *had* to. God help me, I loved her. Yes – There it was. I loved her – and she knew it: unless she was blinder than a baby bat.

I realized that Alain had asked me a question and I tried to pull myself together. 'Sorry,' I said.

'One of those rough-necks – you probably didn't have time to distinguish them – but one of them works for Cartier.'

I looked at him steadily. His voice was even, but was there, once again, at the back of his eyes, something of the bitter personal animosity I had come to hate in him? Were we even now doomed to drift apart, divided by this venomous passion of his against the Cartiers? Suddenly, the St Michel affair loomed over me and a dragging fatigue

234

took possession. It was great to be surrounded by so many good friends and well-wishers, but what I desperately needed was an educated ally, someone whose support was backed by an intimate understanding of the personalities and problems involved. I knew I could count on Nick, but his occupation made him cautious. For a moment, in this room, I had almost come to hope that Alain de Courvel and I might at last talk, that to him I might confide some of the disturbing apprehension that was gripping me. Now, yet again, I was unsure.

Madeleine wanted me to remain at the flat for the rest of the day, but when Louise suggested that she collected Felipe's car from behind the Square and drop me at the hotel on her way home, I seized the opportunity of a few minutes alone with her. I would fetch my own car later, when arms, legs and eyes seemed in slightly better agreement with one another.

Alain left before us, first, he said, to see Blanchard at the Police Centrale, then Nicholas with a report of his findings on the police case. 'I'll ring you,' he said.

When Louise arrived with the car, I made considerable play of the difficulties of getting downstairs and into it, which had precisely the result I'd hoped for: at the Royale, she took the car round to the private car-park and said, 'I'd better see you safely up to your room.'

We got some odd looks as we passed through the foyer and a careful avoidance of any eye contact at all from the lift man, who took us all the way up to the fourth floor without once turning his head. I tried not to limp too noticeably until he had gone, but managed a strategic stumble on the way to my door and was gratified to feel Louise's hand come gently to my arm. Once inside the room, however, I realized that gentle arm-touching was about all I was likely to get if I overdid things, so made a gallant show of rallying my physical faculties to the extent of making it over to the bookcase where I kept my drinks. Now, however, the arm-touching was rather more firm than gentle.

'No, thank you,' she said.

'No?'

'No. And neither do you.' She took the bottle from my hands and placed it back on the tray. 'Aspirin, alcohol and bangs to the head do not go together,' she said. 'As you well know.'

There was only one thing left, so I did it. It was a long, lingering kiss, very warm, very satisfying – up to a point.

'Does anything else?' I asked her.

'What?'

'Go together?'

She smiled, and I kissed her again, but then, rather more quickly, she detached herself.

'Not at this moment,' she said.

'I can't think of a better one.'

'You will,' she said. 'You will.'

I watched her as she picked up her handbag from the settee and walked towards the door. I made no attempt to stop her, but when she turned there, I met her smile with my own.

'You can bank on it,' I said.

NINETEEN

Chief Inspector Blanchard was a suave gentleman whose manners were impeccable. Nevertheless, he wouldn't let me see the Rochas brothers when I approached him the next day, and he would give me no indication of when the men being held were likely to be released. When I declared that he had no right to continue to hold them without charging them, he gave me a long look and suggested that possibly, as a native and a policeman, he could claim to know a little more about the laws of the island than I.

'That being the case,' I said, 'you should know that what I say is true.' I was bluffing and we both knew it, but, in the absence of anything better to throw at him, it was all I could do.

He didn't answer, but the smile that came to his face and the way in which he picked up his coffee cup were as near plain insolent as mattered.

'I shall be in touch with Monsieur Nicholas Le Marnet,' I said rather unwisely and he was quick to see his advantage.

'That is good, M'sieu. There is no one better fitted to instruct you in our legal procedures.'

I was so infuriated that I walked out without asking whether Louise could see her brothers. The thought of going back in again like a forgetful schoolboy was almost more than I could bear, but for Louise's sake I forced myself to do so and received, as I anticipated, a further helping of humble pie. Blanchard was cold and to the point.

'*Non*,' he said.

I was still incensed when I rang Louise from my room, but she calmed me down with her usual gentle reasoning and cool commonsense.

'I know Blanchard,' she said. 'He's too shrewd to act outside his rights and it will not help to antagonize him.

237

Leave it for today, Angus. We'll try again tomorrow. Monsieur Le Marnet has done all he can, too, for the moment. He rang me last night. Also Monsieur Laurent. He said he and Monsieur Despard had both been in touch with Blanchard and he assured me that the most Blanchard will do is to hold Felipe and the others in custody for a day or two as a warning. He said it was better to accept it quietly than to risk giving cause for further action.'

I'd forgotten about Despard and Laurent. '*They* weren't arrested then?'

'They weren't there when the trouble started. They'd left. It was only the men on the platform with Felipe who were held and those who got into the fighting.'

'*Why* weren't they on the platform? They were the other evening at the village hall.' Suspicion was once more raising its ugly head.

'I expect because it *was* evening. They are both extremely busy men. Monsieur Laurent told me that they wanted to be seen there yesterday, but it was not possible for them to stay.'

Lucky for them.

'I must have a word with Nicholas,' I said.

'Not today, Angus. There is nothing you or he can do, and today you should rest.'

'Will you hold my hand if I come out and see you?'

I heard a soft sound of amusement.

'Say eight-thirty?'

This time she laughed properly. 'Oh, very well. Eight-thirty.'

It was a long time to eight-thirty and I was restless. In addition, I didn't want to have to think about the other major problem on my mind. I knew that sooner rather than later I would have to find some resolution of the unease I felt about Simone and all the troublesome implications that had begun to form around her, but right now I almost welcomed the chance to involve myself in a battle of a cruder, more direct kind. Accordingly, I ignored Louise's advice and went to see Nicholas at his office.

The girl on the reception desk there was young and clearly Spanish. I wasn't sure which startled her the more, my battered face or the fact that I had no appointment. At all events, she went off to an inner office to consult her oracle. This turned out to be a middle-aged Frenchwoman, who was obviously annoyed at being disturbed and not much mollified by my appearance. However, she mellowed a little when I explained that I was a personal friend of Monsieur Le Marnet's and that my business was extremely important, and after an uncomfortably penetrating scrutiny she put out a hand and lifted the receiver of one of the telephones on the desk. After a slight pause, she spoke into it: '*Pardon Monsieur Le Marnet, il y a un Monsieur Logan qui voudrait parler avec urgence . . . Oui, il est ici . . . Bien.*'

When she replaced the receiver and looked at me again it was, I fancied, with a shade less hostility.

'Monsieur Le Marnet has a client with him at the moment, but he will see you next,' she said. She managed to make this concession on her part sound like a summons and I thanked her with due humility. She acknowledged the performance with a curt nod and swept off into her private sanctum, leaving me to the rather breathless regard of the little Spanish girl. Altogether, it was something of a relief when, about five minutes later, I heard Nick's client departing and Nick himself appeared in the doorway. He took one look at my face and recoiled.

'My *God*!'

'I know,' I said. 'But it's only window-dressing. Nothing broken.'

He looked at me for a while as if he didn't believe me, then he grinned and motioned to me to follow him upstairs to his office.

'I shall do what I can, of course,' he said when we'd both sat down, 'but in the short term Blanchard holds all the cards, I'm afraid. He *could* – though he won't – call it inflammatory behaviour in a public place, leading to

239

incitement to riot, which is an offence, if proved, punishable by imprisonment up to one month.'

'But that's bloody ridiculous.'

He nodded. 'Blanchard probably knows that as well as you or I, but if he's called to put down a free fight in a public place he's got to take action of some sort, if only as a deterrent.'

'So why the hell didn't he round up a few of the *real* troublemakers? There were plenty of them. *I* know. I was there.'

'The trouble is, *they weren't* – by the time the police arrived on the scene. Could you pick out any of them in a line-up? The one who attacked you, for instance?'

'Well, no. But Alain said he'd collected a few names.'

He sighed. 'I keep telling him, all the good that will do is that Blanchard will question them, they will deny it and we're left with the onus of proof. By the time the law arrived, nobody seemed to know *who* had started it. You can't arrest a couple of hundred people.'

'Nick, you can't doubt that this was a put-up job?'

He sighed again and spread his hands out across the desk. 'Whether I do or I don't is of absolutely no consequence. Privately, I may agree with you that Blanchard's position in this is somewhat dubious, but what we can prove and what we merely suspect are two very different things.' His face, as he looked at me, screwed itself up into one of his expressions of special concern. 'Angus, try to stop Alain shooting off in that paper of his. He will only get himself into trouble and make matters a lot worse than they already are.'

'Could they be?'

'They certainly could. At the moment, all Blanchard can do is hold Rochas and his friends for a day or so. He can't make a charge stick in court without taking statements from almost everybody who was in the square. In fact, the more likely it is that he has been bought, the better our chances are, because, if he has, he won't risk provoking too many counter-charges. So tell Alain to leave the harassment to me. I shall keep at him, but within the limits of the law.

Rochas and the others will be back home within three days,
I promise you.'

'Louise Rochas wants to see her brothers.'

'Yes. I've spoken to her. I'll ask Blanchard, but he is
within his rights to refuse and I have advised her to accept
his decision without argument if he does.'

When I left him, a young woman with a small baby in her
arms was struggling up the stairs. Adoption? Shot-gun
wedding? Or just nobody at home to mind Junior while you
consult the wisdom of the law? Whichever, Nicholas –
good, worried old Nicholas – would cope.

The Rochas farm seemed unusually quiet when I arrived
there that evening. This, I realized, was not because of the
absence of the brothers, but because it was a Saturday when
most work on the island traditionally stopped at midday.
On weekdays, it was not unusual to find work still being
done well into the evening hours.

The French windows of what I thought of as the 'garden
room' were open and I went in that way, calling out my
arrival as I did so. I heard Louise answer from somewhere
at the back of the house, and presently she came in, smiling.
She indicated the drinks tray on the sideboard.

'Help yourself.'

'What about you?'

'I'll have a dry sherry, please.'

While I poured two Finos, I told her of my meeting with
Blanchard and of the conversation I had had later with
Nick. She listened in silence, sitting on the settee near the
open windows, through which, every so often, came a
refreshing scent of flowers. She had drawn up two small
tables, one at each end of the settee and I carried the drinks
over and placed them carefully on their respective mats. I
offered her a cigarette, but she shook her head.

'You go ahead, though,' she said, and she reached across
to another table near the window and produced an ashtray,
which she placed beside my glass. As she leant over to do
this, I caught a subtle whiff of perfume and felt myself

241

responding to the close physical presence of her. I'd known – and, to some extent, satisfied – sexual desire a few times since Maggie died, but this was the first time I'd felt the kind of uneasiness that goes with deep emotional involvement. Did I dare hope it was mutual? I wondered. These things often were. But you couldn't bank on it. Women were adept at playing it cool. You could get frost-bite trying to figure out whether they meant it or not. And by the time you'd finished, nine times out of ten they were bored witless. The moral of all this being that in love, as in war, irresolution is death. This being so, I decided to speed up the rituals a little. Delicately, mind. I asked her to play me something on the guitar I'd seen in the music room. She looked surprised, but obediently got up and went to get it. She played a stately chaconne, followed by a slow sara-bande, and then something unmistakably Spanish, full of sad, Moorish undertones, haunting and incredibly beauti-ful. It did the trick for both of us. I moved over, took the guitar from her hands, laid it carefully down on the settee and kissed her. It was the second time in twenty-four hours.

But it wasn't the last.

It turned out that all the predictions were correct. Blanchard released his prisoners three days later and the first thing that happened was that Jaime de Castro lost his job. Worse, Alain's promise to find him another transpired to be empty, because he, himself, had a raging row with his editor and walked out. It seemed the latter had taken one shocked glance at the article which Alain had written on the affray in the Place de Justice and had adamantly refused to print. I remembered Nicholas's warnings, which had proved all too justified, and I wondered what Alain would do. I was more worried, however, about young Castro, who now looked set fair for the position of the party's first official martyr. It was to be hoped that the school authorities would prove more humane in the case of Antonio Rodriguez. Then, there was Felipe himself. It would be interesting indeed to see what Max would do in the matter. Of the others, only young Luis Garcia had to answer to an employer and he was still young enough to adapt himself with the minimum of inconvenience to whatever came along.

By lunch-time that day, it was clear that neither Max Cartier nor Bernard Corlander planned any disciplinary action against Felipe or Garcia, and the irony of this amused rather than surprised me. It was part of the Corlander image, this pretence of benevolent non-involvement.

During the course of the week, it became clear that Nicholas's interventions were having results. He did nothing dramatic; in fact, it almost seemed that he was doing nothing at all, yet a number of things happened, more or less overnight, that I knew he was directly responsible for. The first was that Rodriguez was interviewed by his headmaster and, after a severe warning of the possible repercussions of further participation in public disturbance, left the room with the assurance that his job, at least for the moment, was safe. Next, Jaime de Castro received a letter from a director of Maillard's informing him that the firm had reconsidered his position and in view of his past record and his obvious, though misguided, sincerity, etc., etc., were prepared to reinstate him, provided he would give a guarantee that his behaviour in future would not reflect discredit in any way whatsoever upon the firm's good name. Whether Jaime would have felt able to give such a guarantee was a question that fortunately didn't arise, as, in the time it had taken Nicholas to do his stuff with Maillard's, André Laurent had installed the young man in his own offices down on the wharf. In so doing, he had declared his interest for all to see, which finally convinced me of the man's good will.

Alain's position remained doubtful. His editor, it seemed, made several attempts during the week to bring about a reconciliation, but Alain's resentment at what he regarded as a demeaning restraint on his exercise of his professional function went too deep to be healed over a span of days. I felt more than sorry for Madeleine, who expressed no opinion on the matter, at least in my presence, and seemed as resigned to this development as to everything else in her life with Alain.

On Thursday, the island's paper announced that the decision of the Lands Committee on the Iturbi affair would be raised before the Grand Council on the following Monday. I thought uneasily of Guy and wondered for the umpteenth time how an obstinate old man who was determined to put his head into the lion's mouth could possibly be protected. My vague apprehensions on this score took on a sharp reality at mid-morning when, sitting over a tepid cup of hotel coffee, I was handed the telephone. From an ageing, tearful, female voice at the other end I learned that Pierre Bouchier had fallen down the cellar steps at the Manoir Mont Vert and broken his collar-bone.

My first reaction on hearing what had happened was to reflect that in the three and a half weeks, give or take a day, since I had been on the island I had been about as much help to all with whom I had come in contact as a piece of string to an expedition falling off a mountain. Two people had been seriously injured, eight clapped in gaol and two had lost their jobs, and at the end of it all I was no nearer the truth about the death of Maurice de Courvel.

Pierre's story, as heard from Madame later that day, was typical of a household inhabited solely by elderly people. The cellar steps at Mont Vert had been in need of attention for some time. The original stone steps had been replaced by a wooden staircase when Nicholas and Imogen were children and this in turn had become rickety, a fact which Pierre had apparently considered unworthy of being brought to Guy's notice since only he himself ever used the steps. His sense of security seemed to derive from his faith in his ability to count up to seven, the seventh step having been the potential hell-raiser. That the seventh step should thus have been his downfall, collapsing completely and flinging him some six feet to the ground, seemed as inevitable as the law of gravity itself – except for the fact that only three weeks previously, at Madame's insistence, Pierre had repaired it. Since then, the old lady affirmed, it had been as firm as the top of her solid old kitchen table. Pierre had had wood sent up from the village specially and had replaced the whole step. She was adamant that he had made a good job of it; he had never done a shoddy piece of work in his life, she passionately claimed, and I believed her, even while the analogy that kept presenting itself to my mind was of the well-charted dangers of putting new wine into old bottles. This, of course, was the reasonable explanation. It should have satisfied. But it didn't. Once again, all the things that pointed to the possibility of sabotage – the timing, the implicit elements of threat – were subtly obscured, this time by the cloud of doubt arising from the frailty and vulnerability of an anxious old man exposed to a potentially dangerous situation. And once again, any attempt to pin the blame anywhere outside the range of the accident seemed hopeless.

If any comfort at all could be drawn from the situation, apart from the fact that Pierre was at least still alive, it was that now, for sure, Guy would be compelled to give in. I was almost sorry this was so when I went to report to him after I had seen Pierre in hospital.

'I know how you feel, sir,' I said, 'but at least everyone knows where you stand. You took it as far as you could.'

He looked at me without speaking, and his face seemed to have lost colour and got thinner in the space of just a few hours. I felt a sudden stab of foreboding as I studied him, but I had no idea why until he spoke.

'Yes,' he said at last, pausing for a moment, lost in thought. Then he looked up into my face again, straightening himself as he did so. 'This makes no difference, Angus,' he said. 'I shall not withdraw.'

I must have looked as I felt, for he smiled gently, like an old man with a child. 'I'm sorry, my boy. I know how *you* feel. But there it is. I must do what I am sure is right.'

I drew in my breath, closed my eyes and then opened

them again, but he was still there, standing straight and firm, with that gentle smile on his face. 'You can't possibly be serious,' I said. But I knew he was.

'Oh, yes. Never more so. You see, Angus, I'm not being brave, or even – as you might think – stubborn.' (I was past smiling at this.) 'I am merely being logical.'

I waited helplessly. If he was going to be academic at a time like this!

'Don't you see?' he asked. 'No, clearly you don't. The point is that nothing worse than this can happen. No, it can't,' he said, forestalling an expected contradiction. 'If this was treachery – and I am beginning to agree with you about that – then it is about the worst possible thing they could have thought of. They have created a situation of abominable suffering for the two people I value as much as anyone else left to me in this world. But if I give up now, I shall neither help them nor anyone else on this island. If I go on, they can do nothing more to me that matters, but I can at least try to break their power. I *shall* try to break it. I owe that to those like your friends, Señor Rochas, who are also trying. Who knows, even if *we* don't succeed, the fact that we did what we could may encourage others, and one day perhaps this island will find its way back to reason and sanity.'

Old as he was, his eyes held the hardness of youth as he said this, and I felt sick.

'We can't put the clock back,' he said. 'We don't want to, or, at least, we shouldn't. Seigneurial rule is finished on La Roque. That is as it should be. We did our best. We were for our time. All that matters is that the new law shall be a good one; and that the *people* shall decide. Without duress. Without fear. Without seduction. The duty left to us now is to ensure this. So, you see, Angus, I have to go on just this little longer.'

I stared at him for a long time. The worst part was that I knew he was right. I thought of Maurice. He must have felt the same, for he and Guy were of the same mould. Yet he had given up. Again, the everlasting question. But now

Guy's eyes remained on mine and I knew I was licked.

'Right,' I said briskly, 'that's it, then.' A thought struck me. 'What about Madame? Could she perhaps come here with you until Pierre is out of hospital?'

His face relaxed into a smile. 'She could,' he said, 'but she won't. In any case, I'm going home, my boy. I should never have left. Don't worry. I very much doubt if there will be any further incidents of this particular kind. They tend to betray their perpetrators after a while. Our enemies are too clever for that.'

Once again, he was right.

'O.K., sir, but in that case I'm moving in with you – and *I* should have done *that* in the first place.'

A small chuckle signified his submission and we eventually managed to convince Nicholas and Stéphanie of the inevitability, if not the wisdom, of the proposition, so that in the evening, after an early supper, I took him home. There, we found that Madame had meanwhile made some arrangements of her own.

'My grandson is coming,' she said. 'Marcel, Monsieur,' she said to Guy, pursing her lips and nodding ominously, clearly in confirmation of some dire knowledge that they both shared. To me, she added: 'He is seventeen, Monsieur, and – ' she measured with her arm to a point high above her head – 'right up to here. And strong!' She nodded vehemently again and her dark eyes flashed fiercely. 'He is a blacksmith, Monsieur,' she finished simply.

I moved out of the Hotel Place Royale with considerable satisfaction. Not that I had any tangible reason for suspecting any interference with my personal belongings, but I had never felt secure on that score and I therefore paid my bill with a gratification that owed nothing to Corlander's tariff terms.

The following evening, Nicholas and Stéphanie came to see whether they could persuade Guy to change his mind and go back with them, but he would have nothing of it, and eventually, after a supper served very creditably by the magnificent Marcel, they gave up and went home.

I slept badly that night. It had nothing to do with the strangeness of the room. It was because, here at Mont Vert, I was more conscious of the reason I had come to the island than anywhere else on its surface. And with that consciousness of the mystery surrounding the death of Maurice there returned, in full force, the mystery of his daughter. I had to face that mystery, and I had to do so without any further delay. I was conscious of an urgency that was not wholly to do with the sense of violence that had begun to surround those I cared about, but was also in some indefinable way connected with Simone herself. By morning, I had made a decision. I would go and try to talk with Simone. The thought filled me with foreboding, but I could see no other way.

First, however, before joining Guy at breakfast, I went down to the cellar. I had taken a cursory look at the steps the previous evening, but this time I studied the whole situation carefully. From the house, the cellar was approached through a door just beyond the kitchen. This led immediately on to the wooden staircase that had been Pierre's *bête noire*. This seemed reasonably secure at the top, but the steps above and below the broken one were extremely hazardous. Whether they had been weakened by the collapse, or had previously been uncertain, it was impossible to tell, as was also the cause of the collapse, as Madame had been correct in saying that the wood was new. It looked as if the nails had been torn out, arguably by Pierre's weight on them, and it hardly seemed unreasonable to doubt an old man's efficiency as a carpenter.

There was, however, another entrance to the Mont Vert cellar and this was outside the house at the bottom of some stone steps which led into a small, almost weed-covered basement about three or four yards from the kitchen window. Here, there was a small wooden door that Pierre kept 'locked' by means of a simple 'hook-and-eye' type of fastening, the only purpose of which, I was told, was to keep the cats out. It was obvious that anyone who wanted to enter the cellar secretly could have done so through this door at almost any time between eleven o'clock at night, when Pierre habitually retired, and six in the morning, when he customarily made his rounds. I found that the door opened easily and with barely any noise, but inside there was nothing to arouse suspicion. The boiler that heated the Manoir's water supply was here, together with coal and wood in separate compartments bounded by loose bricks. There was an axe, a chopping block, several buckets and a couple of shovels, plus a few dirty rags, cans of oil, the usual empty cardboard boxes and several piles of old newspapers.

Back upstairs, I asked Madame who chopped the wood.

'Oh, that is my *second* grandson, Monsieur,' she said, smiling proudly. 'Jean-Pierre. He is the brother of Marcel,' she added, giving the distinction an unmistakable emphasis.

I nodded and returned her smile, resigned yet again to the inevitable *impasse*.

'He is fourteen and he works with his great-uncle – you remember him, Monsieur? – Pierre's brother, Armand? – in the gardens here?'

Oh, yes, I remember old Armand, all right: another lily-white character, about as likely a candidate for treachery as the Archangel Gabriel; been with Guy – like the other two – for as long as I'd known the family, and then some. I stifled a curse, smiling brightly, and went to join Guy over breakfast.

Neither of us spoke much over the meal. Guy looked tired and strained behind the usual smiling courtesy, and I had a great deal on my mind. Afterwards, Marcel drove Guy's big car up to the front door and the old man and Madame went off to visit Pierre in hospital. With the house to myself, I stood for a while at Guy's study window, staring out over the gardens, the domain of old Armand and young Jean-Pierre. The view was soothing, but the urgency I had felt throughout the night returned now in full force, and I went over to the old man's bureau and picked up the phone. With the receiver half-way to my ear, I changed my mind. This time, I wouldn't ring. This time, I'd try the tactic of surprise.

There was no answer to Simone's bell at the house at St George's. At the third ring, however, the ground floor window opened and a face, framed by an unruly mass of auburn hair, appeared in the gap.

'Hullo, there. She's not in, I'm afraid.'

I went to walk over to the window, but she waved me back.

'Hang on. I'm coming out.'

A few seconds later, a shadow loomed against the stained glass of the door, which opened to reveal a large, untidy young woman wearing a long cotton skirt, and a blouse that looked as if it had been used to wrap cheese in. The ends of this were tied together in the front, separating skirt from blouse and giving the whole ensemble a look of the Spanish gypsy, Andalusian-style. With the glorious hair, the concerted effect was of a wild, unco-ordinated mass, redeemed – and this without question – by superb blue eyes and a complexion like pure alabaster.

'Hullo,' she said again. 'You're Angus.'

'And you're Rose.'

'That's right. Are you going to look after her?'

The abruptness of the question shook me. 'Sorry?'

'Well, *someone* should.' Her eyes, which continually seemed to hold a hint of mischief in them, took on a quizzical look as she cocked her head to one side. 'You'll have noticed it, I'm sure.'

I was still floundering for an answer when she went on: 'Well, you've seen how it is. Her old man was a swine, her brother never comes near her, her pa's dead, and even her kid – poor little pigeon – never utters. If ever a girl needed a friend – '

Friend. I grasped at this with relief.

'Yes,' I said, 'she does, and I am. At least – ' I stopped, uncertain where I was heading.

'Yes?' She looked at me keenly.

'Well – ' I paused again. 'The problem is,' I said, 'she may not see it that way.'

She didn't answer for a moment, but continued to look into my face with a shrewdness I would have found disconcerting in anyone I trusted less than I instinctively did her.

'Well,' she said at last, 'you can only do your best.'

'Yes,' I agreed. 'That's all.'

I turned to go, but at the gate I looked back.

'She's up at the house very likely,' she said.

I nodded. 'Thanks.'

There was no smile on her face as she stood there, watching me. But the human sympathy that seemed to emanate from her in waves was with me long after I had turned the car and driven out of her sight.

I parked just inside the gate at St Michel and walked up the drive to the coach-houses. Simone's car was there as I'd been led to expect, but there was no sign of her and the yellow door was closed. When I tried it, however, it opened and I stepped inside with a show of resolution I was far from feeling and closed the door behind me. I went up the stairs quickly, making no effort to be quiet, and on reaching the landing I saw that the door of the sitting-room was open. Inside, Simone was standing near the table, waiting. Her eyes, fixed on the doorway, were wide with apprehension, and when I appeared she neither moved nor spoke.

I moved towards her, and when we were close enough to touch each other I drew the copy of *Adam Bede* from under my arm and held it out to her. Her eyes moved from my face towards the book, but it took her a second or two to recognize it even though the binding was the same as on her own Blackwood copy and the title was clear. When the significance at last hit her, the effect was no less disturbing than I'd feared. I heard a sharp intake of breath; her face lost all colour and her eyes, lifted again towards mine, stared wildly. She had to struggle to speak, but, when her voice came, there was a strength and a passion in it that shook me.

251

'Damn you!' she said. 'Damn you to hell! How *dare* you!'

And before I could see what was coming, she brought up her arm and caught me full in the face with a blow that sent all the good old healing processes into instant and bloody retreat.

TWENTY

Of course, I had it coming to me. I don't deny that for an instant. In a curious way, it was almost a relief: a sort of purge of all the guilt I'd been feeling over the past few weeks. But I'd never been attacked by a woman before – and when I say 'attacked' I don't mean any of your mildly vicious pokes with a wet umbrella in a bus queue; I mean 'attacked' as according to dictionary definition: 'to fall upon violently: to assault: to assail with unfriendly words . . .' By way of self-defence I grabbed her flailing hands and forcibly pulled her down into a sitting position on the bed. It's difficult to belabour someone when you're sitting down. Unfortunately, it doesn't stop the unfriendly words. Out of loyalty and affection for Simone, I shall not repeat them all. Suffice to say, that some of the French ones were new to me – though their meanings were indisputably clear, and in olden days women had been rolled down hills in barrels for far, far less. Eventually, she exhausted herself and fury was replaced by a tearful, vicious logic.

'I thought you were a friend. I've trusted you ever since I was a child. I thought you'd come here because you cared for Father, because you wanted to pay your respects. But all the time, you've been spying on us – I suppose for your damned magazine. And now you've actually been in this room, and you've been poking among my personal things. This book – ' she raised the copy of *Adam Bede* and I instinctively ducked – 'you actually *took* this away and kept it. You – '

'No, Simone,' I interrupted, 'I didn't.'

'Yes, you did. You actually – '

'I didn't. *Listen* – ' I tightened my grip on her hands and looked hard into her face. 'That book is not yours. No – ' as once more she tried to protest – 'it isn't. It's a copy I

253

borrowed. And,' I added quickly, 'I did *not* tell the person I borrowed it from why I wanted it.' That was not wholly true, but neither was it wholly *un*true. 'Look, Simone – ' Still holding her hands, I bent closer towards her – 'you're right about me poking around where I had no business to. Quite right. I've felt badly about it. But that's why I came here this morning, openly. Because I wanted you to know. I wanted you to talk to me. I wanted to try to explain to you that everything I've done is because I *am* a friend. It's why I came to the island – not for my damned magazine, as you put it. I came because what happened to your father shocked and grieved me very much. You *know* what I felt for him. And for you, Simone. You *know* that I care deeply what happens to you and little Hélène, for Alain, too, for that matter: you're the only family I've got. I've gone about all this in the wrong way, I know. I've loused everything up – '

'*No!*'

The sudden, unexpected contradiction came almost as a shout. The fierceness of it startled me; but it was the look on her face that alarmed me even more. It was agonized; and what happened next disturbed me almost as much as had her previous outburst. Without warning, she wrenched herself away from me and collapsed on to the pillow in a fit of uncontrollable weeping. Her whole body seemed to be torn by great, racking sobs and every so often she beat the pillow with clenched fists and rolled her head from side to side as though in actual physical agony. For a second, I was stunned, both by the suddenness and the terrible violence of it, then, tentatively, I put out a hand to her.

'Simone – '

But she only jerked further away from me, and all I could do was sit there beside her, helpless and shattered. I had never in my life witnessed anything quite like it and inwardly I cursed myself to hell for having precipitated it.

It seemed to go on for ever, but gradually I realized that she was growing quieter. The sobbing turned to a muted sort of moaning and her hands, clasped now round her head, became still.

'Simone – ' I bent towards her again, circling her head with my arm and placing one hand over hers. 'Simone. Please. Forgive me, Simone.'

For a while, she neither moved nor answered. Then I saw her head lift a fraction and gradually her will yielded to mine. As she slowly straightened, I took her face in my hand and turned it towards me. Poor Simone! She was a sorry mess, with the tears blotching her pink, swollen face and swimming still in the great green eyes. She had snatched her glasses off earlier, and now, as she replaced them, they sat for a moment slightly askew on her nose. It was a child's face, pathetic in its vulnerability, and there was a terrible aching inside me as I straightened her glasses and smoothed away the pale wisps of dishevelled hair from around her cheeks. I found a handkerchief for her and she blew her nose. Afterwards, looking at me, she gave a great sigh.

'I'm sorry,' she said.

As the pain hit me, I knew there was only one answer. I bent forward and kissed her, as gently as I knew how, on the cheek. Immediately, she moved her whole body towards me, and I held her close without speaking for what must have been a full minute. When she stirred, it was only to bury her head further into my shoulder and to cling to me more closely.

'Oh, Angus,' she whispered.

'I know, love, I know,' I said, and I rocked her in my arms like a baby. Then, gently, I sought to disengage myself.

'Simone,' I murmured. Then, as she moved to bury herself again, I resisted her more firmly.

'Please, Simone. Please try to tell me.'

For a while, I thought she was not going to respond, but then, reluctantly, she straightened and looked at me. Her face was pale again now, but her eyes still had the huge, hurt look of a child.

'Even if I did,' she said, 'you'd never know. Never. You couldn't. It's been terrible.'

'Try me,' I murmured.

'Everything I had . . . everything I touched . . .

everything that meant a thing to me . . . all taken away. One after the other . . . destroyed. And nobody cared. Nobody.' She paused. 'Not a single sodding soul,' she added with the sudden brutal coarseness of unendurable anguish.

'That isn't true, Simone.'

'It *is* true!' And now she was almost shouting again and her face was hard with rekindled passion. 'How can *you* know?' she demanded, glaring at me. 'How can you know *anything*? You were never here! Now, you come back and you want to know all the answers. Just like that! Why we did this and didn't do that. As if we were all puppets. On little strings. Waiting for you to come back and jerk us all into action. You, the famous, successful Angus Logan!'

I stared at her, aghast. 'Simone – '

'Oh, yes,' she said bitterly. 'Father always said you would make good. He set great store by you. You were going to come back one day and set us all to rights! Well, you came too late! You want to know what happened? Why everything went wrong? Why Father killed himself? Because of me! That's why – because of me!'

I shook my head. 'No, Simone.'

'Oh, *yes*, Simone!' she mocked. 'Yes, yes, yes,' she reiterated with a hard, angry emphasis. 'I did all the wrong things. I fell in love with the wrong man, so I had to be punished for that. So he died. And then I *married* the wrong man, so my baby died. And then Father . . .' her voice broke . . . 'Father turned against me at the end. He wouldn't talk to me. Every time I tried, he . . .' her voice failed her again and she fought for composure . . . 'he just stayed silent. All the time, silent. As though – ' She stopped altogether, staring down at the handkerchief she still held, twisting it over and over between her fingers. But I couldn't let her off. I couldn't show her any mercy now.

'As though, what?' I insisted.

'As though he despised me,' she finished. And now there was a distant look on her face, a remote, closed-in look, mingled with hopelessness as she contemplated a past that she could never change.

'Yes,' she said. 'That was how it was. Alain made him sad, but me he despised.' She paused, looking down again at her hands, and then, more, it seemed, to herself than to me, she whispered: 'He knew, you see.'

I waited, hoping she would go on unprompted, but she just sat there, lost within herself, almost as if she had forgotten everything that had immediately preceded this moment, or no longer cared. These sudden changes of mood disturbed me almost more than their effects. It was as if she were incapable of sustained, rational discussion, even of retaining any clear memory of such.

'Knew what?' I pressed. 'What did he know, Simone?'

She looked up at me as if she had just remembered I was there.

'He knew,' she said.

'Yes. But what, Simone?' I decided to go for bust. 'Was it about the baby?'

For a moment I thought I'd hit the spot again: that another avalanche of emotion was about to come. Her face puckered alarmingly and her eyes filled once more with tears. But this time she only stared at me, the far-away mood still upon her.

'He died,' she said.

'Yes, I know.'

'He had pneumonia. He was only nine days old.'

'Yes. I'm very sorry. It must have been terrible for you.' I stopped. Then, softly, looking straight into her face, I added: 'and for Raoul.'

It was flash-point. I hardly knew what to expect. I only knew that to persuade a festering wound to discharge its poison you sometimes had to use force. I saw horror come into her eyes, and her whole expression changed from a dream-like vagueness to one of menacing intensity. She sat perfectly still, locked in a rigidity that I knew was pitched a hair's-breadth short of panic. At last, her lips moved and I bent to catch the whisper.

'I don't know what you mean.'

'Oh, but you do, Simone.' I took her hands again in both

257

mine. 'You were in love with Raoul, and he with you. You used to meet here in this room – '

'No *one* knew that!' she interjected fiercely. 'No one! No one knew that!'

'True. You kept your secret well. *I* only guessed because of my abominable prying. And this – ' I touched the copy of *Adam Bede* where it lay on the bed beside us – 'and your note, and my rotten intuition. So far as everyone else is concerned, I imagine it's still generally accepted that the reason you two didn't marry was because poor old Raoul *couldn't* have children. But that wasn't quite true, was it?'

Her head jerked as she swallowed hard. 'You seem to have got it all worked out to your satisfaction. I suppose you've been discussing it with everyone behind my back.'

'I've discussed it with no one, Simone. I only saw it for myself last week when I found your kitchen window downstairs open and succumbed to the temptation. Yes, I know – ' as I saw her mouth twist in distaste – 'it was unforgivable. But I was desperately concerned. You were holding back from me. Once, we'd have talked. Now, you wouldn't. I sensed there was something troubling you that was worse than any of the things you and Alain had so far told me – '

'*He* never knew,' she interrupted passionately.

'And your father? You said just now – '

'Not that!' She looked anguished again. 'I didn't mean that.'

'What *did* you mean?'

'I – ' She stared at me wildly. 'I – oh, stop it!' She wrenched her hands out of mine and flung herself down again on to the pillow. 'Leave me alone!' she cried, her voice muffled. 'Go away! For God's sake, go away!'

It was heartbreaking, but I couldn't leave it at that. Lies and evasions had choked the life out of Simone, had turned her beautiful, healthy child into a mute, and had – I was certain of it – killed a fine old man. Now, the truth lay half-exposed between us. I could feel it, smell it. We were almost there. Already, I was certain I knew its nature, but

258

for her own sake as much as anyone's Simone had to admit it.

I bent and placed my hand on her shoulder. '*What* did your father know, Simone?'

She tried to pull away, but I held her by both shoulders now and drew her forcibly up towards me. Her frustration, when she felt herself powerless against me, bordered on hysteria.

'Leave me!' she cried. 'God damn you! Leave me!' But as I felt the hot tears falling on my hands, I sensed also that this second crisis between us was passing.

'Tell me, Simone,' I insisted. 'Tell me. *What* did your father know? Was it to do with the baby? *What* about the baby?'

'Let me go!' Still she fought me and still I hung on, and, as her frustration reached unendurable proportions, so, at last, her resistance snapped. 'All right, all right! He knew what I felt about it. . . . He knew that I wanted. . . . ' She caught her breath, and then it came. 'He knew I *wanted* it to die!'

'Like Hetty Sorrel.'

'Yes – *No!*' As the significance of what she had begun to say hit her, she gasped and her eyes bored into mine with a desperate intensity. 'I didn't *kill* my baby! Good God, is that what you thought? Did you think – Oh, my God!' Her hands went to her face and covered it as she fought for control.

'Hetty Sorrel didn't kill her baby either,' I said. 'Not really. She just let it die. Today, she would be treated with infinitely greater compassion because of what she had suffered.'

Slowly, she uncovered her face and looked at me. 'You think so?' She paused and her face took on a bitter sadness as her thoughts wandered off again into the past. 'I didn't kill my baby,' she murmured, 'but I did let it die. In here – ' She touched her abdomen. 'It was still-born. Only Nature – the old hag – wouldn't let it stop breathing. She let it go on pushing its way where it wasn't wanted.'

'But *why*, Simone? *Why*? Your baby was conceived in love.'

'Conceived in love. Oh, yes – ' Her mouth twisted in a mocking smile. 'We women are supposed to set great store by that sort of thing. Well, it's not going to be much comfort when the only father her child knows is a man he's going to grow up to loathe. And when he realizes that his mother is only living because she hasn't got the courage to die.'

'Oh, Simone – ' It was all even worse with her than I'd feared. 'Is this what he's done to you?'

'He?' she queried vaguely.

'Your ex. He found out, didn't he? About you and Raoul. About the baby. It was blackmail, wasn't it? Your marriage. He wanted to use you against your father. And later, I suppose, when he met Phyllis and felt he'd squeezed you dry, he wanted out.' I sighed. 'Yes, if your father "knew" anything, it was probably this. Not what you felt about the baby. But that Corlander was threatening to expose you. You never told Raoul? About the pregnancy?'

She shook her head. 'He was so desperately ill.'

'Yes. I can understand that. But it was a pity. No, Simone, your father didn't despise you; he just despaired. Don't you see? He was probably being blackmailed, too, before the end. He'd feel – ' I nodded several times to myself as, piece by piece, the pattern fell into place in my mind – 'he'd feel that if he were no longer here, the main incentive would be gone, that, now you were divorced, Corlander would eventually grow tired of putting pressure on you over the house, and you'd be free. That divorce was not our Ray's cleverest move, was it? But I suppose the enchanting Phyllis had a lot to do with that.'

I'd got a bit carried away with my reasoning, but now I realized that she was staring at me with a strange expression on her face. I took one of her hands in my own. 'I'm right about this, aren't I, Simone?'

She didn't answer, but continued to look at me in that rather odd way, as though she were seeing something for the first time. I hoped that, in time, as the truth about her father got through to her, the guilt she had carried around inside her for so long would finally die away. I squeezed the hand I held. 'I *am* right, aren't I?' I persisted.

And now, at last, I saw her head move in an almost imperceptible nod. Her lips parted and the look in her eyes seemed to me to be one of relief. 'Yes,' she said. 'Yes, you're right.' She paused for a moment, and then, as though a key had been turned, it all began to come tumbling out.

'He said if I didn't marry him, he'd tell everyone about Raoul and me, and about the baby. He said he had evidence. I don't know whether that was true, but I didn't dare risk it. I hadn't told Raoul that I was pregnant. I couldn't have borne him to feel he had to marry me because of that. Ray knew. He knew I'd do anything rather than have it all come out. He said I had to pretend to be madly in love with him, and after we were married I was to tell him everything I heard Father discussing with his friends, especially those who were members of the Assembly. He said he would want to know dates of meetings, and the people concerned and everything I could find out about them – '

'About the people?'

'Yes. He was insatiable. He just never let up, though I implored him to leave me alone. After we were married, it was worse. He tried to make me turn Father against Alain, so that everything would come to me when he died. Father had always said that the whole of St Michel – both the house and the estates – would come to us jointly. Both of us were to have equal rights to live here – we could convert it for the use of separate families if we wanted – and we would share the upkeep of it and the income from the plantations. Ray didn't like that. He wanted me to have it all. So he tried to make me influence Father against Alain. I – I couldn't. But it happened, anyway, when Alain went off on his own. It broke Father's heart. I – I couldn't do any more. Oh, Angus – ' She broke off, her face distorted. 'It's all been so terrible! Don't you see . . . I couldn't bear to think of our baby growing up surrounded by all this – this – greed and corruption, and all the lying and stealing, and the hating. I *wanted* him to die! Yes, I *wanted* it! It was wicked, awful! I know it was, but I didn't kill him, Angus . . . I didn't neglect him. He was sickly from the beginning and instead of willing him to live, I willed him to die! Oh, Angus!' She threw herself towards me and I held her hard and close while the agony of remembrance closed over her.

There were no tears this time, but somehow that silent suffering was worse. I tried to counter its deadly restraint by whispering endearments to her and stroking her hair, treating her as one would a precious, unhappy child. Perhaps that's what did it. I don't know. But suddenly she lifted her head from my chest, her whole body seemed to stiffen, and before I realized what was coming her arms were around my neck and I was on the receiving end of a kiss that was about as childlike as a lovesick sailor's.

I should like to say that, for old time's sake, Simone and I made love. I should dearly like to say that, because, as I've mentioned before, there is a part of me that has always loved Simone, and probably always will. But even as I sat there with her arms around me on that unmade bed in her secret room, stubborn instinct refused to be fooled. In a moment hardly propitious to rational thought, it told me that, despite what others may have believed, Simone had never seen me as a lover. And she didn't now. All that was happening now was something I'd seen in sterner natures than Simone's at moments of unbearable emotional strain. Maybe, as I've said, it's the sympathetic response of another human being that does it; the fact is that so long as things stay tough, everything holds up, but, given a kind word, the whole nervous system seems to collapse and one's reflexes start behaving in some very odd ways. Simone's, it seems, had run amok. By comparison, her earlier hysteria had been no more than a mild test-run.

I take no credit for having realized this: nor for further

perceiving that, for Simone, in that anguished few minutes
of time, I was not Angus Logan but a convenient strip of
ectoplasm for the use of one Raoul Cotarde. I'm glad I *did*
realize it, though, because, while it didn't exactly help me to
lie back and think of England, it did at least save me from
making the appalling mistake of resisting to the point where
Simone would have inferred rejection. For all that, it was
very necessary to think of *something*; when a woman
you've always half-fancied suddenly takes you in her arms
and starts caressing you as though life was going out of
fashion, there's a limit to the latitude you can allow the
lecher in you. So I thought of everything, from curtains –
which I could see just over Simone's shoulder – to potted
plants – an example of which sat just below the curtains –
to smugglers, street-fights, broken steps and collar-bones,
and finally – mercifully – Hélène. And that did it. I
thought of grave, incomprehensible little Hélène, strumming on her piano as she waited mutely for her life to come
into some sort of acceptable focus, and I found the will to
do what was necessary. I found my voice and spoke to
Simone in a flat, everyday tone as, at the same time, I began
very gently to pull away from her.

'I think it's time we went now, love, don't you?'

For a moment, I thought it hadn't worked. Her grip
tightened and she raised an arm to pull my head back down
towards her, but then, quite suddenly, her arm dropped
back on to the bed and I felt her go limp. As I straightened
up, she offered no resistance but simply lay there, staring
up at me with huge, wondering eyes. I smiled at her and her
lips moved.

'Angus – ' I barely caught the whisper, but nodded
reassuringly.

'It's O.K.,' I said and patted her hand.

She raised the other one and covered her eyes. 'Oh, dear,
she murmured. And then, after a second's pause, 'Oh, my
God.'

'It's O.K.,' I said again.

'I just wish you'd meant it,' I said when she didn't

answer. 'But even though I know you didn't, I shall still treasure it for ever and aye.'

'I'd rather you forgot it.' Her voice was barely audible.

'No chance. You can't begrudge me a memory, Simone.' '*He* wouldn't,' I added.

At that, she dropped her hand and looked at me again. Then she sat up, propping herself on her elbow. 'I want to go home,' she said.

I stood and held out a hand to her. 'Shall I drive you?' I asked. 'I can always bring you back another time for your car.'

She shook her head. 'I'm all right now. I'd rather go alone.'

We went out together and she locked the front door behind her.

'I won't break in any more,' I promised, earning, as I'd hoped, a flicker of a smile.

When we reached her car, I held the door open for her and she stood for a moment looking at me. 'You were right,' she said, 'I *didn't* mean it.'

'I know.'

'But I wish I had.'

'So do I.'

She got into the car and I closed the door.

'Thank you,' she said, but I knew it was not for my chauffeurial courtesies.

'You're welcome.'

I watched her as she reversed the car into the coach-house gateway and turned and drove away, and it was not until she was out of sight that I allowed the events of the past hour to wash over me. When they did, I had only one consuming desire – to find a means, *any* means, to present Ray Corlander with his full and final account. I had no possible way of knowing that, without realizing it, Simone had just cleared the path and taken the first fateful step towards such an end.

TWENTY-ONE

It was a bad weekend: there were just too many problems all at once, too many worries. The predominant ones, of course, concerned the situation at Mont Vert, where the anxiety over the possibility of a fairly prolonged spell of hospitalization for Pierre was adding considerably to the tensions arising from Guy's coming battle with the Grand Council over the Point Rouge issue. Then there were the after-effects of what I'd come to think of as 'The Battle of the Town Square'. From Felipe I gathered it was rumoured that the so-called People's Party were taking advantage of the somewhat blackened image of the New Islanders (the fancy, and perhaps rather over-hopeful, name which the Rochas faction had come up with) and were planning to put up a candidate to challenge Felipe for the St Michel Deputyship. As the parish of St Michel was the largest and most influential on the island, this augured a conflict every bit as crucial to future developments as the Point Rouge affair.

'We don't know who they've chosen,' Felipe told me, 'but you can depend on it, he will be *formidable*.'

I had my own private suspicions about this, and I was right. The People's candidate for representation of the parish of St Michel in the Island Assembly was to be Max Cartier – whose primary representation, I had no doubt whatever, would be the aims and purposes of the Corlanders, *père et fils*.

This revelation arrived with the morning paper on Monday as Guy was preparing to set off to meet his peers in the Council. He made no comment beyond what was implied in a rather tight smile and I answered it in kind. The news, however, increased my determination to force Ray Corlander to a confrontation. Simone's confirmation of his vile coercion of her, and its implications for the death of her father, made a showdown imperative. The fact that here, as ever, I could not have met Nick's eternal requirement of 'proof' bothered me not at all. I didn't need proof. I'd seen for myself what marriage to this moral cripple had done to Simone; I'd witnessed her anguish on her realizing that I knew. Everything in the story I'd ultimately succeeded in wringing out of her checked with the facts as I knew them. Who needed proof?

What I *did* need – and I at least had the good sense to see it – was some sort of an excuse. Simply to tear round to the Rivage d'Or and take the swine by the throat would just as simply put me behind bars before Blanchard got round to sinking his teeth into his mid-morning *brioche*. It needed thinking out, and the immediate moment was not ripe.

At ten o'clock, Marcel got out the old Rolls and drove Guy into town. Normally, the official car would have come up from Porte Hilaire to collect the old man, but Marcel expressed a praiseworthy, if somewhat disrespectful, distrust of this arrangement and insisted on driving Guy himself. I watched them depart slowly down the drive, the old man and the boy – the former too old for what lay before him, the latter too young even to hold a driving licence in England – but both ten feet tall in courage and in pride. It seemed to me in that moment that these two represented something invincible: the wisdom of the past in partnership with the promise of the future, fulfilment with aspiration. As individuals they might be overwhelmed, but surely what they stood for would prevail, as historically it ultimately always had. Sure: but 'ultimately' wasn't enough. Not for them. Not for La Roque. Nor for me.

After they had gone, I went out to the kitchen with the idea that Berthe might be in need of some muscle around the place in the absence of the excellent Marcel. Her reaction to this, however, was to press me, more or less literally, to a seat at the kitchen table, whereupon she set about making me coffee, which she served with *croissants* hot from the oven. The old woman had borne up with the stoicism of her kind and generation to the shock and worry of the last few days and I knew that neither she nor Pierre would have thanked Guy had he allowed himself to be intimidated by his fears for their safety.

While I drank my coffee, we talked of the old days, and then I wandered back into the breakfast room, where I had left unopened my only item of mail, a bulky buff envelope forwarded on to me from the Royale. I knew what was in it and was half-inclined to leave it where it was, still unopened. However, I changed my mind and felt a certain wry amusement when I saw my Editor's scrawled note across the top of the 'pull' of my article: 'Turned out nice again.' From his point of view it had. He had made good use of the material I had sent him, and had I not been so personally involved in the subject I would have felt a touch of satisfaction in the result. It was all there: the story of the Seigneurs, the story of Maurice de Courvel, Seigneur and scholar and family man, and the story of an island kicked out of paradise by its own greed, and suffering the first agonizing pains of self-knowledge. I had known when I had sat down to write this story that it would stir up feelings on the island. Now, when I saw it in cold print, I was more than ever aware of the fact. In two or three days, copies of the magazine would be on the island's news-stands. It would be interesting, to say the least, to see what the reactions would be.

I wanted very much to see Louise, but I was reluctant to leave Mont Vert until news of the events in the Assembly reached us. Meetings of the Grand Council were open to the press, but not to the public, so I rang Alain's flat to see if he still had access to sources at his office that could provide us with information as to how things were going. Madeleine answered the phone.

When I explained the purpose of my call she told me that Alain was in fact in the Assembly at that moment.

'Officially?' I queried.

'Yes,' she answered. 'He made it up with Rochard on Friday and went in this morning as usual.' She gave a little chuckle. 'I suppose it would be truer to say that Rochard made it up with *him*. You know Alain.'

I did.

'Anyway,' she said, 'as soon as I can get hold of him, I'll get him to call you. But don't worry,' she added, 'I'm sure all will go well.'

I thanked her and returned to the kitchen, where I asked Berthe where her husband kept his carpentry tools. She looked surprised, but led me to a small store-room off the kitchen. This appeared to be a depository for general household equipment, and inside a wall cupboard near the door I found what I wanted – nails, a hammer and saw, and, underneath, in a drawer crammed with miscellaneous nuts and bolts and pieces of wire, a folding rule. Armed with these, I repaired to the cellar, where I spent the next ten minutes or so working out the extent of work needed to make good Pierre's wooden staircase. I then went back up to the kitchen and told Berthe that I intended going down to Porte Hilaire, but would be back within the hour and should thenceforth be in the cellar if wanted. She gave me the kind of indulgent smile you would bestow on a helpful child and, emboldened, I pinched a second of her *croissants* and left by the kitchen door.

In the Petit Fond district of Porte Hilaire there is a small timberyard where my father used to get wood for repairs to his boat. It is an old family business and was run in those days by a man my father used to called 'Old Henri'. Today, he had been succeeded by 'Young Henri'. We spent several minutes exchanging reminiscences before I explained what I'd come about. He then led me through to the back yard, where he selected some lengths of wood of the quality he estimated I required. When I protested that this was far more than I needed, he said it was for old time's sake and that wood like this would 'always come in useful'. He insisted on carrying the stuff out to the car.

There was no news awaiting me at Mont Vert, so I went straight down to the cellar and commenced work. By lunchtime, I'd done little more than strip away all the broken woodwork and measure up and cut the wood for four new steps with their side supports. I had told Berthe that I would have my lunch with her in the kitchen, and after I'd washed my hands at the big sink where she did her vegetables we sat opposite each other across her old wooden table. It was then that the memories came flooding back, memories of the kitchen at St Michel, where Alain and Simone and I had so often had our meals with Melanie, the elderly Jamaican cook-cum-housekeeper-cum-nurse, who used to rule our lives in those boisterous days. Melanie, who had been hugely fat and wise, had had a pet canary which she called 'Honoré' and kept in a large gilt cage on the dresser, and we always had to pay our respects to 'Honoré' before we got any food. Melanie said 'Honoré' was pining for a mate, but she was afraid to give him one in case he ate it.

After lunch Alain phoned. The Chamber of *Conseillers* had broken up for lunch but it was too soon to predict what the outcome of their debate would be. Guy had made a brilliant speech, he said, but had had to stand up to some extensive counter-argument from what Alain called the 'Cartier-Corlander mob'.

'So you wouldn't like to hazard a guess.'

'Not at this stage. No.'

I went back to work deeply uneasy.

By four o'clock, there was still no further news. I had completed all but the final step, but the heat in the cellar had given me a thirst, so I went up to the kitchen to enquire whether Guy's resources extended to a bottle of beer. Berthe had forestalled me and had embarked on what was for her the unfamiliar task of making a pot of tea. She had a tray already laid and had been on the point, she told me, of calling me up to the drawing-room. I thanked her and again sat myself down at the kitchen table, having first taken a cup and saucer from the dresser and invited her to join me. After a certain amount of persuasion, she allowed me to pour her a cup of tea, but declined to sit down, and it was while she was toddling off to her vegetable sink with her cup and saucer held in front of her like a lighted lamp that the telephone rang. I called out that I would answer it and slopped my tea on her crisp white tray-cloth in my haste to

269

get across the room to the extension. To my surprise, it was Nicholas's voice at the other end. He thought I'd like to know that his father looked like having carried the day. 'He made a rather good speech, I understand,' he said.

Looked like? I queried, and he explained that it was not unknown for the Grand Council to run to more than one sitting before a decision was made. He didn't think it was likely to do so this time, however, because at four o'clock the members had agreed to take merely a short break for refreshments. That was almost certain to mean, he said, that afterwards they would proceed straight to the vote. He wouldn't be able to let me know the outcome immediately because he had to go out to the other side of the island to take instructions for a will.

'But I thought you would like to know the position. We still can't be one hundred per cent certain, but a reversal now would certainly be quite unprecedented.'

'In other words, Corlander's had his chips,' I said, taking a certain perverse pleasure in converting his guarded legalese into the homely vernacular.

'Yes,' he said, and I could almost feel him wince.

'Good.'

I should have felt triumphant, but anxiety, I suppose, is habit-forming; or maybe relief brings reaction. At all events, returning to the cellar I felt oddly subdued.

Half an hour later, I reported to a delighted Berthe that the cellar steps were now once more safely negotiable, cutting short her emotional expressions of gratitude with a request for another cup of tea. Alain had still not rung, and the fact made me uneasy. Surely, if there were no complications, he would have let me know by now?

It was just after seven when they arrived. I was in the drawing-room when I heard the car coming up the drive and went to the door to meet them. At the same time, Berthe came bustling out from the kitchen and we stood at the top of the steps while Marcel brought the Rolls round in a slow, dignified sweep and stopped, facing back the way he had come. As he sprang out and began to help Guy up the steps, we went down towards them. Guy's appearance was a shock. He looked worn out. His skin had a bluish tinge and his dark eyes were bloodshot. At sight of him, Berthe burst out in a torrent of French: '*Monsieur! Que vous êtes fatigué! Ah, Sacré! C'est terrible! Marcel! Imbecile!*'

Poor Marcel looked startled at this unjustified and unexplained attack, but he was too worried about his master to protest, and without a word he continued with him up the steps while I gave Guy my arm on the other side. In the hall, we helped the old man out of his coat and then led him into the drawing-room and to his chair by the window. Madame, who had hovered anxiously round us all this time, pushing doors open, moving furniture out of the way, now hurried off to get us something to eat. To save Guy going into the dining-room, she said, she would bring us our supper on a trolley. It was doubtful whether Guy even heard her. I had never seen him so weary, and his colour and the strain in his eyes continued to bother me. I glanced at Marcel, who returned my look with a question:

'Cognac, Monsieur?'

He spoke quietly, glancing at Guy, and I nodded. I was grateful to him. The boy might have the build of an adolescent gorilla, but inside he was all mother-cow.

The brandy did the old man good. His face took on a little more colour and he seemed to notice his surroundings properly for the first time. He smiled at me. 'We've won, you know,' he said.

'Yes, sir, I know.'

'You heard?' He sighed deeply. 'Yes,' he said. 'It was not easy, but we won.' He smiled again. 'We looked in to see Pierre on the way back.' So that was why they'd been so long. I should have known. I could imagine how that other stalwart old campaigner had received the news.

'How was he?' I asked.

'Coming along.' But his face clouded and he took a sip of his cognac and then sighed. 'I'm being a nuisance, I'm afraid.'

'Not on your life! But how about going up to bed? I could bring you something up.'

He waved the suggestion away, shaking his head firmly and making an effort to draw himself up in his chair. 'No, no,' he said. 'Certainly not. I shall stay here.'

But he didn't. After finishing his cognac, he apologized again for causing us worry and said he thought that perhaps he would go to bed after all. I called Marcel and, together, we helped the old man upstairs to his room, where Marcel stayed to help him undress. Some twenty minutes later, he returned to the drawing-room and told me that Guy would like me to go up.

'Is he all right?'

'*Oui, Monsieur. Mais, très fatigué.*'

I found Guy sitting propped against a pile of pillows, his thin brown hands resting on the white sheet. His eyes were closed when I entered the room, but he opened them as I approached the bed and he again tried to smile. 'Sit down, my boy.' He indicated a nearby chair. 'You must forgive me, but it's been a long day and I suppose I'm not as young as I thought I was.'

'You should get some sleep,' I told him.

'Oh, I shall. But first there is something I must ask you. Tomorrow I will tell you everything that occurred in the *Conseil*, but now there is something *you* must tell *me*.'

'Can't it wait, too?'

He shook his head. 'No. I want to know, Angus, whether you have discovered anything. About Maurice.'

I hesitated and he noticed it.

'It is important to me, Angus.'

This was difficult. For all my love and admiration for this old man, I could not bring myself to tell him what I now knew about Simone and the baby, yet without this revelation the mystery of Maurice's suicide remained. And Guy, despite his exhaustion, was looking at me shrewdly. He was not going to be easily put off. I decided to temporize.

'Well, Sir,' I said, 'I've no proof of anything, but I believe I've found a more than possible reason for what happened, something that ties up with what you felt.'

'Yes?' His face was eager now, and I had to steel myself

against the urge to satisfy his need to know.

'As I said, sir, I've no proof, so, as it involves someone else, someone still living, I'd rather not commit myself. All I feel I can say is that it's my opinion you were right; Maurice *was* in fear, for someone else, someone who, like most of us at one time or another, had been a bit unwise and put themselves in the kind of position some swine could profit from.'

He looked at me heavily. 'Blackmail. You're sure?'

'To my own satisfaction, yes.'

'So – that was it.' He drew a deep breath, looking past me towards the window. 'Poor Simone,' he murmured. 'It had to be Simone, of course. For Alain he would have given much, but not, I think, his life; because of her, you see.'

I said nothing. Having accepted the possibility of some indiscretion of Simone's leading to blackmail, he would not consider the matter again. The details, even had I felt free to supply them, would not interest him.

'Poor Maurice,' he added softly. 'If only I had known. Surely he could have trusted me.' He turned his head for a moment and looked at me, then his gaze went back again towards the window. 'But no. No, he would keep it to himself.' He looked at me again. 'What will you do?'

'I don't know. Murder, probably.'

For a second, he looked startled, almost as though he believed me. 'There is nothing you *can* do,' he said. 'Better to leave us now, Angus; go back to England. We shall sort out our problems eventually. There are some good young ones on the island, ready to fight. But no matter what happens, now, we can't save *him*. At least you and I know the truth. Leave it there.'

It was the most he had said since his return and his face shone from the compound of effort and emotion. I wanted to avoid tiring him further, so I nodded my agreement.

'Try to sleep,' I said. 'The battle's over for today, anyway. Could be, the war, too. Who knows?'

'You think so, Angus?' His look was anxious, almost pleading.

'Could be. Who knows?'

273

Guy remained in bed throughout the next two days. Madame insisted he should and, rather to my unease, he submitted. Each time I went up to see him, however, I realized more clearly why. The old man was not merely tired; he was ill. On the Thursday morning, without consulting him, I told Marcel to telephone the doctor, who came with commendable speed and proceeded to give the old man a thorough examination. I was again surprised, and to some extent concerned, to find that still Guy made no demur. He and the doctor, Roger Le Jeune, were old friends, it was true, but the Guy Le Marnet I recalled from the past had been anything but a complacent patient, and I had been warned by Berthe that he would probably be very cross with me. Instead, he suffered the examination with a gentle, albeit rueful, smile and listened to the catalogue of his sins afterwards with patient penitence. His system was exhausted, the doctor told him, and he must have complete bed rest for a further three days, after which, if he felt like it, he could move downstairs and sit in his chair. He was not to attempt to walk anywhere, nor to do anything more taxing than read a light book until further orders. Guy waved a deprecating hand at the end of all this, but promised nevertheless to obey. He then instructed me to see that Le Jeune had a glass of madeira before he left.

The doctor declined the drink, but complied with my request for further information on Guy's condition. It was, he said, serious; typical of his kind, however, he would not commit himself as to exactly how serious. The old man's blood pressure had been rather higher than it should have been for some time now, he said, and recent undue strain hadn't helped.

'He's been building himself up for a fall,' he said. 'We must just hope this will be the extent of it, but. . . .' He shrugged. 'He will need watching, Monsieur.'

We watched: for three whole days, constantly. At the beginning of the fourth, at just after three-thirty in the morning, Guy Le Marnet died. He did it with no fuss, but with great sweetness and courtesy. He patted Madame's hand, pressed Marcel's arm and to me endeavoured to speak. I bent to catch the words. 'Thank you for coming,' he said.

The news seemed to get round the island faster than those of us who were nearest to its source could assimilate it. Nicholas and Stéphanie, who arrived, still in their night attire, too late to catch a last sight of Guy's departing spirit, reported later that among the numerous telephone calls they had received many had been from people they barely knew.

The biggest problem was that of breaking the news to Pierre. I offered to do this on the family's behalf, but would gladly have opted for a brisk rub-down with a rubber truncheon if it would have afforded an effective alternative. Driving back to the Manoir, I was haunted by the sense of silent reproach which had seemed to emanate from that narrow hospital bed. Perhaps it was an illusion, springing from my own guilty conscience *vis-à-vis* Guy's actions; perhaps, alternatively, it was simply and solely a grief too deep for words. The fact remained that I couldn't shake off the feeling that at the core of Pierre's wordless response to Guy's death was a criticism of all of us who had had any part in the old man's initial decision to stay on in office. I wondered, too, how much self-blame was there: the feeling that had he, Pierre, been present, things would have been different.

My own reactions were equally complex. Guy's death had opened up an abyss of suffering, in which the obvious strands of grief and personal loss seemed to reach back far beyond their immediate source in this death of one very dear and valued friend. Guy's life, like that of Maurice's, had been inextricably interwoven with the life of the island; thus, in a strange way, his death seemed to signal something irrevocably final in the island itself. Whatever happened next, nothing would ever be quite the same again. The Rock that had sheltered my boyhood had gone; from henceforth, it would remain only as a memory. Time had marched on, and there was nothing I or anyone else could do about it. From this thought I derived a certain relief; personal guilt could perhaps now be subsumed under a general, all-blanketing sense of regret. It was something to tell myself, anyway.

Nicholas moved into the Manoir for the three days before the funeral and we had our own share of telephone messages and personal callers. Alain and Simone came together, fortunately missing Max and Imogen, who stayed only as long as was decently possible. Imogen was her usual nauseatingly gracious self, but Max was clumsily embarrassed, no doubt aware that his recent political gesture could hardly fail to have been interpreted in this house as a vote of no confidence.

Max's awkwardness, however, was as nothing compared to my own the following morning when I opened the front door myself to the first caller of the day. For a moment, I was so disconcerted that I could only stare back in sheer disbelief at the figure that stood there. But there was no mistaking those glasses, nor the short, squat figure itself in its clerical grey suit and sedate dark straw trilby hat.

'Monsieur Logan.' He bent his head and gave me the toothy grimace that passed with him for a smile and said he had heard the news and wished to express his and his wife's deep sympathy to the Le Marnet family. The man amazed me. He appeared so devoid of any sense of guilt or shame as to make of amorality something almost akin to virtue. He and his misbegotten son had set in motion the first real division the island had known in its four-hundred-year history, a division that had now cost a second life, and here he was, as bland as a bottle of barley water, offering his condolences to the family that had just acquired one of the best possible reasons for wishing him in hell. What was more, I was convinced that at that moment, in his own grisly way, the man was sincere. Once again, I was aware of that repellent magnetism that flowed from him, producing, as it had before, simultaneous reactions of fascination and revulsion. Something of this confusion of thought must have shown in my face, for he hesitated as I stood back for him to enter and regarded me quizzically. 'Perhaps some other time?' he asked in his thick, accented English.

'No. No, it's all right,' I answered, and he stepped past me into the hall, removing his immaculate hat as he did so. It was the first time I had seen him without a hat and I was surprised at the difference it made. With his thinning hair, shot with silver-grey, and that watchful, obsequious air of his, everything that had seemed sinister about him retreated. In the immediate context of death, he looked more like an undertaker than a murderer, however theoretical the interpretation of the latter might need to be. I led the way into the drawing-room, hoping that Nicholas would remain in his father's study where he was sorting through some papers.

Corlander took the chair I offered him, but I remained standing; I'd hoped it would give me an advantage, but it only succeeded in making me feel like a very new and inexperienced housemaster in the presence of an extremely gifted sixth-former. To boost my morale I lit a cigarette, and then felt flippant; I hoped Guy would understand.

'I'm afraid Monsieur Le Marnet is a little occupied at the moment,' I said. 'I'm sure you understand.'

He raised a white, well-manicured hand. 'But of course! Please, Monsieur Logan, do not trouble yourself. My wife and I wished merely that Monsieur and Madame Le Marnet should know of the deep regret and sympathy which we feel for them at this time. I'm sure I speak for my son also, who is out of the island at the moment.'

'Oh? I didn't know.'

'Yes. He has been in Europe over the past few days. He will be returning tomorrow evening. But I imagine the funeral will be tomorrow, will it not?'

'Yes.'

He spread his hands and then clasped them together in front of him like a plaster saint. 'It is very sad. Monsieur Le Marnet and I were – as you would say, Monsieur Logan – on different sides of the fence more often than not, but always I admired him. He was – forgive what may seem a presumption – a *good* man. Such a very rare quality, is it not? I wonder sometimes if people realize just *how* rare. He was honest. And compassionate. And wise. Oh, yes, Monsieur Logan, so very wise. He knew, you see, that both sides in an issue make mistakes, that we are all fallible. But in the end he remained where he stood. Oh, a very rare man, Monsieur Logan, believe me.'

I stood with my cigarette poised half-way to my mouth, staring at him through the cloud of smoke that rose from it. If I could have buried the man then and there, I would have! His past duplicities were undeniable, yet once again he had succeeded in producing in me that sense of doubt, the nagging fear of an injustice being done, the sense that, even at his worst, he was more to be pitied than loathed. Yet this was the man who had at least surely known of, if not actually condoned, the obscene pressures that had led up to Maurice's death and who now, by reason of the same greed and megalomania, had contributed to Guy's. I had always prided myself on having some understanding of human nature, but this man, with his suave pragmatism *vis-à-vis* human conduct, was something new. He seemed to have no more sense of guilt over the worst aspects of that conduct than the wolf that devours the kid. Guy and Maurice were both dead as a result of his activities, or those of his son. Guy, the 'good' man, by Bernard Corlander's own assessment, had suspected graft and corruption, and Maurice, I was virtually certain, had been blackmailed. No matter that this man had possibly some curious, unsqueamish kind of honesty of his own, no matter that his motives might, to himself, be justified by a certain brutal fidelity to his own sense of social law – the survival of the fittest – and no matter what nameless devils had terrorized his past, the fact remained that the island would have been a far happier place had he and his cursed son never come to it. – Or would it? Had Madeleine been right? Was La Roque its own blunt instrument when all was said and done? There was a historical precedent, I told myself, for the guidance of those who hoped to find that the response of human nature to sweetness and light would be consistent patterns of the same: the Garden of Eden, they'd called it.

He stayed just the correct length of time, and then, clearly concerned to observe the proprieties, he rose and left as quietly as he had come. I watched him as he drove away down the drive, then I returned to the drawing-room to pour myself a stiff Scotch. With the bottle still in my hands, however, I changed my mind. It was too early for a drink. The damnable thing was that I couldn't shake off the feeling that it was probably too late for just about everything else.

It looked as if the entire population had turned out for Guy's funeral. The number of bowler hats and black suits on show would have amazed me had I not known that for any self-respecting Roquennais male the shame of being arrested stark-naked in the Place de Justice would seem infinitely more endurable than being caught without your bowler and black suit at a family or Seigneurial ceremony. In the event, the combined smell of moth-balls and incense was formidable on a relatively empty stomach and I was glad when the proceedings moved out to the graveside. There, as the Le Marnet children, erect and resolute, dropped their small posies of roses on to their grandfather's coffin, I kept thinking of that other funeral but a few weeks ago, and my eyes kept wandering towards Maurice's still fresh grave just a few yards away. Once, I noticed Alain's doing the same, and I saw Simone, who had positioned herself between the two plots, quietly detach a few flowers from the posy she carried and place them on her father's grave. It was difficult to see her expression behind her glasses, but I suspected she had been crying. I saw Louise and her brothers in the churchyard, and, with them, Madeleine, keeping discreetly in the background. Old Pedro Calvaro stood with his daughter and the Garcia family; after the coffin had been lowered and we turned to walk back towards the waiting cars I saw a short, stocky

279

figure in a dark straw trilby hat move quietly away from the press of people near the shadowed lych-gate and vanish from view. For what it was worth, Bernard Corlander had meant what he had said.

In accord with island custom, only members of the extended family returned to the Manoir afterwards. There, under Stéphanie's direction, and with Marcel's help, Berthe presided over a cold table augmented by coffee and a variety of wines. A short, staunch figure in black silk, she had carried to Guy's grave a cluster of his favourite flowers, the huge, wide-eyed pansies of St Michel. Now, unsmiling but sharply attentive to every need, she was serving him still, seeing that those he had cared about were cared for in their turn. It was good to know that she and Pierre would themselves never lack. From Nicholas I had learnt that, predictably, Guy had left a sum in trust for them for the rest of their lives. It was also agreed that they should remain at the Manoir, to which Nicholas and Stéphanie had decided to move on a permanent basis, keeping the Villa as a week-end retreat until such time as it might be needed as a home for one of their children. They planned to modernize the interior of the Manoir and to engage extra staff to help Berthe. As far as the plantations were concerned, Nicholas seemed to think that, with Molina's help, he would meet with no insuperable problems in their running while still maintaining a full-time involvement in his law practice. 'After all,' he said, 'Father did it for years until he retired, and he was alone.' This oblique reference to his mother, who had died giving birth to Imogen, reminded me that among the many strong links that had bound Guy to his friend, Maurice de Courvel, had been this shared tragedy of personal loss. Come to think of it, none of the three families had had much luck in this respect. Edith Cartier had been widowed shortly after the war broke out.

I thought at first that Simone had decided not to join us at the Manoir after the funeral, but then I saw her appear hesitantly in the doorway of the drawing-room, looking around her until she spotted Nicholas and Stéphanie. After exchanging a few words, however, she slipped away again as unobtrusively as she had come. To his eternal credit, Alain managed at least fifteen minutes in close proximity to the Cartiers before allowing himself an escape from the required courtesies. By then, I figured, the temptation to pour his drink down his old enemy's neck must have afforded quite an impetus to his retreat. In his turn, Max seemed unduly silent, even given the nature of the occasion. He stood apart, flushed, and drawing copiously on Guy's whisky. Imogen, on the other hand, clad in a particularly elegant version of the 'little black dress', had never shown herself to be more odiously capable of adapting herself to the moment. From her shining patent-leather shoes to her radiant, sleeked-back hair, she oozed all the right ingredients like an over-filled cream bun, and I marvelled that Stéphanie's habitual kindly tolerance never once failed her. For myself, I felt a nausea even more desperate than that generated by naphthalene and incense, and I was grateful to the unfortunate Marcel, who, entering the room with a large tray of sandwiches, caught his foot in the leg of a chair imprudently positioned just inside the door. By a show of sheer choreographic wizardry, he succeeded in avoiding the apparently inevitable, but was unable to prevent two sandwiches from sliding to the floor. Swooping on these with the zeal of a watchful scrum-half, I made for the kitchen, where I remained in the role of general factotum, grade three, until I heard welcome sounds of departure. I then crept guiltily out of the woodwork – just in time, for my sins, to catch Max and Imogen making their farewell speeches at the open front door. At the sight of me, Imogen feigned a mixture of astonishment and rapture.

'Angus, love, where *have* you been?'

Silly questions invite silly answers, but I managed to resist quoting the famous rhyming pussy-cat and simply gestured expansively and murmured something about trying to be helpful. She had the sense to let this pass without comment, and with Max nodding pontifically, to convey, apparently, his profound understanding of the matter, the two of them departed down the steps to their car.

The following evening, Louise and I made love. Speaking for myself, the moment couldn't have been more appropriate. The experience of loss acts like any other vacuum: it creates an emptiness that has to be filled sooner or later, by something, or someone. I was lucky: for me, comfort was at hand, and it was human. This time, I *knew* Guy would understand.

TWENTY-TWO

I spent most of the next day trying to make myself generally useful at the Manoir. I took Berthe to see Pierre, helped Stéphanie move furniture and talked to Nicholas about his plans for the future. In the evening, as the sun cooled a little, I piled the kids into my car and took them down to the bay for a swim. Later, when they had gone to bed, Nicholas and Stéphanie and I sat up late, talking. It was pleasant and as I looked at them, noting the easy relationship between them, I kept thinking of myself and Louise: in particular, my mind kept returning to the events of the previous evening, when, by what had seemed almost a miracle, I had found Louise alone at the farm. The brothers, it had appeared, had gone across the island to Sommières to help an old friend celebrate his coming wedding. As soon as she had told me this, I think we'd both known what was going to happen: although right from the beginning matters had seemed to operate of their own volition.

It had all started conventionally enough. I'd driven up to the farm at about half-seven and we went into the 'garden-room' for a drink. But then I began to talk, and somehow I couldn't seem to stop. I told her about my boyhood on the island, about my father and about the way he died, and all about the time I'd spent afterwards with the de Courvel family at St Michel; and then I told her about Maggie, how I'd first met her in a Prom queue outside the Albert Hall, and finally lost her in the smoke and rubble of the London Blitz. I must have talked for at least twenty minutes, and all the time she had just sat there without a word, nursing her drink and looking at me. Afterwards, we went upstairs. It was Louise's idea really; cross my heart. All I said was couldn't we find somewhere more comfortable, and *she* said we could provided we were careful, and *I* said I was *always* careful. So we went upstairs: by tacit agreement, you might say.

In the event, due to a bed that was demonstrably too small for two people, we came together with a gratifying promptitude. The first impact over, however, we tried to do things slowly and gently, each of us savouring the preliminaries, wanting to hold them out for as long as we possibly could before letting ourselves be lost to each other in the ultimate maelstrom of climax. When it came, it seemed – to me, at least – to be perfectly timed: like the moment in a trapeze act when catcher and flyer meet in a miraculous union high above the abyss of space. I heard her breathe my name several times over, her voice finally fading away on a long sigh, while I held her as if to save us both from drowning.

It was dark when we awoke, and we panicked. We had no idea whether or not the men had returned; consequently, the procedure of getting me dressed, into my right mind and out of the house was performed with infinitely more speed than grace. Nor was it helped by the fact that we were both trying hard not to laugh; it didn't seem right so soon after seeing poor Guy to his grave. But shock and laughter go together like smoke and fire, and, as I've said, I somehow knew that the old man would understand. Maybe I was kidding myself, but in a funny sort of way I was certain that if he could see us, he'd be laughing, too.

I was still thinking back over it all long after Nick and Stéphanie had gone to bed. What had happened between Louise and me was a complication I hadn't bargained for: but in that respect it was hardly different from almost everything else that had come my way since I'd arrived on the island.

Next morning, Nicholas decided to check on things in his office, and left while Stéphanie and I were finishing breakfast. We were still doing so when Marcel called me to the telephone in the hall.

'Who is it?' I asked him.

He raised his shoulders apologetically; I still hadn't

managed to teach Marcel to ask telephone callers their names.

'A lady, Monsieur,' he said.

Well, nominally, I suppose, he was right. It was Imogen.

'Hello, angel *chéri*. What beautiful shining armour we're wearing this morning! From now on, *chéri*, I shall call you Galahad.'

'Why not? I've been called worse.'

'Oh, darling, I'm *sure* you have.'

I hadn't the least idea what all the sarcasm was in aid of and I had no intention of giving her the satisfaction of feeling that I was curious; so I waited, and presently she came out with it: a copy of the magazine containing my article on the island had arrived with the daily papers in the Cartier household and she wanted me to know that she thought my piece was 'wonderful' and that I must be a great comfort to my Editor. The touch of venom in the honey amused me. I imagined her sitting up in bed with her breakfast tray in front of her and the pile of papers and magazines which she and Max were probably in the habit of taking scattered around her. Clearly, there had been some discussion between them before Max had left for his office, and it wasn't difficult to imagine what his own reactions had been. The Cartiers were piqued, not to put too fine a point on it. With luck, I reflected, it might just be the end of a beautiful friendship. At least, this time, Imogen didn't invite me to dinner.

The next call was from Felipe, who reported that the magazine was selling so fast in Porte Hilaire that newsagents were running out. (My Editor's monkish face, beaming with satisfaction, rose before my inner eye). Reactions on the whole were fairly favourable, Felipe said. While one or two people were resentful of criticism from an outsider, most, he said, seemed to feel that I had merely said openly what they had been thinking secretly for a long time. 'Coming after the Point Rouge verdict,' he added, 'I think it will give courage.'

If so, then, fortuitously, my activities would for once seem justified.

I was a little concerned as to how Nicholas would see things. From what Felipe had said it seemed more than likely that someone would make it their business to manoeuvre a copy of the magazine on to Nick's desk before the morning was out. I wished that I'd talked to him and Stéphanie about it sooner; they were, of all the people most immediately concerned, the ones I least wished to hurt, but there was nothing I could do about it now. I tried to explain my motivations and feelings to Stéphanie on the principle of better late than never, and her response was, as ever, honest, understanding and direct.

'Whatever you've written, there will be those who will approve and those who won't. Most people will respect what made you do it; those that don't aren't worth bothering about. As far as this family is concerned, you can count on us, as you well know.'

I did, of course, and Nicholas confirmed her support when he returned just before lunch. He had, as I'd guessed, seen the article, and his final comment was characteristically cautious.

'Be careful, my friend. You don't need me to remind you that human nature is never so nasty as when it's ashamed of itself.'

He had just poured us some sherry and we were sitting in the study drinking it when, once again, the telephone rang.

This time, it was Alain, and instinctively I tensed. I had as much as possible avoided making any direct reference in the article to Maurice's immediate family, but this was not likely – nor was it intended – to be construed by Alain as a compliment. I wasn't surprised, therefore, to hear the bitter edge back in his voice, nor the old tone of cynical banter.

'Well, well,' he said, 'scratch an Englishman and you'll find a St George. Or is it a touch of Savonarola, perhaps. The dragon slain with pious exhortation. So much tidier than the sword – and, of course, safer.'

I decided to meet him on his own ground.

'Sharper, too, don't you think?'

I heard the slight hint of a laugh. So we weren't *quite*

back to square one. I was glad of that. Alain had saved me in a bad spot and I wasn't going to forget it, but it would be easier to remember it if we could stay friends. I congratulated him on his return to work and thanked him again for his recent services in the field, and was gratified again to hear a small sound of amusement, followed by what I took to be an agreeable grunt, before he rang off.

But, of course, it was Louise's comment, when I received it that evening, which meant the most of all to me; like Nick's, it was cautionary, even, I felt, a hint critical.

'You might just as well stand in the middle of a bull-ring waving a red cape,' she said. 'I hadn't realized how dangerously you people make a living.'

'Does it make a difference?'

It was a pertinent question, but she didn't answer it directly; she simply smiled in that provocative way that women do when they want to keep you hanging in there without committing themselves too openly.

During the next couple of days it became clear that the island was sharply divided in its opinion of me. Letters appeared in the paper, more or less equally expressing praise and condemnation. The advice of the latter proponents was, in substance, identical: 'If you don't like us, there's a plane leaving in the morning.' One letter was particularly interesting, primarily on account of the signature at the end of it. It was André Laurent's. The man's style was blatantly rhetorical and his sentiments almost quaintly old-fashioned, but the overall effect was of a compelling sense of integrity. Laurent wrote of his disgust concerning the affair in the Place de Justice and had some forceful things to say about the 'inherited rights of the island people to speak their minds in public without fear of harassment, legal or otherwise' – a phrase which would not have given Blanchard much joy, assuming he could read. The letter then went on to lament the accelerating decline of these rights and other such democratic aspects of the island and referred to my article as a 'salutary warning', which he exhorted his fellow Roquennais to heed before it was too late. Finally, he spoke of the recent action of his 'old friend and colleague of many years, Guy Le Marnet, who, in fulfilling his traditional duty to stand guardian over the interests of the island people, had laid himself open in his advancing years to possible calumny and personal attack.' Sadly, he wrote, in removing Guy Le Marnet from the battle altogether, fate had robbed the island of its foremost champion, a 'veritable soldier-prince in the old tradition'. He concluded: 'If any feel this to be to be to their advantage, let them be warned that there are still those who will not allow this island to be sold in the market-place, piece by piece, to the highest bidder. If recent events in the Assembly of *Conseillers* do not convince them of this, then future action must.'

It was by no means a veiled threat, which both heartened and intrigued me. I asked Felipe if in fact it had any substance and he reported that already there had been a dramatic increase in interest in the New Islanders party and growing support for himself in connection with the coming St Michel elections.

'Good for Laurent,' I said.

'That is true. But in this case it is you who must take the greatest credit, Angus. Your words have reached so many people who would not normally bother to attend a meeting or take much interest in local politics. Many of these people are influential. It is true they listen to men like Laurent and Despard, but it is what you have written, and *where* – the implications of international coverage – that have finally shocked them out of their sleep.'

'Well, maybe – but don't imagine you're out of the wood. You've seen how cunning and vicious the opposition can be, and that could be just for starters. They're not going to hand over their precious vested interests without putting in some pretty dirty fighting, I fear.'

'Don't worry. They won't catch us again as they did the other day. We shall be ready next time.'

I doubted it. But who was I to talk? I was by *no* means ready for what happened next.

It came in two parts. The first occurred that same evening when I was packing the children's wet swimsuits into the boot of my car, which I'd parked on the slipway leading down to the beach at St Michel between the Church of the Fishermen and the garden of the old convent. Its present occupant, Corlander Senior, must have spotted me from one of his top windows because just as I was about to round up the squad and take them home for supper, his gate opened and he stepped out on to the slipway with the obvious intention of accosting me. There was no possibility of evading him without the most blatant rudeness, which is something I prefer to avoid even with people whose guts I'm not particularly partial to.

He was, as ever, immaculately dressed, in a light linen suit and green silk tie, his bland, bespectacled face shaded by the ubiquitous straw. As he came up to me, he gave his usual small bow.

'Mr Logan. A pleasant evening.'

I nodded an acknowledgement and he glanced towards the beach, where the four young Le Marnets were engaged in a friendly attempt to mutilate each other with seaweed down near the water's edge.

'You have your quiver full.'

'Fortunately, on a temporary basis only.'

He chuckled. 'It is a good place in which to bring up children. They, of course, do not realize how fortunate they are. One asks oneself sometimes whether the parents do either. When life is always so good, it is hard to appreciate that it can ever be otherwise: that there is a price that must be paid.' He paused, and I waited in silence for what was to come.

He took a small cigar case out of his pocket and extended it towards me; when I declined, he selected one of the small, thin cheroots for himself and lit it with a silver pocket lighter. Through the first haze of aromatic smoke he looked at me with that enigmatic expression of his which I found so maddeningly difficult to define.

'Mr Logan,' he began, 'you and I never did have that

little talk I promised myself the pleasure of. This is possibly not the most favourable occasion, but we must take what opportunity we can.' He paused, pursing his rubbery lips and looking down at his cigar in a ruminative way. 'Mr Logan, you have travelled a great deal. You are aware of the risks one takes in visiting communities that are in a state of transition. And, of course, that is just how it is with us on La Roque at the moment. We are like a woman who decides to grow her hair; the beginning is neat and the end may be glorious, but the intermediate stage is often disconcerting, to say the least. It would be a pity if she were to be judged on her appearance at such a time, you will agree?'

I had no idea what I was supposed to say to this, but the man's unctuous tone irritated me and I had neither the inclination nor the time for philosophical discussion.

'I wasn't aware – ' I began, but, divining my mood, he raised a soothing hand.

'*Please*, Monsieur.' His lips parted in an amused smile, which only had the effect of further increasing my irritation. 'Don't be offended. I merely wanted to make a point, which, since I seem to have annoyed you, I will get to without further preamble. It is this. You have made certain comments in public as to the way in which things here are done. I think you are hasty both in the conclusions you formed and in your public expression of them. Perhaps, had you had more time in which to study all sides of these matters, you would have felt differently. I should like to think so. In these circumstances, there is always a danger, don't you agree, that one can do oneself and one's friends a disservice? It would be a pity if that were so in this case.'

'Is this some sort of threat, Mr Corlander?'

I had felt my anger rising during this last delivery of his and I was having difficulty in speaking, but incredibly there was no sign on his face of the intent to intimidate which I had so potently sensed in his words. All that showed there was that same soft amusement. There was no doubt about it: there was a great danger of underestimating Bernard Corlander, and I had come very close to it.

'Good gracious, Mr Logan!' he said. 'You've been reading your own copy, as they say in the advertising world. Threats? Why should we be so melodramatic? I was merely expressing my regret that you appeared to have formed such a low opinion of us, and my anxiety that you should give us the benefit of the doubt. I'm sure your friends would wish that. After all, they will be here after you have left.'

There it was again: the implied menace. He was referring to Felipe and Louise, the Orthoz brothers and old Calvaro, Alain, Madeleine and Simone – yes, even Simone, confused and helpless as she was: all my friends, in fact, and all who did not accommodate themselves to his arbitrary will. He had lost on the Iturbi issue; his grip had been weakened; no doubt he felt his power on the committees to be in danger. It rankled. So now he was warning me, and now I knew it and knew where I stood with him.

'Think about it, Mr Logan,' he said, still in the same lulling tone. 'Nothing is black or white. We do our best and the result will be a more profitable economy for *all*, not just a few. Give it time, Mr Logan; give it time.'

I didn't answer and he nodded pontifically, his head cocked on one side like a wise and benign garden gnome; then, with a final crooked smile, he turned back up the slipway and disappeared through his garden gate, leaving me staring after him, feeling about as challenging as something on a pin.

Some of my repressed feeling must have got through to the children, for they came immediately I called and climbed into the car without posing a threat to a single door-handle or transferring the contents of the ashtrays to the floor.

When I told Nick and Stéphanie about it, however, they laughed.

'Let that be a warning to you,' said Nicholas. 'You can't win them all. Considering that you and Father have just bloodied his nose between you, I think he's let you off lightly. So far,' he added with a sudden sombre change of expression.

Later, I realized that Bernard Corlander had, in fact, done me a good turn. The frustrated fury he had aroused in me against himself was easy to channel in the direction of his son, whom I now knew I was ready to tackle.

Here again, though, I was taken by surprise. The following morning, just as I was about to take off round the plantations with Nick, Marcel exercised his newly acquired major domo talents with the announcement:

'M'sieu Raymond Corlander on the telephone for M'sieu Logan.'

As we stopped in our tracks, Nicholas gave me a small, commiserating smile. There was a touch of the I-told-you-so's about it, but he was too considerate to put it into words.

Corlander's voice was less jarring on the telephone than in real life, but that I put down to the wonders of technology. He had heard, he said, that I was now staying in the St Michel area and would appreciate it if I could find time to call in at the Rivage d'Or to see him.

'May I ask what about?'

'You may, but I would prefer to speak with you direct.'

'When?'

'Later this morning? If you ask for me at the bar.'

I agreed and he rang off. Nicholas looked at me enquiringly, but I could tell him no more than Corlander had told me. I had my own feelings, however, about the coming interview. Corlander's tone of voice had hung somewhere between curt and hostile. What was coming was a showdown. Which suited me just fine. But I preferred not to reveal anything of this to Nick at the moment.

The bar of the Rivage d'Or Hotel was crowded with the usual Saturday morning complement of well-heeled island businessmen and their wives and girl friends mixing with equally favoured holiday-makers. Rather than fight my way to the counter, I beckoned over a nattily-attired young lad gathering empty glasses and told him my business. He gave me a smart '*Sí, Señor*' and, putting his tray down on a vacant table, went to a door at the back of the bar, knocked discreetly and went inside. A few seconds later he reappeared and hurried across to me.

'*Por favor, Señor,*' he murmured and escorted me back to the door, which he had left open behind him.

In a room that only needed a couple of flags to make it worthy of the embassy of a top-ranking power, Ray Corlander sat at a huge leather-inlaid desk, holding a half-empty glass of milk. This he drained as I entered, imperiously holding it out to the young lad to take away. He then sat back, staring at me over his sundry impressive aids to executive living, all with their embossed-leather lids and velvet trimmings, and gestured half-heartedly towards a nearby chair. When I ignored the invitation, he shrugged and got to his feet. He walked over to a small bar in a corner of the room and took a bottle down from one of the shelves.

'Scotch do you?'

As I still didn't answer, he looked round enquiringly, the hand holding the bottle half raised.

I shook my head and he grimaced, replacing the bottle without helping himself. Obviously his trip to Europe had been unsettling.

Back behind his desk, he remained standing, looking at me with a sullen expression on his pink, fleshy face.

'I thought it was time we had a talk,' he said.

'I agree.'

He looked slightly surprised, but went on as if I hadn't spoken.

'I don't quite know what your motives were in coming back to the island, but for a man who claims to be honouring the dead you've been making a helluva lot of trouble for the living.'

'That's tough.'

'I'm glad you think so, because sooner or later it's going to come back on the people you seem to see as your friends.'

'If that's a threat, Corlander, you should take lessons from your old man. He's got more style. But what I have to say to you will do for the pair of you. I grew up on this island. In a very real sense it's my home. What happens here, and to the people I care about, matters to me. I take it that's not too difficult to understand? You're right, I came here to honour the dead, and I'm not in principle resistant to the apparent inevitability of the fact that the old order changeth. But what I've seen here convinces me that the pattern of change on this island now is a bloody unhealthy one. The king is dead, O.K., but the money-grubbers are not averse to sitting on the throne. Unless something's done pretty damn quick to prevent it, everything that's decent and good here, everything that men like Maurice de Courvel and Guy Le Marnet gave their lives – *literally* – to preserve, will get flushed down the drain. I don't care to see that happen. More to the point – when people who matter to me are threatened by it, I don't *intend* to see it happen. So there's your answer, Corlander, and now we've disposed of it, there's a question or two I have for *you*.'

'*You* may have disposed of it, Logan, I haven't. What you wrote in that damned article of yours was a bloody presumptuous interference in affairs which, despite your touching sentiments, are no concern of yours. You may have influenced certain weak-minded people to your point of view, but I'm giving you fair warning – '

'Forget it, Corlander! I'm warning *you*. I didn't come here today because you asked me to; I came because you obligingly opened a door which I was about to kick in, anyway. You and your father have done a good job in a relatively short time of destroying what has taken hundreds of years to build up. Between you, you've been carving this island up to suit your own ends, and you've got a few greedy people going along with you. But that's not what I'm here about. I despise what you're doing and how you're doing it, and I shall continue to support those who are trying to stop you. But what lies between you and me, Corlander, is something very much more personal. Yes – ' as his eyebrows went up – 'it concerns your relationship with the de Courvel family, which, as I've already explained, I see myself as being a part of.'

'What the hell are you talking about?' His face now was dark with a mixture of perplexity and anger.

'I'm talking about what happened to Simone, and how it affected her father. Oh, yes, I know all about that, Corlander. I know you put pressure on Simone to marry you when you discovered – God knows how – about the affair she'd had with Raoul Cotarde. I know you blackmailed her to gain some advantage in connection with the St Michel estates. I suspect that when the marriage proved too irksome to you, or less helpful than you'd hoped, you transferred the pressure to Maurice himself. I believe he killed himself to rob you of your motive against Simone, and I'm here to tell you, Corlander, that unless you abandon your schemes concerning St Michel and leave Simone alone once and for all, I shall find a way of letting enough people on this island know what happened to ensure that you never get another vote of confidence from anyone. I'll drive you clear into the sea, Corlander, don't think I won't.'

Having at last found the opportunity to face him, I'd got a bit carried away, and at the end it took me by surprise to find that he looked less disturbed by all I'd said than I had anticipated. A sardonic look had replaced the fury on his face, and he seemed almost to be savouring something.

'You've got proof of all this, of course,' he said eventually.

'Enough,' I replied. I'd decided beforehand that, if necessary, I would bluff him. It didn't worry me; eventually he would take fright – even if I had to provide some practical assistance towards that end.

But now, as he looked at me, a sudden uneasiness came over me. A slow, sneering smile had come to his face, and with deliberate insolence he kept me waiting while he got up, went over to the bar and poured himself a drink. He took a swig and then walked back to his desk, where he placed the glass on a small leather coaster. Leaning back in his chair, he regarded me with what I was now aware was amused contempt.

'You're a fool, Logan. But I didn't think you were so

bloody far gone as to believe a single word our poor little sick Simone would tell you. For God's sake, man, don't you know she's a case? Don't you realize that but for the grace of God, and who she is, she'd be locked away?'

For a moment, there was a murder in my heart. As the rage tore through me, every nerve and instinct within me clamoured for the relief of instant physical retaliation. Fighting for control, I dared not move or speak, and, seeking to avoid the provocation in his taunting face, I found myself staring at the elegant grey silk scarf negligently tucked into the neck of his fine white shirt. It would be so easy to fasten my hands round that scarf and to use it to throttle the life out of him where he sat.

Something of this must have transmitted itself to him, for he rose suddenly from his desk and backed slightly away from it, as though ready for immediate retreat.

'Watch yourself, Logan! And you can put your bloody hands back in your pockets, because what I've just told you is the truth and you'll sodding well have to live with it! You wanted the truth. Hear it then. I didn't blackmail your precious Simone into marriage – or anything else. *She* came to *me* – You know, of course, that she's a nympho – '

'Why, you rotten – ' And now I rose, too, and we faced each other, both of us all too well aware of the enormity of the danger that lay between us.

I heard him draw a deep breath and he moved still further back towards the window.

'Now, cool it, Logan, because all I'm telling you is what you've asked for. Simone de Courvel, your innocent little girlhood sweetheart, offered herself – with every art at her disposal, I might add – oh, yes – ' as he saw the slight move I made – 'oh, yes – plus the extra inducement of her influence over her father – in return for marriage. She told me the affair with Cotarde had been a mistake and was over, and that she had secretly been in love with me for a long time. What she *didn't* tell me, my friend, was that she was pregnant, and that what she was really hoping to do was to trick me into accepting her bastard as my child. She got away with it, too, long enough to get me into her bed with all the solemn sanctions of her church to make it all nice and legal and respectable. Oh, she wouldn't have any monkey-business beforehand! It was marriage or nothing, and she had us at the altar within weeks – *said* it was because she couldn't bear to wait till I got back from a trip to Europe. Well – ' he laughed sardonically – '*that* was true enough, as I damn soon found out! It came as a shock, I can tell you, to find that my eager little bride had a bloody bun in the oven! And let me tell you something else, Logan, maybe that poor little sod of a kid didn't live long enough to look a lot different from any other little perisher of his age, but as far as *I* was concerned, if he could have got up and walked with a limp, he'd have been dear old Raoul himself, fresh back from the wars.' He stopped to draw breath, and as I stood there, staring at him, I felt my blood turning cold inside me.

'So you see,' he continued, 'your dear little Simone is about as sweet of heart, as innocent of guile, as a cageful of starving monkeys. She tried to play me one of the dirtiest deals in the book and I almost fell for it.'

He took another deep breath and leaned forward across the desk, his puffy, pale blue eyes glaring into my face with a baleful intensity.

'You'd better believe this, Logan, because, understand this, my fine, Puritan hero, *I can prove it!*'

TWENTY-THREE

How long I stood there, staring at him, I don't know. Maybe, one day, I'll have forgotten the whole sickening incident. But I doubt it. The hell of it was that I *knew* he was telling the truth. I didn't need his rotten 'proof', though he insisted on shoving it down my neck; I knew in every nerve of my body that there and then, for the first time, I was hearing what had really happened. There's no way you can rationalize this kind of intuitive knowledge. There's just some precise conjunction of fact and feeling that mind and body seem simultaneously to recognize and accept. Looking back, I think I'd known even on that evening in the coach-house, that Simone was lying to me. I remembered the curious shift of mood at the end when I'd given her my explanation of her father's attitude to her: the strange sense of what had seemed relief, the sudden rush of confidence with which she had told me the 'truth'.

Knowing what I did now explained so many other things: the odd way in which Simone lived her life – as though in a kind of fearful flight from reality – her evasiveness and, most particularly, that manifest sense of guilt that seemed always to haunt her and to make it impossible for her to relate to other people in a consistently stable way. It had been this inability in her that I had first noticed; one minute, she would seem perfectly normal, the next, she would appear awkward, withdrawn, almost rude, in her anxiety to escape even the most undemanding social pressures. But did all this put together necessarily imply the serious abnormality that Corlander had so brutally suggested? It was this – with its inevitable prognosis – that had upset me most of all: more even than his foully contrived 'proof', which consisted of a tape he had taken without Simone's knowledge of certain stage-managed conversations he had had with her. In these, he had manipulated her into repeating her avowal of love for him, her desire for marriage and – most damning of all – her willingness to provide him with such significant snippets of information relating to her father's public affairs as came her way. In these exchanges, his own contributions had been judiciously phrased and edited so as to seem relatively innocuous. His *tour de force*, which remained word for word in my mind, was on the de Courvel estates:

> (Corlander) – St Michel is a heavy burden on your father. Do you think he will one day let me take it off his shoulders?
>
> (Simone, hesitantly) – I – Perhaps . . . I don't know.
>
> (Corlander) – His caution is understandable, but perhaps you can help him to trust me. It would be a good basis for our marriage, wouldn't it?
>
> (Simone, with obvious anxiety) – Oh, yes. Oh, I'm sure if – if you will give him time . . . I – I *will* try.

The tremulousness in her voice was something I should remember for ever. That she should ever have been so humbly conciliating to this nauseating wretch made me in that moment almost hate her. And it was then, with a horrifying clarity, that I finally understood Maurice. Corlander, tired of his marriage to Simone, had used this tape on Maurice himself in an attempt to destroy the family pride which had been the basis of Maurice's resolution to hold on to St Michel. 'Why not?' he said to me with a scornful smile on his face. 'He had a right to know what the apple of his eye was up to. He didn't want to believe about the kid at first. This he *had* to believe.'

And Maurice had heard Simone eagerly agreeing to using her influence on him; had heard the abject compliance in her voice and had known that there and then he stood completely alone. Justine was dead; Alain was a stranger; I – God knew where *I* was! Simone had become his one safe anchorage, the centre of his life – and now here she was, his only and dearly loved daughter, a smiling cheat, ready to sacrifice everything he treasured to keep her own reputation intact and ensure a socially acceptable future for her child. Worse – much worse, from Maurice's point of view – she was prepared to betray the safety and security of scores of faithful estate workers, some of whose families had a tradition of service in the plantations of St Michel going back almost a century. As I fought to retain my charity and compassion for Simone, I knew that this same battle had been Maurice's – only with an agony infinitely worse, an agony that at the end could not be endured.

For two days after my interview with Corlander, I kept out of everyone's way, taking myself out in the car immediately after breakfast on some pretext or other and staying out until supper time. I knew my behaviour was both perplexing and worrying to Nick and Stéphanie, but I could do nothing about it for the simple reason that while I was unable to talk about what had happened, conversation about anything else was also impossible. Looking back, I realize that had I only taken Stéphanie into my confidence, or gone up to the farm and told Louise the whole story from beginning to end, the ultimate horror so soon to come upon us might never have happened. But when reason deserts us, fate or the devil, or whatever, steps in, often in the form of some casual fortuity or coincidence, behind whose mask we are unable to detect the lurking malevolence.

So it was that on the Monday morning I found myself standing in Maurice's study at St Michel. Why I had gone there, I don't know. It was as though some irresistible magnetism had drawn me back there, as if I had to confront the old man's spirit for the last time, to tell him – tell him what? As I stood there, looking round me at the now familiar disorder, I tried to see the room as it had once been, as though perhaps I might find in that peace and quietude that I still remembered the stability I sought. As I did so, I became aware of a sound. I turned, and there she was. It was uncanny: a recapitulation almost exactly of that very moment of my first visit here over six weeks ago.

Simone – alone this time – was standing in the doorway of her father's study, staring at me, and her grey-green eyes were wide with surprise and apprehension.

As though in obedience to some well-rehearsed piece of theatre, I followed the same script as before:

'Hello, Simone.'

It was she who broke it. The fearfulness left her face and she gave an uncertain little smile. She glanced around her.

'It's all a terrible mess, isn't it?'

It was. But not just the room.

Even then, we might have escaped without disaster. If I had said nothing to any effect, we might both have gone our separate ways undisturbed. As it was, seeing her there in her father's room, the room in which, because of her, he had killed himself, I felt a sudden revival of all those feelings of anger and resentment which had temporarily taken possession of me in Corlander's office in the Rivage d'Or. If I had been strictly honest with myself, too, I would have had to admit that my vanity was wounded by her inability to confide in me with absolute honesty and trust.

And so it was that we each stood, unaware, on the brink of tragedy. It only needed a word: the wrong word. And I said it.

I took two steps towards her and held out a hand. 'Simone,' I said, 'why did you lie to me?'

The shock was instant. Her face flooded with colour and then turned deadly white. Behind her glasses, her eyes were enormous and the look in them filled me with foreboding.

'I know everything,' I said. 'I know, Simone. Why you married Corlander. What you told him you would do. And,' I added, 'what you *didn't* tell him.'

Still she didn't answer.

'Surely you knew I'd try to understand. Even what you promised concerning your father. For that matter, you could have trusted *him*. Why didn't you? Why didn't you tell him about the baby? In heaven's name, he was your *father*! And God knows he loved you enough. Why did you have to turn to a swine like Ray Corlander?

301

She muttered something, but I didn't catch it.

'What did you say?'

With a suddenness that took me by surprise, she flung her handbag on to the floor and sat down on what must have been the only chair that wasn't littered with something. From there, she stared at me with a hostile intensity.

'I said, you *still* don't understand! In spite of the fact that you're still going round behind my back, asking questions and talking about me! That's what everybody does. Poor little Simone! Caught with her knickers down. So had to make the best of a bad job. – Well, that's not sodding well how it was! And I don't *want* their pity! I married Ray Corlander because I bloody *wanted* him! Do you hear me? I *wanted* him! You know, "wanted, desired, lusted after".' She thrust every word at me with a fierce, crude emphasis, her eyes glaring into mine, while I stared back at her in horror: at a stranger I had never known existed. I tried to speak. 'But Raoul – ' I began.

Her lips twisted into a smile, but there was no warmth or kindliness in it, nor in her eyes, which mocked me.

'Oh, yes, Raoul,' she said. 'I did love him, in the beginning. But he didn't love me.'

'That's not what other people thought.'

'*Other* people!' she flared. 'There you go again! Always other people – all talking, whispering, pitying. So much for what *they* knew! Raoul Cotarde didn't love me. He wouldn't marry me. Oh, he made plenty of excuses about his health, but if he'd really loved me, as I'd loved him, he would have married me anyway. I didn't want his baby, because he didn't want *me*! Ray Corlander did.'

'For God's sake, Simone, all *he* wanted was St Michel!'

'That's not true! Not at the beginning, anyway. Afterwards, he turned cruel and horrible and I was afraid of him. He kept threatening me, and I came to hate him. I hate him now, because he's the one that's told you all these things, isn't he? *Isn't he?*' she repeated angrily.

I ignored this. 'Simone, why didn't you go to your father when you knew you were pregnant? He would have understood. He would have given you all the love and care you needed.'

'Oh, yes! Poor little Simone! What a shame! Daddy's poor little erring daughter! No, thank you! I've told you, I didn't want pity. Neither his, nor anyone else's. And I don't want yours! At least Ray Corlander never offered me that.' She flashed me a sudden arch glance. 'He was better-looking in those days, you know. Quite a catch.'

I felt sick.

Just as suddenly, her mood changed, and her face went dark. 'But it all changed. He began to threaten me. Said if I didn't help him to get St Michel, he would tell my father about the baby, and everything else.'

'Everything else being that you had promised already, before you married him, that you would give him confidential information. Did you know he had evidence of this on tape?'

'Yes. He said if I didn't get him what he wanted, he would play it to my father.' Her face crumpled and she looked near to tears. 'I couldn't have borne that.'

'God help us, Simone, didn't you know he *had* played it to your father?'

Her face seemed to turn to stone and she stared up at me uncomprehendingly.

'What!' The whisper was so low I barely heard it.

'Didn't you *know*, for Christ's sake?'

Her eyes, distraught, continued to bore into mine. 'Why did he do that? He didn't have to . . . he promised . . .' Her voice trailed off and an odd look came to her face. She seemed not so much far away as in another dimension altogether. Some strange metamorphosis appeared to be taking place within her, and although I could not have explained it, even to myself, I feared for her.

I didn't know what to say, but a move of some kind – *any* kind – to break the spell of her silence, seemed vital. I moved closer to her and held out my hand. 'Let's go home,' I said. 'It's all in the past now. We must try to forget it.'

It was a clumsy bromide, and I wasn't particularly proud

of it, but I didn't expect the reaction I got.

She looked up at me for a moment as though trying to take in what I'd said. Then, her mouth trembled and I thought she was going to cry. It was several seconds before it dawned on me that she was laughing. Not, however, in mirth; rather more, I felt, from a kind of anguished self-mockery, something terribly close to the complete break-down of despair. It continued for so long that, despite the sympathy I felt for her, I had to fight against a surge of irritation, which I knew could spell disaster. I was also thoroughly alarmed. Corlander had been right; there *was* something wrong with Simone, and if now, suddenly, she became worse, *I* was to blame. I felt a desperate need for air, but I couldn't leave her here like this. I bent and touched her hand.

'Come along, love, let's go.'

She stopped laughing, to my relief, but the look she gave me was worse. To my acute disquiet, I detected a sly coquettishness. Her lips curved into a provocative smile.

'*Love?*' She tilted her head and the smile taunted me. 'Am *I* your love, Angus? I thought it was someone else. *Am* I?' she repeated, and she stood up and moved closer to me.

Christ, I thought, as memories of the coach-house flooded over me. Involuntarily, I took a step backwards, and suddenly she was laughing again. Only this time it didn't last. Almost immediately, she stopped, and her expression turned hard. For a second, our eyes met. God knows what mine showed of the blue funk I was in; but hers chilled me to the heart. Never again would Simone and I meet in the old sweet assurance of friendship and mutual trust. The knowledge of this hit me like a physical blow, but even as I wrestled to assimilate it, she wheeled away from me and walked towards the door. Behind her, her handbag still lay, forgotten, where she had flung it. I went and picked it up and touched her arm with it and she paused, looking down at it for a moment, bemused. Then she took it from me and, turning, stared past me into the room. I felt she was doing what I had done: that she was seeing it as it had once been, seeing her father, perhaps, sitting there in his chair. Her lips moved and I strained to catch the words. Even in the stillness of the empty room her voice was barely audible.

'He shouldn't have told him. He promised.' Her eyes retracted from their long gaze into the past and focused on mine. There was a cold fury in them, and inwardly I shivered. When she spoke again, her voice was still scarcely above a murmur, but it trembled with the intensity of barely controlled emotion.

'I *hate* him. He killed my father. He *murdered* him. I *hate* him.'

She choked on the last three words, and before I could respond she turned again and hurried from the room. Seconds later, I heard the front door slam shut behind her and then her feet, outside on the drive, breaking into a run. I was still standing there, caught in a hiatus of uncertainty and apprehension, when the engine of her car roared into life and the wheels skidded into motion on the gravel.

Only then did I seem able to move. But the uncertainty was still with me as I followed her out to the drive. It increased with every mile that I drove back towards Mont Vert, so that by the time I arrived there it had grown into a powerful but indefinable premonition.

That night I dreamt again that, as before, I was back at St Michel, but this time, by some weird transposition in time and events, only the house itself was as I had known it. Everyone in it, including myself, was of the present – Maurice and Guy (who were also there), both old men, Alain, Simone and myself as we were now. There was a pervading atmosphere of distrust – something utterly alien to the St Michel I had known – and of an overwhelming sense of threatening disaster. In a final, frightful reconstruction of ancient Oedipean fantasy, Simone suddenly produced a gun and shot her father. I woke in the shock of this and lay sweating and staring into the darkness around me.

* * *

After breakfast that morning, I herded Nicholas and Stéphanie into Guy's study and told them all about it. They listened in silence until I'd finished, then Stéphanie glanced at Nick.

'Your father was right, wasn't he?' she said.

He nodded.

'About what?' I asked.

'About her being besotted by Ray Corlander. At least at the beginning. Afterwards, of course, she did change. Poor Simone – ' She sighed heavily. 'If only one could have realized – '

'I don't think it would have made the slightest difference. Simone *is* a very sick person, Stéph. This is what is worrying me most of all. Her troubles are far from over. And there's Hélène – You don't think – ' I left the question unfinished, but they both looked at me sharply.

'Oh, no!' Stéphanie said quickly. 'Oh, I'm sure she wouldn't do anything that would hurt Hélène.' She turned to Nicholas. '*Would* she?' she queried, her normally serene face reflecting a new and powerful anxiety.

Nicholas didn't answer, and she turned back to me. 'Could you somehow get her up here?' she asked. 'Tell Simone the children have invited her to stay, perhaps? What do you think?'

'I'll try,' I said. 'If it doesn't work, I'll see whether Louise can work something out. God knows what, but you never know. I must go and talk to her.'

'Yes,' said Stéphanie. She paused. 'I think,' she added eventually, 'you had better do that right away, Angus.'

By a lucky coincidence, Hélène was with Louise when I arrived at the farm. The lesson had ended and both of them were out on the drive, playing with the small black-and-white puppy which I'd seen before and which apparently belonged to one of the workers.

As I got out of the car, Louise came over to me.

'You couldn't have come at a better time,' she said.

'How's that?'

She glanced towards Hélène, who was kneeling on the

grass verge, shaking something which the pup was gripping with its teeth. 'We have a small problem,' she said. 'She came up on her own today.'

'On her own?'

'Yes. Apparently, she came on the bus by herself. Carlos found her walking up the lane over an hour before she was due. I've been trying to find out the reason, but I haven't got there yet. What was worrying me was how I would get her back. I didn't want her going on her own again, but I've got another child due in ten minutes: The odd thing is that I haven't heard a word from Madame Corlander. She must have *put* her on the bus, surely, but it seems strange that she didn't make it the later one. I rang her to see if she was coming to fetch her, but there was no reply.'

'Look!' I said, 'it was about Hélène I came – '

'Oh, I *see*!' she said and looked relieved.

'No, I don't mean that. I know nothing about her coming by bus. No, it's something different.' I glanced back again at Hélène, who was now being pulled by the little dog, via the connecting bone, or whatever it was, round the corner of the field. 'Look,' I repeated, 'the problem is a bigger one than you thought. It's a long story, and I'll tell you as soon as we have a suitable time, but if I tell you now that Simone Corlander is probably having, or about to have, a mental breakdown, have you any ideas how we can keep Hélène away from her for a few days without either of them knowing why?'

Her face had gone grave during this brief explanation; now she spoke quickly and decisively.

'She can stay here. She won't mind. She's already said she wished she lived here.'

'Good. Then I'll go and see her mother. What can I tell her?'

She thought for a moment. 'Tell her,' she said, 'that we're holding a field party for the pickers, and Hélène's been invited.'

I kissed her. 'Thank you. That should do it.' I opened the car door. 'I'll see you,' I said.

All the way to St George's, I was worried. Why had Hélène gone up to the farm on her own? Why had Simone not contacted Louise? Why was she not answering her telephone? Where was she?

When I arrived at the house, the front door was ajar, and I could hear Rose's and a man's voice coming from the ground-floor flat, the door of which was also slightly open. Upstairs, Simone's apartment was empty. There was not even a cat in sight, despite the usual olfactory evidence. Returning to the hall, I knocked on Rose's door and it was opened by a dark, burly chap with a black beard, his check shirt and linen slacks much the worse for time and paint.

The modern Primitive, Julian, no doubt. He made no answer when I explained my mission, but stood back and made a sweeping gesture with his arm for me to enter. Rose was ironing in the small kitchen that led off from the sitting-room, but she switched off the iron when she saw me and, after rather perfunctorily introducing me to her partner, she offered to make us coffee.

'We've been worried, too,' she said as she unplugged the iron from its socket and substituted the kettle. 'I was going to ring you if she wasn't back by lunch-time. She went out very early – oh, about seven-thirty, wasn't it?' she asked Julian, who nodded. 'Then, we *thought* we heard her come back – that was about nine, or a bit after. But later, I went up to see whether everything was O.K. because last night we thought she'd seemed a bit odd.' She frowned. 'Sort of faraway, if you know what I mean. Anyway, when I got up there, there was no sign of her. Nor Hélène. It was strange, because we'd definitely heard the door shutting around nine, hadn't we?'

Julian, who had perched himself, cowboy-fashion, across a kitchen chair, his arms resting on the back, nodded again. Not a great communicator, our Julian.

'What you heard was probably Hélène leaving,' I said. Rose stared, and I told her what Louise had told me.

'Good God! Don't tell me that kid went all out there by herself!'

'Apparently she did.'

Rose looked at Julian, who shook his head as though in disbelief.

'*Could* she have done that?' I asked. 'I mean, what is she – eight years old? Does she know her way to the bus station? Presumably, she'd have to go there, and then find the right bus. Could she do that?' A new thought struck me. 'Shouldn't she have been at school, anyway?'

Rose shook her head. 'No, it's *Jour de Parlement*. Don't you remember?'

'Oh, yes of course.' It was the twenty-fifth of October: the commemoration of the founding of the first island parliament, a public holiday. I'd forgotten it.

Rose switched off the kettle and began spooning coffee from a jar into three cups.

'The answer to your question,' she said, 'is yes, she probably *could* manage it on her own. She *does* know her way to the bus station. And she *had* been taken up to the Rochas place by bus once or twice when Simone's car was out of order. – You remember?' she asked, looking over her shoulder at Julian, who signified his usual assent.

'Only a couple of times, though, wasn't it?' he said.

'That would be enough for Hélène.' She poured hot milk from a saucepan into the cups and handed me mine. 'Sugar? No? – well, that kid might not have *said* much, but, believe me, she missed *nothing*. You only had to tell her, or show her, something once, and she'd got it. Know what I mean?'

'Yes,' I said. 'O.K., she could do it, but why *would* she without her mother?'

'Homing instinct,' said Rose promptly.

'Uh?'

She handed Julian his coffee and led us out of the kitchen into the sitting room, where she gestured me to take a chair. Against the wall just inside the door there was a battered old settee, littered with what, to my untutored eye, looked like scraps of paper haphazardly daubed with paint. Various items of discarded clothing shared what space there was

309

left – a dirty blue cardigan in need of darning, one green-and-red patterned sock and a pair of paint-stained moccasins – and presumably not to disturb this impromptu exhibition Rose perched herself on an arm of the settee, where in my opinion she put the whole display in the shade. Stirring her coffee vigorously, she proceeded to enlighten me.

'Most kids of her age, if their mums went missing, would stay put, press their noses to the window-pane for a bit, and then probably start to howl, whereupon someone like me would go pounding to the rescue. But our little pigeon isn't like most kids of her age. Think it out for yourself. For a start, she's never really had a mum and dad. No offence to Simone, of whom I'm very fond, but you know what I mean. For a very little girl, that kid has had her troubles. So she backs off. Can't say I blame her. Then along you come: take an interest in her, introduce her to someone who'll teach her to play that damn piano of hers. Well – ' she shrugged, slopping her coffee in the process – 'what do you expect? For our little Hélène, whether you like it or not, Angus Logan, you're a sort of dad until something better comes along, and Señorita Rochas – well, she's become a kind of mum, someone to make her feel at home, because when she goes up to the farm there's someone waiting specially for her, other kids turning up, a piano, and someone who cares about the thing like she does. I tell you, that kid's found a place where she really wants to be, and so – when she's frightened, confused, feels herself abandoned, what does she do? She makes for that place, and she'll get there if all hell breaks loose!' She stopped, breathing hard, her natural vitality exuding from her in warm waves of feeling so palpable that, for a moment, I forgot my worries and gazed at her in admiration. Julian, I saw, was doing the same, a small, affectionate smile lurking somewhere behind the black, manly bush.

'Well,' I said at last. 'That explains a lot.'

We all laughed, each of us, I felt, glad to be rid of some of the tension that had been passing between us.

'Do you have any idea', I asked, 'where Simone might have gone? I mean, is it her day for doing anything special, which she might have forgotten when she fixed for Hélène to go for her lesson?'

Rose shook her head. 'Not that I know of. Anyway, she only ever pottered round the shops: nothing regular. And she was only talking about the kid's lesson last night – or maybe it was the evening before. She could hardly have forgotten it that soon.'

I wondered about that. In her present state, it seemed to me to be a distinct possibility.

'O.K.,' I said. 'If anything should crop up, ring me on this number – ' I fished my notebook out of my pocket, scribbled the Mont Vert number and then tore out the page and handed it to her – 'You needn't worry about Hélène any more. Señorita Rochas will keep her as long as is necessary. I'll let you know if I come up with anything myself.'

Rose glanced at the scrap of paper I had given her and then placed it between a framed photograph and a small brass candlestick on the mantelpiece.

'Do *you* know where she might be?' she asked.

'I think so. She's probably gone up to St Michel. In fact, I'm fairly certain she has.'

'St Michel!' She looked startled and I realized that she was thinking of what had happened when another member of the de Courvel family had gone back to St Michel while of unsettled mind.

'It's all right,' I said, 'she's got a secret place there.' And I told her about the room in the yellow coach-house.

She sat down heavily on the arm of a chair and her eyes were bright with tears.

'It's all so goddamn awful,' she said. '*Isn't it?*' she demanded of Julian, rounding on him as fiercely as if he were in some way responsible.

He looked back at her with apparent calm, but the tension was back in his eyes. 'Yes,' he said.

Rose was silent for a moment and then she looked up, concerned afresh. 'But why?' she demanded. 'Why should she go there today, when she knew Hélène had a lesson? And if she had to go for some damn reason, why didn't she tell me, so I could look after the child?'

'Because,' I said, 'she's ill, Rose. I've been feeling it, without really taking it in, for some time. She's gone back there because that's where she feels safe. In a sense, her father did the same, but I don't think Simone – '

I had been about to say that I didn't think Simone would do anything foolish; but then, suddenly, something struck me clean under the heart like a blow from a fist.

'God, no!' I whispered.

Rose started up, and, mechanically, I put out a hand to restrain her.

'Stay where you are. I'm going up there. Don't do anything; not anything, until I ring you.'

She said nothing, and I could still see her standing there, her eyes wide and horrified, as I moved from the room and out of the house.

TWENTY-FOUR

Once out of town, I put my foot down hard, but as I raced up the lonely stretch of the Côte du Nord towards St Michel, I became uncomfortably aware of the dichotomy posed by a full mind and an empty stomach. The fact of the matter was that I hadn't eaten since breakfast at seven-thirty, and it was now nearly two. Even in my agitated state, it was obvious that hurtling through the lanes like a drunken dodgem driver was inadvisable and I made a conscious effort to slow down. Despite this, I reached St Michel in record time and had swung from the lane into the drive before I realized that something I had seen glinting from under the long grass near the gate was in fact a bicycle. I was still wondering whose it was as I drew up with a screech of brakes in front of the coach-house driveway. There, however, something else caught my eye: a human figure, moving quickly away under the trees where the garden bordered the plantations. What the hell was Pedro Calvaro doing here? Was the bicycle his? If so, why was he now scurrying off through the plantations leaving his machine lying in the hedge near the gate? In any case, he must have heard and seen the car; why hadn't he stopped to speak to me?

As I got out, I noticed that under the archway between the two coach-houses there was another car. With relief, I saw that it was not Simone's; but what workman would turn up on *Jour de Parlement*? Well, *someone* had, it was clear, for the front door of the yellow house was open, and inside there was a strong smell of paraffin, mingled, I was vaguely aware, with something else. The place appeared to be empty, however, and, recalling that I'd seen no trace of Simone's car, I was about to turn and leave when I suddenly realized what the other smell was. *Smoke!* I looked up the staircase and saw the first grey cloud curling round from the landing. At the same time, I heard an ominous crackling sound and in obedience to some reflex impulse I slammed the front door shut behind me and leapt towards the stairs. As I went, I tore a handkerchief from my pocket and wrapped it over my nose and mouth, stumbling on the top step as I tried to tie the cotton ends behind my neck.

The landing was smoke-filled, but free of flame; the open door of the lounge, however, revealed a lurid cavern. I tried to swallow what air there was down into my lungs and then made a dash for it. At first, the room seemed a cauldron of flames and smoke, but then I realized that only the end nearest the door was so far affected, the seat of the fire being the bed, which looked like some ritual funeral pyre. At sight of it, all rational thought deserted me. I forgot that I'd seen no sign of Simone's car: forgot everything, in fact, except the horrifying fear that on this bed I would find her body, that, like her father before her, Simone had chosen to return to die in the place that had been most dear to her. But as I lurched, gasping and choking, towards the bed, I tripped over something lying on the floor beside it. Groping and peering, I made out the shape and feel of a human body, and, frantic with apprehension, I grabbed hold of a pair of legs and began pulling in the direction of the door. The weight of the body surprised me, as did the fact that, for some peculiar reason that I couldn't understand, it kept getting caught up in what was left of the carpet. Once out on the landing, I changed position, moving round to the head of the figure to get my hands under the shoulders. It was then that I saw something that knocked what was left of my breath clean out of my body. The figure I had been trying to rescue was not Simone's: it was Ray Corlander's, and sticking out from between the shoulder-blades was what looked like the wooden handle of a large carving-knife.

What happened immediately after that has become a blur. How we got out, whether I carried Corlander or dragged him down that short but steep flight of stairs, God knows. All I do know is that as I collapsed on the grass and cobbles outside the front door, Paulo Garcia, his son, Luis, and old Pedro Calvaro all materialized as though from nowhere. With them, they had buckets and a reel of hosepipe, and Paulo ran with this under the stableyard arch, while Luis dashed with the other end into the house itself. Meanwhile, as Pedro knelt anxiously beside me, I choked and was sick, and then leant forward on my knees trying to get my breath. At the same time, I pointed back to where Corlander's body lay several feet away, the side of his face to the ground, the knife clearly showing between the shoulder-blades.

'Sí, sí,' muttered Pedro. 'It is no use. 'E is dead.'

I was having difficulty in opening my eyes properly, but I fixed them as hard as I could on his. 'What happened? You were here. I saw you. Where is Madame Simone?'

He shook his head. He looked terrible. His hands, I noticed, were shaking as if he had a palsy.

'Have you raised the alarm?' I demanded.

He nodded. 'They come now. And Luis, 'e look for Madame, but we cannot find.'

I tried to struggle to my feet and was immediately sick again. My stomach and lungs were in revolt and my whole body was raw with burns and bruises. Behind me, however, I saw that the flames were no longer shooting up behind the cracked glass of that upper window, and there was an acrid smell of damp ash in the air. It should have been a relief, but only one thought consumed me: I had to find Simone. From my knees I looked up again at old Pedro. 'You saw her, didn't you?'

His lips moved, but no sound came.

'You saw what happened?'

Anguished, he shook his head, but I had no mercy on him. I staggered up and grabbed him by the shoulders. 'Don't lie to me, Pedro! You saw! Did she do it? What happened? Did she start the fire?'

'No! No! No! No!' He was beside himself now, wringing his hands and rocking from side to side as though in intolerable physical pain.

'What do you mean? Who, then?'

'*I* did it! *I* started the fire!'

'Oh, for God's sake!' I turned away, exasperated, reeling as I did so, but at that moment Paulo appeared beside me and took hold of my arm.

'Is true, Señor. Pedro start fire. But the other, no! That is not true!' 'E lie!'

I believed him. 'What about the police? Have you called *them*?'

No one answered me, and I swore. 'What the hell did you think you were going to do about *that*?' I jerked my head in the direction of Corlander's body.

Still no one answered. 'Have you got your car?' I demanded of Paulo.

'Sí.'

'Then you come with me,' I ordered. 'You, Pedro, go home. Luis, make him. And then you call the police. Do you understand? You call them *now*. Then come back here. There'll be questions to answer. For God's sake, say as little as possible. Keep your head. If you have to say something, then stick to the truth. You came up with your father and your uncle. Don't offer any explanations if you can help it, and for God's sake no confessions. But don't start telling a whole string of lies. It won't help anyone. And, Luis, make your *uncle* understand that!'

The young man nodded and I left them to it, followed by Paulo, who put out a hand every now and then to guide my somewhat uncertain footsteps. As we went down the drive, I asked him how he and the others had come to be on the scene after I had so clearly seen old Pedro hurrying away from it. He told me that the old man had arrived at his cottage in a state of great agitation and told him that St Michel was on fire and that he had seen me making for the coach-house. They had collected young Luis and raced back here in Paulo's cab.

'You say Pedro started it?'

'Sí. 'E did it for the best, Señor. But then 'e see you, so try to put it out again. But fire, it is a clean thing. It bring all things back to the beginning. All as if nothing 'appen. You know?'

I swore. I *did* know. 'He must have been mad! You can't get away with things like that. Doesn't he realize that?'

He shrugged. Clearly, he thought the point academic.

'I want you to go to Porte Hilaire,' I told him, 'and bring Monsieur Alain back with you. He will be needed. And keep your eyes open on the way. If you see anything of Madame Simone, come back for me straight away. I shall be somewhere down in the Bay. If you can't find me, try to take Alain to her. And if that fails – because the place will be crawling with cops by that time – well, God help us, you'll just have to tell Blanchard. There'll be no other way. You've got that?'

He nodded vigorously, glad to have something to do. 'Sí, sí, I understand! I will do this!'

'Right. Get going, then.'

He hurried off down the drive towards his cab, parked beside the gate, and I went back to the Citroën. I had told Paulo he would find me in St Michel's Bay, but, in fact, I hoped to God that my visit there would prove unnecessary: that at the Rivage d'Or I would find that Phyllis Corlander, at least, was safe. The implications were impossible; yet so was the thought that Simone de Courvel had murdered her ex-husband. But I knew that she had. I knew it with a cold certainty that grew clearer the further I went, until, when I reached the coast road again, it was as lucid to me as the blue, transparent waters of the bay. I knew exactly the moment at which she had made her decision. In my mind, I could see it taking place within her, as she had sat there in her father's study, staring at me after I had told her about Corlander's betrayal of her with the incriminating tape. *I*, then, was responsible. *I* had been the one to open her eyes. A terrible sickness was in me as I drove. It was useless that cold reason argued that I could not possibly have known – not in a million years – the secret that Simone was harbouring: that the grave disorder to which her mind had finally succumbed must have been slowly forming long before, and would inevitably have found its outlet. All I could think of was that Simone had killed her ex-husband in mad, blind hatred, having, presumably, somehow persuaded him to

317

meet her in the coach-house, and that now she was somewhere at loose on the island, suffering God knew what devils, and planning – what?

Desperation was still gripping me when I reached the top end of the bay, and I braked fiercely as I swung under the lemon trees that lined the drive of the Rivage d'Or, and stopped with a grinding of gravel outside the handsome glass doors. The commissionaire visibly went into shock at sight of my appearance. However, when I brushed aside his first tentative expressions of concern, he came quickly to the point and told me, no, Madame Corlander – that is, Mademoiselle de Courvel – had *not* been there at any time during the morning, and, no, Madame Corlander had *not* left the hotel. She was, in fact, in the Terrace Bar at the moment, checking arrangements for an evening party. Did Monsieur wish to see her? No, Monsieur did *not* wish to see her, but Monsieur was damn glad to know that at this moment in time Phyllis Corlander's only worries were logistic ones.

Outside again, I stopped to think. Phyllis, then, was safe. Was there anyone else who could possibly come within the range of Simone's distracted brain? Alain had accused Max Cartier, but that came within a different province altogether. Simone had known of Max's growing affiliation with the Corlander camp, but had not seemed particularly concerned. Even allowing for her present state of mind, I couldn't somehow see the Cartiers as her next victims. Probably there *were* no further potential victims – except Simone herself. On that score, it was imperative that she be found. And already I knew where, if anywhere, that would be.

Before I got there, however, I saw Paulo's cab coming towards me. We stopped and he got out and came across to me. My eyes searched his in the blinding sunlight.

'Have you found her?'

He nodded without speaking.

'I'll follow you.'

It was silent and beautiful down in the Arle Valley. The

sun was still high and the waters of the reservoir formed a luminous sheet of gold, dappled at the edges by the dark, filigree shadows of the overhanging trees. Her car was parked at the roadside, the door open, her handbag on the floor beneath the passenger seat, its contents spilled. At the water's edge, under a young acacia tree, we found her shoes. In the brilliant sunlight it was possible to see almost every curve and inlet of the broad reservoir, but nowhere, over the whole length and breadth of the calm, quiet water, was there anything else of her to be seen. Nevertheless, we walked almost halfway round before we gave up. Then we went back to the road in silence and I shut the door of her car.

'Go on down to Porte Hilaire,' I said. 'Fetch Monsieur Alain back to the house. I'm going back there now. The police will be there by now, I expect. I'll tell them about this.'

He nodded again, but still didn't speak. In the sunlight his face was a round, shining mass of corrugated anguish. I left him and walked slowly back to my car and got in, waiting in the heavy lethargy of someone drugged or drunk until he started the engine of the cab and moved away. For something like a quarter of a mile I could see him as he went down the valley road, driving fast but with none of the panache normally so characteristic of him, and all the time my brain seemed to be set in a rigid lock that prevented all movement or even feeling. Small, irrelevant details, such as the bald white patch on Paulo's distant roof-top where the sun touched it, the croak of a hidden water bird and the sweet smell of mimosa, all assumed a curious distinction as they filtered through my consciousness. It took a considerable effort of will to reach for the ignition and, when the engine flared into life, to put the car into gear.

The fire tender was already out in the lane heading back for Porte Hilaire when I arrived at the Manoir, but Blanchard was still there, standing on the cobbles outside the coach-house door while three of his uniformed men prowled in and out. The cold anger with which he received me was even more abrasive than his sarcasm had been, but I didn't blame him. People who left a murder scene and then came back again when it suited them could not expect to rate high on a police popularity poll. He started by having my fingerprints taken, and then wanted to know what I had been doing here in the first place and why, when I'd discovered the fire, I had left it in the hands of an old man and a boy and gone off on some investigation of my own. I interrupted his interrogation to tell him about Simone's car on the bank of the Arle, and he stopped dead in his tracks, staring at me with an expression impossible to gauge, before turning and snapping out an order to two of his men to go to the spot I'd described.

When they had gone, he returned to his attack on me with a new waspishness. My explanation that I had come to the Manoir on the off-chance of seeing Simone, whom I knew had been doing some painting up here, clearly failed to impress him, as also did my story that, having seen the worst of the fire doused by Paulo and Luis, I had left in order to go and rouse Simone at her home, having sent Paulo to do the same with Alain. We had both found Simone's car on the way. It was worrying to see old Pedro still hovering around the garden; I had no idea what, if anything, he had told Blanchard and could only hope that he had been his usual non-commital self. In typical police fashion, Blanchard gave me no help. I couldn't even guess what he knew or did not know, but it began to dawn on me that my own personal position *vis-à-vis* Corlander's body was a none too happy one. At the same time, I was worried about having told Blanchard that I'd thought Simone might be up here, painting. The possibility that I'd lied about not finding her here would now be very much in his mind, as would all the implications connecting her with the murder. I waited miserably for him to follow this up, but he seemed suddenly to lose interest in me and went back into the house.

Taking advantage of the respite, I went over to where old

Pedro was standing on his own on the edge of the drive. The sight of him, abject and terrified, drew upon the pain that was locked inside me and our eyes met in a shared wretchedness. There was a question in his.

'I'm sorry, Pedro. I was too late.'

I saw the tears appear on his grizzled old cheeks, but could find no words of comfort for him.

'Where?' he whispered.

'The Arle.'

He said nothing, but a great sigh seemed to come from somewhere deep inside him and to shake his whole frame. A harsh, rasping sound succeeded it and he turned away. I did the same, but everywhere I looked I saw her car, with its opened door, the handbag and scattered shoes, and the sunshot waters of the reservoir. And again, for the millionth time, I was tortured with the feeling that I had let her down, that I should have known, should have sensed, the danger she was in, should have stayed with her, protected her – though God alone knew how – from the devils that had drawn her with such vile implacability to her end. But all the time, I knew in the still centre of my being that such thoughts were vain. I could not have helped her then any more than I could help her now. She had gone from my life as suddenly and shockingly as her father had done, and the world they had once represented for me was as dead as they were.

Meanwhile, here in this one, questions remained unanswered. Pedro had said he had started the fire, Paulo had confirmed this and indicated that the old man had done it to 'clean' away the evidence of Simone's guilt. But if this was true, it meant that either Pedro had actually *seen* Simone plunge the knife into Corlander's back – if so, why had he been around to do so? – or, alternatively, he had found the body afterwards – in which case why had he come with such certainty to the conclusion that Simone was responsible?

I became aware that the old man had turned again and was looking at me. I heard him draw in his breath.

'Do they think it was 'er, Señor?'

321

'I don't know. Probably – unless they've decided it was you or me. But unless somebody's been very clever, they're bound to have found prints on that knife.' I gave a wry grimace. 'I messed it up, didn't I, old man? Your nice clean way. Maybe it *would* have answered. I don't know. You can never be sure with modern forensics. The trouble was – ' I sighed heavily – 'I thought *she* was in there, you see.'

He nodded, the old, gentle look returning to his eyes. 'I know, Señor. You did good.'

Good! The irony of my blundering progress towards the truth concerning Simone and the bull-headed confrontation that had finally set her off on her path to destruction struck me afresh and I groaned aloud.

'Señor – ' The old man was picking up the vibrations between us faster than his command of English could cope with them. 'You must not – It is an old, old trouble. It go back long, long way. It had to – to – ' he searched for the words he wanted, holding his hands up as though weighing something.

'Burst? Come to a head?' My own hands simulated an explosion.

'Sí!' His face cleared. 'That is it! It must come!'

I looked at him keenly. 'Pedro, you knew Señor Maurice better than any one of us. He must have told you many things. Did you know about – ' I jerked my head back towards the coach-house.

'Sí. Señor Maurice, he not tell everything; but I know. Señora Simone, too, she not say, "this", or "that", but I know. I help her with house there. Furnish room. Paint furniture. I come today to paint. That is how I hear what happened.'

'You *heard*? What?'

'I am in stable, Señor. Painting. I see Señora Simone come, but she not know. Then come other car. Then terrible screaming, Señor. Terrible. And man shouting. Then – '

He paused and for a moment covered his mouth with his hand as though forcibly to prevent further revelation; then slowly his hand came down again and he swallowed. 'I 'ear sobbing, Señor, then – I try to decide – but she come running out and I see 'er go.'

'So then you went in and found the body.'

'Sí.'

'And started the fire.'

'Sí.' He swallowed again, his agitation painfully apparent. 'Señor, I tell Blanchard I do it, but – ' he gestured despairingly – 'but he no believe. So – ' and now a fierce resolution showed in his eyes – 'if they say it is 'er, I shall say she kill to save 'erself. From *'im.*'

I shook my head. 'Pedro, dear old fellow, listen to me. Unless you thought to wipe that knife – which you wouldn't have because you thought your good clean fire would do the trick – then trying to pull the wool over Blanchard's eyes is only going to do Madame Simone more harm than good. It will also get you and your family into a lot of trouble. If you are questioned, you must tell only the truth. Believe me, anything else will do nothing but harm.'

The desolation in his face as he stared ahead of him was heartbreaking. His mind, I saw, was back in the past. When he spoke again, his words had the quality of gunfire:

'I *'ate* that man!'

'Yes – well. We all did. But he's paid his due now.'

'*Never*! Death, it is too easy.'

'Perhaps not, Pedro. Who knows.'

He sighed again. 'Sí.' He was about to say something else, but there was a stir outside the coach-house, and a car drew up. I recognized it.

What do you say to a man whose son your 'sister' has murdered? I didn't know the answer to that, so I patted Pedro on the arm and moved away down the garden, turning under the trees which lined a path running parallel with the drive. From here, I was able to see Paulo arrive back in his cab with Alain sitting beside him. They both saw me, and Paulo stopped. I stepped off the path, threaded my way to the wire fence, a single strand about two feet high, bordering the drive, and stepped over.

Alain's face, as he watched me approach, seemed to have got suddenly thinner, the olive skin drawn tight over the cheekbones, giving his dark eyes an almost cadaverous intensity.

'Have they found her yet?' he demanded.

'You know – ' I glanced at Paulo, who nodded – 'you know what happened?'

'Yes. But have they found her?'

'I don't know. I think not.'

'Why in God's name did she do it? Garcia here says there was some accident involving Corlander and she went off and threw herself in the reservoir. Is that true?'

I tried to summon the strength and will to tell him, but an accumulation of hunger and emotional strain made the explanation, even to my own ears, sound brutally perfunctory. I expected him to press me, but he didn't. Instead, half-way through, he got out of the cab and, indicating the vacated seat, transferred himself to the back. Sitting down, it was better, but even then I faltered, anticipating the worst when I came to my own part in his sister's collapse. To spare us interruption from Blanchard's men, Garcia backed out of the drive and drove us round the lanes until the recital was finished. Then he drove us back, parking, ironically, directly behind Bernard Corlander's car. As he got out, Alain threw me a glance. To my surprise, there was no trace in it of the accusation I had expected.

'Don't blame yourself, Angus. All this goes back a very long way. Sooner or later – ' He sighed.

It was almost word for word what old Pedro had said, but for once I was less than impressed by the Roquennais tendency to conceal the deepest thoughts and feelings within an oyster-like camouflage. Perhaps, in this case, any other attitude would have proved equally useless, but I couldn't help wondering whether, like myself, Alain de Courvel would not for the rest of his life writhe under the whiplash of self-vilification whenever the memory of his sister returned to him.

TWENTY-FIVE

Simone's body was never found, despite intensive searches of the reservoir. One theory held by the police was that she hadn't died there at all, but had wandered on down to the banks of the Arle river itself, where she had either, in a confused state, stumbled into the water by accident, or had made the decision to drown herself. Either way, if this hypothesis were correct, the possibility of her ever being found was remote, for there are places where the Arle is full of a thick, binding weed whose roots go so deep as to defy penetration. The Spanish name for this weed, translated, is 'Corpse Grass', the French, 'Fisherman's Shroud', both being apt indicators of the likely fate of anyone unfortunate enough to get caught in the stuff.

The post-mortem on Corlander showed that he had died as a direct result of a knife wound that had penetrated the heart from the back, but two sets of prints were found on the handle of the knife, suggesting that a struggle had taken place. One set was established as belonging to Corlander himself, while the others were found to match those taken from various objects in Simone's apartment. However, as neither of the protagonists in the drama was available for questioning, the police were unable to bring criminal proceedings. For this small comfort, I drew a deep breath of relief, but at that stage Nick was still deeply worried.

'There's still the coroner,' he said.

'But surely that's just a formality. I mean, it's not a trial court, is it?'

'No, but there is a fifty-fifty chance that he could bring in an open verdict.'

'Meaning?'

'Meaning that *should* any further evidence come to

light – Simone's body, for example – the whole business could be reopened.'

'Christ!'

'Then, there's old Pedro. He will have to give evidence, and Bernard Corlander will have the right to question him – '

'Oh, my God!'

'Well – that's the right of relatives at an inquest. He will have to tell the truth, but no more than the truth, heaven help us!'

In the event, Pedro was both truthful and subdued, having been bullied, threatened and cajoled beforehand by Nick, who applied to represent him and who, in the restricted question-and-answer context of the coroner's court, managed very skilfully to emphasize the old man's age, his long service and known devotion to the de Courvel family and to show that, in starting a fire, he had acted from a combination of panic, fear and blind, unreasoning loyalty. His subsequent desperate efforts to reverse his actions had saved him by the skin of his teeth from police action, a decision of Blanchard's which, in terms of his own security in the community, was possibly the wisest the inspector had ever made.

My own blundering intervention was held to have been justifiable and responsible. But I had one bad moment when Bernard Corlander rose to comfort me. For the first time since I had known him, I saw the man as vulnerable. The corners of his rubbery mouth twitched as he made to speak, and his eyes, behind those huge glasses, held no trace of the mild mockery which I had so often sensed in him. His nerves lay close to the surface, and they were raw, as were my own and those of so many others in that room.

'Monsieur Logan,' he said. 'You put yourself at some considerable risk that day. My wife and I wish to thank you for what you did.' He stopped, turning as if to move away, and then, as if remembering something, turned back again. 'Thank you,' he said. The voice was so low that I barely heard it, but as he moved to his seat I felt sick with shame.

God, didn't the man *know* that I had done what I did for Simone? That I had thought that *she* was in that burning room, that in all probability, had I known it was his blighted son, I wouldn't have moved a finger to save the swine! – Or would I? The fact was I didn't know, and probably never would. If Corlander thought he did know, and it gave him any comfort, well, good luck to him!

The final verdict was 'Death by Misadventure'. No one ever doubted that Simone Corlander, née de Courvel, had slain her ex-husband while of unsound mind, but it was equally certain that, with the possible exception of Phyllis Corlander and certain of Ray's closest adherents, there was not a single individual on the island who did not derive considerable satisfaction from her evasion of the consequences of her action.

In the aftermath of the hearing, the island as a whole moved solidly behind the de Courvel family, encouraged by the fact that, released from constraint after so long, the Garcias and old Pedro began to talk at last. The result was a steady trickle of truth, half-truth and rumour, all of it deadly damaging to what was left of the Corlander faction. Within a week of Ray's funeral, we heard that Phyllis Corlander had left the Rivage d'Or, bound, some said, for London – which seemed to have brought her full circle. I could feel no pity for her. She had known what her man was capable of, even had she not realized the details of his culpability; she had been content, as long as it profited her, to turn a blind eye.

For some reason, however, that I could not possibly have defined, I was conscious of a certain regret when I learned that Bernard Corlander and the crippled Dorothea had also disappeared. No one knew where they had gone, or how, although there were rumours of a mystery boat anchored off the pier at Pointe Ste Marie for several hours late one night. Next morning, it – and they – were gone. I asked Nick if he thought the departure was permanent.

'I don't know. No one seems to have been instructed to sell the house or to wind up his affairs, which may or may not be significant.'

'Surely he wouldn't just leave everything wide open?'

'Well, it's impossible to tell whether he *has*. Bernard Corlander always did operate through a highly efficient team of functionaries. I wouldn't put it past him to be still doing so from a distance.'

'Until the dust dies down.'

'Precisely.' He gave a quizzical smile. 'Missing him already, are you?'

I grimaced wryly. 'O.K., so the bloke had about as much charm as a cornered octopus, but there's a kind of Quasimodo ugliness that generates sympathy even while it repels. When all's said and done, I suppose you can't blame a creature for creation's bad jokes.'

In a sense, too – though I didn't say so to Nick – I felt the island needed the challenge of a Bernard Corlander. The seigneurs had gone for ever, and with him both the inspiration and the government which they had provided. Felipe's party would now carry most of the island with it, but there was still too much idealism in it to be safe in a high wind. Maybe all that was needed was experience, but experience took time, and the right mixture of entrepreneurial vision and hard-headed administrative acumen was not acquired in ten easy lessons; like genius, it had to be recognized, grasped and given its head while it lasted. And, like genius, it didn't necessarily have to come smelling like a rose. In Bernard Corlander, I felt I had identified some of the basic qualities; without his evil son, there was a chance, I believed, that he might have spear-headed a viable new order and economy on La Roque. Well, perhaps it would yet be. Perhaps, one quiet night, a boat would reappear off one of the lonely bays of the island, and the lights would go on again in the old convent house of St Damien in the bay of St Michel.

Meanwhile, there were decisions of an immediate nature to be made. After discussions with myself and the Le Marnets, Alain gave instructions for a headstone to be erected beside his parents' graves. On it, was carved simply:

Simone de Courvel ·
Fille de Maurice et Justine de Courvel, Manoir St Michel,
Née le 19 février 1923. Morte 25 Octobre, 1959.

After I had seen it, I drove down to the Arle, needing in some strange way to seek catharsis through recollected pain. Guilt still haunted me. I could not forget that it had been from a few crude, blundering words of mine that Simone had fashioned the key to her final hell before finding freedom under these sunlit waters. Could it really be that she had been blind so long to what her father had suffered on her account? Could infatuation so distort? Could fear so dehumanize? – And could I, at nearly forty, ask such bloody silly questions? Could I, having gone my own sweet way for the best part of twenty years, return now expecting to find a company of Olympians? I had been inexcusably idealistic, using these people to bolster my own inadequate sense of family and my need of some compass-point or bench-mark by which to orientate my own transient existence. I had served these people ill. Now, seeing them for the first time with the dirty hands and grubby faces of common humanity, I knew that I and they really did belong. These were my people, my family; I owed to them a knowledge of myself that I had never had before. Just what I intended to do about that, I was not yet sure. It was a decision for the future, and there were still present decisions to be made.

The most pressing of these was what to do about Hélène. What was left of St Michel was now hers, but to whom did she herself look for her shelter and security? Alain was her nearest blood relative, and he and Madeleine were prepared to have her, although their circumstances made the position difficult, to say the least, as they themselves realized. Nicholas and Stéphanie, for their part, wanted her at the Manoir Vert, but while the greatheartedness of the offer undoubtedly did a very great deal for inter-family relations, I don't think anyone seriously believed in the possibility of Hélène settling down successfully with the bouncy, extrovert young Le Marnets. While challenge can often be good therapy, it was not what Hélène needed now; her problems demanded a background that would be more neutral, more certain, on which she could poise herself with confidence before taking her first small leap into life. Meanwhile, she clung to Louise with a tenacity that was touching.

While we all thought about it, I decided to fly back to London to sort out some of my own neglected affairs. Once I got there, however, I regretted it. The dank, chill London air was intimidating after so many weeks of warm sun, added to which I found that the matters I had left unresolved on the island intruded to such an extent that I was unable to settle down to routine chores. I didn't realize it, but I was moving towards the next major decision of my life. It was while talking to my Editor that I began dimly to appreciate this fact.

'Well,' he greeted me, 'you certainly stirred up a hornet's nest over there. Reading between the lines, that is. You must be glad to get back to peaceful old London. Although, there's a job coming up down in Aussie land – '

'Sorry, Henry.'

'Eh?'

'I'm not over on a visit. Didn't I mention? I've got unfinished business back on the island.'

'What kind of unfinished business? Woman kind?' He turned on his kindly, understanding grin, which never failed to make me hopping mad. 'Come on, Angus. You've always been able to love 'em and leave 'em.'

'Not this time, Henry.'

'Oh, dear, oh, dear.' He sank his bald head in his hands and pursed his lips. 'She must be very special,' he said, looking up at me from under arched eyebrows.

'She is.'

'Beautiful, eh?'

'Very.'

'Let me guess – blonde, blue-eyed, aged about twenty-five.'

'Close, Henry, close. Blonde, blue-eyed and aged about eight.'

*   *   *

330

It was on the following Monday that the letter arrived from Louise, and my last doubts dissolved. I read it several times, carefully.

I have had to tell Hélène that her mother is dead. Madeleine rang and asked me if I could bring myself to do so. She said Alain felt Hélène should be given an explanation for her mother's absence, and that excuses wouldn't do, but neither she nor Alain could face it. Oh, Angus, that poor little one! She didn't shed a single tear or ask a single question. I found myself weeping because she could not. What has happened to this little girl is dreadful. And what is to become of her? I keep asking myself if we have done the right thing. She reminds me of some tiny animal, peering out of a hole in the ground, frightened to come out any further in case someone steps on it. I am so worried for her, Angus. If things were to go wrong for her now, I don't think I could bear it.

After I had finished reading, I poured myself a whisky and sat for a long time staring at the bare, wet branches of the plane tree outside my window. Then I picked up the phone.

It was raining again when I flew in over the island. As I hurried across the tarmac, I had the curious feeling that life was repeating itself. A plane slowly descending out of a world of unreality. Questions to be asked. Answers to be given. Only this time, it was others who were coming in from uncertainty, and I it was who must answer them. As I neared the Reception building, I saw them, two slender figures, standing close together, behind the glass windows of the lounge.

To my surprise, Hélène was smiling as I approached them. It was the first time I had seen her smile, *really* smile. I took her in my arms and hugged her, and she hugged me back. Inside me, something seemed to slide into place. This had been the first question. Now, it was answered.

The second was more complicated, but in the end it, too,

answered itself. Immediately after supper that evening at the farm, Louise settled Hélène down in the spare bed which she had temporarily set up beside hers, and then returned to where I was sitting out on the loggia, sipping Bénédictine.

'She's tired,' she said, 'but she wanted so much to come with me to meet you. She said she hoped you would stay longer this time.'

It seemed perfectly logical at that moment to ask her what she thought about adoption, and whether she considered that people of mixed nationalities should marry.

It was not what I had come to the island to discover, but if the spirits of the dead do indeed watch over their own, then Maurice de Courvel, I felt, would have been well content with the answers I received.

Romantic Suspense

Three outstanding romantic thrillers by great modern authors, in the marvellous storytelling tradition of Evelyn Anthony and Helen MacInnes.

In Safe Hands   Jane Sandford

Kate Harper was just a student but she was also the only child of the toughest Secretary of State for years. So she was kidnapped and held hostage for his resignation. Or that's what the kidnappers' leader, Irish doctor Conor, told her. Then, from the outside, new and unexpected dangers threatened her – and the kidnappers. Suddenly Kate was no longer safe – in anyone's hands.

The Servants of Twilight   Leigh Nichols

To his mother, Christine, Joey was an ordinary six-year-old boy. But to the Servants of Twilight he was an evil presence who must be destroyed. An encounter with a threatening old woman began a terrifying ordeal for Joey and Christine – a nightmare of horror that only the love of one man could enable Christine to survive.

Stillwatch   Mary Higgins Clark

Investigative journalist Pat Traymore was in Washington on a red-hot assignment – to find out about the Senator tipped to be the first woman Vice-President. But Pat had horrifying memories of the city, for something happened to her there as a child that scarred her life. Now her search for the sinister truth unleashes powerful and menacing forces against her . . .

FONTANA PAPERBACKS

Winston Graham

'One of the best half-dozen novelists in this country.' *Books and Bookmen*.

'Winston Graham excels in making his characters come vividly alive.' *Daily Mirror*.

'A born novelist.' *Sunday Times*.

The Poldark Saga, his famous story of
eighteenth-century Cornwall

ROSS POLDARK
DEMELZA
JEREMY POLDARK
WARLEGGAN
THE BLACK MOON
THE FOUR SWANS
THE ANGRY TIDE
THE STRANGER FROM THE SEA
THE MILLER'S DANCE
THE LOVING CUP

His immensely popular suspense novels include

THE WALKING STICK
MARNIE
THE SLEEPING PARTNER

Historical novel

THE FORGOTTEN STORY

FONTANA PAPERBACKS

Fontana Paperbacks: Fiction

Fontana is a leading paperback publisher of both non-fiction, popular and academic, and fiction. Below are some recent fiction titles.

- [ ] GLITTER BABY Susan Elizabeth Phillips £2.95
- [ ] EMERALD DECISION Craig Thomas £3.50
- [ ] THE GOLDEN CUP Belva Plain £3.50
- [ ] A THUNDER OF CRUDE Brian Callison £2.95
- [ ] DESERT QUEEN Julia Fitzgerald £3.50
- [ ] THE GREEN FLASH Winston Graham £3.50
- [ ] UNDER CONTRACT Liza Cody £2.95
- [ ] THE LATCHKEY KID Helen Forrester £2.95
- [ ] IN HARM'S WAY Geoffrey Jenkins £2.95
- [ ] THE DOOR TO DECEMBER Leigh Nichols £3.50
- [ ] THE MIRROR OF HER DREAMS Stephen Donaldson £3.95
- [ ] A SONG IN THE MORNING Gerald Seymour £2.95

You can buy Fontana paperbacks at your local bookshop or newsagent. Or you can order them from Fontana Paperbacks, Cash Sales Department, Box 29, Douglas, Isle of Man. Please send a cheque, postal or money order (not currency) worth the purchase price plus 22p per book for postage (maximum postage required is £3.00 for orders within the UK).

NAME (Block letters) _____

ADDRESS _____

_____

_____

While every effort is made to keep prices low, it is sometimes necessary to increase them at short notice. Fontana Paperbacks reserve the right to show new retail prices on covers which may differ from those previously advertised in the text or elsewhere.